T0385373

Anne O'Brien is a *Sunday Times* bestselling author and has sold close to a million copies of her books globally. Anne gained a BA Honours degree in History at Manchester University and a Master's in Education at Hull, working in East Yorkshire for many years as a teacher of history. Today, she lives with her husband in the Welsh Marches in Herefordshire, where she writes about the many forgotten women of history.

Also by Anne O'Brien

*A Marriage of Fortune*
*A Court of Betrayal*

# ANNE O'BRIEN

# The QUEEN and the COUNTESS

ORION

First published in Great Britain in 2025 by Orion Fiction,
an imprint of The Orion Publishing Group Ltd.
Carmelite House, 50 Victoria Embankment
London EC4Y 0DZ

An Hachette UK Company

The authorised representative in the EEA is Hachette Ireland,
8 Castlecourt Centre, Castleknock Road, Castleknock, Dublin 15, D15 XTP3,
Republic of Ireland (email: info@hbgi.ie)

3 5 7 9 10 8 6 4 2

A CIP catalogue record for this book is
available from the British Library.

ISBN (Hardback) 9781 3987 1124 2
ISBN (Export Trade Paperback) 9781 3987 1125 9
ISBN (Ebook) 9781 3987 1127 3
ISBN (Audio) 9781 3987 1128 0

Typeset at The Spartan Press Ltd,
Lymington, Hants

Printed and bound in Great Britain by Clays Ltd,
Elcograf S.p.A.

www.orionbooks.co.uk

To George, as always, with much love.
And with my thanks for listening and agreeing with me
in all the right places.

# The
## 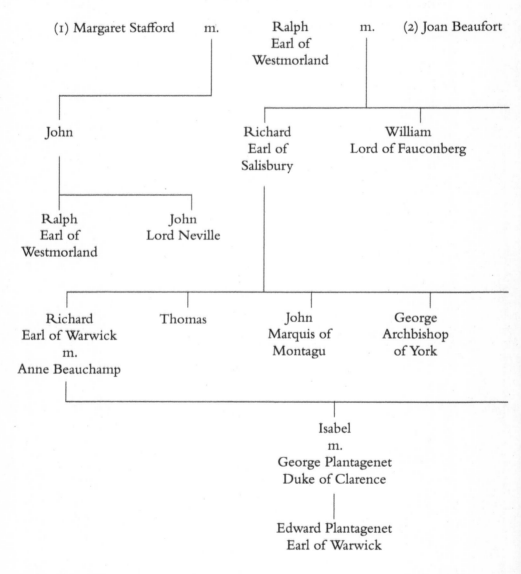 Neville Family

(1) Margaret Stafford    m.    Ralph    m.    (2) Joan Beaufort
Earl of
Westmorland

John          Richard        William
Earl of       Lord of Fauconberg
Salisbury

Ralph          John
Earl of        Lord Neville
Westmorland

Richard      Thomas      John      George
Earl of Warwick          Marquis of    Archbishop
m.                 Montagu     of York
Anne Beauchamp

Isabel
m.
George Plantagenet
Duke of Clarence

Edward Plantagenet
Earl of Warwick

Edward
Lord
Bergavenny

Cecily
Duchess
of York

+ 2 sons,
3 Daughters

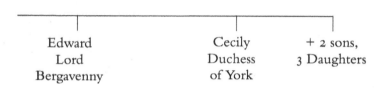

Katherine
m. William Hastings
Lord Hastings

Margaret
m.
John de Vere
Earl of Oxford

+ 4 daughters

Anne
m.
Richard Plantagenet
Duke of Gloucester (Richard III)

Edward of Middleham
Prince of Wales

# The
# Lancaster and York Kings of England
# *and the* House of Tudor

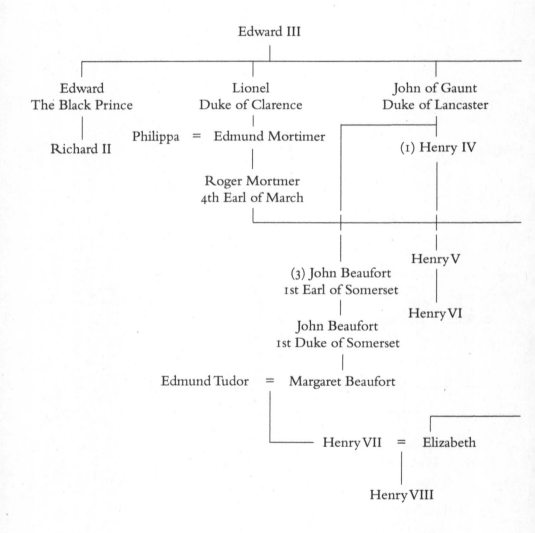

Edward III

Edward
The Black Prince

Richard II

Lionel
Duke of Clarence

Philippa = Edmund Mortimer

Roger Mortmer
4th Earl of March

John of Gaunt
Duke of Lancaster

(1) Henry IV

(3) John Beaufort
1st Earl of Somerset

John Beaufort
1st Duke of Somerset

Henry V

Henry VI

Edmund Tudor = Margaret Beaufort

Henry VII = Elizabeth

Henry VIII

– (1) Blanche
– (2) Constance
– (3) Katherine Swinford

Edmund
Duke of York

——— Anne Mortimer = Richard          Edward
Earl of Cambridge

Richard = Cecily Neville
3rd Duke of York

Elizabeth Woodville = Edward IV          Richard III

Richard          Edward V
(Princes in the Tower)

# *Prologue*

## Anne, Countess of Warwick, Middleham Castle, 1480

I dreamed last night. I dreamed that it was the Love Day, so many years ago, when it seemed that all enmity between York and Lancaster might, with the aid of a miracle, be reconciled in harmony, all past wounds healed, all hostile words obliterated in expressions of lasting friendship. All swords sheathed.

I smiled at my lord Richard as he walked in the procession through the streets of London, for I was young and full of hope. In my dream Richard, Earl of Warwick, darkly impressive, gleaming in courtly robes of velvet and satin, returned the smile.

It was a marriage, arranged for me as was customary in families of my status, with the high-powered Neville family with its formidable flow of royal blood in its collective veins. It was a marriage that brought me rank and authority within my own household and in the realm. It blessed me with a family of two affectionate daughters and a husband who did not neglect my comfort and security. We lived in the luxury appropriate to one of the greatest magnates in the realm. I had no fears for the future. How could I have been afraid when Richard commanded wealth and a dangerously well-organised, well-armoured retinue?

All that was now stripped away; my estates proscribed, my

husband dead as a traitor, one daughter lost in childbed, the other alienated from me in trust and affection.

Today I awoke with the rising sun, as I did every morning, to the knowledge that all my expectations on that Love Day had been trampled underfoot, some of that trampling without doubt beneath Richard's metal-clad feet when he was in battle array. I awoke to another day of isolation, of despair, of heartbreak. Of loss. Richard would not smile at me again, unless in dreams.

How I wished that I could return to that Love Day when I could not see the future. But I could not return, and that future was here with me now, a bitter experience, a cruel existence of loneliness and abandonment. A marriage that had brought me such happiness and contentment had damaged me beyond repair and brought me to my knees.

How much I had lost. All the love that I had been able to give and to receive was destroyed in a battle for political dominance.

But I would not weep. I would never forget the contented times when our household was united at Middleham. One day the trust between my daughter Anne and I might be restored. My grandson, the child Edward, might provide the healing power between us. I would hold on to that dream.

Nor would I ever withdraw from my battle to retrieve what was my own inheritance.

## Margaret of Anjou, Queen of England, Château de Dampierre-sur-Loire, France, 1480

When I dream, if indeed I do, I do not dream gently. I sleep fitfully, remembering when I wake the scenes of blood and destruction that stalk me during the dark hours. All hours are dark to me. I wake to the misery of bleak reality.

I remember the past, but what use dwelling on it? All I held dear has been removed from me by the terrible meld of military defeat, vicious hostilities from my enemies, and even foul weather. From a time when the crown of a royal consort, as wife of King Henry of England, was mine to wear, now I have no claim on it. From a time when I furnished my palaces and castles with cloth of gold and tapestries and the finest beds, now I live in poverty, on the charity of others in a country where I would not choose to be, at the whim of my omnipotent cousin, the King of France. My gold coronal has been sold to a French merchant to raise money for my cause.

My marriage alliance with King Henry of England had raised me from a poverty-stricken princess without a dowry worth speaking of, to a woman capable of standing beside him to keep a tight hold on the royal power in England. Lacking in dowry I might be, but had I not brought that most essential alliance between England and France? I was praised and lauded for it, until, with Henry's weakness, it had become necessary for me to take that power into my own care, quickly showing that I could do so with some skill and much success. How many foreign princesses would be willing to lead an army into battle, would engage in negotiation and alliance-making? I had done all I could to save the crown for my husband and my son.

Now that same authority, which my enemies claimed I stole unjustifiably, has been taken from me and I have been abandoned. My marriage has brought me low indeed.

To recall the past only makes my present more desperate.

My memories of my lord Henry, my royal husband, grow insubstantial and shadowy until all I remember is his weakness, his appalling inability to grasp the power with which he was born, and yet I can never forget my son, my golden Prince Edward, full of life and a resolution to win high praise on a

3

battlefield. How can I not allow him to walk at my side through these meagre rooms that I am forced to inhabit? I sometimes hear him laughing. I hear him demanding the crown that is his by right to wear. He whispers in my ear that he will fight and win the next battle against the House of York. He will restore me to the heady position of King's Mother.

It will never be.

My son lies, a cold and lifeless body, beneath the tiled chancel floor of Tewkesbury Abbey.

My health declines, pain an endless companion, living with me as vividly as my son. There is nothing for me to do but await death.

There is no comfort for me. Age falls on me like dust onto the surface of a well-carved coffer, pressing down, obliterating past beauties. The cruelty of life has left me with nothing or no one to fight for. I can think of neither the past nor the future with any bright hope. Even my faith in the Blessed Virgin seems to be a weak creature, deserting me in the darkest hours of the night.

# I

## *A Love Day Reconciliation, London, 25th March 1458*

**Anne, Countess of Warwick**

I really did not wish to be here, and yet there was a terrible fascination about it all. There was the trumpet-blast, which meant that they must at last be approaching. Thank the Blessed Virgin; it had taken so long, but now the culmination of this inconceivable ceremony was in sight. Despite the sun it was winter-cold, with a touch of frost still in the air. I flinched. My heavy veils did not muffle the screeching when a young lad, standing on the step above me, was trying to hold a tune on his pipe. It was stridently off-key but did not stop the singer at his side from bawling the words to this new ballad that had become the rage on the streets of London.

*Love hath under-laid wrathful vengeance.*
*Rejoice England! Our lords accorded be.*

Rejoice indeed. Unfortunately, there was little rejoicing in my household.

I moved to escape the piping with no little difficulty. The steps leading into St Paul's Cathedral were crowded with those come to watch and marvel. Duchess Cecily of York, my aunt by marriage, muttered at my side that she could think of better things to do with her time than push through a flea-ridden mob of ignorant Londoners.

Not long now. The increasing roar of the crowd heralded the approach. Cheering, shouts of acclamation. The people of London were enthusiastic and well mannered, despite the ale consumed so early in the day. Despite the clash of wills at St Albans when Englishman had fought against Englishman and had spilt blood. Was that all now over, the hostility, the death and desire to kill? I should have been rejoicing like the tuneless singer, but there was a sharp element of doubt in my mind, like a grain of wheat in a shoe at harvest.

I glanced at the two women who stood on the step below me. Alice, Countess of Salisbury, my mother-in-law, shrouded in fur and displeasure. Beside her was Cecily, Duchess of York, my husband's influential aunt, equally muffled in sable and transparent veiling. The thin smile directed up at me was as disbelieving as my own.

'Here they come, at last,' she murmured, 'unless they have murdered each other on the road. If I had my way, I would have banished all knives and swords.'

'The murder may come after the ceremony,' I said.

'Pray God this farce is all over soon,' said Lady Alice, holding a square of linen to her nose as she sniffed. 'I need a fire and a cup of warm wine.'

Here they walked in a stately show of power preceded by royal heralds, magnificent with tabards and trumpets, the spring sun brilliant on the red and blue and fine gilding. The highest born in the land followed behind in solemn procession. There was nothing warlike about this gathering. No warhorses, no armour or war-banners. No swords in evidence except those sheathed in jewel-studded leather. No taint of blood and death. All was an essay in sumptuous soft velvet and silk and damask, hats adorned with feathers, light glinting on the royal crowns. Here was a deliberate statement of quiet peace and unity.

I stepped sidewards again into a space, that I might, unimpeded, see the participants. There they walked, two by two, and what a shock it was for all to see. Who in their wildest dreams would have paired these couples together, after the horror of St Albans, when the Duke of York and his adherents had challenged King Henry's right to choose his own ministers? And how successful that challenge had been in the streets and gardens of the town. The Duke of Somerset had died in those streets. So had Lord Clifford and the Percy Earl of Northumberland; Lancastrian magnates done to death, while the call to arms from every side had been *A Warwick! A Warwick!* My husband, Richard Neville, the Earl of Warwick, the leader of the attack on the royal forces, revelled in the clash of arms while I remained at Warwick Castle and, as ever, worried that he might not return unscathed.

So much for my sleepless nights: my worst fears were not realised. Richard had been unharmed. King Henry had survived with nothing worse than a fleshy arrow-wound in the neck, while the Duke of York had proclaimed his loyalty to the wounded King and escorted him back to London, still King, but did not everyone know that his crown was now dependent on York's good will? All I could do, a mere woman, a looker-on, was pray that the deaths at St Albans would bring them all to their senses.

'Will this bring peace?' I asked Duchess Cecily, who had followed me into the space.

'I think not.'

Yet here they were, the combatants in that bloody battle, united in amity: Queen Margaret, leading the way with the

Duke of York, hand in hand, as if the greatest of friends rather than the most vicious of enemies. Then my Neville father-in-law, the Earl of Salisbury, reluctant and saturnine, yoked with Henry Beaufort, Duke of Somerset, heir of the dead Duke of Somerset at St Albans. Another pairing of fervid enemies who would spit on the other and run him through with a sword rather than offer aid in battle. How did their hands manage to clasp in such comfortable harmony? How did their expressions manage to express complacency rather than revulsion at what was being asked of them?

Then came the man I was here to see. To admire, for was that not the role of a wife? It was my silent role, for I rarely spoke of it. Richard Neville, Earl of Warwick, hand grasped in hand with Henry Holland, Duke of Exeter, whom he despised as a hound despised a feral cat that haunted the hearth. Clad in dark velvet and sable fur, the Earl of Warwick was every inch the arrogant magnate who had made a name for himself in the recent clash of wills. I knew him well. The arrogance was no mere show, nor was the ambition that coated him from head to heel, just as surely as the rich fabric. Yes, I admired him, his stern features, his precisely carved lips that could equally smile or snarl. I might fear the extent of his ambition, but he was kind and generous to me.

How much gritting of teeth had it taken to get these protagonists to participate in this procession? How many sweating palms – for they had been forbidden to wear gloves. Skin must adhere to skin in friendship. Richard's face was a picture of bland acceptance. Only the line between his brows might indicate his loathing of this façade of camaraderie.

And then came the King, the sixth Henry, who had ordered this procession to be made, walking alone in royal robes of velvet and ermine. Even with the crown on his head his slight figure was far less impressive than the allies of York, yet the cheering increased. Was he not King? He beamed on his subjects and raised his hand in acknowledgement, his rings glittering.

How could this seemingly frail man unite this disparate group?

'The King is optimistic,' I murmured.

'The King is a fool if he thinks a Love Day will put all to rights,' Duchess Cecily replied.

It had taken months of negotiation, but Henry had succeeded, or at least it seemed that he had, when he had negotiated for clemency, and for reparations for the death and destruction at St Albans. But could he keep them together? The air around us was alive with unspoken hostilities. Richard caught my eye as they climbed the steps, from where they would disappear into the sombre depths of the cathedral to give thanks for this ostentatious healing. A wry curve of his lips, the slightest twitch of his dark brows, his watchful eyes that today were as darkly black as a storm-cloud. It was impossible to know what he was thinking although he had been vocal enough when we had broken our fast together that morning.

'It is a sham! A mockery! A travesty of all the hatred that bites below the surface, and everyone knows it.' He had thrust aside the platter of meat and bread, scattering crumbs. 'You know it, I know it. The only one who is still living in a dream of myth and legend is the King. I have no appetite for this.'

'But you will still do it,' I had observed, accepting the political necessity, despite Richard's reluctance.

'I will because I must, but God forgive me if my heart is not in it and my hand flinches from the clasp with that viper Exeter.'

He left me to my own repast, but not before planting a kiss on my coifed hair in passing. As the door closed behind him I could hear him growling about wolves in sheep's clothing, but whether this referred to himself or his present partner, the Duke of Exeter, I did not know.

I was almost within touching distance of the King. How had he achieved the unachievable? It was assuredly not the work of Queen Margaret, who was now standing on the top step, turning to face the crowd with a wave of her free hand, clad in blue and white as if she were the Blessed Virgin herself. There was none of the celebration that could be read in Henry's wide smile. The Queen was not in any mood to rejoice, despite the regal authority of her trailing velvet robes, her face turned to bestow recognition on the noisy crowd, her burnished hair carefully plaited to support her gilded coronet.

'She detests all of this,' Cecily observed. 'You can see it in the set of her jaw, but I have to admire her self-control.'

'Her loyalty to the King is without question,' I agreed.

'What choice does she have?' Cecily asked with a fatalistic shrug. 'It is the duty of every wife.'

'Who's to know where this will lead us? Will it bring us happiness or tragedy?'

My words, offered without too much thought, struck against my heart. Where would we all be led in the coming years? I thought that this Love Day would have no lasting blessings, and yet I hoped beyond hope that it might be so.

'Best not to think about it,' Countess Alice commented with another sniff.

They began to move again, in solemn, silent procession, into the dark reaches of the cathedral where they would give thanks for this return of peace, leaving me to consider what I had seen. Whatever happened in the future, I would have no place in it but to watch and follow the dictates of my husband. I knew the limits to my power and influence, as did most women. A wise woman could whisper in her husband's ear but whether he listened would be beyond her control. Whatever my thoughts on the matter, Richard was planning that we should leave England, to go and live in the great fortress of Calais. In return for his valuable services to the Duke of York's cause at the Battle of St Albans, Richard had been made Captain of Calais; an impressive honour, of which he was suitably aware.

And now, despite this parody of a Love Day, of King Henry still beaming with good will, the sun making of his golden crown a halo, there was no pretence of where the power might lie, or that Richard had his share of it. At York's behest, it had been the Earl of Warwick who had carried the King's great sword when they had escorted him back through the streets of London. A victory parade indeed.

I wondered what the Queen was thinking behind her regal façade. My own thoughts were interwoven with anxieties. Those who challenged the God-given power of the King could be accused of treason; traitors could come to sticky ends. All my life, as far back as I recalled, had been tied to the heraldic colours of Richard Neville, Earl of Warwick, for good or ill. Duchess Cecily must have seen the fear momentarily writ large in my face. She patted my arm.

'All will be well, Anne. Our menfolk will not willingly reject the authority they have recently gained. King Henry will reward them with high office at Court, as is their right, and thus the days of the Duke of Somerset are numbered. You'll soon have Warwick back under your feet, and be wishing him at war again. Is it not the same in all families such as ours?'

'You can always send him to Calais on his own,' Countess Alice suggested.

'I think I would prefer to know what he is doing,' I replied.

'I have learned,' Duchess Cecily observed, 'that with the

Neville and Plantagenet families, sometimes it is better not to know.'

We exchanged a smile, but it was a grim recognition. Did we three women not know that there was neither humour nor reconciliation in this Love Day? A dark and forbidding entity rumbled beneath the damask and fur and gold. At that moment an errant cloud covered the sun, dimming all the grandeur, as if in a terrible foreshadowing. An omen indeed, some would say.

## Margaret of Anjou, Queen of England

I allowed my hand to rest limply in his. There was nothing of reconciliation in this hand-clasp, only a hard-won mockery of amity as I came to a halt on the top of the shallow steps, turning to look back at the procession following me. My impulse was to release my hand from that of the Duke of York, but that I must not do. He had a firm grip, and one I disliked, as much as I disliked him. I could imagine him gripping a sword in his battle for power. He was my enemy, but this was a show of unity and it must not be broken now, not after all of my lord Henry's planning to heal the terrible wounds of the past year. Love Day forsooth! But I would play the part to the bitter end, kneeling before the altar in the cathedral in derisive penitence.

Those on the lower steps had also come to a halt, waiting for me to continue. All my enemies, and the enemies of my husband if he would actually acknowledge it, were here in one place. York, Salisbury, Warwick. Not only my enemies, but those of my son. I knew it as if it were written in blood. If they had their way, my son, Prince Edward, would never be offered the crown or the throne of England.

And then there was my husband, Henry, King of England,

looking more than kingly on this festive occasion that was of his own making. There was even a confidence about him as he bowed his head to his subjects, who cheered and wished him well. A man of peace, of erudition, a man who had secured victory here against all the odds. There were no signs today of the cruel instability of his mind when he had recognised no one, not even me, his wife of a goodly number of years. He had not even registered the birth of his son until the mists finally passed from his inner sight. But today, in appearance at least, he was truly a king again. Had I not personally supervised his choice of vestments, insisting on the royal colours of blue and red with a thick edge of ermine? Had I not been present to ensure his grooming was fit for a king, his fair hair shining?

A cloud appeared to obscure the sun. I saw no omen, merely the threat of a deluge of rain, which might mar the King's hard-earned grandeur, leaving him drenched like a half-drowned rat.

What I desired more than any one thing on this abominable day was that I had my son here with me, to show him to the people whom one day he would rule, but this was not the time. I knew when to bring him, Prince Edward, the hope of our reign, into the centre of this disgraceful show of power, and it was not in this procession. I would bide my time and make my own decision.

Behind me Salisbury cleared his throat in impatience. I must move on. We would give thanks for peace and unity. I looked over the faces once again, finally on the expression of the man at my side, the dark saturnine features much like those of a raptor with their sharp edges. I did not trust them, I did not trust him. York had an eye to the crown. He had royal blood in his veins from two royal sons of King Edward III, which would stoke his ambitions.

Could my lord Henry keep these raptors, this pack of wolves, at bay?

Perhaps not, but I could. I must. And with my help my lord Henry would prevail. I would never allow any attack against the inheritance of our son.

Over towards my left I could see the treacherous wives enjoying the achievements of their menfolk, the women of York, of Salisbury, of Warwick. I owed much to Duchess Cecily for her kindness to me in the early days of my marriage when conception was difficult, but gratitude could easily wear thin. As for Alice and Anne, they were coated with the same mire as their lords. Warwick's wife caught my glance. She inclined her head but with no hint of any undue loyalty. Indeed, her stare was surprisingly judgemental. What did she see for her family? Power. A golden crown. I could see nothing but war. I turned and, still harnessed to York, I led the procession into the cathedral. I would indeed dedicate myself to the Blessed Virgin for this day of peace, but that did not mean that I had to believe that it would last beyond the week.

'Come, my lady. Let us kneel and give thanks. Our lord the King has high hopes of his miracle of healing.'

I turned to look at York, whose eyes glinted with the triumph of the occasion, and managed a smile.

'As do I.'

At last he released me, allowing me to wipe my hand surreptitiously down the luxurious nap of my skirt, flexing my fingers. Whatever happened, this vicious show of unity might fool many in the crowd that had witnessed it, even if it were all a disturbing falsehood. Like trying to sweeten the stench of a midden with a shower of rose petals.

Here they were, these allies of York, striding into the cathedral, as if treason had never been their plan. Here they were, prepared to kneel, heads bent, proclaiming their loyalty, while I kept my anger rigidly suppressed beneath a gracious expression. Henry was smiling, accepting, willing to grant York's petition for forgiveness, whereas I knew well their ambitions, this group of over-powerful magnates. York desired above all to wield power, to remove our faithful Somerset from my lord Henry's side. Henry must never accede to York's control of government. The Duke of Somerset could be relied on, and I would stand beside him. It was a diabolical situation. I could only thank the Blessed Virgin that I had carried a son and heir for my lord the King.

Walking forward between the bright banks of candles ordered by my lord Henry to illuminate our glorious union, I knelt before the altar, troubled with the weight of what we might face. Until the day that Prince Edward was old enough to take power into his own hands, what was the role of the Queen in this troubled Court? Intercessor? Peacemaker? Intermediary? All of them feminine skills, advising the King so that he might make the right decisions. Instead, I would take Henry and his government firmly in hand. Henry needed no protector, no constable. Unless I took on that role.

As for York and his allies, they had made me an enemy, as they attempted to make Henry a worthless puppet, obedient to their desires. I would never forgive them for it. But perhaps I would have to do so. I would consider it when my temper was less heated. I wished that Henry would not smile so ingratiatingly at York, at Salisbury and at Warwick. Did he not know that he was smiling at men who would bring him down and strip him of his power?

I needed to know what my enemies were planning so that I might pre-empt them, but of course it was impossible to win the confidence of any one of them.

My attention was taken again by the little knot of women standing together in silent strength as their husbands nominally accepted the authority of royal power over them. I envied their friendship, their family alliance, their solid connection, the manner in which they bent their heads to speak softly with each other. A touch of a hand. A turn of the head. A smile, the meeting of eyes, even a frown and a hint of anxiety. I envied this close-knit community of well-born women. I had no one to speak with except my waiting women, but they could not be confidantes of the Queen of England, and that is what I needed.

Should I consider these women, appeal to them, one woman to another? Yet what would I achieve when they were wed to the enemy? There would hardly be a compassionate ear amongst them. I turned my gaze away from them, towards the cross and the crucified Christ, but my thoughts remained anchored in my uncomfortable isolation. Would it not be useful to know what was being said in those households, what future plans were being made? Were the allies of York even now, when they had been thoroughly subjugated, contemplating another grasp of royal power, to imprison Henry or to even do him to death? I could never discover that. Or could I? From a woman in those households it might be that I could discover news of inestimable value.

Not from Cecily, Duchess of York, despite her kindness to me. She was too loyal to York and too politically astute to serve my purpose. Nor Alice, Countess of Salisbury, a woman with whom I was little acquainted.

My eye fell once more on the tallest, the youngest, Anne Beauchamp, Countess of Warwick, enveloped in costly fur, her veils intricately wired. She might be a little older than I, but not by more than a handful of years. She had her own young family. An interesting woman, self-contained, quietly spoken, confident in her position in society. Perhaps she would be a confidante, or, more importantly, an unsuspecting informant. That is what I needed. An ear in the enemy camp, even if a female one. Did not a woman know what went on in her own household?

I needed a campaign of my own, and one of which my lord Henry had no knowledge, for he would assuredly denounce my lack of honesty. I no longer cared for honesty. This was a battle for the survival of the House of Lancaster.

# 2

# *Significant Beginnings*

## Anne, Countess of Warwick

My marriage had been negotiated when I was eight years old. I was not informed of this impending alliance, but overheard the discussion, listening at doors as any child of eight years might do when she escaped the cleric who was teaching her to read. My opinions, my desires, my attractiveness to my future husband, or him to me, were all irrelevant, as they were to all daughters of noble families. My mother and father were planning for the future. My father, Richard Beauchamp, Earl of Warwick, and my mother, Isabel Despenser, both with powerful names, sought suitable connections for their Beauchamp children.

'The Nevilles are interested,' my father stated behind the closed door, probably raising a cup of red wine to toast the success of the coming negotiation.

'And they have enough Beaufort royal blood in their veins to be attractive to us.'

My mother had her own smattering of royal blood, as she often told me. It meant nothing to me.

'Then let it be so,' my father agreed. 'Anne and my heir Henry will wed two of the Neville children. Richard and Cecily.'

And that was my marriage, and that of my brother Henry,

agreed upon. I would have no inheritance other than my dower. That much I did know.

'It will be a good marriage for Richard Neville,' my mother observed. 'If his father had not wed the daughter and only heir of an earl, and thus become Earl of Salisbury through her claim, the Neville sons would be no more than mere north-county knights. Salisbury will be looking for a wife from a formidable family for his son.'

So his name was Richard Neville. I did not know him.

'He is only six years old,' my father said. 'A marriage in name only, of course.'

I would not leave home. Not yet. I made a rapid departure on hearing my father's footsteps approaching the door.

What difference did this decision make to my childhood and my own anticipation of becoming a Neville bride, wed to a boy of whom I had no knowledge? None at all. Marriages in our families were arranged by signatures on a document. By negotiation and decisions over dowers and jointures. All was a matter of sought-after alliances, of money and power. Had it not always been so? One day we would meet, be wed, and would live together. I would carry the Neville heirs for the future. If I was fortunate there would be some affection between us.

Thus, my future was something to be accepted, not feared, certainly not worried over. The days of my childhood were no different now that I was an affianced bride. It might not even happen. So many affianced children never reached the church door together through the exigencies of death and disease and battle. It did not occupy my mind to any degree other than that one day with good fortune I would wed and go to live at Middleham Castle with Richard Neville.

I hoped that at least he would be amenable.

Thus I was not raised to consider that I might one day hold

any attraction as a bride of some value. Unlike my great-great-grandmother Johane de Geneville, who had become through marriage the Countess of March and was a major heiress in her own right, I was never intended to be an heiress. A daughter of a second marriage for both my mother and father, I had four older half-sisters, as well as my full brother Henry who would inherit the Beauchamp titles and estates. As a younger daughter I was not raised to see myself as of vast importance even though I was part of a formidable household, my father holding court and military office throughout his life. Richard would never have expected that I bring him so much direct power or wealth, or even a title. My brother Henry became Earl of Warwick on our father's death and soon had a daughter of his own.

But death brought rapid changes; the unexpected death of my brother Henry, and then, most unfortunately, Henry's tiny daughter, left me, at twenty-one years, old enough, even as I mourned their loss, to see the importance of the repercussions of these deaths, as the one survivor and the Beauchamp heiress. Richard Neville had gained a jewel of great price in that eight-year-old child. Through me he inherited all my father's lands and titles, and thus became Earl of Warwick. We were one of the most wealthy and powerful families in all England, and I a far more valuable wife than Richard had ever anticipated.

What of me? I regretted my brother's death far more than I valued my stepping into his high-born shoes as Countess of Warwick in my own right. There was no ambition in me to share power, or direct policy. Was I not raised with a belief in loyalty and duty, as were all daughters? All I looked for was a family of my own, living in peace, with sons to carry on the inheritance, daughters to wed into attractive marriages, and a husband with whom I could build a friendship, and who would not find me an impossible wife to live with. Richard did not seem dissatisfied with me as a wife, nor was he averse to my company. How could he be, when with the Beauchamp deaths I had brought him the unexpected but highly valuable Earldom of Warwick? Valuable wives were worth their weight in gold coin and Richard wore the title with much dignity and self-esteem.

As a child, how could I have known that my brother's death and thus my inheritance would set family against family? I should have known, and quickly learned the truth. When battles were fought on English soil, personal vendettas would play a major role in the spilling of blood.

I had no regrets about the marriage arranged for me. I would never have wanted any other fate than to be wife of Richard Neville. Not even when our future was turned upside down; not even when Richard became a landless outlaw, stripped of his lands and attainted for treason. Even when we disagreed, I was where I belonged. It was a treasure to be held close and protected.

My abilities soon proved to be considerable, well polished in my father's household. I could manage my own affairs as a wife of a great magnate. I could oversee the keeping of accounts in the hands of my steward and the supplying of the major fortresses that we held with all the necessities for a life of luxury. Such skills came to my fingertips. This is what I had expected of my life, to manage the households of a powerful and wealthy magnate. I had never foreseen that he would become such a figure of authority, of charisma, of forceful competence in the government of England.

But I was not the political animal that Queen Margaret was. I had no role in the government of the kingdom, nor did I ever wish it. And yet there lived in me the strength of will of that great-great-grandmother Johane de Geneville, who had faced grief and loss and treason in her life, but had striven to see the restoration of her family's fortunes. I determined to be a worthy successor to her as wife of Richard Neville, Earl of Warwick. Would I fight and struggle for legal recognition, as that distant Johane had done? I was no fearsome raptor. But I would do all in my power to protect my family. Perhaps I was not so different from our She-Wolf Queen after all.

Sometimes I yearned for a quiet life with my family. Richard's ambitions to impose his will on critical matters of government were not mine; indeed, they often reduced me to despair, when the outcome might be decided on a battlefield, redolent of instant death or terrible mutilation. Living with such fears, I just wished that Richard was more often at home, in our castles at Warwick or at Middleham, and not involved in some distant campaign that did not involve me. Perhaps this Love Day meeting of enemies would be the first step on the road to my hopes being fulfilled.

## Margaret, Queen of England

How had I come to this situation, where covert threat and danger hemmed me in on every side? As with all women of royal birth, I had no choice in the matter.

'A marriage has been arranged for you.'

My father, Duke René of Anjou, announced this in the wake of a royal courier, sent by the King of France to impart important news. It was no more than I would expect. A marriage to a man I did not know, but a man of considerable power.

I would be Queen of England.

'I am gratified,' I said. 'I will be honoured to accept the role expected of me.'

My marriage to King Henry of England was simply a step in the ongoing lethal chess game between England and France. Both sides desired a peace settlement. How to achieve it? Henry sought a French bride and King Charles VII was not averse to it, to tie the English King firmly into some level of friendship. I was niece to King Charles and of an age at fourteen years to be the perfect choice. I smiled at the image in my looking glass when I returned to my chamber to contemplate the prospect. I would be Queen of England within the year.

Many Englishmen would have said, and did so, sometimes in coarse language, that I lacked experience, lacked knowledge. The experience would come to me with time but the knowledge of the value of power was already embedded in me. I knew what was due to me and my husband, King Henry. I would allow no man to strip away even an ell of it, the length from the tip of my elegant middle finger to my royal elbow. Inheritance was everything. God's anointing was supreme.

'You will step into this marriage with utmost assurance as a daughter of France,' my father had said. 'And a daughter of Anjou.'

It was true. I came from a line of women – strong women – who were accustomed to wielding power. Not that they sought it. That was not the role of a woman, as I had been well taught. But when it became necessary for a woman to wield authority they were quick to take hold of it. The women in my family had the ability and self-confidence to grip the reins of government and make those critical decisions to safeguard the realm.

I lacked for neither that ability nor that confidence.

'It is our role to hold our enemies to account,' my grandmother had instructed me.

This lady, my paternal grandmother, was the famous Yolande of Aragon. She was left as Regent in Anjou for her eldest son, ruling the duchy and resisting English military incursions. It was said of Yolande that she possessed a man's heart in a woman's body. It was my ambition to also possess such an impregnable heart.

My mother, Isabelle of Lorraine, sadly dead before my marriage, proved equally to be a woman of renown. When her husband was held captive, waiting for a ransom to be paid, Isabelle took the power of the crown into her own hands and fought the wars in her husband's name.

I spent eight years with my grandmother as a young girl, taking for granted that politics, wars and administration were discussed by women at every turn of the stair. It was a natural element for women in my family, much as the air that we breathed. When I set foot in England I knew that I would make my mother and grandmother proud of me. I would be a worthy child of their skill in holding what was their own with the firmest of hands. Neither of these two women whose blood I shared shrank from taking power if their position was in danger. Neither would I. I would be a sure and certain help for my new husband. He was twenty-three years old and thus a man with some experience.

What I did not know was if England would value a strong woman as queen to rule over them. Or would I be expected to be a silent and dutiful companion? I would soon discover.

'Be sure to tell my lord Henry, King of England, that I am grown to be a woman of good health and great beauty,' I said when arrangements were first made for us to meet.

What woman would not want her chosen husband to admire her? He must see me as worthy of his regard, as well as the future mother of his son and heir. Sadly I had no dowry of any note to take with me. Health and beauty and high birth must be enough to win the King and his subjects to my side.

'I will tell him, this English King, that I am sending him the White Dove of Peace,' my father agreed, then crowed with laughter, for he knew me well. 'More like a hunting gyrfalcon with sharp talons. I will pray that this English King soon learns to appreciate your value. Perhaps the antagonistic English will even take you to their hearts.'

I soon learned that they did not want a politically active queen, meddling in ruling the country. The English had no wish for me to take on this role. I remembered one sharp comment, although who said it, I had no idea.

'It is not fitting or safe that all the keys should hang from the girdle of one woman.'

Would they find me meddlesome? I hoped not. I hoped that I would have no need to be so. But with the fragility of my lord Henry's health, I had begun to fear that it might be so if I was to secure the inheritance for him and his son. I would not be averse to having the keys of the kingdom hanging from my girdle, and I would challenge any man who tried to stop me. I would lead an army into battle for my lord Henry if I was called upon to do so.

# 3

## *Love Day Reconciliations Under Attack*

### Anne, Countess of Warwick

Having made our protestations of good faith in St Paul's, we were now gathered to celebrate in Westminster Great Hall, all together, past friends and enemies, under the aegis of our King who continued to glow in the success of his venture. Wine was handed round beneath the lambent gaze of the gilded, carved angels above our heads. What did they make of this interweaving of old enemies?

The mismatched pairs for the Love Day were now separated, clearly in relief, while it seemed to me that the whole magnificent space held its breath in tension as if it was expected that swords would be drawn after the first draining of the wine cups. Would it not have been better to have disbanded and gone home after the thanksgiving? It must have been Henry's command to celebrate and raise our cups in mock jollity at this false return of good will. I would like to have been hopeful, but I was not naive. As Richard had said, this was a sham.

I remained aware of the Queen, noting how endlessly watchful and protective of Henry she was, after the months of vacuity that had laid him low, withdrawing him with a light hand on his arm from any dangerous gatherings. Also, I acknowledged her sheer elegance of face and form, which outshone the presence of her regal husband. His manner continued to be kindly and welcoming, seeing no trouble building, whereas the Queen's acid expression suggested that she could taste it on her tongue. It might be four years since the disaster at St Albans, but memories were long and full of vengeance.

Suddenly, beneath the ever-watchful eyes of the carved angels, there were the raised tones of an outbreak of ill-temper between the two sides. I looked over my shoulder for those involved. Richard was in the middle of it with his father, as might be expected. King Henry, too, looking anxious, mystified, with Somerset at his side. I took a step, aware that I could achieve nothing in this company, but still reluctant to allow the quarrel to develop. I could hear Richard's voice across the hall, sharply combative.

'Have we not taken an oath of loyalty? Have we not knelt before God in penance? And still we are not trusted.'

I took another step, until a hand on my arm stopped me. It was the Queen.

'Leave them. You can do no good here. I will deal with it.' Margaret; her eyes, momentarily holding mine, were not unfriendly, but held all the authority of the Queen of England. Then her gaze sharpened. 'And where, my lady Countess, will you stand when this becomes a matter of drawing swords again?'

I tried to pacify, as I had been doing all my life. 'Do you think that it will, Your Grace? Has there not been enough bloodshed between Englishmen?'

'Assuredly. Do you tell me that your husband will be satisfied? Is this just a light exchange of opinion?'

The voices had grown louder, more antagonistic, Salisbury joining in.

'How can we ever trust the sly words of the Duke of Somerset? He will always be our enemy.'

They were already moving into dangerous waters.

'I do not always know my husband's mind in this matter,' I said. Could I have offered a weaker reply? I recoiled at the thought, but it would be well to be circumspect in this surprising exchange of opinion with the Queen.

'But you see his ambition. He must speak of it when you break your fast.'

'His ambitions are not always mine, but I will stand with my husband, of course,' I said. 'As will you, with yours. You have more power to determine events than I do, Your Grace.'

For a moment I thought she would deliver a sharp reply, but instead her lips curved in what might pass as a smile: 'You speak truth. Let us pray for an amicable solution, one that will please all, Countess.' A wry comment but an honest one. 'Sometimes I fear our prayers will be useless. Meanwhile let us find comfort in our children.'

'I do, my lady. I am sure that you find solace in the birth of your son.'

As if an inner candle had been lit, the Queen's face glowed.

'You cannot imagine the pride I have in him. He is the light of my life. To give birth to a son is so vitally important in a family such as ours, is it not? I consider it imperative when inheritance is an issue. Is it not a wife's duty?' Then, at a further outburst of choler from the gathering of warring men: 'I am needed. Perhaps we will talk again later.'

She left me alone, to fight against the bitter truth of her words.

The unexpectedly complex conversation with the Queen, brief though it was, had left me with the dregs of a long-standing anguish. On the surface, her initial response to me had shown a willingness to condemn me as the wife of her enemy Warwick. But then there had been that acceptance of our pleasure in our families, the joy that must be experienced by any wife and mother in her ability to carry a son. It had surprised me. I would never have expected that harmony with the Countess of Warwick was in the Queen of England's mind.

No, I had mistook her intent, I decided, as I watched her approach the furious magnates. There was no friendship here. It had been nothing less than a brutal affirmation in my presence, that the birth of a boy was critical in a family such as ours. Some would say that Margaret was merely turning a knife in the very personal wound of my failure.

## Margaret of Anjou, Queen of England

'Let us not break the good will of this day, my lords.'

Relieved to abandon the Countess and any attempts to be conciliatory, I strode to stand beside my lord Henry in the squabbling array, keeping my voice soft, persuasive, but with despair in my heart. My husband the King was increasingly incapable of leadership, while my son – my only son and probably always would be – was a mere five years old. How could we hold the magnates such as York and Salisbury on a tight leash?

'It has been a magnificent occasion,' said Henry. 'I thank you all for your participation. God will bless us in our ventures to bring peace to this country. It is wrong that we should shed English blood, Englishmen fighting against Englishmen.'

'It is difficult when those Englishmen claim powers that do not belong to them,' Somerset replied, in no manner mollified.

'The Battle of St Albans is over, my lords,' I said. 'We must ensure that it will be the last between us.'

'We will threaten neither you nor your crown, my lord,' Warwick replied, addressing himself to the King rather than to me, which was quite in character. 'Are we not your loyal subjects? Whatever the Duke of Somerset might imply, we will not raise arms against you. Those days are past, and will not return.'

Facile, empty words. I believed none of them. So far, they had got what they wanted. York had become Constable of England, as he had always intended, Warwick appointed the influential Captain of Calais, while so many of our most valuable and loyal allies lay dead in the streets and gardens of St Albans after the fierce fighting, the true blood of our supporters shed by this rabble that followed the self-serving Duke of York.

I pinned a smile to my mouth, masked my rank hatred, and raised my cup. No good to be had in stirring up the lees of even more ill feeling at this point in the game.

'Let us drink to the future, my lords.'

'As my wife says –' My lord Henry nodded '– let us be merry and give thanks to God.'

They complied, of course. More outright enmity would be reserved for a later date.

'To peace.'

'To unity.'

'To England.'

As I led Henry away to a less contentious grouping, I turned my head to give a small nod of achievement to the Countess of Warwick, certainly a woman with whom I might have had some kindred spirit in a different life. I thought it would not happen. Her husband might just be the most bitter of my enemies. I must keep my own counsel and hope that my lord Henry remained in good health. He had removed his crown and held it lightly in his hand as if it meant little to him. I resisted the urge to take it from him, to run my fingers through his dishevelled hair, straighten the jewelled collar on his shoulders, and replace the coronet, as if crowning him with my own hands.


## Anne, Countess of Warwick

Now what was the Queen plotting?

At that moment when it would be natural for the celebration to end, there was a flicker of vibrant movement under the great arched doorway. One of Margaret's ladies-in-waiting, who had been with her since she had first come to England, Katherine de Vaux, stood there until the Queen, her face glossy with pleasure, beckoned her forward. With her was a child clad as a page, fair hair neatly combed under a jaunty feathered cap, his small body encased in a tabard emblazoned with the royal colours of crimson and azure and gold, much like a miniature herald. This was no place for a child. Surely the Queen should send him back to the nursery, yet anticipating no displeasure, the child walked steadily forward until he stood in front of his mother. It was of course Prince Edward of Westminster, the royal heir. The apple of Margaret's eye. The light of her life. The child who, with true legitimacy, would stamp on York's hopes of taking the throne when King Henry died.

The boy bowed, his movements polished for one so young, but then he was being raised as the future King. Margaret put her hands on his shoulders, turned him round so that he faced the gathering. She raised her voice, speaking clearly with all the authority that her husband lacked.

'My lords.'

All attention was caught at her clear, high accents.

'Here is your future King.'

She looked around, willing them to acknowledge the boy, how he made a comparison with his father even though so young and inexperienced. The child was polished and confident. His smile was one of pure delight to be here in our midst. The magnates dutifully bowed to their future King. The women curtsied, as did I.

'I would present to you my son,' the Queen said, unnecessarily, but she would make her point. 'The heir to the crown. I thank God for this blessing. Does not every man need an heir, particularly a man of power?' She curtsied in all due reverence to King Henry. 'It was my honour to give birth to a son to secure your inheritance, my lord. My failure to give you a son would have been a failure indeed.'

Henry raised her to her feet, bending to press his fingers lightly against the child's cheek. It was well done to restore good relations, to centre it on this bright child. As she walked past me, the child's hand in hers, her glance towards me was truly one of victory. It seemed to me that I knew immediately where her thoughts lay. Had her words not announced it? She had a son and I did not. Hers was the victory and I had failed.

It was a sharp blow to my heart, my emotions frozen in that instant. No intimacy bloomed in her cold heart. I should not have been surprised that Margaret could show such a depth of malice, but then she saw her husband and her whole security under attack. She knew my weakness. I had been able to produce for our Neville line only two daughters, while Richard's family throughout the generations was fecund with handfuls of healthy sons. I had no son.

I might have read it as pity in Queen Margaret's glance. I did not. I read it as triumph and I turned away to hide my sense of failure, regretting that I allowed it to hurt me so much.

## Margaret, Queen of England

A victory in a minor way. Well planned, perfectly executed, I knew that it would be good to make these lords remember that the King had an heir. As for the Countess of Warwick, it had been impossible not to read the brief flash of emotion in her eyes; all the regret, all the sorrow of failure. Of course. In fairness, I had forgotten. She had no son of her own, only two girls. Even as I rejoiced at my son's presence in that hall, I felt the pang of guilt. I knew what was in her heart, from the days when I feared that my lord Henry and I would never conceive after many years of intimate marriage. My words to her had been thoughtless, less than compassionate, even if it was not wilful cruelty. I must try to right that wrong.

But for now, my own inability to conceive was in the past. My son would rule England in the glory of a true monarch. York might be Constable of England but that was a post dependent on the good will of the King. I would ensure that it would be a temporary one. When my son was old enough, he would stand at his father's side.

Approaching the door where I would hand him over to my waiting woman again, my son laughed up into my face, a hint of mischief in a task well executed.

'Did I do well, *Maman*? Did I make you proud of me?'

'Indeed you did, my son.'

'*Quand est-ce que je porterai la couronne d'Angleterre?*' he asked, his eyes searching the room for his father. '*Comme celui que porte mon pere?*'

'*Quand tu seras adulte, mon fils,*' I replied. 'But you must speak in English when you are at Court. You are an English prince.'

I kissed him, then looked over to where Warwick's wife stood beside her husband. Did Warwick ever blame his wife for her inabilities? I was sorry to have stirred her grief. I would write to her, but I would be careful. If nothing came of it, I would have lost nothing. She should be honoured that a queen should even consider communicating with her.

And yet here perhaps was the opportunity to build a bridge with the Countess, albeit a flimsy one. Any information of affairs in the Warwick household would be of value to me. Friendship? I would not call it that. Merely a means to a political end.

# 4

## *An Exchange of Correspondence Two Weeks After the Love Day*

**Margaret of Anjou, Queen of England, to Anne, Countess of Warwick**

By the Queen.

It is in my mind to sue for forgiveness, although you will understand that it is difficult for the Queen of England to so debase herself.

If you believed that my delight in my son at that uneasy Love Day celebration was a deliberate attempt to enhance your own pain, I must assure you that it was not, and I ask pardon for it. I had in truth forgotten that you had only daughters. It may well be that you will still have a son, and I hope that you will, even though sons can break your heart. It is so easy to envisage the death and loss of a son on a battlefield. I pray that Prince Edward will not break mine.

Can any level of amity ever be maintained between us? What can I say to you that is not as much a travesty as that procession through the streets of London? I have no compassion, no sympathy, no understanding for the Duke of York and his allies. They want power that is not theirs to take. I fear for my lord King Henry in what must be a coming conflict. I fear for my son who is so young and must be guided in his thoughts and actions.

This chasm between us is not of your making, nor of mine, but as long as York and Salisbury and Warwick have a desire to seize power from my lord the King, then there can be no real understanding between us.

Yet, if you can discover a willingness to communicate with me, I think that I would find gratitude in my heart. I would regret losing the opinions of a well-informed woman who has some intimate knowledge of the burdens I bear and the animosity that affects our families.

I ask that you will forgive any uncharitable comments I may have made.

Written at Westminster by a clerk in the employ of the Queen.

Signed by: Margaret
Queen of England

## Anne Beauchamp, Countess of Warwick, to Margaret, Queen of England

I received your letter at Warwick Castle with some degree of astonishment. I was unsure how I should reply, or even if I should, but I have decided to do so.

I feel the pain you have expressed, and return it. I fear that there is nothing more that can be said between us. I, too, saw the pretence of the Love Day. Was it not clear to all? A mummers' play to achieve a feigning of friendship between old enemies. A complete misrepresentation of the emotions of those present.

You must realise that my lord of Warwick sees the Beaufort Duke of Somerset as an enemy to our rightful position in the realm. Somerset is driven by a need to destroy us. My loyalties are to my lord of Warwick and the allies of York, as yours are to King Henry and the Beauforts.

There can be no true intimacy between us, yet I will continue to pray for you and your son, even if you will not pray for my family. Any friendship, even by correspondence, would be impossible in the circumstances, although we managed a semblance of courtesy in Westminster Hall. My lord of Warwick would not be in favour and although I will make my own choices of whom I will befriend, I will not deny him his authority in matters of loyalty. It would be seen as a betrayal to preserve an understanding with you, of which he was unaware.

Yet, as I write, I am unwilling to abandon the light connection we have attempted. It eases a pain in my heart that your flaunting of your son was not a deliberate act to wound me. I understand why you saw a need to present him to the great magnates.

Was it deliberate that you made use of a clerk to write the letter for you, rather than forming your apology in your own hand? I accept of course that the signature is your own.

Written at Warwick Castle in her own hand.

Anne

Countess of Warwick

# 5

## *Conflict and Disaster at Ludford Bridge, October 1459*

### Margaret, Queen of England

This was an act of treason, as clear to me as the waters of the River Teme that tumbled and roared between its banks. We were standing, my lord Henry and I and the royal army, on what would inevitably become a battlefield. This was treachery, as blatant as could be manifested. King Henry had raised his royal banners. York and his allies had responded with theirs displayed.

A challenge. This was war.

The festivity of the Love Day, in all its appalling outward reconciliations, was not long lasting, as anyone of sense, anyone but my lord Henry, would have foreseen. Now here we were after a long and wearying journey to track down our enemy, the supporters of York. At last they were in sight: York himself, his two eldest sons the Earls of March and Rutland, together with Salisbury and Warwick, all drawn up on the flat land beside the bridge over the Teme into Ludlow where York held a most impeccably defensive castle.

All our enemies together in one act of perfidy.

They would be punished. Had Salisbury not shed more Lancastrian blood only a few weeks ago just north of here at

Blore Heath? My lord Henry could no longer afford to be forgiving. Love Days would never be repeated; Henry could afford no more dramatic joining of hands. I would make sure of it.

I nudged hm.

'Go forward and make York retract. Order him to disperse his troops.'

Henry nodded, mounted his warhorse and gave his commands. We advanced. Henry must be seen to lead his troops, to put down this insurrection, and take his revenge.

There were the heraldic colours of the traitors, the rebels, protected by hastily dug ditches and sharpened stakes. Before the range of their troops I could see cannon on carts. They were much outnumbered, but they intended to make a stand and they had the power to hurt us. Henry must not draw back now into uncertainty and cowardice. I pushed my horse into a trot to ride beside him as our heralds proclaimed the promise of pardons for those who would stand down and make amends; there must be some here who would desert York and proclaim loyalty to Lancaster.

This was my lord Henry's plan. I did not approve. Those who stood against us should never be pardoned. Oh, yes, they would willingly retake their oaths of fealty, kneeling in respectful homage, only to break those oaths when they saw a need. They had proved it too many times for trust to lie between us, but my lord Henry, as always, was in a mood to be compassionate. I would be wasting my breath to tell him to issue the order to attack.

'Do you know the importance of today?' Henry asked as I pulled up beside him, masking the fear that sat deep within me, for within the day we could all be dead on the battlefield. But fear must not be allowed to rule. I knew that we must fight. We had no choice.

'It is the day before our son reaches the celebration of his sixth portentous day of his birth,' I said.

'Of what value is that?' Henry demanded pettishly. 'It is the twelfth day of October, the day of the Vigil of St Edward the Confessor,' he explained. 'How can I not offer the hand of friendship to those who face us here?'

'Very easily,' I replied. 'York would rejoice at your death!'

A blast of gunfire rent the air and sent the pigeons flying in panic from the trees along the river bank. I closed my hand on Henry's reins, relieved that our son, Prince Edward, was safely ensconced to the rear with his own bodyguard. Another blast, and we saw the smoke rising from Yorkist cannon.

'The allies of York do not seem to be in the mood for reconciliation,' I said.

Henry turned to one of the heralds. 'Discover what is afoot. Why do they fire without a parley?'

We waited, Henry with growing impatience, until the herald returned.

'Rumours have been spread, my lord, that the King is already dead. Therefore our enemy cannot be charged with treason. They are prepared to fight.'

'But I am still alive.' He looked at me in habitual uncertainty.

'And our enemy must be made to realise it,' I stated, any remaining patience dissipating. 'God's blood, Henry! Come with me.'

The light was fading, but there was still a low sun, sufficient to illuminate a dramatic scene. I sent Henry out before his troops in those last rays, the light glinting on his armour, on his helmet and the golden standard behind him, on his gauntlets as he raised his hand in acknowledgement of the forces against him. It was a magnificent gesture.

There were no more cannon shots, but still no attempt at a parley.

What there was instead was a most valuable defection.

After a light repast of bread and wine, I sent my lord Henry to bed, where he might rejoice that the Confessor had indeed answered his prayers. I was more grateful to Sir Anthony Trollope, who had been lured by the sight of his King, alive and glowing in the light from the setting sun, to cross the line between York and Lancaster, complete with his garrison of prime troops from Calais. A man I would do well not to trust on a battlefield, but how could I not be elated that the Earl of Warwick would feel the slight. Was Warwick not Captain of Calais? Now some of his best troops would take the field against him.

That night I knelt at my prie-dieu with gratitude in my heart.

Tomorrow we would see who would emerge the stronger. God would be with us. I even spared a thought for the Countess of Warwick who might receive ill news after the battle. I would mourn for her inevitable loss, but only when my lord Henry and the Prince were safe and victorious and the Yorkist threat wiped out once and for all.

## Anne, Countess of Warwick

This was what I had feared, but it was a manoeuvre over which I had no influence. Richard had gone to war with his father Salisbury and his uncle by marriage, the Duke of York. I and my two daughters had been ordered to take up residence within the vast protective walls of Warwick Castle. Duchess Cecily was at Ludlow, closer to the fighting than I would have liked. Countess Alice was at Bisham Abbey.

41

'When will father be here?' my elder daughter Isabel asked, bright-eyed and unaware of any danger.

'When he has won his battle.'

'Will it be soon?'

'I expect that it will.'

I thought that it would, and somewhere in the West. Had Salisbury not been successful at Blore Heath, killing Lord Audley, a notable supporter of the King? For certain Henry was no leader of men on the battlefield and, to my knowledge, Queen Margaret had not yet taken to donning armour and leading the affray. If they were in danger my embattled family could always take refuge in Ludlow Castle. The progress of the conflict was not clear to us, but I was not unduly concerned. I told myself this as I drew an optimistic picture for the girls, even as I knew, in my heart, that every battle was dangerous. A random arrow. The blast of a cannon. The heavy blow of a sword from an expert swordsman. A chance fall from a terrified horse. Lives were lost even in victory.

The Love Day, not a year ago, had failed, the joined hands now clutching swords.

'There's a dog howling in the stables,' observed young Anne. 'When a dog howls inside someone will die.'

'Who told you that?' I asked, taken aback, for Anne was not quite four years old.

'Our nurse.'

Who should have known better, but omens were rife in warring households.

'We will pray for your father,' I said, dispatching them to the chapel.

'And for the hound? Perhaps it is in pain.'

'Yes, and for the hound, too.'

My nights were troubled, my days spent in waiting for news,

listening for every new arrival. When it came, it was Richard himself who rode into the outer bailey in a bustle of orders and scurrying men. I met him in the Great Hall. I was given no time to even greet him, much less ask after the events that had driven him here.

'We leave today.' His greeting was clipped and impatient, his voice harsh.

'You have lost a battle,' I remarked.

'It could be said that we have lost it. A feather in the Lancastrian cap!' His face was austere as he turned away to converse with his steward, unwilling to elaborate. Defeat would not sit well with him. I was not unduly worried. Not yet.

'You are not harmed as far as I can see,' I said as he returned and took my hand in a belated greeting. His clothes were shrouded in dust, which transferred itself to me when he pulled me closer and kissed my cheek. At least he spared a moment to embrace me, but it was brief and his mind was elsewhere. All I could think of was that he was alive, even when he was already marching towards the staircase to our private chambers.

'Where are you going?' I asked conversationally, lifting my skirts and following him.

'Calais.'

'Am I coming with you?'

'Yes. Should I leave you here, to be picked up by a Lancastrian force and offered to me for ransom? You would be too expensive.'

'Do I have any choice in this?'

I saw no reason why I and our daughters should leave this safety and flee across the country. Surely Warwick Castle was quite strong enough to withstand a siege, but then I caught the short temper in the gleam of his eye as it fell on me.

'None. Absolutely none! And don't even try to pronounce a reason why I should allow you that choice.'

It was still in my mind to insist that we stay, but reading the determination in the set of his shoulders, I went into fast retreat.

'Very well, but only because I have no wish to be dragged indiscriminately from my own castle and tossed onto horseback.'

'Excellent. We have no time for such frivolity. Get your women to pack some travelling coffers.'

At least he managed a smile, his face, normally so still and controlled, brightening and softening as it rarely did except for a few men or women save myself. For a brief moment I considered my reluctance to ride across country with an army in pursuit. Was there not strength in his argument? If there was danger for us, Calais was the obvious place to take refuge, a fortress where we had lived for many months with Richard as captain of that formidable military base.

'Don't stand there, Anne,' I was chivvied. 'Organise your women and the girls. Garb yourselves for a long ride.'

So I obeyed, as of course I would. I would find out later what had happened to stir the devil in him.

We were on horseback before I had the opportunity, the girls riding pillion behind two of Richard's squires. There was obviously no time to travel by litter, and our luggage would follow later. With a sidelong glance, I considered that dark, fine-boned face, the eyes grey like winter rain, yet lit with the fire of ambition that was rarely absent.

'Are we being followed?' I asked, kicking my mare to keep abreast of him.

'It may be that Lancaster forces are hot on our trail already,' he said as we clattered over the drawbridge and headed south.

'Well? What happened?' I asked.

Setting a fast pace, he ignored my question; instead, he explained his plan of action.

'We will catch up with my father and nephew Edward of March on the road.'

'So we are all in flight.'

'Yes.'

'Is this as dangerous as it sounds?'

The lines of displeasure bracketing Richard's mouth were heavy. Things had not gone well, and his reply was sufficiently moody to suggest a disaster.

'York and his son Rutland have gone west into Wales. They will head for Ireland where they can make a base in Dublin. We will go across the Channel and take refuge in Calais until better days.'

There were two names missing. 'What about Duchess Cecily? What about your mother?'

'My mother is intent on accompanying York to Ireland. Duchess Cecily was still at Ludlow when we left, with the younger children. She may have gone with York, but she may have stayed and simply closed the castle gates, praying that they hold. Not an enviable situation with a Lancastrian army on your doorstep.'

I thought about this. So we were all under threat, and scattered in all directions, like autumn leaves. Something had indeed gone badly wrong. I could not believe that King Henry had won a battle against the might of the Yorkist forces.

'So Henry won,' I suggested in some disbelief.

Richard's quick temper boiled, his hands clenching, causing his horse to toss its head as he kicked it into a smart canter. 'God's blood! We never fought! We never came close enough to even draw a sword!'

He rode off to the head of the cavalcade that was showing signs of slowing down. When he returned, the whole having picked up speed, he continued the conversation as if there had been no pausing.

'They were too strong for us. We might have risked a confrontation since Henry was keen to make peace and might not force a full-scale battle. But that bastard Anthony Trollope, God damn him, changed sides, taking his men – my men – from the Calais garrison with him, leaving us with no choice. We were just outnumbered.' Richard's expression of sour disgust said it all. 'We abandoned the army at night, under the pretence of returning into Ludlow to collect supplies. By the time Henry rose next morning from his prayerful bed we had gone. But they will be on our tail.' He paused, scowling ahead at some unpleasant thought. 'It goes ill with me, to flee and abandon our troops. They were not warned of what we intended. We can only hope that Henry treats them with generosity and turns all his ire on us, the leaders. I would not have done it, but York thought it politic to remove ourselves from what would have been certain death. If we had been taken prisoner, there would have been no reprieve.'

Realising what they had done, I was as horrified at the outcome as he was angry.

'Does it not matter to you, that you abandoned your men? That you left them unprotected to the ravening Lancaster wolves?' I challenged him, in spite of being short of breath from our rapid progress.

'I like it not, but better that than all of us ending up in the Tower with an axe poised over our necks. Henry might be keen to pardon us, but his officers would not. Somerset would call for our heads.'

'Nor would Queen Margaret be lenient.'

'No, she would not. She was with him at Ludford Bridge, strengthening his backbone. You can imagine the quality of her advice, to destroy any noble supporters of York. I expect the royal army will be allowed to take its revenge on Ludlow. After the deliberate destruction we allowed at St Albans, the Lancastrian soldiers will be out for blood.'

'And revenge on us?'

I knew the answer before he gave it.

'Attainder will be our punishment. As foresworn traitors, our lands will be confiscated. Our lives forfeit. We knew the risks when York raised his standards at Ludford Bridge, but we had hoped for a better outcome.'

How bleak a picture, but Richard had taken that risk. To raise arms against the King was treason, and this was not the first time. Fear churned within me, all but choking me, as I considered our future and that of our daughters. As well as the fear, I experienced an unwelcome deluge of resentment. Richard had put us all in danger. There were no certainties now.

'Was it worth it?' I asked. 'Was it justifiable to challenge the King?'

His glance was patently hostile. 'You know the answer to that, Anne. Have you not been party to so many discussions? It is not the King that we oppose, but the men he takes as his advisers. It was more than justifiable to challenge Somerset who sat at the King's side, at the head of the army.'

I understood the cause of this hostility between Richard and Somerset without asking. How could I not, since my own inheritance was partially to blame? The enmity went further than a struggle for power as a royal adviser. It was all about inheritance of land. I had older half-sisters from my father's first marriage. Their husbands, one of whom was a Beaufort, demanded that my inheritance should be shared with them, thus robbing Richard of a considerable quantity of the land I had brought into our marriage. It made for a lasting animosity between us and the

Beaufort Dukes of Somerset. I might have some compassion for my half-sisters, but my inheritance on my brother's death was engrained in law. Through my marriage it had now passed into the hands of the Nevilles; it was as legalistically simple as that. Richard would deal with the resulting hostility in his own formidable manner.

'How can you ask if it was justifiable?' he repeated, his brows drawn into a frown.

'How can you accept that we might lose everything?'

'I don't accept it.' His voice rose into a harsh croak as the swirling wind whipped our breath away. 'How can you think that I will simply stand aside and allow Somerset to take what is ours.'

'I do not accept it. You ill-judge me. I am the reason why you have the title and land to lose in the first place. It is mine too. Did I not bring it to you with my maidenhead? A Beauchamp can be quite as proud as a Neville.'

'As I know.' The tight-lipped anger simmered beside me. 'On this occasion, my combative wife, just do as I ask.'

'I am not the enemy here, Richard,' I replied, fending off his ire. Richard exhaled slowly and I saw his brow smooth a little, his hands relax a little on the reins.

'As I know. Forgive me. The whole thing has been a mess of bad planning.'

Which was as much of an apology as I would get, but I had known him long enough to accept that it was sincerely meant, and I would accept it, even though I wished that he would not attack whoever was closest when fury twisted a knife in his gut.

'So it may well be Calais for ever,' I said.

'Until Somerset is sent by King Henry to be Captain there, and drive us out.'

It was becoming worse and worse. I could think of no

adequate response to this woeful summing up. If the port of Calais was barred against us, what then? Richard must have seen my set expression, for, in a welcome gesture of atonement, he stretched out a hand across the space to clasp mine where it gripped my reins.

'It will not happen. Not if I have anything to do with it. I promise you, we will be safe in Calais and then when the time is right we will return. We will set this injustice aside. One day all our lands will be returned. I'll not let them go.' He released my hand to tuck a strand of hair beneath my travelling hood since it had started to rain. 'Not even the smallest plot of land of Neville and Beauchamp will be allowed to fall into the hands of Henry and his grasping Beaufort allies.' He grinned through the rain. 'The gifts of your maidenhead will continue to be treasured by a Neville lord.'

It was comforting, of course, and I returned the smile. I had to accept it, but at that moment, with two small, fractious girls, I could not be optimistic. We rode on through the wilds of Dorset, stopping at friendly houses, hoping to reach the coast before the royal troops caught up with us. Once we reached Calais we would, at least for the foreseeable future, be safe from attack and be able to draw breath and plan.

When a loose-limbed hare crossed our path, leaping into the undergrowth with one of our hounds snapping at its heels, it made me draw rein for a moment, recalling my daughter Anne's recounting of an ill omen. To meet a hare on the road signified an event of some disaster.

'What is it?' Richard asked.

'Nothing,' I said. 'Nothing at all.'

I could not afford to be drawn into despair by chance ill omens. I would refuse to believe in their power.

*

It was a hard journey, full of fear and anxiety, where every hoof-beat might herald Lancastrian troops, come to arrest or kill. Richard's ability to organise and commandeer vessels was remarkable, as was his patience in the circumstances. How impressive he was, even when events conspired against us and the captain claimed that they knew not the way to Calais. Unperturbed, Richard ordered the sails to be raised and with predictable expertise he himself took the tiller.

'We will get ourselves to safety in Guernsey if nothing else,' he determined.

And I was sure that it would be so. Richard undertook nothing by halves.

Yet it would be the second day of November, on the back of a turbulent sea, that we arrived in Calais, news hard on our tail, and not to Richard's liking. Ludlow had been sacked and Duchess Cecily was taken prisoner to Coventry where she must exist in fear for her life at the hands of a vengeful queen, to whom I might write in utter desperation, although I did not think it would have any effect. She would not listen to any pleas from me and would certainly not respond. Why would a queen write to a subject so tainted in treachery as I?

So much for the soft overtures from the Queen to the Countess.

All was at an end.

Yet I might just take advantage of that connection. Richard need not know. I would do nothing to harm his strategy for our survival, and if my petition could gentle a hard heart, then so much the better. If I could wring some compassion from the loins of a cold queen, then it would be a task worth undertaking.

The coast of France and the port of Calais came into view. Richard appeared at my side to lean on the rail.

'Thank you, my inestimable wife.'

'For what?'

I was still feeling ruffled at the manner of our departure.

'For not making the journey more difficult than it had to be. And no, you are not the enemy.'

I read the lingering restlessness in him and regretted my intransigence. When he held out his hand, I placed mine there. We were safe and I was appreciated, perhaps beyond what I deserved.

# 6

## *An Exchange of Correspondence After Ludford Bridge*

**Anne, Countess of Warwick, to Margaret, Queen of England**

Written from Calais.

There is no necessity for me to write this, because you will know the outcome of the events at Ludlow far more clearly than I, and no doubt be rejoicing in the success of the royal campaign against my family. How can I blame you? I understand that your loyalties to your husband the King and to your son's inheritance are paramount. Do I not feel the same towards my own husband of Warwick and the future of my daughters?

This is the terrible outcome that faces me. I admit to despair. The refusal of both sides to compromise has handed you victory and driven me and my family into exile to Calais. If we are driven out of Calais, too, we will be homeless, penniless, forced to live out our days dependent on meagre charity in some foreign court.

If you have any compassion, if you have any fellow-feeling for women caught between two warring factions, I beg of you to encourage the King to reopen negotiations once more, to invite York and Salisbury and Warwick to return. I am in exile, Countess Alice is in Ireland, separated from her husband, and Duchess Cecily is under your duress in Coventry as far as I am aware. I beg that you will consider our plight and restore us to home and family.

I know that King Henry will listen to your sage advice. Otherwise, the country might be rent in two by war that will never be contained.

When you first came to England you were heralded as a Dove of Peace. We need that Dove more than ever at this present time.

Your loyal subject, writing in hope,

Anne

Countess of Warwick

**Margaret of Anjou, Queen of England, to Anne, Countess of Warwick**

By the Queen.

Written in the hand of her clerk.

Why do you even attempt to sway my judgement? You will fail. I am well aware of what has happened. Nor is there any need for me to respond except that it is necessary for me to make all things plain.

I have no regrets for what has happened to you and your family. What did you expect, when York and his allies raised their banners in the field against the King's forces? That was the time for compromise, for coming to terms, if they had the courage to do so. Instead, they were cowards. They fled, knowing the penalty for their actions. To raise arms against

the anointed King is treason. What did you, Countess
Anne, foresee when your menfolk decided that they dare no
longer face the rightful King and his army?

There could be no compromise. There could be no
forgiveness. I would never petition for my lord King Henry
to hold out the hand of friendship, nor will I in the future.
It must be permanent exile for those who threaten the
peace of this land. A return to England will lead to their
inevitable death.

It is my intention to make the most of our victory, and
ensure the banishment of York and his allies for ever. I wish
you well of your stay in Calais. I doubt that it will be for
long. Would it not be unacceptable for a traitor to remain
on English soil? You will be driven out within the year. As
for the Duke of York, he will probably remain in Ireland
to the end of his days. There will be nothing for him in
England, or for his sons.

I trust your daughters are safe with you. Perhaps you
should consider taking refuge in Ireland, or at the French
Court, if you think you would be made welcome.

Our previous attempt at establishing any sort of affinity
was predictably short-lived. This is the ending for us. It can
be no other way. Once again you will see that this reply is
not written in my hand. I do not correspond with traitors
in exile, or their wives. You can expect no mercy from me,
and certainly I have my lord the King's ear in all matters of
state.

You say that I came to England as a Dove of Peace. That
was indeed so, but those days are long gone. Of what value
is it for me to breathe dulcet tones of sweet reason when
all around is bleak hazard? You will discover that I can be a

She-Wolf of France if I must fight for the true inheritance of my son.

Signed by:

Margaret

Queen of England

# 7

## *War on the Horizon in Coventry and Calais, 1460*

### Margaret, Queen of England

We were in Coventry, the town where we had made our head-quarters after the foolish Ludlow challenge by a hostile Duke of York. It was early morning and a late dark dawn, with heavy clouds as the year drew to its close when I decided that it was a good opportunity to spend some time with my son. It was so easy to leave him to his tutors when urgent matters of state demanded my time. He might be only six years old, yet still I needed to oversee the depth of his education as a good mother should, even the Queen of England.

'You should not be here, my son. Come and read to me,' I said, discovering him in the stables, urging one of the reluctant ostlers to saddle his pony for him, even though it was barely light. 'Show me how well you are learning your lessons. Bring with you the book you are enjoying.'

Willingly enough, the Prince sat beside me on the cushioned window-seat in my private chamber in our comfortable lodgings and began to turn the pages of a well-thumbed book of the tales of King Arthur and his knights. He began to read, carefully but fluently. He had learned well. I was proud of him.

'That is very good,' I said when he had read the tragic tale of the final battle. 'Who do you admire most?'

I thought that he would say Arthur, because he was King. Or Lancelot because of his adventures. Or any of the famous knights who fought with valour and chivalric intent.

'Mordred,' he replied without hesitation.

It took me aback.

'Why Mordred? He was a traitor. He fought against the rightful King Arthur.'

My son looked up at me with serious consideration.

'But he died in the battle. He was a brave soldier.' He looked down to trace one of the flamboyant pictures in his book with his forefinger. 'I like his dark armour and the black cloak. I like his white horse, and his great helm. Look how he wields his sword. I would like to ride into battle as Mordred did.'

'It might be better that you admire King Arthur for his gallant deeds.'

'Oh, I do, *Maman*. But I much prefer Mordred.'

It worried me a little. There was a lesson here that my son must learn. That treachery, however flamboyant and magnificently garbed, must not be admired. To hold Mordred up for hero-worship was no better than admiring the Earl of Warwick because he rode into battle in superb Italianate armour with the dramatic banner of the bear and the ragged staff fluttering above his head.

'Here is some advice, my son,' I said. 'Do not be taken in by outward display. Look for the loyalty in men's hearts, not the quality of his armour or his horsemanship, or the fairness of his face.'

'So I must admire my father the King, even if he does not ride into battle?'

'Exactly that.'

Did he understand? Perhaps not. My son was still very young, but it was never too young to learn the value of loyalty over treachery. Even though I must protect him from the vicissitudes that surrounded us, I would ensure that he became proficient in assessing the value of the men who would one day surround him at Court.

'Must I admire the Duke of Somerset, though he has a harsh voice and scowls at me.'

'Even the Duke of Somerset, who will never let harm come to your father or to you.'

The Prince closed the book on the dramatic images of Mordred.

'But I must not admire the Earl of Warwick.'

'Not the Earl of Warwick. Nor the Duke of York.'

Somewhere my son had absorbed the hostility that was threatening our Court. Satisfied with what I had achieved, sending the Prince back to his tutor with dire warnings if he absconded again to the stables, I decided to make another necessary but probably equally uncomfortable visit and chose a cushioned carved chair beside Henry in his private chamber. The King looked up from the psalter he held in his hand, his finger marking a page. The room was cold and he had not chivvied his body servant into lighting a fire, but at least he wore a heavy damask robe enhanced with fur at cuff and neck.

Since he had not thought to do so, I lit a candle at his elbow.

'My dear Margaret…' He smiled as if he had not expected to see me, and would indeed rather continue reading.

'What are you planning to do with these traitors who have proclaimed their treachery in flight?' I demanded with the briefest of salutes to his cheek, frustrated by his lack of involvement in this deadly issue. 'A decision must be made.'

I had been surprised to learn that the rebel birds had flown far and wide from Ludford Bridge. I was not willing to allow them to escape our clutches and plot their return in the safety of Calais or Ireland. My lord Henry must be made to see the danger of allowing them any freedom.

Henry continued to smile. 'I will forgive them if they are willing to return and petition for mercy.'

I had not broken it to him, the wanton destruction of Ludlow that had been undertaken in his name. His heart was too soft to deal with such necessities of punishment, but mine was not. The town deserved no compassion from us. I was sorry for it, but treachery must be dealt with, so to allow our forces to run amok, to rob and drink the taverns dry, had seemed to me to be a suitable punishment. Unfortunately, the Yorkist leaders were now fled out of our immediate grasp.

'I would advise against that, Henry.'

'Why?'

'Because you need to show the weight of your royal hand, to stop any further insurrections.'

'Yes, of course. That would be good policy. Can I not still show leniency and God's care for all my subjects?'

'Leniency would not be good policy. What will you do with the Duchess of York and her younger children?' I pursued the train of thought since he was concentrating, his eyes on mine. 'They are still here in Coventry under your power. It might be good policy, as you put it, to show the Duke of York that, if he values their lives, he must come to terms with you.'

'Duchess Cecily? I like Cecily. I do not wish her to be sent to the Tower.'

'So do I like her, on occasion, but we must do something with her.'

He considered, discovering a strangely apposite solution to the problem. 'Perhaps we should send her to live under the control

59

of her sister Anne, Duchess of Buckingham. There is no doubting the loyalty of Buckingham to my cause. I would trust him with my life. To send her there will keep her from contacting her husband and plotting his return.'

An excellent decision.

'That is kind,' I agreed. 'It will be a gentle imprisonment and will certainly keep her from meddling. But what about her relatives?' To stop him returning to his book, I took the psalter from him and gently closed it so that he would concentrate on me. 'What about Salisbury and Warwick?'

'Pardon would be best. If I can win the friends of York to my side...'

I sighed but remained determinedly amiable. 'I would say an attainder would be more appropriate.'

'But that would condemn them as traitors.' He blinked his anxiety. 'Should I not have mercy?'

'Better to have justice! Your son's inheritance may depend on it, my dear lord. To use an attainder and brand them traitors will be a lesson to all. Their vast possessions will also fall into your hands. It must be done.'

Henry thought about this, picking at the sable of his cuff, to the detriment of the fine fur.

'Then I must show a heavy hand now, as you say, but I must be allowed to offer pardons in future if they will make their peace with me.'

'Of course.'

I smiled and took his thin, restless hands in mine. York, far too ambitious, would never make his peace. Nor would Salisbury and Warwick. There would be no pardoning. My son's inheritance would be safe. If it could be arranged that York should meet his end in Ireland, it would be a blessing for us all. It was all falling into place for me as our hold on the crown grew stronger by the day. I had achieved everything I wanted. And yet I could not rest, for our enemies were still alive and it was possible to return from exile. What would happen if they set foot on English soil again in triumph?

I regarded Henry with some remnants of affection even though his refusal to face the situation drove me to an unqueenly impatience. We no longer shared a bed, nor had we done so since he regained his mental strength. If Henry visited my chamber at night, it was to read to me some gem of erudition that he had discovered in a missal or a book, urging me to pray with him. The days of our earthly passion had long gone. But the loyalty between us was as strong as ever and I would fight to the death for his right to wear the crown.

I had come to England, a foreign princess, without authority or reputation or dowry, but Henry had seen the value in me as a wife and consort, showering me with affection and precious gifts, making me feel welcome. Henry had given me sovereignty at his side in this realm and I would not willingly hand it over. If York and his treacherous friends had their way, it would be York's hands to grasp the reins of power and determine all policy in England. Henry seemed oblivious to that danger; I would not allow it to happen.

Oh, I was aware of my situation. Of my increasing unpopularity. Henry's disastrously feeble mind had cast me without protection into the savage arena of political fighting. Some said that I was oblivious to all but the need to protect the inheritance of my dear son. Perhaps that was true. In my mind I had no choice. Henry's withdrawal from the real world had made my son vulnerable.

My mind began to turn over possibilities to eradicate the dangers. First the attainders. Then the confiscation of lands and money, to destroy York and his associates. Duchess Cecily and her children dispatched to the control of her sister. What then should be done about the Duke of York, to keep him out of England? We would appoint the Earl of Wiltshire as Lieutenant of Ireland. That would keep York in check. As for Warwick in Calais, I thought of the Countess's request for compassion. I could not afford to have any. I folded Henry's hands between mine.

'I would suggest that we oust Warwick from Calais. We should send Somerset with a fleet to take up the captaincy there. That should remove the Yorkists from their most valuable base.'

'Do you think so?'

'I do. It is too dangerous to allow them to keep a foothold on English soil, even if it is across the sea.'

'Very well. Somerset will become Captain of Calais.'

I breathed gently, perfectly satisfied with what I had achieved. All I needed now was some clever rumour and propaganda to destroy any popularity York might still have. It should not be difficult.

'You are smiling,' Henry remarked.

'I am planning.'

His gaze sharpened, as did his mind. 'Do not be too hard-hearted, in my name.'

'No. I will only do what will be good for you and our son.'

How I wished my lord Henry had more strength of will, more vision of what needed to be done. But if Henry would not, then I must do so.

'What are you thinking now?' he asked, peering to look at me as he bent to retrieve his psalter from where I had placed it on the floor beside him.

'I am thinking that when the Parliament meets, every lord and bishop in attendance will take an oath of loyalty. To you.'

'But have they not all taken an oath of loyalty to me? At my coronation?' Henry frowned mildly, abandoning the book when I pushed it further aside with the toe of my shoe.

'They have. But now they will take an oath of loyalty to me and to the Prince our son as well. Is that not the strongest means of ousting York from the centre of government? Somerset and all those of a like mind will willingly swear their allegiance to you and your family.'

'Yes.' He reached for his cup of warm spiced ale, now probably gone cold, from the coffer beside him and sipped, before abandoning it with displeasure. 'It will be a good plan. You always know what is best for me and our son. Now may I have my psalter back?'

'As long as we are agreed on an attainder against the York faction.'

'If you wish it.'

I patted his arm and returned his psalter to him.

A necessary plan. Victory for me.

Duchess Cecily would indeed be dispatched to her sister. I hoped it would be an uncomfortable stay. As for the Warwick and Salisbury wives, Anne and Alice, long may they live in Calais and Ireland. Or wherever the Neville family must take refuge when Somerset ousted the Earl from his captaincy. I did not care as long as it was not without the bounds of England.

As I had warned the Countess of Warwick, I could play the role of She-Wolf most effectively if need be. It gave me more satisfaction than Dove of Peace.

## Anne, Countess of Warwick

For me, as the French countryside blossomed into summer in the heat of June, it was a time of anxiety. For Richard it was one of exhilaration, in spite of our exile from home. The news that followed us to Calais was what we expected. My letter to Margaret had gone unheeded. Had I ever thought that there would be a solicitous reply? The She-Wolf had indeed replaced the White Dove.

'I have been declared a traitor,' Richard announced, 'together with York and my father. We have been placed under attainder. Our lands are forfeit,' he bared his teeth in a specious grin, 'but that will not stop me ruffling the royal feathers at every opportunity.'

The constant ruffling at sea made a return to England an impossibility unless the political storm-winds changed, to blow to our benefit. At least the Duke of Somerset had not managed to set foot in Calais. We had now been in residence here for six unsettling months. All was comfort and undeniably free from attack, but how many times had I made it my task to help Richard put on his armour, piece by piece, dismissing the squire who would have undertaken the office? Too many times to count in those busy months of naval campaigns against Somerset, snatching at as much time as I could that we might be together.

But today was different. Richard's battle armour was already packed into its numerous coffers and carried down to the quay where his ships awaited him.

'I am fearful,' I informed him, holding out his brigandine so that he could shrug into the plated jacket. This was no battle garment, faced as it was with leather insets within the dark blue silk, held together with gold rivets. This was a garment to demand a loyal admiration from those who saw him set foot once again in England. In Kent where he could be guaranteed much support.

'That is not a Beauchamp characteristic.' He turned to look at me, shrugging the garment into place. 'Since when have you been lacking in courage?'

'Since the day that the Parliament of Devils in Coventry proclaimed us traitor and confiscated all our lands. Since you have taken to piracy and naval campaigns against Somerset. I always worry about you when you are gone. But not as much as today.'

'Today is no different.'

'Then why do I have presentiments of disaster?'

I fastened the laces of his brigandine with unsteady fingers.

Richard had had no intention of living in hiding, of cowering in terrified exile, waiting for the edge of a sword or the head of an arrow from one of King Henry's minions. He had immediately taken the initiative, thriving on the energy and success of his campaigns, enjoying the popularity amongst the forces at Calais, which had needed reinforcement after Anthony Trollope's despicable defection. He had not found it difficult. Nothing like conspicuous success to win friends. Piracy on the high seas against any Lancastrian ships that were ill-fated to cross his path in the Channel won him much regard. Capturing Somerset's ships to prevent him from landing, so thwarting Margaret's decision to appoint him Captain of Calais and ousting Richard, had given him much pleasure. Not only that, he had led a successful raid on the English port of Sandwich.

Fortunately, Queen Margaret was unable to reach us to put a stop to it.

'We have had an incredibly successful series of manoeuvres. I have been in no great danger,' Richard said. 'Why should you worry now? If you are going to act as my squire perhaps you can find me a pair of gauntlets. The heavy kid ones.'

'No great danger?' I repeated, discovering beneath a cushion the finely embroidered gauntlets that I had worked for him in bright hues and gold thread in the early days of our marriage. 'Even when you risked your life to sail to communicate with York in Ireland? If you had been caught by a Lancastrian ship on that desperate planned voyage, I would have been mourning your death.'

I was prickly and lacking patience. As with all women, all I could do was wait at home and deny the fear, no matter how wearing it might become.

'I agree it needed care,' Richard said, dealing efficiently with the final brigandine straps, 'but it meant that we would be well organised on our return. York and I planned it in detail. It will be an invasion to reclaim all that has been taken from us.'

'And you brought your mother, Lady Alice, back with you. For which she is grateful. And so am I.'

'I had little choice. She insisted!'

I thought about the uncertain future as I sat on the bed and held the gloves palm to palm in my lap. I knew the answer yet still I asked it, as Alice came unannounced into the room.

'Why not just accept the promise of a pardon?' I asked, knowing his reply before it was made.

'Do you believe in it, even if it is offered?' Lady Alice asked.

'I might consider Henry's word, but not Margaret's. And not Somerset's advice offered with a forked tongue, which makes Henry's word always suspect.' Richard pulled the velvet folds of a chaperon down over his hair. 'I will never accept a pardon. It is as empty a promise as a sailor's flask of ale.'

'How have we slid into warfare?' Alice bemoaned. 'In all the years of my life, I could never have dreamed it.'

66

'You know why.' Richard surveyed the chamber for anything that he might have forgotten, his eye latching on an assortment of weapons. 'You have heard the propaganda that she has been spreading over us, like dung on a newly planted field. York has been painted as the devil himself, plotting to bring down the King and his family.'

'While Henry is the generous King who faced his enemies on the battlefield,' Alice added. 'The King who has been wilfully betrayed by you and your father.'

'God's blood. How can anyone accept that mythical image as the truth? They saw him at St Albans. He looked the part, but was quick to retire into the tanner's house when that stray arrow found its target. At Ludford Bridge he did not even have to loose his sword in his scabbard.' Richard fixed a rondel dagger to his belt. 'When we reach England we will reply to those offensive lies. We will remove all of the councillors who make the most of Henry's weakness for their own ambitions. Shrewsbury, Wiltshire, Beaumont, even Buckingham. And of course Somerset. We will remove them all and surround Henry with loyal supporters.' He strode towards me and clasped his hands around mine and the gauntlets, as if to make a sacred oath. 'You don't fear my failure, do you? Do you not believe in my powers to take this force to England and prevail over those who would deny my name and my title?'

I stood so that our eyes were on a level as the thought crept into my mind, not an unexpected one, for did it not hover over me every day? Would Richard not be quite as uncontrollably ambitious as those he would remove? As for York, he would demand to be re-appointed Constable of England to dictate Henry's actions. If their planning brought victory, they would be in a position to take such power. It seemed to me that there was little between any of them.

And that was why, for me, it was different from Richard's previous short-term departures. They had been fast and skilful campaigns, to attack and retreat, with the enemy forced to retire, unable to do any damage. This was to be a full-scale invasion, to take Richard back to England with a strong force, to overthrow any opposition and march on London. June was a fair month for an invasion.

'I will pray for your success,' I said, determined to suppress any desire to become emotional. 'And no, I don't have any presentiments of your failure. You will doubtless return crowned with a laurel wreath of victory.'

Richard smiled briefly, but when Alice touched my arm I read the same anxiety in her face. 'We will both pray,' she said. Then asked the question that I had not. 'When you are victorious, do you remove the King, or do you keep him as a puppet? Does York seek the crown for himself?'

'No, it is not our plan to remove King Henry. He can keep his crown, but we will take control of his royal person and of London. I expect that York will become Constable again. Is that not the height of his ambition, despite all that royal blood in his veins?'

I would not have wagered on that. 'And will you challenge Margaret's propaganda with your own?' I queried.

'Of course. Would you expect less?'

No, I would not. Richard had a talent for devising propaganda, not surprising since the penalty for the attainder placed on his head was death. He would be as brutal as Margaret's attack on him. He pronounced a summary of it: there was nothing new, but it would raise support when he arrived in England.

'This is the word we will spread in London.' He was now pulling on his gauntlets, eager to be gone. 'The lack of justice from the crown. The overbearing power of the lords who support the

King. A conspiracy to murder York and all those with royal blood in their veins. We will promise justice and honest government in the King's name. We will rid ourselves of the over-powerful magnates. We will rid ourselves of Somerset.'

'By raising an army when you land,' I added.

I knew he would. Richard would get his army from the dis-affected subjects in Kent, always ready for rebellion, as well as in the Midlands where his own strength lay.

'Yes. There will be battles. Henry might compromise again, offering pardons with both hands, but I suspect that Margaret will not.' He caught up his sword and sword belt. 'Nor will Somerset. Now, it's time I set out, for the tide is good for sailing.'

We followed him out onto the battlements from where we could see the fleet that would take him to England. It was an awe-inspiring sight, with banners and pennons; Richard's bear and ragged staff, dramatic in red on white, Salisbury's multi-coloured flags already flying on the masts. The impressive personal retinue of soldiery proclaiming the badges on their breasts. Salisbury was there on the quay with York's eldest son Edward, the young Earl of March, a formidably striking young man of some height, with gilded hair as well as a ready tongue and a winning smile for any passably comely female.

For a moment we stood and assessed the busy scene.

'Ned relishes the thought of battle,' I said, watching him as he marched impatiently up and down the quay.

Richard laughed. 'Ned relishes any activity. Keeping him restrained is the problem.'

'When you go to London,' I asked, 'what do I do? And the girls?'

Was the answer not clear enough already?

'Remain here. I will bring you back to England when all is at peace again. Until that day you will rule here in my name, as you always do. I rely on your good judgement. I will not leave you here longer than necessary.'

There was a warmth in his promise. I longed to be back in Warwick Castle, or Middleham. I must be patient. I must not spend every day in nameless anxieties, looking out over the sea towards England. I must live my own life here in Calais, albeit a struggle, for I seemed to be losing the ability to harness patience, when once I thought I had far more than Queen Margaret could lay her hands on.

'I will leave you to say your farewells.'

When Lady Alice descended the steps to give her blessing to her husband and nephew, I turned to Richard.

'What do I say to you that I have not said before?' I asked, studying the fierce hunger for action in his face. He was keen to leave but was willing to give me this moment of his time. I said what any wife would say. 'Take care. Do not take too many risks – or no more than usual. I will worry until the day I see you again. Pray God it will be soon.'

His reply was just as banal and predictable as my farewell.

'And you will be safe here, until the day when the attainder is lifted and York is back at the King's side. Only when I am sure that you will be under no threat will I bring you home.'

He leaned in to kiss my lips to seal the promise.

'Richard...' I stopped him as he turned to leave me. He swung back and smiled.

'You know that I will think of you every day and hold you close in my thoughts.'

'As you will be in mine.'

'Except when you are on a battlefield.'

'Except then.' He laughed aloud, before dropping into serious thought. 'I need you with me in England, as I always do.' He stroked my cheek gently with his gloved fingers. 'Do we not make a formidable Neville-Beauchamp alliance?'

It pleased me, colouring my cheeks at such a commendation. It was an accolade that would remain with me as, within the hour, I watched them depart, with Alice beside me and the girls. I leaned between two of the crenellations to see them as they went aboard. The girls were waving even though they would be invisible at this distance. How tragically empty had been the Love Day promises; the Parliament of the Devils had proved that. Twenty-six of those lords aligned to York's policies had been attainted. There would be no peace with this black cloud hovering, and now it was outright war.

'What are you thinking?' Alice asked.

'That my father, the famous thirteenth Earl of Warwick, despite a lifetime of war and battle, died at peace in his bed in the end. Why should our menfolk not do the same?' I shivered in the light wind. 'Rather than see a bloody death on some distant battlefield.'

'I agree,' said Lady Alice. 'But I think that there is more on your mind than that.'

'I was thinking... what is love?' I mused.

'Is love important?'

'Not in marriages such as we make.'

'That is true. We are fortunate indeed if love becomes a part of the alliance.'

'Did it become so for you?' I asked her. We had never spoken of it.

'No. And yet I have come to care for him.'

'Do we not all care for a husband, unless it is a marriage of cruelty and neglect?'

'You could never accuse Richard of that.'

71

'No, I could not. I never would.' I spoke honestly. 'There is a warmth between us. It is enough.'

What did a wife seek in a husband, in families such as ours where the marriage had been made for political reasons? A friendship. A care, a concern. A willingness to talk and ask opinions. An interest in my daily life, in the world of the nursery. A consideration when he rode into battle that I as a wife would worry. The thought for me, to buy gifts, to consider my enjoyment. To rule my own lands well as behoved the man who took them in my name, as my husband. A man of stature and influence, who could be admired, even though I lived on the periphery of his life and always would.

Did I not have all of these attributes to hand in Richard Neville?

By now his vessel was ready for departure, sails being hoisted. We had been married in name for twenty-six years. There was little about him that I did not know – his strengths, his talents, and his faults. I was not blind to his faults. No wife should be.

'You cannot expect the love of which the minstrels sing,' Alice said as we descended the steps, the girls bounding down before us.

'Nor do I.'

Love between Richard and me was a private matter. A touch, a smile, a shared memory. Often unspoken, but undeniable. Love was a cup of wine in our chamber when Richard returned unharmed to Middleham from a long campaign. Love was a shared opinion as we broke our fast, when Richard actually listened to what I might say. Love was forgiveness after sharp words. We did not need to announce it from the crenellations of the castle keep. We knew what was in our hearts.

Yet sometimes I wished that he would announce it rather than leave me feeling abandoned. Now he was gone, and as always, the thought was vivid in my mind.

*You might never see him again.*

It was enough to make me wish to weep.

On a whim I ran back up the steps to watch them finally leave harbour. The sky was azure-bright, the waves lapping gently, the breeze just sufficient to belly the sails to drive them to England. I imagined the wind whipping Richard's hair into a tangle, wrapping his heavy sea-cloak around his thighs. Ned would be looking forward, his hair a gilded halo. All was well. There was no portent here of danger. That is, if I was not aware that the ships were armed with death-dealing weapons from bow to stern.

*Do we not make a formidable Neville-Beauchamp alliance?*

Pray God that we would continue to do so.

# 8

## *Despair at Northampton, July 1460*

**Margaret, Queen of England**

Blessed Virgin, have mercy on me. On my lord Henry. On my princely son.

Here was a desperate situation that I could never have envisaged. Warwick and Salisbury and March, all three returned to England like ravening wolves despite my efforts to keep them at bay. Even worse, we heard that York was planning to sail from Ireland to meet up with them. No doubt Countess Cecily was planning to escape her sister's eagle eye and ride to welcome him home.

I must not allow this to happen.

'You must march south,' I advised my lord the King as we knelt together in the chapel at Coventry after the prayers at the end of the service of Prime. 'You must take your troops and put a halt to this invasion.' I gripped his arm, digging in my fingers. 'It is imperative.'

'I will, my dear Margaret. But you and the Prince must remain here in safety in Coventry.'

He stood and drew me to my feet, his hand over mine. It seemed to me that the Duke of Somerset had been too free with his advice to Henry. This was not what I wanted at all.

'I cannot stay here when—'

'It is best,' Henry broke in, an unexpected urgency in his grip, in his voice, 'and Somerset advises it. Do not come to me, under any circumstances, unless I send you a token. If there is some trickery afoot, I do not want you to fall into York's hands. Keep the boy with you.'

His face was a mass of anxious lines, but his eyes were stern. There would be no bending him.

'Very well.'

I hid a sigh. Henry was full of energy, determined to keep his crown, which encouraged me. And was not this the best of ideas? Prince Edward was the heir. How dangerous if both Henry and our son fell into York's hands. Best to keep the child under my eye, in safety here in Coventry.

There would be a battle. Neither Warwick nor York would step back again from conflict, and I must, as all wives must do, simply await the outcome. I wondered if Countess Anne was in Calais still, awaiting the results of Warwick's invasion. I would pray that God ensure that he was defeated. And the rest of this Yorkist rabble. However despicable it might seem, I would pray that she received the worst of news.

## Anne, Countess of Warwick

Would it be today? Would my life be turned on its head today, on a day when the sun still shone, white clouds hovered on the horizon and seabirds swooped in drifts of white? Surely these blessings were too auspicious for bad news.

I was waiting in Calais, doing what I had vowed I would not do, counting each moment of time as it dragged past, awaiting the news of a battle that might bring victory and allow me to return home. Or news of Richard's death on an English battle-field. The uncertainty nibbled at my mind like a starving rat, waking or sleeping, with one question uppermost.

Where was Richard?

If he was dead, what should I do? What would be best for two daughters who bore his name, daughters of a traitor?

In such amenable voyaging weather, there would be travellers to Calais who would carry some news. It was the constant perturbation as we watched the empty sea that was the hardest to bear. Then there, a mere smudge on the horizon, came one merchant vessel as dawn broke, a sturdy craft engaged in the wine trade. I was down on the quay before Lady Alice had even risen from her bed and broken her fast. I would discover any disasters before she must hear of them.

'What do you know?' I asked, calling up to the captain of the little vessel who was still standing at the stern, to supervise the unloading of his cargo.

He jumped down to the quay and clutched his cap to his chest as he bowed.

'Little, my lady. When last we heard, your men were marching on London. They were making good time through Kent.'

'Were they made welcome?'

'Ay. Thousands were flocking to march with them.'

Which I would have expected from the men of Kent, who had a name for insurrection. It was comforting. Kent was a county where Richard had many followers.

'Where is the King?'

'In Coventry, as far as we know.'

'And the Queen?'

'She's with him, so they say, spurring him on to tighten his grip on his crown and wipe out his enemies.' There was the faintest sneer. 'I doubt it will be a peaceful outcome.' His brow

THE QUEEN AND THE COUNTESS

wrinkled in thought. 'I would say that your lords will be in
London by now.'

They were alive. The campaign had still to be fought out. My
heart settled a little.

Lady Alice and I held each other's hands as we prayed that
night.

'Where is father?' whispered Isabel, as she did every night.

'I have no idea. Pray for him. God will keep him safe.'

Lady Alice's hand tightened on mine. I prayed that it would
be so.


## Margaret, Queen of England

My prayers to the Blessed Virgin for a resounding victory were
unanswered. The news, brought to me at speed, could have
no truth in it, for all was a disaster, a catastrophe beyond my
imagining. I shut myself in my chamber, unable either to eat or
drink, nor talk to anyone in my Court. I banished my son to his
own chambers. I could not even find the words to pray. What
should I pray for in this scene of devastation? The pain around
my heart was too great to bear.

We were defeated. Panic and chaos had inflicted our troops.
And treachery. Lord Grey of Ruthin, on whom we thought we
could rely, had defected to the forces of Warwick and York's
son, the Earl of March. Even the elements had raged against
us, when rain had swamped the battlefield. Our water-logged
cannon could not even be fired.

It had been at Northampton, I was told, where I had been
waiting, safe in Eccleshall Castle for news of the battle. A
battlefield of our choosing where we should never have expected
defeat, even though we had refused negotiation. Quite rightly,

Warwick and his weasel words had been denied access to my lord Henry.

What despicable revenge Warwick took, viciously proclaiming that he would speak with the King, or die in the field. He did not speak with my lord Henry, but neither did he die. It was our captains who had been hunted down and slaughtered. I covered my face with my hands. Oh, their deaths were impossible to quantify. Buckingham. Beaumont. Shrewsbury. Thomas Percy and Lord Egremont. Our most valuable and influential leaders in battle. The whole terrible slaughter in less than a half-hour, and Warwick had emerged untouched.

And what of my lord the King?

I sought out my son, discovering him in the stables, feeding apples to his favourite horse, where I enfolded him in my arms, even when he squirmed to be set free. I told him nothing of our defeat, that his father was taken prisoner, and into the possession of our enemy the Earl of Warwick. The Prince was still too young to be burdened with such matters. From the battlefield my lord Henry had been escorted under guard, by Warwick's orders, to Delapre Abbey. Was he still there? All I knew was that he was not yet dead.

I should have been there with him, to snatch him up from danger. Fury robbed me of clear thought. He had been discovered sitting in his pavilion, while Buckingham had been hacked to death outside, trying to protect him. Henry should have been led to freedom long before that could happen. Why could he not have removed himself from so parlous a position when he read the outcome in the flight of his soldiers?

But all that was in the past and I could not see what would happen next. Taken to London, I presumed, and locked in the Tower, a puppet, with Warwick pulling the strings. A convenient death? At least York was not landed yet in England. I hoped that

THE QUEEN AND THE COUNTESS

all would wait on his return before decisions were made about my lord Henry's future. I gripped Prince Edward's hand in what could only be a panic. I must keep him under my regard.

What could I do? To whom must I turn for advice?

There was no one.

It behoved me to make my own choices, for the safety of all of us. It was in my own hands to take command of our cause. I released my son, returned to my chamber, where I rebraided my hair, secured a golden coronet, and changed my garments to some semblance of regality. This was not the time to malinger and mourn. My son was safe with me. Now I must rescue King Henry from the hands of the enemy.

But, as my women tied my laces and pinned my veiling, my mind could not concentrate. I did not know what to do. All I knew was that I must rescue him quickly. Would my lord Henry give up his crown for the sake of a monkish tonsure and a paternoster at Delapre Abbey? He might, if Warwick made the offer and added a new psalter for good measure. The Earl of Warwick had a persuasive way with words, and, to my regret, my lord Henry was not to be trusted.


## Anne, Countess of Warwick

There were more sails, which I thought were not merchant vessels, growing clearer by the minute in a frisky wind. It was into the warm days at the very beginning of August and we were still without trustworthy news. We continued to live as if nothing could possibly go wrong. And yet it could. There had been rumours of a battle at Northampton, but the outcome was uncertain. Some said the King had carried the day. Some said that it was Richard.

I watched from the wall walk, Lady Alice with me. Would this be the Duke of Somerset come to drive us out again?

And then there were banners that we recognised. We could see figures on the decks. The pennants lifted and fell in the increasing wind; the waves were beginning to gather. A storm was coming but they would make port before the tempest hit us.

'I do not see my lord's colours,' Lady Alice observed in the calmest of tones.

No, it was not the Salisbury heraldry. But there were those of the Earl of Warwick.

'It seems that my son Richard is alive,' Alice said, still as calm as if discussing the return of the wine dealer, 'but what of my lord Salisbury?'

Once more anxious wives, we were on the quay before they had made anchor. My heart beat so hard that it was deafening, until Richard leaped down from the vessel. Only then did my blood cool and settle. He had returned from another war without apparent injury.

Lady Alice was immediately beside him before he could draw breath, hands outstretched in a plea. 'Your father. Is he in health? Why is he not with you?'

'The best of news.' He took her hands, smiling over her shoulder to where I waited before he kissed his mother's cheek. 'He is in good health, mother, and remains in London. All is well. You may breathe easily again. You know that he is a cat with nine lives. He was not even present in the battle, but remained to keep order in London while Ned and I took to the field.'

Alice laughed softly while I watched them together, mother and son, the easy relationship, as Richard moved to me, taking my hands, saluting my cheek too. I had been willing to wait. He was here, once more under my care even if the future time was unpredictable. He was alive.

'We have lived in a fever of concern,' I said with the faintest reprimand as I returned his embrace.

'But here I am in one piece to reassure you.'

We would speak of more personal matters together when we were alone but for now he talked with the girls, then we sat over ale while he told us what we needed to know. There had indeed been a battle at Northampton. While Salisbury had remained to hold London, my lord had marched north with his cousin Ned and my lord Fauconberg, until they had met up with the King's forces on the banks of the River Nene. Thus I received a rapid survey of events that had taken so many weeks.

'I presume that you won the battle.'

'Yes.' He raised his cup in a toast, the glow of victory still in his eye. 'Our men fought well in a day of heavy rain and much blood, although we spared the soldiery. We were not so tolerant of the Lancastrian leaders. Many of the King's men tried to desert and join us, but in their flight drowned in the flooded river.'

I left it at that since Richard seemed not to wish to speak of it. He had not been so reticent over the previous clash of arms at St Albans.

'And the King?' Lady Alice asked.

'Unharmed, but a prisoner. I escorted him back to London, and left him there in his own rooms in the Palace of Westminster, in the care of my father.'

'Was York not there?'

The slightest of frowns touched Richard's brow and he ran a fingertip around the chased rim of his silver cup. 'No, he is still in Ireland for all I know, in spite of all the plans we made when

I risked my freedom to sail to Ireland. He should have returned by now…'

He glowered into the dregs in his cup. I rose and refilled it.

'Why are you here?' I ruffled his hair in passing. 'Not that we are not more than pleased to see you.'

'To reassure you.' The frown was dispelled and his displeasure with York's absence dissipated into his previous satisfaction. 'I thought that I had neglected you for too long without solid news.' There was the care for my peace of mind that I wished for. He looked up at me where I still stood beside him. 'And I have a plan to meet up with Somerset at the port of Guisnes tomorrow. He is isolated there and must assuredly hand the town back to us if we attack. All has gone well for us.'

Ah! So this visit to Calais was all part of the political struggle. I should have known.

'I thought we would not be your prime importance,' I said. 'And what then?'

'Then, because you are always of prime importance to me, and my lady mother, I escort you back to England. Duchess Cecily is at Baynard's Castle in London, waiting for York's return. She has been released from her sister's care, which I am sure they both rejoiced over, although her sister will take her widowhood hard. Buckingham was killed at Northampton.'

A breath of grief marred my pleasure. 'I am sorry. I liked him.' Our families were not untouched by the battle.

'He was a man of sense, even though he fought for the King. But that aside, I thought you could join my Aunt Cecily in London until the whole is settled. Do you agree?'

'Yes, I would like it above all things.'

Lady Alice was already halfway across the room, intent on giving orders for our possessions to be packed into their travelling coffers. I did like the thought. Much as we had comfort and safety in Calais, at least at Baynard's Castle I would not be far from the action. I might see Richard more often than at the wane of each moon. There was one piece of news lacking in this information. It was essential news indeed.

'If the King is your prisoner, where is the Queen? Where is the young Prince?'

Margaret would no longer be in control of the King. Was she, too, a prisoner? I could only imagine her anguish if she had been separated from her son.

'It is not certain,' Richard admitted, encircling my wrist with his hand. 'She was at Eccleshall Castle when the battle took place. I would wager on her collecting all the troops she can muster to rescue Henry and make life difficult for us. Our problems, my dearest wife, are not yet over.'

## Margaret, Queen of England

Prepare for flight! Remain here at Coventry! Negotiate for help!

So many conflicting possibilities. A night of contemplation made all clear to me. No, I had no one to give me advice that was any better than my own decision. I really had little choice. I could give no immediate aid to Henry. I might like the prospect of launching an attack on London to rescue the King, but I must rest on the goodwill of Warwick and Salisbury not to harm him. Had it not been Warwick who had shouted across the battlefield at Northampton, alerting his own forces though the rain and the clash of arms, that the King and his foot-soldiers, who were merely obeying orders, should not be touched? Only the nobles. Only our commanders. If he had wished the King to be spared on the battlefield, I must rely on his generosity to keep him safe still.

It went against the grain to give thanks for Warwick's tolerance, but so it must be. Yet still my lord Henry was far beyond my authority until I had an army to command. What of the Prince? Therein lay another problem. My son must be kept from harm at all costs, and I must put myself in a position to recover his inheritance. We could not sit here in Coventry, awaiting another Yorkist army under Warwick or indeed York, when he finally returned from Ireland, for I was certain that he would return now that the King was kept under duress in London. I could not deny it; I did not have the forces to oppose any direct attack. I would lose any such battle.

I sent for Prince Edward, and for the steward of my household.

'Prepare for flight. We go west.'

It was as simple as that. All we could do was take flight to Wales, making for the massive fortress of Harlech, a tortuous journey of well over a hundred miles, and then from there sailing to Scotland as fast as it could be arranged. Remaining in Wales would be too dangerous and would give me no help of any magnitude. I needed foreign help, an army, money to buy troops. Would the Queen of Scotland come to our aid, one queen to another? She was the one woman who would understand my predicament, a widow and Regent for her son, the young King of Scotland. I was no widow, but I was certainly a woman alone.

I was not unrealistic, although I hated the prospect. There would be a price to pay, of course, to encourage the Scottish Queen to aid me, but I must reimburse her with whatever she demanded. I could not allow Henry to become a permanent puppet of the Yorkist lords.

What price would I be prepared to offer in recompense for Scottish aid?

If it meant that my son Edward must wed one of the Scottish

princesses, some day in the future, then it was not completely unacceptable. Besides, marriage alliances could always be broken before the participants reached the marriage bed; it did not necessarily have to be binding. I could make the agreement in return for an army, but with an annulment in mind if events fell in my favour and I and my son and husband could return to London in triumph.

I would promise anything I could to restore our hold on the English Crown, even if it meant handing over English territory in the North. I would do it. A King's crown and the King's life were worth a fortress or two.

I turned my face towards Scotland. It was my only hope, the only beacon of light in a dark world.

# 9

## *Hopes and Fears, 1460*

### Anne, Countess of Warwick

My daughters and I, accompanied by Lady Alice, returned to England, where we settled into Baynard's Castle in London as if we had never been in exile. Richard forbade me to consider Middleham. If the Queen collected an army in the North, Middleham would be in the centre of enemy territory. So it was London where, he said, he could keep an eye on us.

King Henry remained comfortably accommodated in his own royal chambers in the Palace of Westminster. Richard and his father Salisbury held all under control in a tight fist, organising a public display of thanksgiving with King Henry at its centre, in St Paul's Cathedral. Queen Margaret, we learned, had taken herself into exile to Scotland to petition for money and military support to aid her return. Duchess Cecily, already in residence when we arrived, kept us informed after her enforced residence with her sister, while her youngest children became reacquainted with my two girls. There was much laughter as well as some grumbling from the two young boys, George and Richard, that they were kept away from any fighting. There would be no battles, their elder brother Ned informed them, although he clearly hoped that there would be.

Meanwhile, Duchess Cecily set off in a travelling litter, in an outrageous splendour of blue velvet, the equipage pulled by four pairs of fine horses, to meet her newly returned lord of York at Hereford, from where they would return to London in glory.

'Will this herald a time of peace?' I asked Richard as the litter and escort pulled out of the courtyard in a flutter of falcon and fetterlock banners and pennons.

I was not certain. Nor was he.

'It will all depend on what it is that York demands on his return. If he is belligerent in his quest for power, then I doubt it. If he is content to keep Henry as King with himself holding the reins as Constable, then it may be so. As long as Somerset is removed. But if York does have an eye to the crown for himself then we may have trouble on our hands. The lords will not support him in it.'

'And above and beyond all, Margaret is still a distant and unknown player in the game,' I said as the dust settled and we returned within.

'Indeed she is. I would say that she will not remain distant and unknown for long.'

He would say no more.

'Will you allow me to visit the King?' I asked on a sudden whim.

Richard's brows rose. 'Why would you wish to?'

'I thought he might be lonely.'

'I doubt he will notice a lack of visitors as long as he has his books and prayers, but yes, if you wish. I'll arrange an escort for you. I doubt he would want to see me.'

Yet Henry was pleased enough to greet me, and even more the books that I took with me, French books of tales of chivalry for the occasion when he might tire of his prayer books and psalters. He appeared to be in good health and well groomed, untroubled by his situation. He rose to his feet and approached as I entered the room.

'Countess of Warwick, it pleases me to have your company. You are most welcome.'

I curtsied, indicating that my servant place the books on a coffer within the door-arch.

'Are you comfortable here, my lord?'

'Of course. They have allowed me to keep my own servants. And I see you have brought books for me.'

He lifted one and began leafing through the pages. He seemed to have little more to say to me. Then he looked up. Would he ask after his wife and son?

'Next week your husband, Earl Warwick, is arranging a pilgrimage for me to go to Canterbury. I will enjoy that. Will you go too?'

'No, my lord. I will remain here with my daughters.'

'Of course. But I will pray before St Thomas for you.'

I did not stay much longer. The fate of his wife and son seemed to have little interest for him. It saddened me that he should be so unaware of his precarious position. I did not speak of it to Richard.


**Margaret, Queen of England**

*'Domine, Jesu Christe, qui me creasti.'*

My hands were clasped so tightly together that my knuckles shone palely in the shadows of this unadorned Scottish chapel where I knelt before the crucified Christ, riven with pain on the cross. So, too, was I torn apart as I used the words that my lord Henry himself had written and frequently used.

*Lord Jesus Christ, who hast created me,*
*Redeemed me, and preordained me unto this that I am,*
*Thou knowest what thou wouldst do with me;*
*Do with me according to thy will, with mercy.*
*And I pray your blessing on my lord Henry in his travails.*
*Amen*

In the silence that followed I slid my gaze to one side, to the serene face of the statue of the Blessed Virgin, and uttered a most undutiful comment of my own.

'It may be that a wife should not take issue with the decisions of her husband, but before God, I cannot condone this utter stupidity. How could he agree to such an abomination! How do I forgive him for this outrageous attack on his sacred inheritance?'

I closed my eyes so that I might not see the condemnation on that composed face. My fury, when I heard what had come about, was beyond my keeping silent. Now I turned my wrath on the Duke of York.

'May God consign your soul to the depths of hell where you will exist in permanent torment!'

I cursed York, even though I should not have been surprised at what he had done on his return in regal triumph, banners unfurled, claiming his own royal blood. Announced by trumpeters, the royal arms of England displayed with his own, he might have already been King. But I also cursed my lord Henry in the same breath.

'How could you accept this destruction of your son's birthright? How could you agree to it? Do you not understand what you have done?'

Of course he did not. I groaned at the magnitude of what had been achieved by York at Westminster and covered my face with my hands. It was as much an achievement as a victory on a battlefield, and with no bloodshed, merely a signature on a document. All willed away at the stroke of a pen. York was back, in an aura of authority, and had persuaded Henry into accepting what was called an Act of Accord. Before God, there was no accord in my mind.

The terms were spelt out in a letter brought to me by a courier to my accommodations at the Scottish Court. Had it been sent to me out of malice, or as a warning of what had been done? There was no signature to it. I crumpled it in my fist after the first reading.

Henry would remain King and wear the crown for the length of his life. At least he was safe, the only good news to be gleaned from the whole disaster. On his death, the crown would pass to the House of York, to York himself if he were still alive; if not, to his son and heir, the Earl of March. My son had been utterly disinherited, and Henry had, in his foolishness, in his weakness, given his acclamation.

I smoothed out the letter and read it again. It made for no better reading on the second attempt. Our son would never rule under the terms of this agreement. It was all York's doing. When he placed his hand on the empty throne at Westminster and claimed it for himself, there were not many of the lords who raised their voices in approval. Even Salisbury saw the need to remonstrate. And yet the Act had become law.

'I will destroy him,' I announced when ushered into the presence of the Queen of Scotland in her austere audience chamber. 'I will celebrate the death of the Duke of York.'

'But you will need an army first,' the Scottish Queen, Mary of Guelders, commiserated, yet saw possibilities for herself in this situation. A foreign-born bride like myself, severely garbed in dark damask, her hair close-confined in gold mesh, with jewels shining on collar and cuffs, she was a woman of power as well as wit and intelligence. Surely she would respond to my need.

'Give me the men, your grace. Give me the money to pay my English forces. A loan will do it, a loan that I will repay when I take back what is mine. Are you not Regent for your young son? You know how important it is to preserve the future power of your children.'

Queen Mary indicated that I should sit beside her, and leaned close to speak in confidence.

'I will give you what you need. But there will be conditions.'

'Name them. I will pay.'

'It may mean the exchange of English land into Scottish hands.' Her dark eyes were lit with the possibilities. 'Do you have the authority to agree to that? Indeed, would you agree to some of your northern fortresses becoming my property?'

'I will consider it, Your Grace.' I, too, had suggestions to make. 'As you, Your Grace, might consider a marriage between my son and your little daughter.'

It would not be an unacceptable match, and it would buy me time.

'We will meet again to discuss such heavy matters,' Mary replied with a thin-lipped smile, her pale skin without blemish despite the weight of the regency on her slight shoulders. 'Rest assured I will not let you return to England empty-handed.'

As we made some initial agreements I watched my son, who sat on the floor and played with a monkey belonging to the royal children. His innocence. His enjoyment of life as he encouraged the little creature to climb onto his shoulder, its gold chain looped around his fist. He laughed aloud as the creature ran its fingers through his hair and removed his hat. The Prince did not know. He did not yet understand what had been done to undermine his future. To wilfully destroy his birthright.

'Do we go hunting, madam?' he asked when I removed the monkey and returned it to one of the servants.

'No, my son.' I managed a smile. 'We are to return to England, within the week.'

'I will like that. Will I have a monkey when we are home again?'

'Perhaps.'

I would give orders for my supporters to march south with me. I could wait no longer for a Scottish army. What if York, dissatisfied with the Accord, snatched the crown from Henry's head before I could get there, and placed it on his own?

All hope would be lost for us, and for Henry, too.

I had already sent petitions to the French King for safe conduct for myself and the Prince if all fell out badly. I could no longer have any faith in my lord Henry. However regretful it was, the days of my regarding him as the man who would guide my life and confer on me a position of authority were long gone. I must hold that authority for myself, as the Scottish Queen held hers in her own kingdom.

I took Prince Edward's hand in mine to return to my chambers, regretful that although the Scottish Queen might appear pale and fragile with soft words, she had proved to be a master of hard bargaining.

I had to promise to hand over the town and fortress of Berwick to the Scottish Queen. It would not be a popular decision in England and would doubtless create more enemies for me. As I rode south, to return to my own kingdom in a gown of fine black velvet and a black veil, given to me by the Queen of Scotland, I hoped that the outcome of this campaign would be worth the gamble. But why should I doubt it? When I had taken back what belonged to my lord Henry, I would exchange this mourning-garb for a gown of azure and gold silk as I rode into London in triumph.

## Anne, Countess of Warwick

We were placed on a war footing with news of Margaret's approach, crossing the border into England from the North. We watched as our forces gathered to leave London to hold them at bay.

'I suppose this invasion is pre-empted by the Accord,' I remarked to Richard.

We were all uneasy over it, Salisbury still sharply condemning the arrogant irresponsibility of his brother-in-law's actions, although York seemed sublimely optimistic.

'This invasion would have happened anyway,' Richard replied, 'as long as Henry remains in our hands. The Queen would never sit in Scottish exile for ever. She must make a push to return.'

'I think that it was a mistake,' I said, with enough political acumen to weigh up the repercussions of what York had done, finding them dangerous.

'Do you now? Are you a traitor to the Yorkist cause, madam Countess?'

Richard's words were mischievous, but his expression was grave. The danger of a battle was breathing down our necks.

'I think that you feel the same. Even if you are not as openly damning as your father has been.'

'It has not made matters easy for us,' he admitted. 'Many who might have been our allies dislike so overt a display of greed for power.'

'Yet you remain loyal to York.'

He shrugged a little. 'It is a family matter. It is necessary to remain loyal. What would you have me do? Give my allegiance to Henry and the Queen?'

Which Salisbury, approaching, overheard with a grimace.

'I will pretend that I did not hear that. We are ready to depart.'

Father and son embraced with much hearty male wishing of good fortune and success.

'We will meet again after the New Year when the Queen has been driven again into flight for her life,' Salisbury announced.

On which optimistic note we all parted company. York marched north, with his second son, the youthful Earl of Rutland, as well as Salisbury and Richard's brother Sir Thomas Neville, intending to make a base at Sandal Castle. Richard would remain in London to keep a strong Yorkist presence amongst the belligerent lords who might still cast in their lot with Lancaster.

'Do you wish you were marching with them?' I asked him as the courtyard at Baynard's Castle emptied, a strange stillness settling after the noise of the Yorkist retainers died away.

I could read it in his face.

'Yes, but if we all leave London it would be a weakness. Someone has to stay and hold London, in case of any disaster. The populace might consider an uprising if they think they can rescue Henry and give him back his power. We will keep all safe here until they can return.'

His eyes were sombre, his tone hard-edged.

'Do you foresee such a disaster?'

Richard shrugged off any concerns. 'York has enough experience to hold his own and push back any rabble that Margaret may have managed to bring together. Sandal Castle will provide him with an excellent fortress. I doubt it can be taken quickly in a siege. I think – I hope – we will see another Yorkist victory.'

He watched the final exit of soldiery. 'It will be interesting to see how Ned shapes up in the West when he faces the Welsh and the forces of the Earl of Pembroke.'

I was not sorry that Richard was staying but said nothing as he walked over to wish success to York's heir, who, despite his lack of years, had been given his own command and would march west to hold off any Welsh interference. A young man in his first venture.

Richard and I enjoyed one of our rare evenings together, in our own chamber, Richard clad in a long gown of finest woollen cloth, not an item of armour in sight. He stretched his legs to the fire, studying the flames through narrowed eyes, a cup of wine in one hand, his thoughts I would wager not as comfortable as his demeanour. Meanwhile Duchess Cecily had to more or less lock her sons George and young Richard in their chamber. It was too much for them to bear, their two older brothers going off to war while they must stay at home.

'At least daughters don't give us the same headache,' I said.

'No, but their marriages might.'

'There is time enough for that. Where will Margaret look for a wife for the Prince?'

'Possibly France. Possibly Scotland.'

A silence fell between us since Richard had no desire to discuss what the future would hold. As long as York did not allow arrogance to override his good sense, we might hold off the invading army. What would be in Margaret's mind? Victory, of course. She would never accept her son's disinheritance. If she must lead the army herself, she would do so. It would not take a letter from her to enlighten me as to her thoughts. What had we to say to each other now? Were we not firmly in two enemy camps?

When the silence became uncomfortable for me and Richard's

thoughts troubling, I produced the board and the ivory chess pieces, challenging him to a game. We were well matched, for my skills were as keen as his, until I made a chancy move with one of my knights, allowing Richard to capture my red queen. He picked up the exquisitely carved figure and enclosed it in his fist.

'What are you thinking?' I asked

He was staring at his closed fist, but now looked up at me.

'That you are beaten. Your King is now in danger and I see no hope of your saving it.' He opened his hand so that the little Queen lay rigid on his palm in her crown and stiff robes. 'I wish it would be as easy to capture King Henry's red Queen. I fear it will not be.'

'Do you have a sense of York's defeat?'

He shook his head and returned the chess piece to me. 'No. I expect that York will return to London with my father and brother, glorious with confidence, with the captive Queen in tow. They will defeat her as easily as I seem to have defeated you tonight.'

'My mind was not on the game,' I excused myself. And indeed, it had not been.

'Then come and give all your attention to me, before I must leave you once again,' Richard replied.

It was an invitation that could not be refused by a woman of imagination. Within the confines of our own chamber, the world shut out by solid doors and thick curtains, Richard donned a different role from the one seen by our household, by the Court, by our enemies. The harsh world of the warrior-lord was cast aside, replaced by the softer words and the enticing kisses of the lover. The sword-calloused hands became gentle. His voice whispered in my mind rather than bellowed across a battlefield. The scarred body was hidden in velvet shadow, except for the caress of my fingertips. Here our private world shrank to the encompassing of the great bed with its carved tester and embroidered hangings, all rioting with the carefully stitched fertility of abundant leaves and flowers.

'Is your mind on this game?' Richard asked, his lips against my throat.

'I think that you have caught my attention,' I said, equally catching my breath.

These were infrequent moments in our lives, when we could withdraw from the demands of those who needed Richard's talents elsewhere, but ones that we treasured. We still hoped that I would quicken again and give birth to the much-desired son.

The next morning Richard went off to deal with affairs in the city while I sat with Countess Alice and Duchess Cecily and considered the future and the fate of our family. I thought that I might never see Margaret again. If York achieved a victory on the battlefield in the environs of Sandal Castle, Margaret, rather than risk imprisonment, must flee for the life of herself and her son. Perhaps that would be for the best, for all of us.

'What does Richard say about the threat from the Queen?' Duchess Cecily asked.

I set another stitch in an altar-cloth, considering a reply that would not increase their anxiety.

'That it will not come to fruition,' I said.

I did not believe it. Perhaps neither did he.

# 10

## *A House in Mourning, December 1460*

**Margaret, Queen of England**

'Look up,' I ordered my son.

I had no compunction in making so young a child aware of the actions we must take against those who would destroy us. The Prince needed no prompting, for indeed most of our soldiers were glancing up as they marched past. There on the gateway reposed in bloody array the heads of our enemies.

My thoughts were strangely conflicted.

Those who might wish me ill said that I was there at the battle at Wakefield, and at the aftermath in the city of York. That it was I who gave some of the more vicious orders in the destruction of our Yorkist enemies. I was not present at the battle in the environs of Sandal Castle near Wakefield. I did not watch or order the encirclement of my enemies or their subsequent slaughter. The honour was due to my loyal captains, Somerset and Devon. They fought magnificently. The tragedy of St Albans and Blore Heath and Northampton was paid for in Yorkist blood. Those traitors who were not cut down on the field were caught in flight and summarily executed.

Did I give those orders?

They might not rest on my shoulders, but how could I mourn such a mighty revenge? The blood debt of St Albans has been repaid in kind. The loss inflicted on us at Northampton had been wiped out. The loyalty of my forces was vindicated in this destruction of those who would depose my lord Henry the King.

And yet still it rankled that the decisions to take so many lives were laid at my door. I did not regret it but nor did I seek it. If the Yorkists had not risen in treachery, they would be alive today and I would be beside my lord Henry in Westminster. Instead, I was still far to the north in Scotland when those Lancastrian swords and daggers had drawn Yorkist blood, when I gave thanks for it.

I could not worry about the events that I could not change. I must seize the opportunity offered to me and make it my goal to take London back from the hands of Warwick, who still controlled the city and held my royal husband in captivity. Riding swiftly from the Scottish border, I gathered my forces in York and began the long march south. As we left through Micklegate Bar, I drew my horse to a halt, taking the reins of Prince Edward's mount to pull him to a standstill. He was riding beside me, for I would not allow him out of my sight.

'Look up,' I repeated.

For there, teeth bared in their skulls, grinning down on us in a mockery of joy, was the evidence of our debt paid. There the head of the Duke of York and his son Rutland. Of the Earl of Salisbury and his son Sir Thomas Neville. Their heads leered in death for all to see and deride, York's with the sodden remains of a paper crown, since he had spent much of his life proclaiming his royal descent. For a moment nausea gripped my belly but I quelled it, breathing deeply. I had not given the order for this ultimate punishment, but I could afford no compassion. I would not have hesitated to command this bloody display of treachery if I had been present and it had been asked of me. Thus the end of those who would threaten me and mine. York's heir, the Earl of March, was too young to be a threat to me, even if he still had an army under his command, somewhere in the West. Surely the Earl of Pembroke, Jasper Tudor, with an array of Welsh forces, would cut him down where they were campaigning in my name. Warwick worried me, of course. He remained in my thoughts, but now my troops had tasted victory, we would face him and destroy him too.

I raised my hand.

'Thus die all traitors.'

The soldiery around me cheered.

Still there was a nibble of concern as we turned south. It was essential that I take London and Henry back under my supervision. I did not think it would be an easy thing to accomplish, yet I smiled at my son, who sensed the excitement around him, before I looked back a final time to where York's dead eyes followed me. I could not afford a siege of London, particularly if they locked Henry in the Tower. The city must invite me in and return my lord the King to me.

Here was another worry. By that disgraceful Act of Accord, Edward of March, now the new Duke of York, was also heir to the throne instead of my son. He must be cut down too. The Act of Accord must be repealed, the true inheritance of the House of Lancaster must be restored.

Was the Countess of Warwick in London, with the rest of the Yorkist women who would be weeping in grief and fear? There would be many widows in that household.

I had no regrets for what had been done in my name. I would take responsibility for it, tomorrow and tomorrow if need be. It might be that I would have to. I could not afford the weakness of a woman.

## Anne, Countess of Warwick

We were a house in mourning, of black-garbed women, of whispered grief. The New Year, usually a time of merry-making and gift-giving, in those days after the battle was one of sorrow and heartbreak.

Even the children were silent, absorbing the atmosphere of death and loss.

York. Salisbury. Rutland. Thomas Neville.

All dead. All dead and their bodies mutilated in an act lacking in generosity towards those seen as the enemy. Even Rutland, still so young. All either cut down on the battlefield or brought to their deaths in the aftermath when the Queen's captains had no mercy. Both Duchess Cecily and Countess Alice each lost a husband and a son to Queen Margaret's cruel campaign. She may not have been present, but her commanders knew well her commands. Rutland died by Clifford's knife, in reparation for his father's death at York's hand at St Albans. So many bad memories laid to rest in vicious bloodshed.

'How could my lord have marched out of the safety of Sandal Castle?' Duchess Cecily demanded in despair, not for the first time. 'How could he have had so little sense of what might happen? Was he tricked? Was he so full of self-aggrandisement that he believed that he could wipe out Margaret's army so easily?'

She stiffened her spine and refused to weep for her loss of husband and son. We did not howl in agony. Instead Baynard's Castle gritted its teeth around us in muted conversations. Our grief was one of silent agony and fervent prayers for the souls of the dead. Richard had lost a father and a brother.

'I am so sorry,' I said to him, when the news was broken. What other could I say?

'I cannot talk about it.'

There was no penetrating the grim armour that he donned in his own mourning. I tried and failed. He would not talk to me about his loss, not then and not later, until ultimately I gave up trying.

We women talked of those we knew and loved, of course we did, letting our memories run free, as if they were still alive and would return to London any day. But we knew they would not. They were gone from us for good, their bodies maltreated. We could not think of that. To die on a battlefield was one thing, but to be dragged out and executed, their heads displayed and mocked, as was York's with a paper crown, all to satisfy public bloodlust. Salisbury might have escaped the battlefield, but was captured, hauled out from Pontefract Castle and beheaded by his tenants, who it seemed had no love for him. His head had joined that of his son and the Duke of York on Micklegate Bar. Rutland had been hacked to death on the bridge in Wakefield.

All those dreams and hopes lost on that battlefield and its aftermath. Cecily's long journey to welcome home her lord from Ireland had been for nothing.

'Where are their bodies now?' Countess Alice asked, eyes wide and dry in shock.

'We know about their heads, which still adorn the gateway in York,' Duchess Cecily replied, her brittle features set in anguish.

'But what of the rest?'

'Richard thinks that they lie at Pontefract,' I said. 'They have not been further defiled, but are buried there in quiet graves.'

Richard was rarely at home, concerned with the restive mood in London. In the end I waylaid him on his departure after a rapid breaking of fast, even when I knew that he was impatient to be gone, for by now I needed my own comfort. My emotions were escaping my control. He had slept in his own chamber so that I would not be disturbed by his coming and going.

'Why do you leave me alone for so long?' I demanded at a turn of the stair, on a sudden spurt of anger.

He looked up, retracing his steps towards me.

'What has happened?'

'You know what has happened. Here it is like living in a mausoleum to the dead. I have taken the running of the household from the shoulders of Duchess Cecily, which I am perfectly capable of doing. Your mother spends all the time on her knees in helpless prayer, too stoical to weep. You aunt has adopted a spine as straight as a halberd. Yet they are so fragile I think they would shatter at the least touch and I am afraid to talk to them. I just wish they would howl their grief from the rooftops. Everything is muffled, pressing down on us in a thick blanket of horror. It meets me when I rise in the morning and is still a terrible companion when I go to bed at night.' I took a breath. 'And you are not here to talk to me! Should I be afraid? What is happening beyond London?' I paused. 'And I am lonely.'

I knew this was not what I should be saying, but the unexpressed misery that invaded every corner of Baynard's Castle had begun to take its toll.

'Now your aunt is considering sending her younger children to safety across the sea with the Duke of Burgundy. Do we send the girls as well? Would it be safer for them too? I don't know what to do. Would you care to give me some advice?'

At least he looked surprised.

'Anne...'

I turned my face away into the shadows to hide my sudden embarrassment at my own depth of emotion. 'Don't be sympathetic or I will shriek my frustrations and weep on your neck!'

'I think that you have already shrieked them.'

Gently he pulled me up two steps towards him and rested his chin on the top of my head, to the detriment of my veiling. I rested my brow against his shoulder.

'Kissing me will not help. I need news and what your thoughts might be. I need to talk about all of this, not smother it as if it were a rare wine in an old barrel.'

'Then let us sit together and I will do what I can to ease your burdens.'

He led me down the stair to where there was a window embrasure, cold and draughty with an uninviting view of the fast-flowing Thames, but with a stone seat set there, while I suffered a blast of icy guilt.

'Forgive me,' I said at last. 'You have so many problems of your own. I should not burden you with this, but indeed there are some things I need to know.'

I felt him sigh against me.

'I should not have left you in ignorance. I forget that I have a wife who is just as capable as I am of seeing what is happening. The insurrection, the uncertainty. The possible danger to London.'

We sat together in silence for a little while. When he closed his arms around me, since the space demanded it, at last I wept on his shoulder, all the pent-up tears of the last days. Eventually, when I sniffed and wiped the tears on my sleeve, he asked:

'What do you wish to know?'

'What Duchess Cecily wishes to know: what possessed York to leave the security of Sandal Castle?'

'I cannot imagine.'

'How could the Queen be so vindictive as to put their heads on Micklegate Bar? They were men of birth and honour. It was not fitting. As for the crown on York's head...'

'Don't speak of it,' he interrupted, but I would not be quiet.

'Why will you not allow me to mourn such losses with you?'

It had hurt me that he would not. And there it was, the anguish in his eyes, in every line of his face. I touched his cheek with my fingers in regret and kept my own counsel. It would help him to speak of it, but he would not.

'Because the pain is too strong; I cannot allow it to escape my control. Not yet. I'll not talk about it, Anne. The loss is still too great.'

'Forgive me if I make the grief worse.' But still I would ask. 'Are we safe here?'

'Yes. London still holds to its Yorkist loyalties.'

'What if she appears at our gates with her victorious army? What would be the future for us then?'

He shrugged. Deep weariness had set in and I regretted making it worse. 'It is all in the balance. The Queen is in vindictive mood,' Richard acknowledged. 'She wants London and the return of Henry.'

It was not a hopeful conversation.

'What do you do?'

'Keep the King secure here. As long as he is in our hands the Queen cannot win. It is like a game of chess all over again, and one that we must not lose. We can hold Henry as hostage for the Queen's good behaviour.'

I asked that most difficult of questions.

'If you faced her in battle, would you win, even though York lost?'

It was not a prospect that I liked to any degree. Indeed I feared it, although I knew that Richard would not hold back. The Queen would be full of energy and achievement after her success.

'I pray that I would,' Richard said. 'I have a debt to call in for my father and brother.'

'What of Edward of March? What is Ned doing?'

'He is young and inexperienced, but he has a fine mind. I do not fear for him on a battlefield.'

I thought he was being encouraging. Edward was only eighteen years old. As for Richard, I clung to his optimism. Surely Richard would be successful when he took an army to meet with Margaret, as one day he must.

'Do you worry about London changing its loyalties?' I asked, fearing a mob baying outside the walls of Baynard's Castle one morning when we awoke. 'Could we hold out against such an attack?'

He showed his teeth in an expression that contained no humour at all.

'I doubt it. We are spreading the news that the Queen's northern hordes and Scottish rabble are being permitted to rob and pillage because there is no money to pay them or feed them. If they march into London no one will be safe. It will be a repetition of what was done at Ludlow, on a vaster scale. London will not open its gates to such a threat. I knew that the Queen could be a woman driven by revenge. I did not think her capable of such an act of malevolence as she inflicted at Wakefield. There may be forgiveness for her in Heaven but there is none in my heart. She will remain my enemy until the day I die.' He wiped the remnant of tears from my cheeks. 'Have I reassured you?'

'Thank you. I promise not to make a habit of inflicting my worries on you, railing at you as if you were my enemy.'

'It will be a relief. For now, we deal with the approaching army. I will do all in my power to keep you and my family safe. Better here than at Middleham.'

It was a terrible prospect. Would even the walls and

fortifications of Baynard's Castle keep us from attack? Sometimes I wished that we had stayed safely in Calais. And yet it was better to be here rather than in isolation.

'Do we keep the girls here with us?' I asked, returning to practicalities.

'I think it best. I understand my aunt's anxieties, she has lost so much, and we don't yet hear enough of Ned's achievements in the West to decide how dangerous our situation might be, but I think we will stay here.' He must have read the quickly masked concern in my eyes, and pressed his lips to my forehead. 'Have courage, Anne. All is not yet lost. I am not destined to die on a battlefield quite yet.'

'Or ever, I hope.' I managed a poor attempt at a smile.

His arms were strong around me. I could hold fast to the thought that it was so, but all my hopes were shrouded in impenetrable thick shadow. I would weep for Richard's own losses in private. What he had not spelled out in so many words was that, with the Queen still in the ascendant after Wakefield, there would assuredly be another battle in the very near future, and now Richard must fight for his honour and his family.

# II

## *An Exchange of Correspondence After the Battle of Wakefield*

**Margaret of Anjou, Queen of England, to Anne, Countess of Warwick.**

By the Queen.

In the aftermath of the Battle of Wakefield, I have had some consideration for you and your terrible loss. Not that I regret the outcome at Sandal, or the display of heads above the gateway in York. Those who dare raise their standards against the rightful King must accept harsh justice when it is meted out. I have no regrets for the punishment my forces inflicted on those who were fooled by York's lies.

When I first came to England as a bride for King Henry, I was young and full of hope. I had been told that my role was to bring peace between England and France. I also saw it as my role to heal any wounds between the powerful magnates at the King's Court. I worked hard to do so, and my lord Henry was equally driven by a vision of a country living in peace and prosperity, without war or conflict. I was proud of him and what we could achieve together in a realm where men could put aside their weapons and exist in amity.

I learned a hard lesson in those early years. The families who surrounded the King with their advice and desires were not interested in peace unless they held the power to dictate its direction. Such conflict was outside my remit. How could I have called a halt to that bloodshed at St Albans? Any efforts on my part were bound to fail.

Henry, for his part, was too forgiving.

From that day, the Love Day, I realised that I must fight for my lord Henry's authority. I will not stop. If it demanded the deaths of York and Salisbury and their sons, then so be it. I will be no man's White Dove of Peace, not even a She-Wolf. I swear that I will be an Avenging Angel wielding the Sword of Justice.

Be thankful that my enemy Warwick was not one of their number at Wakefield. If he had been there at the battle, his bloody head, too, would have adorned Micklegate Bar and you would be mourning a husband.

Do you take flight into exile again? Assuredly, there is no place for you here. The Earl of Warwick cannot be trusted and has too much influence in his freedom. There are too many who will listen to his clever words. Who was it who has spread the rumour that my forces are without discipline and will rob and steal without compunction? Who was it who has done all in his power to turn the citizens of London against me?

Taking my lord Henry on pilgrimage to Canterbury was a despicable attempt to win the King's support and that of the country.

My lord Henry will take power again. He and I will rule England in peace, and my son will be the heir. I will ensure that the Act of Accord is repealed as soon as I reach London.

Do not be lulled into a sense of security. I curse you and your family for what has been done to mine. I will work for the death of the Earl of Warwick.

This is written in my own hand. It was not something I would leave to a clerk. My feelings are too heartfelt, too bitter.

Margaret
Queen of England

## Anne, Countess of Warwick, to Margaret, Queen of England

I could not believe that you would exert yourself to write such a letter. Did you truly wish to rub salt into my wounds and those of my family? You have brought such grief on our household with these deaths. How could you rejoice at what you have done? And not just York and Salisbury but their sons, young men who should have been granted mercy. I understand that battles bring death and bloodshed. I accept that. But is such glorying in it appropriate for a Queen of England? I think not. Nor for any woman.

Did you shed any tears over what you brought about, robbing women whom you know well of their husbands and children?

Your victory is my despair.

I do not need to hear of your apportioning guilt and punishment. How could you have treated those men at York with such degradation? If a battle is fought, then men are killed. Do their bodies need to be defiled afterwards, in such a despicable act?

Exile? I know what it is to be in exile, as do you, although your experience in Scotland was brief enough. You will know that my lord of Warwick will never accept exile. You have made a life-long enemy of him. He will dedicate his life to the restoration of the fine reputation of his family.

Sometimes what appears to be a victory comes with a heavy price. I trust that you do not live to regret what you and your commanders have accomplished. Whether you were present or not seems to me immaterial. It was all done in your name.

In a spirit of reconciliation, of compassion, which you apparently lack, I have been to visit King Henry in his chambers in Westminster. He has more forgiveness in his soul than you. It should be some solace to you that he is well and in good heart.

There is no solace for me.

Anne

Countess of Warwick

# 12

# *Losses and Rumours at St Albans, February 1461*

### Margaret, Queen of England

'Henry, my lord! My dear lord. At last!'

I felt my lips stretch into a smile; it seemed to me that I had not smiled in weeks, but this was a superb achievement, the best that I could have hoped for. Against all the odds, my lord Henry and I were reunited. I had rescued him from Yorkist hands after their army was trounced on the battlefield.

'Margaret. My dearest one. I have prayed for this day.'

His eyes were damp with emotional tears. Mine were not.

I knew when and how to take advantage of affairs. From York, leaving behind the grimacing heads on the gateway, I had gathered my army of Scots and northerners, all loyal to Lancaster, and pressed on against the Yorkists. Who would have wagered their coin on a victory for me? Perhaps there were many who would, after the Yorkist debacle at Wakefield. I, too, had been confident and had taken Warwick by surprise at St Albans where he had brought up an army to block my path.

Nothing must be allowed to bar my route, to take London and put Henry back where he belonged.

As my lord Henry took my hands in his and kissed them, I

could not take my mind from the battle and how disastrously Warwick had failed. What a victory for me. I would forever give thanks to the Blessed Virgin for this seventeenth day of February in this troublesome year of 1461. Warwick defeated and many Yorkist traitors dead. Warwick still lived but had been forced to flee for his life. Was this not the beginning of the end of Yorkist insurrection? Not the street fighting of six years ago but all-out conflict on a battlefield outside the town of St Albans where once Henry's troops had been ravaged.

Before the cut and thrust of battle had begun, I knew that first I must discover where they were holding my lord Henry and rescue him, so with that in mind I sent out some trusted captains to discover him. I was certain that he would not be allowed to take the field, being too valuable as a figurehead, thus the relief when he was escorted into my camp. His royal tent had been pitched beneath a large tree a mile away across the heath. There was no intention in Warwick's mind of him fighting or leading the battle, just as I had thought. Warwick had known the limits to his value. It was not to lead an army into battle.

Nor would he lead my army. I would never put him in that position again. Our forces wore the livery of young Prince Edward, every man proclaiming his allegiance with a red-and-black band decorated with ostrich feathers. A proud moment for us all. Henry would merely be here as the crown-wearing figurehead, as much as with the Yorkists.

Meanwhile Henry was led into the centre of my camp.

We had been seven months apart. Countess Anne had told me that he was in good heart and health. My first thought: how weary he looked, and dispirited, unhappy with his situation. His face, usually so calm and unlined, showed a deep crease between his fair brows. He was wearing a gold and jewelled coronet, most inappropriately, but someone had clad him in armour suitable for his status. Beneath the coronet his hair looked lank and unwashed. I returned his welcome with a kiss to his cheek, thus our reuniting in public was a tender one, if brief, to give heart to our supporters. A clasp of hands, a touch of lips to cheek; it was all that was necessary.

'Thank God you are restored to me,' I said, pleased to see the warmth of colour rise in his face.

But I knew the truth at last, and my apparent pleasure was a mockery of the real situation that had been finally proved to me on that day. I had acknowledged my lord Henry's weakness of mind and body at the Love Day. I had been supremely conscious of it at Ludford Bridge, and afterwards at Coventry when there were decisions to be made. Here at St Albans, when I watched him approach me, I knew in my heart that any leadership in this realm for the hope of Lancaster must be taken into my hands. My lord Henry was hopelessly incapable of resisting the demands of his enemies, failing as both husband and King. All I could think of was that in the Act of Accord he had disinherited his own son and agreed that York and his descendants would rule after him. I would never forgive him for that, nor for his behaviour on the battlefield at Northampton where, when taken prisoner, he had been discovered hiding in his pavilion as men prepared to fight and die for him. At least in this battle at St Albans, where my men had found him sitting under a tree at some distance from the fighting, it had been Warwick's decision, refusing him any opportunity to participate in the battle. Which I considered good policy in the circumstances.

The respect I had once held for him had also died in that moment, a cruel death.

But York was now dead and the Yorkists were on the run. I felt the authority returning to me again, accepting what I could achieve in the aftermath of this battle. I took Henry by the arm and drew him apart from my commanders, who were celebrating our success. Here was an opportunity to restore honour and respect to the King, and proclaim the heritage of Prince Edward, despite the wording of the Act of Accord. I had a plan.

'Why did you do it?' I demanded, unable to keep myself from an attack. 'What made you sign the Act of Accord?'

Henry regarded me solemnly. 'York asked it of me.'

'But why...' What use in pursuing this frightened hare? 'Now that you are free,' I said, 'it would be good policy if you drew all eyes to your young son as your true heir. No one must be in any doubt.'

'Of course.' He beamed at the boy who stood by my commanders, watching me. 'What would you have me do? And have you bread and ale? I have been given nothing to eat for some hours.'

I tried not to sigh.

'You may eat soon. But first – a most sacred ritual.' I whispered in his ear. 'Will you do it?'

'Yes. If you think it is wise.'

I beckoned the Prince over and we returned, a little group of three, to stand in the midst of our jubilant soldiers. I could not help but regard the two standing together, father and son, the comparison between them was so obvious. Nothing could be clearer. As the proud regality of my lord Henry had slid away with the years, it had settled on the shoulders of the young Prince All hope would rest on the boy. Now at this singular moment in time I would gain him the royal approval and recognition of his father. There would be no doubt in the minds of our forces that here was the hope of Lancaster.

'Kneel before your father,' I commanded my son.

The Prince knelt, all grace and confidence, seven years old but already growing tall, and today impressive in a gilded purple-velvet brigandine with a matching velvet cap, a feather sweeping down over his fair hair. Had I not prepared for this particular event, on the chance that Henry would be restored to us? The Prince took off his cap and pressed it to his chest. Henry took a sword from one of our captains – he did not even wear one of his own – and touched the flat of the blade to the Prince's shoulders, first on the right, then on the left, dubbing him knight.

'Tomorrow I will give you your own sword,' my lord Henry said with a return of his old kingly stature. 'You will wear it with pride. Today you are my son and my heir. You will wear the crown of England when I am dead. From this day every man in England will know you for a Prince and a knight.'

It was all that I wanted. The recognition. The acceptance. The denial of the Act of Accord, even though that legal agreement was still hovering over us with all the menace of a hunting raptor. The Prince's face was flushed with achievement as Henry raised him to his feet and saluted him on each cheek, while I caressed my son's shining hair, before forcing myself to an act that turned my stomach with horror, yet knowing that I must not step back from it. I had ordered my forces to fight. I must bear witness to the result of that order. Standing on a slight rise in the ground, I forced myself to look over the battlefield, at the terrible waste, at the dead and the dying, the piles of bodies of men and horses. I must fight for my son and my husband, but this destruction was enough to make me close my eyes to block out the sight, although nothing could stop me hearing the moans and cries of agony. It must be done. God would judge me, but unless I was willing to abandon the Lancastrian cause, I could not retreat from such wanton loss.

I turned my back on the evidence of battle and stalked back to the camp. There was more work to do to make the impression that was required. Better that the Prince take the helm of this royal vessel than Henry. Some would say that he was too young, that I was lacking in maternal love to inflict this particular duty on my child, but my child was Edward of Westminster, Prince of Wales, and must grow into his royal responsibilities. The Prince must learn that sovereignty did not merely mean wearing a crown. There were darker events that he must witness and accept. Events in which he must play a role as Prince.

When Henry had been returned to me, the two Yorkist guards who had been left to protect him were brought too. Lord Bonville and Sir Thomas Kyriell. It was in my mind to make examples of them. Taking Prince Edward's hand, I led him to stand before the two men.

'Fair son, what manner of death shall these two knights suffer?'

He looked up at me, unsure of what I wanted.

'They kept your royal father prisoner against his will. Is that not treason? What do we do with men who are traitors?'

'We chop off their heads.'

'Do we show them mercy?'

'No, never mercy for treachery to the King and his heir.'

His voice piped with nervousness, but he had learned his words well from me.

'So what is your answer, my son?'

He nodded, confidence returning. 'I say, let them have their heads taken off.'

Lord Bonville looked aghast.

'May God destroy those who taught thee this manner of speech.' He turned to me, pleading: 'We did the King no harm. Our task was merely to protect him in case he was surrounded in the battle and wounded. We willingly gave him over to the care of your men.'

I raised my hand in denial. They were executed, their heads

struck from their bodies while the Prince stood at my side and watched. Thus I exposed my son to the harsh realities of battle and ultimate authority. He did not flinch. He did not look away. I was proud of him even though his face paled as the blood soaked into the ground. He would make an exemplary ruler.

I retired to my pavilion to decide on our next step. Why would I spend time in asking Henry? I would of course be blamed by those who thought that a woman should not take such command but there really was no choice for us. Warwick and March, York's son, were still alive to be dealt with. Warwick had escaped from the battlefield; he and his commanders had vanished from sight. I would deal with them later. More dangerous were the rumours coming in from the West where the Earl of March was campaigning with a force of his own. There had been a battle in the Welsh Marches at a place named Mortimer's Cross where Jasper Tudor had been beaten by this Yorkist upstart. I knew what March would do. With a victorious Yorkist army crowing at his back, he would travel fast to pre-empt me and take control of London. I must get there first. London would be made to pay for its support of the House of York. Henry would be restored and the followers of York crushed for ever. March's minor skirmish would be no more than a pebble rattling in an empty vessel.

Glory and anticipation kept me fine company that day. Henry spent the hours on his knees thanking God for our victory at St Albans where I had difficulty in preventing our forces from wreaking havoc. Perhaps I did not try too hard, for I was becoming desperate in my need of supplies.

'What do we do now?' Henry asked as we ate a light meal of bread and cheese and cold beef together, willing to follow my direction.

'We march on London.'

But I was careful to make promises, that I would not despoil and ravage the towns or the countryside, in spite of the rumours that my troops were starving and out of control. The defeated Earl of Warwick was using excellent propaganda to undermine my cause. I would be victorious and, on the day that I entered our capital city, London would pay for its defection from us, but I saw no sense in terrifying the citizens into submission. I wanted above all that the citizens of London should invite us in.

Did I regret what I had done? I would be despised, hated, condemned, but I would have fulfilled my duty to my husband and my son. I spoke to no one of the blood-soaked dreams that disturbed my peace. Henry, it seemed, slept with a guiltless conscience.

I would destroy the Act of Accord with a sword.

## Anne, Countess of Warwick

London was under threat, in the throes of anxious waiting. The gates were guarded and watched; the walls were patrolled to prevent any surprise attack. The people of the city stayed close to home when rumours flew with the speed of eagles, warning us of the revenge that approached. Queen Margaret and her northern hordes were marching south from St Albans with destruction, rape, and pillage in mind.

As for my personal state of mind, Richard had been defeated in the battle, but I knew that he still lived. It was the only source of relief, and meant little to Alice and Cecily, who continued to mourn their losses. King Henry had escaped Richard's control and was back under the orders of Margaret. Richard had lost his figurehead, and he had not returned to London, leaving me with no idea where he might be. They said he was not dead, true, but he might be injured. There was nothing I could do. How painful was helplessness. Even prayer seemed worthless, failing to assuage my doubts. All I could do was reassure the girls that one day they would see their father again.

January stepped into a wet February with no attack, no demands from Margaret, and no return of Richard. When had waiting in the past been so heart-wrenching? February, too, was flying past with high winds and turbulent showers when, under cover of darkness, I was disturbed by the lift of the latch of my bedchamber. I sat up, my throat dry, my heart beating fast, my hands clutching the bedcovers. It could not be good news.

'Who is it?'

'Who might be visiting you in your bedchamber at night?'

There was no doubting the voice. Or the firm step. Or the shadowy outline as he bent to light a candle.

'Richard. Thank God.' I rubbed my face to dash away the remains of sleep and that instant of terror. 'What are you doing here?'

'Trying to give you some good news.'

'Is that even possible? We are expecting Margaret on our doorstep at any moment.'

'And so she may be. And why are we whispering? We will wake no one who is not already awake.'

He dropped his cloak on the floor, followed by his chaperon and gloves with a little puff of dust. He had found time to dispense with his armour, although his favourite brigandine had seen better days, the velvet scuffed and matted, with what I could not guess. There was no sign of battle about him unless it was a mood of despair. His face when he held up the candle was grey with fatigue, his eyes dark with the unimaginable things he had witnessed. And with defeat. Richard would not take kindly to defeat.

'Are you hurt in any way?' I asked.

'I am heading west,' he replied inconsequentially, handing the candle to me while he hunted for a flagon of ale or wine. 'To meet up with Ned. I don't suppose you have any food to hand? My belly growls with emptiness.'

'No, I haven't any food. And never mind Ned.' I took the cup he handed to me, juggling the two offerings until I found a place for the candle on my night-stand, lighting the wick of the one already standing there. 'Are you unharmed?' I abandoned the wine as well. This was no time for convivial discussion.

'Yes.' I heard the grimace in his voice rather than seeing it on his face as the candle-flames drove back the shadows. 'Except for my pride. And how that has suffered. It was a battle for which I can find no excuses. We were taken by surprise and Henry is now back with his managing wife. It was a disaster of planning and outcome. I misjudged the route the Queen would take and so put our defensive forces in the wrong place.' He added on a note of despair, 'I was not blameless in our defeat. Even worse, my brother John is taken prisoner. I fear that Margaret will apply an axe to his neck. I can do nothing to stop it.'

He was beyond weary as he took a long swallow of wine. Blame lay heavy on him, as it would on any man caught up in this conflagration of battles.

'What of Ned? It is so difficult to get reliable news,' I said to deflect his thoughts.

Richard sat on the end of my bed, pushing my feet out of the way.

'I know as little as you except that he has achieved a creditable victory against Jasper Tudor,' he replied. 'A magnificent soldier in the making, so it seems, ready to step into his father's shoes. My plan is to take a force and head west to meet up with him and hopefully bring aid to London. Meanwhile, you must protect yourselves behind these walls. I have no troops to leave here with the London citizens.'

'And how would we protect ourselves?' I asked, shuffling forward, pulling the bedcover round my shoulders, sharing his cup of wine, unwilling to let him go to yet another battle. 'It all seems hopeless to me. Yes, you might meet up with Ned, but you might also miss him on the march. What if Margaret reaches London before you can return? You will come home to a despoiled city and all your womenfolk dead.'

For the first time since he had entered the room his face relaxed, although he could not smile.

'What ifs cannot dictate our policy at this time. The city will do all it can to protect itself.'

'I agree that London will not willingly open its gates, but equally Margaret will not retreat. Who will speak with Margaret, to whom would she be prepared to listen? Not Henry, who has no advice to give. And certainly not you who will be out in the West! I think that the Queen will listen to no one but her own desires. It seems that her conscience has also deserted her. Will she indeed loose her northern rabble on the city in revenge for its treachery in supporting the Yorkists? I fear that she might.'

I took the hand that was not holding the cup, running my fingers over the abrasions from rein and sword, finding it impossible to see any hopeful outcome. The only good news was that Richard was here, safe within the four walls of my chamber, and was alive, and that Ned had won his victor's wreath on the battlefield. Neither held out the eventuality of Margaret's hostile approach being forestalled.

'It may just be possible to scrape some advantage from the bottom of this particularly nasty barrel,' Richard said. 'It has been suggested to the Council that a negotiation between women might cleave through the impasse and win me some time.'

'Who has suggested it?' He shook his head, but my suspicions were strong. I knew well Richard's ability to use persuasive words. 'Will that happen?'

'It has been suggested,' he repeated. 'All is not lost, in spite of St Albans. We lost some good men to the axe. It seems that the young Prince is being raised in the spirit of his mother. But now I must go.'

'Already? Without food? Was it worth the visit of less than an hour?'

'I daren't wait, and my troops are ready to leave. Would you rather I hadn't come?'

Reaching out, he took hold of my hair, neatly plaited for the night, and wound it around his wrist in a possessive gesture that I recognised from more peaceful times.

'No. Never that,' I said. I took his face between my hands and kissed his mouth. 'I am honoured that you should think of my needs when the future creaks in hopeless desperation. I will pray for you in whatever you venture.'

'Of course. The sooner I meet up with Ned the better. Are the girls well?'

'Yes. Isabel is becoming a beauty and Anne has grown like a willow lath. I will give them your love.'

'As I will give you mine. Look for me with an army at my back. Ned and I will save London. Meanwhile the courageous women of this city will do their part.'

An embrace, a kiss, my plait released, a final linking of hands to remind me of his presence in my life when once again he would face a hostile army across the breadth of a battlefield. What could I say to him that I had not said so many times when he went to war?

'Keep safe and know that I will wait to hear from you.'

'I will. I will return.'

And he was gone, with a swirl of cloak and a thump of boots on the stair, leaving events in the hands of the City Council, who feared that a hungry army without control would run amok through the streets, plundering, pillaging and destroying as it went, while I held my autumn-brown plait in my hands, remembering his final gesture of care. Could Margaret be relied upon to stop it? King Henry could not and the Prince was too young to do more than obey his mother.

I told Richard's aunt and mother of the late-night visit. They agreed. A negotiation of women, Richard had said. It might have its advantages in persuasion rather than the honed edge of a sword. We must try anything to prevent more bloodshed.

## Margaret, Queen of England

'It is necessary that I speak with you, my lady.'

I looked up from the document that I was perusing, a letter I was writing to the citizens of London, dictating it to my clerk.

'… *none of you shall be robbed, despoiled, nor wronged by any person that we or our son shall be accompanied with, or any other sent in our name…*'

It was a difficult letter to write since the rumour of my army's lack of food and payment was perilously close to the bone. The City of London did well to fear my forces. Above my head the canvas of the pavilion flapped in a brisk breeze, making it difficult to hear anything that was not shouted. But here was Sir John Wenlock, demanding my attention.

'Of course,' I said.

'Alone, if it please you, my lady.'

'Is it from London? Have they offered to open their gates to us? If so, this letter need never be sent. Come, man. There is only my lord the King and my son here present. Surely it cannot be so personal.'

'I fear that it can, my lady.'

I walked to stand outside my pavilion where we could achieve a little privacy, tucking my veils within the neck of my cloak. It was a nuisance, but at least we could converse at ease. Around us my forces were preparing to continue their march to London.

'I would not have expected to see you here in my camp, Sir John.' I managed a wry smile. 'Do you change sides again? Has York's death made you reconsider?'

He had once been my chamberlain, but times had changed. Now he was a forsworn Yorkist.

'No, my lady. I will still follow the young Duke of York and the Earl of Warwick.'

'Yet you are here with news. What is so personal that it cannot be told in the presence of the King? If either Warwick or March is dead, why not shout it over the whole camp?'

He shook his head, his face grave as he gave me his news, holding nothing back.

I could not have dreamt it. All my triumph over St Albans destroyed in one utterance of a once-loyal retainer who thought that I should know the rumours that were spreading. That had spread like wildfire through the capital. Yet, should I trust him?

'Do you come here in good faith, Sir John?' I asked with cold judgement.

'I do. I thought that, for your kindness to me in the past, you should know.'

'How widespread are these rumours?'

'They have heard them in this camp, my lady. I know that they have come from London.'

'It is a lie! A despicable lie!' I said, all but failing to keep my temper. How hard it was becoming to present an amenable face to the world. I swallowed and tried for a bland expression while the chill within me bubbled into heat. 'And who is the source of this calumny?'

'Difficult to say.' His reply was hesitant, uneasy, as if he really knew but would not say. 'It is a strong political weapon to use against you, my lady.'

For a moment I turned my back on him, regarding the powerful force that I was creating in these armed men, to overthrow the Yorkists. The weapon that was being used against me was not a physical one, would not kill, but was dire indeed. I returned my gaze to Sir John.

'And who is this man who has helped me to commit this act of sin? Is that being talked of? Which man has so lured me that I would join with him to commit so immoral an act?'

Sir John's face coloured, a heavy flush to his temples.

'I think it is not my place to talk of this. Forgive me, my lady. Perhaps I have said enough.'

I could have struck him for his reticence, but it was not his fault.

'Tell me! Don't mince your lying words now!'

He sighed a little. I thought that he resisted taking a step back when my face blazed with my demand.

'You can guess the suggestions, my lady. Men who have served you well over the years and frequent your company. James Butler, the Earl of Wiltshire. John Talbot, the Earl of Shrewsbury. Viscount John Beaumont. All loyal and faithful and comely enough to attract your admiration.'

And all tarred with this despicable brush.

'And where did these rumours begin? Whose vicious words created this story?' I demanded again.

The name given to me by Sir John did not surprise me. It could be only one source. I could have guessed it myself.

'Are you certain?' I asked.

'The French Ambassador says that this is the source of the accusation. He might be wrong, of course...'

I would not wager on it. When Henry had been captured at Northampton I had been angry. When Henry had signed the Act of Accord, giving away my son's birthright, a flame of fury had been lit that almost consumed me. It was nothing compared to the fire that now burned in me at the defamation of my person and the principles by which I was raised.

Perhaps, if I were willing to admit it, it was fear that manifested itself in fury.

With Sir John standing deferentially, hat in hand, awaiting my response, I could find nothing to say. I was trapped in a web of pure propaganda against me. Would the Queen deny the rumours? Of course she would. Was there evidence to support her denial? None. But then, there was evidence of neither my guilt nor my innocence. The rumours were there, and they would abound, whatever I said in my own defence.

'Thank you, Sir John.' I regarded him for a long moment. 'Why did you come here, to tell me?'

'From past loyalties, my lady. I would wish you well, even if not a victory in London.'

He bowed and walked away to recover his horse, while I returned to my pavilion where Henry was seated, leafing through the pages of a book of tales of romance and courage, a gift from the Countess of Warwick, as he had informed me. The Prince was leaning against his chair, looking at the pictures as Henry pointed out the tales of Arthur and Guinevere, of Tristram and Iseult. Ironically, tales of infidelity and dishonour. Prince Edward's shuffling told me that he would rather be practising his sword-play with one of our captains but the illustrations of famous knights still held him at his father's side. I wondered if he had outgrown his admiration for Mordred.

Should I tell Henry? Better that he hear the scandal from me than from the soldiery in ribald comments.

I said nothing. I could not speak of it. It was too painful and Henry did not need to know. Not yet. We had enough to deal with in the coming days. When we had celebrated our victory, then I would tell my lord Henry how my name had been besmirched.

If I considered it necessary.

Until then I would not think of it.

# 13

# A Negotiation of Women

## Anne, Countess of Warwick

Three well-dressed, superbly mounted noblewomen were given the task of approaching the Queen and rode out of London in the direction of St Albans towards the Lancastrian camp. Could they possibly persuade Margaret to keep her distance, or at least to enter in peace, leaving her army outside the walls? I thought they would fail. Margaret had vengeance in mind for her previous defeats and subsequent exile. She would not be easily deflected.

I knew the women well, all three with Lancastrian loyalties, all recipients of Margaret's friendship and New Year gifts. At least they were known to her and would be received with trust and favour. At least she would not have them cut down outside her pavilion or put in chains.

There was Anne, the widowed Duchess of Buckingham, as forthright and proud as her sister, Duchess Cecily. Strongly Lancastrian, her husband killed at Northampton, she was godmother to the young Prince, the perfect negotiator to appeal to Margaret's compassion. Then there was Lady Scales, another Lancastrian widow, who had escorted Margaret from France as a young bride, and who had served her as lady-in-waiting. And finally, Jacquetta, well-connected widow of the Duke of Bedford, who had also befriended the new French bride in the past, and was now wife of Richard Wydeville, a notable Lancastrian. An obvious choice of Lancastrian women to argue for London's safety, the perfect choice. Surely Margaret would listen to their words of wisdom to leave London secure without attack? What men could not solve on the battlefield with sword in hand, women might smooth over with soft words and courteous negotiation. Sombrely clad, they wore no jewels or ostentatious fur. They proclaimed their own importance in rigid spine and straight gaze.

And I became one of their number, because it was my wish, because it was what Richard wanted me to do. Although Yorkist through and through, wife of Margaret's enemy, yet still I would be a valuable addition to this impressive group. I would be there to speak for the powerful Nevilles and the mourning House of York if it became necessary. What I would say, I had no idea. Perhaps nothing at all. But I would bear witness and speak if I could. Any step to save London from invasion and destruction was essential; any step that I could take to give Richard and the Earl of March time to return.

We rode north, well guarded. We had been given a solemn task and we must not fail in pleading for grace for the city. This was a delicate mission by anyone's standards.

Arriving, we were greeted with deference and shown into the royal pavilion where the Queen awaited us. Henry was not there, nor was her son. It was clear to all: women sent to speak with a woman. It was Margaret's hand that was wrapped around the reins of power. There was no value in begging for leadership from the King, even if his freedom had been restored to him.

Margaret was standing, awaiting us, a cleverly wrought coronet glittering in her hair, an ermine cloak resting on her shoulders, shrouding her in its voluminous folds, a message to all that here was the Queen who would direct the future in this battle-torn kingdom. We curtsied. She inclined her head with utmost respect, then gestured that we should sit on the stools that had already been brought for us. Cups of wine were poured and offered by liveried pages, one of whom I realised was the Prince himself. So far so good. All could be destroyed by the wrong word, the wrong tone. I thought that Margaret looked strained and short of temper, as if she had heard bad news, although her words were equable enough.

'Tell me what you wish to say, and for whom you speak. I see that there is both York and Lancaster here present. Some of you I would have accounted friends in the past.'

Her eyes brushed over me. She knew us all well enough. There was no need for introductions. It was the Duchess of Buckingham who spoke up for us.

'You know me well, my lady, for I am widowed in your cause at Northampton. My words are to be trusted. We are sent by the City Council in London, to beg your mercy. To ask for your promise that the city should not be despoiled.'

Margaret sipped in slow contemplation, then answered in gentle tones.

'Nor will it be. Have I not already given my word? I and my husband the King have no mind to rob, despoil or wrong those who are loyal to us. We have no plan to pillage this greatest city of the realm. Why would we destroy what is of value to us when we return to power? Shall we not make our base there when we are come home? There is nothing to be gained in destruction. You accuse me wrongly. Have I not promised fair treatment for the city? ... but I am aware of rumours that do me ill.'

Her lips thinned in a smile, her fair lashes hid her eyes. We nodded obediently. Was that to be the end of the discussion? Were we to believe her promises?

Margaret sipped again, then added: 'But evildoers will, of course, be punished.'

'We would expect no less, my lady. As long as those to be punished are given honest justice.'

'Does the King not always hand out justice in his realm?'

No one saw fit to speak of the two men beheaded after the battle at St Albans. Lady Scales took up the argument for us.

'We hear that your forces riot in the streets of every town they have passed through, and steal what is not theirs. That they are without discipline.'

Margaret replied as smoothly as new cream. 'As I said, it is unwise to listen to rumour. London will be safe from any harm.'

'But we hear that the troops from the North have had no respect for the land through which they have marched. They have robbed and burned at will.'

'Do you believe that I cannot control my forces?' Margaret asked, eyes raised and now glittering as brightly as her coronet in a shaft of sunlight which had angled through the open door-flap. 'The City of London will not suffer unduly.'

'Do you allow your army to enter the city at will, Your Grace?' Jacquetta, once Duchess of Bedford, asked.

'I will make the decisions on who will enter London with me.'

An ambiguous statement that left the question of uncontrollable forces unanswered. We petitioners looked at each other.

'Then the city will not be despoiled,' Lady Scales said.

'No, it will not.'

We had come to the end.

'With such a promise, Your Grace, the City Council will welcome you back and open the gates,' the Duchess of Buckingham replied. 'As do we.'

'For which I am grateful.' Queen Margaret stood, the rest of us hastily following. 'It has been a difficult few months, when all has been awry. It will be good for my lord the King to resume his rightful place and power in his own city, with me and his son at his side. We will enjoy a triumphal entry through the streets and take up residence at Westminster.'

And there it was. Margaret would make the decisions; there was nothing more to say. Margaret had made her promises and all we could do was pray that she could live by them. If not, her army could run amok and we had achieved nothing.

'We will take your generous reply to the City Councillors,' Lady Scales promised.

We made a general move to leave, but Margaret raised her hand to stop us.

'We trust that we will be welcomed into our capital with food and supplies for our troops who have served us so well. We are desperately short of supplies after our long march. Our city should come to our aid.'

'I am sure that the City Council will look on your distress with compassion,' Duchess Anne assured.

'The city will not regret it.'

'Do we tell the Council that your troops will remain outside the city walls?'

'We will decide what is appropriate when we arrive, but certainly I will expect food to be delivered to my forces outside the city gates. If it is not, it will be necessary to take what they need.'

Which seemed to me to be nothing less than a veiled threat. So little to say after such a journey, but we had achieved what we wanted. Margaret would dispense mercy and justice and her troops would be held in check. Margaret had at least promised us no pillage or destruction.

133

I had said not one word, and yet I felt that it had been right for me to be there.

Accompanying us to the door of the pavilion, the Queen put out a hand to my arm to stop me.

'One moment, Countess of Warwick.' The others left us together. 'I would not expect to see you in this company. Do you mix comfortably with those who are loyal to Lancaster? You can hardly claim to be one of their number. Nor did you have anything to say.'

'I will do all I can to help bring peace for England. There was no need for me to speak since you addressed our anxieties. But I will agree that if you return to bring peace to the city, it will be a greater victory for you than the bloody affair at St Albans.'

Her lips tightened again, as did her brows into a bar of disapproval. 'Your husband did not bring peace. He and his Yorkist retainers are to blame for my lord's miseries.'

I would not speak of the deaths she had brought to my family at Wakefield, fighting hard to keep my accusations to myself. Why risk the peace we had achieved now? It was some time since we had last met at the Love Day celebration and it might be wise not to refer to the exchange of letters between us. She was as confident and assured as I always remembered her. And yet it was clear to me that something was troubling her. There was some matter on her mind that would give her no peace.

'Why did you decide to speak with me, Your Grace?' I asked.

'Because your husband, the Earl of Warwick, is the man at whose feet I would lay most of my present troubles,' she said.

And at that I did not fight hard enough to remain silent on critical issues. 'As I recall, Your Grace, you are to blame for placing the head of Warwick's father, uncle, cousin and brother on the gateway in York.'

'Thus are all traitors punished.'

'Yet such an act cannot but cause hostility. My lord will never forget. He will not forgive.'

'Neither will I. You should warn him to take care. If I take London and he is there, I will have no mercy. He is my enemy and that of my lord the King and the heir. I say again, there will be no mercy.'

'I will inform him of your threat. I doubt that he will wait in London for you to capture him.'

She looked at me, an assessing sidelong glance.

'Do you not fear that I will take you as a hostage? How valuable you would be to me.'

I must have looked at her in astonishment. 'I think that you have more honesty than to do that, Your Grace.'

I hoped that she had. I had never thought that she would take such an overtly aggressive action towards me.

'Where my son's inheritance is concerned, what is honesty? Beware, my lady of Warwick. I will not always be as accommodating as I have been today. Or as I have been in the past when we have written as women with some degree of understanding between us.'

A warning indeed.

'I will take heed. I wish you well, Your Grace. And to your fair son.'

The Prince had just returned to his mother's pavilion, still page-clad, his cap pinned with a jewelled feather, smiling at the role he had played. The Queen drew in a sharp breath at the sight of him, stretching out her hand to draw him close, as if she feared for his safety, although why she should so fear in this loyal camp I could not guess.

Then the Queen spoke, frowning at me.

'How despicable it is that this child's reputation is already blackened with false rumour, his inheritance like to be snatched away. The law, as it stands, will find against him taking the crown. His good name is already damaged. And all of it a lie.'

She stared at me, challenging me to claim ignorance of what she spoke. I could not. The rumours were rife in the streets of London where an excess of ale encouraged the ribald gossip of those who had no love for the Queen. Or in the domiciles where the House of Lancaster had little support.

'I have heard the talk,' I admitted. 'Is it true?'

'How dare you ask me that!'

'I thought that it need be asked. Forgive me, Your Grace, if I appear insensitive. Should you speak of such dangerous matters in your son's presence?'

The Queen's glance down at her son was briefly dismissive.

'My son is yet too young to understand, but one day he will know what has been said and will take revenge, I swear it. Would you wish to consider where such false tales started? They are indeed false and any man who speaks them is a liar. I am told that your husband is at the centre of them. Why would you not be fully aware of so vicious an attack on me?'

I frowned. 'You say that my lord of Warwick began the spread of the rumours.'

'The French Ambassador says that it was the Earl of Warwick.'

'He would not do it,' I said.

And yet a cold hand slid along the nape of my neck. Was I so certain? It was as if the Queen could read my uncertainty.

'Can you be so sure? York's followers would do anything to undermine my position. And if my son is not the rightful heir, then who is? Think of that, lady of Warwick. York's heir, with all his legitimate blood, unless Duchess Cecily also chose to make her lord a cuckold. The Earl of March is the heir because of that

136

damnable Act of Accord. I will break that Act, if it is the last thing I do. I will break Warwick too!'

There was nothing I could say that, on this suddenly tense occasion, would be politic.

There was even less when in unbridled malice she added, 'At least I was able to give my lord a son, which you failed to give to your own lord. Some women are not so blessed as I. Was the problem yours? Or his? Could you find no admirer to give you a son to inherit the Warwick title and land? So the rumours accuse me. How simple it must be to bear an illegitimate son, one that will be accepted by your husband as his own. Did you never consider it? They say that I have done so.'

Her grip on the wrist of the little Prince tightened, as if in possession.

I ignored the bitter accusation.

'No, some are not so blessed, Your Grace. I was unable to bear a son. Who is to know God's will? I wish you well of your blessing. A son, of course, means everything.'

'You will have to live with your failure.'

It was true. I had failed. The guilt and the grief were overpowering as I curtsied and left to join the little party that was waiting for me, yet at the door I turned round, sorrow pushed aside, determined not to neglect this opportunity.

'If you wished to heal any wounds with the Earl of Warwick, you might release his brother, the Marquess of Montagu, from captivity.'

The Queen raised her chin. 'I will not. I will see him dead first.'

Had I expected any different? I left the pavilion.

'What did she have to say?' the Duchess of Buckingham asked curiously.

I shrugged as if it were of no consequence. 'Nothing to my comfort.'

All she had said was true. I had failed and Richard must regret it every day of his life.


## Margaret, Queen of England

My son is not a bastard! My son is a true-born child of the King of England!

The meeting had left me stripped to the raw. Oh, I appreciated the attempt at peace-making by these brave Lancastrian women, but it was Countess Anne of Warwick who had left me with a vicious anger. Why had I allowed it to take command, to make the Queen less than queenly? What had made me accuse her so cruelly of failure as a woman and a wife? Should I feel ashamed? To blame another woman for being unable to achieve a male heir, when it had taken me long enough and demanded a pilgrimage from me to Walsingham to give thanks to the Blessed Virgin when I had all but given up hope; now in my cold isolation it seemed despicable. Nor would there be more heirs of my body. I suspected that Henry would get no more children on me.

The rumours hurt my heart: my son Edward a bastard, an illegitimate child, foisted on the King by me. A bastard got in adultery. It was my plan, so the stories said, to force Henry to abdicate and install my changeling child in his place. How could he be Henry's child after so many years of childlessness and Henry's mental uncertainty? Would not the Queen look elsewhere for a child? Surely any cunning women would do so. Oh, the gossipers were cruel indeed. And it had all reached the ears of the French ambassador.

I looked across at Prince Edward now that we were alone again. There was nothing in his appearance to deny it. Edward was growing strongly, my pride and my joy, his features and colouring resembling neither mine nor the King's. He was fairer than either of us, a true prince. One day he would rule this realm more effectively than his father ever could. Did he not have my blood in his veins? He would be a knight, a fighter, a king. Would I not do all in my power to defeat the Yorkists and bring my son to the throne, whoever the father?

There was no doubt at all who was the father of this royal child.

A statement that I would find it impossible to prove.

How I detested those who had damned me with such an accusation, and if it was indeed Warwick, as I fervently believed it to be, it hammered yet another nail into the coffin of my hatred of him.

I still regretted painting Countess Anne's failure is such lurid colours.

I remembered the stricken look in her eyes. Was I becoming the vicious She-Wolf they called me? Guilt swept over me to mingle with the anger.

## Anne, Countess of Warwick

We had carried the news to the City Council with all the optimism we could muster; they promptly proclaimed Margaret's word through the city, that she would keep the peace. Unfortunately, they added the Queen's promise that evildoers would be punished with all the weight of royal justice.

'By the Blessed Virgin! Of what value was that?' Duchess Cecily was damning in her opinion. 'The Lord Mayor is a dolt!

He should never have announced the Queen's reply in quite that manner,' she said.

'I would not,' I agreed, 'and neither would you. Did they not think of the repercussions in the streets?'

'What fools they are!'

For almost before I had returned within the gates of Baynard's Castle, rioting erupted in London as Queen Margaret's words were worried over in parlours and ale-houses. Who would be thought evil? Who would be punished? And would she turn loose those rampaging hordes about which we heard? Perhaps they would be the ones to mete out vengeance against those whom the Queen designated as traitors. It sent a frisson of fear through the city. Would there be such events as trials, or would it be mass slaughter? In an effort to allay fears, the Mayor of London arranged for cartloads of vital provisions to be collected and sent out to assuage the Queen's wrath. Margaret would be won over by the generosity of her loyal city.

I went to the Strand with Lady Alice as the carts made their slow path to the city gates, laden with barrels of ale, canvas-wrapped packages of bread and haunches of meat. Herein might lie our future safety.

'At least it will buy us time,' I said, 'until your son returns with Ned.'

Lady Alice looked unconvinced. As indeed was I.

Then chaos and uproar erupted as law and order disintegrated. Crowds thronged the narrow streets, bellowing their defiance of the Mayor's orders, while we took refuge in a common tavern, watching as well as we could through the grimy windows. Blows were traded as the Londoners, both poor and well-to-do, leaped on and seized the carts. The supplies never made it beyond the walls. No one believed the Queen's promises. Why should the citizens of London give up their provisions? Better to safeguard themselves against a coming siege if that was what was to happen. The bread and meat, the vast circular cheeses and the barrels of ale were all seized and squirrelled away in kitchens and cellars and nearby taverns. The approaching army would go hungry.

'She'll not keep her promises now,' I said as we made our way home through the dispersing melee.

And there in the midst of it all, the supplies being carried away, even more tales were being exchanged to unsettle us:

'Warwick is captured. He'll not be returning to rescue us.'

'As for the young Earl of March? Too young to take on the Queen. Probably already dead out in the West.'

'If they're captured, the Queen will demand their heads. More Yorkist heads to decorate a gateway.'

The blood-stained opinions buffeted us as if we were in a high wind. When Lady Alice quickened her step, her veil pulled over her face in despair, I struggled against the rising hopelessness that gripped me so that I could barely breathe. Was Richard indeed dead? When we were recognised by the Neville arms on our escort's breasts, a cheer went up from the little group of citizens around us.

'Don't believe the bad rumours, my lady. We hear that the Earl of Warwick has met up with the Earl of March and they are now advancing on London. They'll soon be here to drive the Queen and her rabble back from our gates.'

It would be our saving grace.

'Who do we believe?' I asked of no one in particular. 'Who is to say which tale is true?'

'Warwick is alive, my lady. I swear it.'

But what would Margaret do? What would I do in her superbly gilded shoes? Probably I would bring my forces and attack London first, before the Yorkist troops could arrive. We were still not safe. Even if Richard and Ned were free to come to our rescue, Margaret could make us pay for our treachery before they could even be seen on the horizon.

Waiting drained the soul as well as the strength of the body, and until we saw Richard with our own eyes we must exist with it.

# 14

## *The Wheel of Fortune Turns*

**Margaret, Queen of England**

'I am King. I will still enter London and retake my throne in triumph. They will not harm me.'

Standing in the middle of his pavilion, my lord Henry looked incapable of taking any action to ensure his return in triumph.

All had been turned on its head. Victory in London had been within my grasp, and now all was rubble at my feet. The Earl of March, York's spawn, had indeed achieved a destruction of the Earl of Pembroke's army in the West, a deadly blow against the supporters of Lancaster. Even worse, Warwick had fled St Albans only to meet up with March. Now, together, they were pushing purposefully on towards London to save the city.

The despair, the destruction of my plans, put a torch to my temper even as my heart plummeted. Henry, anxious and prayer-ridden, continued to talk of an advance on London, unable to envisage being taken prisoner again.

'I am still King. They will not harm me,' he repeated, his fingers plucking restlessly at his sleeves as he habitually did when his thoughts were scattered in terrible indecision.

'No, they will not harm you,' I assured him, regretting the

edge to my voice, but unable to stop it. 'But to enter London would now be a terrible mistake.'

'It is my own city!'

I turned away from him, unable to reply with any calm, since my mind was rent with possibilities, all of them unpalatable. What to do to safeguard him and the Prince until better times? What to do to restore the Lancastrian strength in England? If I were not careful, all we had achieved at St Albans would be undone. My hold on my forces was already tenuous since London had reneged on its willingness to supply us with food. Would I dare, with a hungry army, face March and Warwick? Perhaps I should try to take London by force, to gain a foot-hold there and hold the capital against the combined forces approaching from the West. But there again, it might be better to remain where we were, ensure a good battle position, and wait for the Yorkists to come to us.

'We should not fight,' Henry said. 'I'll spill no more English blood. We will negotiate. Do I not desire peace in this land?'

'To negotiate will achieve us nothing,' I replied in a harsh tone that I rarely used with him.

I took advice from my captains. Regrettably they spoke with one voice. Not one of them liked our dependence on the men from the North.

'It has lost us support,' Somerset advised with much urgency. 'Turn north again, my lady. Move back out of harm's way, back towards the city of York perhaps, where you can shelter and re-muster your forces, until all is clear.'

'All seems very clear, to me,' I responded as temper drained away in despondency. 'We are under threat from our Yorkist enemies. Does not retreat make me – us – appear even weaker?'

'Better than if we faced another battle in which we were defeated. We cannot guarantee our success against Warwick and

March. The young Yorkist's victory in the West has given him great confidence.'

'I think that we should fight,' the Prince announced.

'You are not of an age to make such decisions,' I told him, ignoring the sulky set of his mouth. 'As my lord Somerset will tell you.'

I turned away from Henry and my captains in sheer desperation. It had to be done. I gave the orders. How aggrieved I was that I had lost the chance to take London, but at least we would escape unscathed, and Henry was tucked firmly under my wing. Once my army was fed and strong, we would come south again, take London and reassert my son's rights.

How often was I thinking in terms of Prince Edward in those weeks, in spite of his lack of age, rather than my husband? I watched him as the boy mounted his horse with such confidence, such ease, prepared to ride beside his father, insisting that he carry one of the royal pennants. With experience and sage advice, and my guiding hand, Prince Edward would make an excellent King. All was by no means lost.

I remembered the stricken look on Countess Anne's face. I had been unforgivably cruel.

## Anne, Countess of Warwick

Richard and Edward of March, now Duke of York after his father's death, rode at the head of their troops into London. What a welcome was given to them. Cheering, Yorkist banners displaying Richard's bear and ragged staff, and Ned's newly adopted emblem of the Sun in Splendour; there was much ale liberated from barrels in celebration.

The fears engendered in the past weeks, the fear of the

northerners, had won support for York. The city was now no longer weak and open to Lancastrian attack, for with Richard came the news that the royal forces were in retreat. The volume of the rejoicing blossomed like a clap of thunder when the news came in.

There was hardly time for me to greet Richard before it was decided to hold an immediate council of war in one of the chambers in Baynard's Castle. How difficult it was not to mourn again, at so many faces missing from the meeting. York and Salisbury and young Rutland as well as two of Richard's brothers: Thomas dead and John still imprisoned. Duchess Cecily embraced her son Ned with fervour. No one seemed to find it unusual that she and Countess Alice and I should sit around the table with George Neville, Lord Fauconberg and the Duke of Norfolk.

It was an interesting experience. The discussion was dominated by Richard, but he made it his policy to ask young Ned for his opinion too. I watched my husband, listened to him, admiring his handling of the situation, winning friends and supporters, allowing others to speak and give opinions. His thoughts, when offered, were balanced, without overt hostility and demands for immediate bloodshed. Here was an opportunity for me to appreciate a master in negotiation, a man born to lead, to take command. I watched the confident play of his hands, his eloquent lift of an eyebrow, the quick smile of approval, with admiration.

When views had been exchanged and argued over, Richard addressed Ned directly.

'My advice, Cousin, is this. We accuse Henry of breaking the Act of Accord, to which he gave his royal assent, by waging war on the House of York. By breaking the Act he has forfeited his right to the throne. If that is so, if London and Parliament will accept it, you will make a bid for the crown of England since you, by the Act, are the legal heir. Do you agree?'

How would he not? Edward of March, Duke of York, king in waiting, Ned, to all here present, raised his cup in a toast to the future. So did we all.

'Hail to the Rose of Rouen.'

It was a most important step. A new King Edward. A Yorkist king, with Richard as his adviser and mentor.

'If this can be implemented, then Margaret will never return to restore Henry or indeed his supposed son.'

Richard proved himself to be so clever with words, for here was the lightest of references to that rumour that had caused Margaret such heartache, but no attention was brought to it. The council of war ended on a note of victory, with much toasting of the coming ceremonies when Edward would be crowned King of England. It was agreed. Before he could wear the crown on his own brow, Richard and Ned must solidify the claim of York. Henry and Margaret must be deposed, executed or driven into exile; only then would Ned, he announced with the relish of the young, take the crown for himself. A young man of some strength of character.

'What do you suppose Margaret will do?' I asked Richard when all had departed and we remained alone, still seated at the table with the remains of cups of wine in which we had toasted our success. 'Will she accept it, if Ned is crowned King?'

'No, she will not accept it,' Richard said. 'What are her choices? Go to Scotland? Back to France? I think that she will collect another army in Scotland and try again.'

I agreed. I could understand her despair.

'Would we be safe?' I asked Richard. 'Would there not always be plans to return? Our new King Edward would be constantly looking over his shoulder. And so would we.'

Elbows planted on the table between the cups and platters, Richard rested his chin on his linked fingers.

'It may be that there will be a final battle to destroy the Lancastrian claim completely,' he said. 'I will give you all praise and honour for your negotiations to prevent Margaret from attacking London but...'

'Thank you, although I added nothing to it...'

'...but sometimes a clash of arms is necessary to end all threats.'

My conversation with the Queen remained echoing in my head, an accusation that I could hardly push aside, for was it not true? I had been unable to dislodge it. Richard Neville, Earl of Warwick, needed a son and heir and I had failed to provide it. Two girls I had carried, both healthy and strong, but not the boy he wanted. Yes, they would marry well but it was not the same.

Watching him as he planned his next sortie, I wondered if he blamed me. He never said so, but who knew what was in his mind when he was not fighting battles. It had remained an inner grief as I had walked away from the Queen in her pavilion. And was it true that the rumour of the Prince's illegitimacy had come from Richard's lips? He would see the value of it; to spread such ideas, falsehood or no, would strengthen Ned's claims. It was so close to the bone.

'What is it?' he asked. He was sitting opposite me, chin tilted. I had not realised that he was watching me, his lips curved into a smile. 'Here I am returned from possible death, about to go out and risk my life once more in the name of a new Yorkist king, and you are very quiet. Some rat is gnawing at your peace of mind. What is worrying you?'

He stretched out his hand across the board. I could just reach it with my fingertips if I did likewise.

'A small mouse, more like. I had conversation with the Queen,' I said.

'Why should that worry you? I am surprised that she took note of you even being present, since I am certain the Duchess of Buckingham would be holding forth on what London needed. My aunt is a woman of strong words.'

Which made me smile a little too.

'Your aunt left Margaret in no doubt about what she faced, but the Queen did speak with me. About you.'

'Ha!' At a stretch, he curled his fingers around mine as his eyes darkened. 'What did she say? Nothing good, I expect.'

'No. Nothing good. She accused you of spreading the rumours about her child's birth. Is it true? Is it true that you were the source of the rumours that the Prince is a bastard or a changeling? That he is not the true heir?'

He did not hesitate.

'Does it matter?'

'I would like to know.'

There was no dissembling in his reply.

'Yes, I did. Why not? When fighting a war, any action is of value, whether it be by sword or word. The use of lies and half-truths can be more valuable than we might guess at. Those who wish to believe it will do so. Those unsure will remain uncertain, and perhaps reluctant to accept the Prince as the next King.'

Richard's handling of the council of war had been perfect; his use of propaganda was ruthlessly without principle. I did not know what to think.

'But is it true?' I asked. 'The illegitimacy of the Prince. Margaret would deny it. It seems a savage blow to make against her, if untrue. She was desperately hurt behind her façade of assurance.'

As if the distance between us were too great, Richard stood

up and walked around the table, pulling up a stool to sit beside me, turning to face me.

'But are not all means justifiable? I would raise my sword against those who support Lancaster, why not use words? It is merely a step in a campaign to oust Henry and make Edward of York King. It has been necessary. If we are to crown Ned, then the Prince's claim must be discredited. And how do we know that it isn't true?' I could sense his patience running out. 'At the end of the day, when the war is won, will it matter whether it is true or false? Do you not understand that? I thought that you would.'

'We don't know, of course.'

But I believed Margaret's helpless sorrow. It would do no good to tell Richard that my sympathies had been challenged.

'It is not for you to worry about,' he said.

How difficult it was to admire someone but despise their undermining of another's peace of mind, in so pertinent a matter as the father of one's own son. Would I have done it? I would never have used such a cruel weapon, but Richard had no such qualms.

'I suppose that I must accept the need for so personal an attack,' I consented, reluctantly. But it still seemed wrong to use such a painful and dishonest method. It was a cold and cruel insight into Richard's character that I had previously been unwilling to acknowledge. And yet this was war, and Margaret would willingly see him dead in battle or by execution. Were not words a better weapon? I leaned forward, turning my face into his shoulder, guilt descending in a deluge. 'Forgive me.'

'For what? I see no need for my forgiveness. You have done no wrong. I understand why you might question my methods of attack.'

I shook my head.

'Anne... It cannot be so very bad.'

'I think that it can. Or you might think so.'

'What have you done?' He lifted my face with a hand beneath my chin so that he could read my expression. 'I cannot believe that it is so very bad.'

'I am sorry for not giving you a son. I regret it deeply.' My penance came unwillingly but I could not hold it back.

'My dearest girl...'

'I am no girl.'

'Is this the Queen's doing?'

I nodded. Discovering that there were tears on my cheeks, I wiped them away with the back of my hand. 'I know that you never speak of it, but is it not what every man desires? A son to take on the inheritance and family name? It will die with you. The title will have to be passed to another. Was it my failure? I am so sorry.'

He wiped away another errant tear with his thumb. His voice, perhaps more used to issuing orders on a battlefield, gentled, as if soothing a favourite horse, which, in spite of everything, almost made me smile.

'Just as I took the title from you, from your father. You must not carry this burden. We have two fine girls. We will marry them well, and one day the husband of Isabel will become Earl of Warwick. You must not let it cloud what we have made together. I do not blame you. Have we not made more of our marriage than many who were joined together in an arrangement made for family aggrandisement? Do we not have a deep affection and respect?'

'Yes.'

And even love, I thought. Was not love contrived of respect and affection? Of trust? And despite the ruthless ambition I had read in his face, all my trust rested in the palms of his battle-hardened hands.

My thoughts returned to Margaret. How similar we were. Both arranged marriages, both to create a powerful alliance. Did she love Henry? Did she have respect for him in his weaknesses? I did not think so. Perhaps she had, as a young wife, but now I saw only tolerance, and sometimes that, too, was strained.

Would I exchange my place for hers? I would not.

But I still regretted the lack of a son. I was well aware that Richard had a daughter, Margaret, born out of wedlock, before he came to my bed, when he was very young. It did not concern me. I knew that he supported her, which was as it should be. I did not know the mother of this child. Since then he had to my knowledge been loyal to me. I might not know, but sometimes ignorance was best. It was comforting.

Queen Margaret and I both had our crosses to bear.

'We will meet after supper,' he said. 'Now I must test the allegiance of the people of this city. Then my time will be yours. We will enjoy the moments we have together.'

We left the empty room where so much emotion had been aired either in a war council or in private. Richard departed to arrange a public acclamation of Ned as King. I took myself to where I knew I would find my daughters, to enjoy their company. I watched them as they challenged each other in a game of fox and geese. Isabel was ten, her hair darkening, her features firming into Neville cheekbones and chin. Anne still a mere child of five years, growing petulant when her geese, the little finely carved counters, failed to hem in Isabel's fox, until I took a hand in the game so that she could crow with success. It all ended with much laughter when the board was upset and the ivory geese scattered over the floor. Still time for me to enjoy them as children, offering them love and care. But then we must consider their marriages.

I might not have a son, but these daughters were of such great value.

# 15

## *An Exchange of Correspondence with Battle Looming*

**Margaret of Anjou, Queen of England, to Anne, Countess of Warwick**

By the Queen.

How hard it is for a Queen to express abject regret and beg for understanding, for exoneration. I saw how much I hurt you. It was unforgivable because it was deliberate on my part. What happens on a battlefield has no bearing on relationships in a bedchamber. It was wrong of me. A woman should have understanding of the anxieties suffered by those of her kind.

I have thought about this, when the dangers of my situation wrap around me and cause my heart to shake with fear. I might blame those who follow the ambitions of the Duke of York, for what they have done to me, but I think I should not lay the blame at your door. I said unforgivable things. I have asked for the grace of forgiveness from the Blessed Virgin.

Even harder to ask it of the wife of the detested enemy. Yet I will do it.

My only excuse is that the campaign to destroy my good name has undermined any courtesy with which I was raised. I have now lived with this calumny against my name for more weeks than I can count. It has haunted me, snapping at my heels, and I have no means of refuting it. How is it possible to produce evidence that no adultery was committed? It wears my spirits down so that they are in the dust beneath my feet.

Nor is there any man or woman with whom I can share my heartbreak.

I have been defamed as a woman, as a wife, as a mother; as a princess brought up in the strictest understanding of morality and honesty. Sometimes I cannot bear it and it has sharpened my tongue. Yet I must bear it for the sake of England's crown and my son's inheritance.

He is indeed my son.

You do not need me to tell you how my good name has been degraded, the despicable accusations used to wrench apart my chastity and my loyalty to my husband the King. You will have heard it in Warwick's household as well as in the streets of London, where my name is fair game to those who would slander it. I know what you will have heard, for it has been repeated to me in all its injustice. I have been guilty of taking power from my husband when his mind retreated into a world of dark shadows and thus was incapable of making the necessary decisions. Yes, I have been guilty of that. Yes, I have encouraged him to fight for what is his by right of royal birth. But dabbling in politics is not acceptable female behaviour. Such impropriety has led to the questioning of my morality too. If I was guilty of seizing that power which was not mine to take, then I could quite readily be guilty of cuckolding my royal husband.

I know the partial guilt of Warwick. Did he not tell the papal legate Coppini that royal power was now disastrously in the hands of King Henry's wife? There is no doubt of his involvement in that. Could he not then have been the source of the other empty talk that has grown in recent months, that my son, Prince Edward, is a child got in adultery? Thus I defiled my marriage vows and my son is a bastard; he is not Henry's son. My reputation has been dragged in the mire. Chastity within marriage is so important for women; the greater the lady, the more should her honour be celebrated through the country. These allegations damn me beyond hope. Infidelity and promiscuity are beyond destructive.

Those accused, utterly without evidence, of sharing my bed have been named. I will not repeat them. It is all false. A terrible lie.

That is not the end of it. If it is too much for some to accept that I have welcomed others into my bed, it has been said, without evidence, that the Prince might be a changeling. How many years did it take for me to carry a child? Eight barren years. If I was incapable, then this child could be an interloper, the child of another nameless woman, taken from her so that I might fulfil my duty. Thus I am attacked as a woman since I could not do what a woman should do. There is no evidence, but repetition gives it an element of truth. No, there is no evidence at all. There has never been any doubt in my lord Henry's mind, nor should there ever be. I have always been a true wife to him.

There are even scurrilous rumours on the wind that I would poison Henry, make my son King and wed the Duke of Somerset. Just another means to attack me by those who fear and hate me. The position I have worked hard to uphold, a dutiful wife and queen and mother, has been dangerously undermined and I know not where it will end.

And yet of course I do know. If the child is a bastard, who would be the rightful King after my lord Henry's death? You know the answer, too, quite as well as I: the new Duke of York. The Act of Accord gives it legality even if the ties of blood do not.

I have poured out my heart to you, perhaps unwisely, with all my fears. There is nothing you can do. Nor do I know that you will have any compassion for me, but as a wife and a mother, I think that you might.

I know that the crown will be offered to Edward of York and that there is much support for it in London. I cannot accept it. I will not accept it. The crown belongs to my true-born son.

What do I say to a woman with whom I feel an affinity when I detest all she stands for, whose husband is my greatest enemy? Yet I will pray for your health and that of your daughters. Perhaps one day we will meet again in better times and such enmities might be healed. I feel that it is an empty hope.

We have been forced to retreat, perhaps to Scotland again. I foresee only an outcome on a battlefield. I do not ask for pity, simply for some understanding, for there is no one else to whom I can unburden myself. I beg of you, Countess of Warwick, offer prayers to the Blessed Virgin for me. And for my beloved son, who has no blemish on his birth.

I regret my heartlessness. You did not deserve it. As a token of my regret, I send you this ring by the hand of my courier. It is a symbol of the friendship that once might have existed between us, but that now seems dead and

157

buried for good. It is a jewel from my own family, thus it
has no Lancastrian attributes that might encourage you to
reject it. In my family the rubies are a symbol of power, the
emeralds of hope. We can both hope for a resolution of this
bloody state of affairs in England, but although I doubt that
we will seek the same outcome, peace would be a blessing.

Margaret

Queen of England


## Anne, Countess of Warwick, to Margaret, Queen of England

Your words to me outside London were deliberately
provocative. They were vindictive. At the same time as
they hurt me to my soul, I understand the pain that you
must feel at the deliberate destruction of your reputation.
As a wife and mother I do understand. My own tardy
pregnancies and my failure to give birth to a son make me
sensitive to such failures in others. Chastity and integrity
in a marriage are so important for women, while men are
free to take others to their bed. It is the way of the world,
and women are easy targets for those who will seize on any
cause with which to blacken their name.

This was an act of war against your good name. I think
there is only one stratagem that you can apply. Remain
stalwart and fight for your son's rights, for recognition of his
legitimacy. You state that the rumours are false. I will not
ask further of you. It is on your own heart and your own
conscience.

As for my lord of Warwick's involvement in the rumour
of your son's bastardy, I know that he is critical of your

taking the reins of power into your own hands and will use any means to achieve his ends. War is his metier.

Although I denied it, I now know that my lord of Warwick was responsible in part for the rumours. I will not excuse him, I will not condone what he did, but neither will I condemn him. So many close to him died at Wakefield. You cannot expect him to show compassion, but I, his Countess, will pray for some resolution that will bring no more bloodshed to either of our families.

Would I ever consider adultery to give Warwick an heir? Would I ever consider smuggling a changeling, a child not of mine, into my bed to give him a son? I do not think so, but sometimes fate leads us down strange and uncomfortable paths. I would not condemn you for it.

I, too, fear another battle. I, too, will pray for the outcome for us all. I can do nothing more. I would say that women are helpless in so many spheres, but you are not. If you can offset another conflict, I pray that you will do so.

I regret your unhappiness. May the Blessed Virgin smile on you, when I cannot.

I admire your courage in continuing to fight for your husband and your son when faced with such personal hostility. I do not think that I would have that depth of courage.

I am honoured by the gift of the ring. I cannot wear it, but I will keep it as a memento of what might have been.

Anne
Countess of Warwick

# 16

## *The Bloody Field of Towton, March 1461*

**Margaret, Queen of England**

Of necessity, we marched north, away from London. It was March, not a season for campaigning, with cold winds and threats of snow, and I shook with fury. It seemed to be the only permanent emotion in my life. Days of contentment and soft affections were long gone. The days when I had been satisfied in the gentle company of my lord Henry had also vanished like sun in mist. How difficult it was to give credence to a man who had no sense of the dangers in which we stood. I felt compassion for his vagueness of mind but, Blessed Virgin, the strain on my own decision-making was complex and never-ending.

Nor, in this cold March, had I any choice but to call on my army again, for Edward, the new Duke of York, had roused the treacherous population of London to deny my lord Henry's worthiness as King, despite his crowning and anointing. Instead, they acclaimed this young Yorkist upstart who had more ambition in his sword arm even than his father, whose head still leered at us as we entered by Micklegate Bar into the relative safety of the city of York. The heads had suffered from the depredations of the weather, and the carrion birds that hopped and pecked at the dried flesh. The remnants of the paper crown had long gone.

I had rid us of the father and uncle and brother. Now all I needed was to see the death or capture of the son on the battlefield.

I was told by my commanders that there would be a battle. Had I not always known it, even as I had fled north? The forces of York had followed us, step by step. Raw anticipation of what was to come shivered through my blood, but I would not retreat from it. It had been difficult enough to flee from the environs of London, encouraging my lord Henry every step of the way.

'Should I don my armour?' Henry asked. 'I will lead my forces and encourage them with my presence. As I did at Ludford Bridge.'

It surprised me that he still recalled that brave show. So much had happened since.

'No. Not today,' I managed to say with a consoling hand to his arm.

I shivered even more. I could think of no worse scenario than to have Henry at the head of the Lancastrian forces. The King would not be asked to fight, and at the same time I thanked the Blessed Virgin that Prince Edward was far too young to take to the field.

'But must I not lead my troops?' Henry asked, eyes wide with what might have been fear as well as duty.

'No,' I reassured him as gently as I could between issuing orders. 'Our captains will lead and carry the day. We will wait here. I will remain with you.'

'You will not be there?'

'No. They know what they must do. We will be safe here.'

'Yes, of course. Behind these protective walls.'

In the end he took no persuading. I did not know whether to

be relieved or heartbroken that so much authority had arrived at my door. What would I have done if he had insisted? Locked him in his chamber, I decided. He was too much of a responsibility on a battlefield, too much of a liability.

'Who will lead the Yorkist army, *Maman*?' my son Edward asked.

'The Earl of March, I suppose. Or the Earl of Warwick, unless there is truth in what we hear of his being wounded.' There had already been a short clash of arms between our troops at Ferrybridge, to secure the crossing of the river. 'Nothing serious, unfortunately, but enough to keep him from the field. I wish it had been an arrow to his black heart.'

'If the Earl of March fights against us, he is a traitor,' the Prince observed.

'Indeed he is.'

'The crown is mine, after my father.'

'Yes.'

'The Earl of March says that he should be King. The Act of Accord says it.'

Where had he heard that? But then it was common knowledge, and he had sharp ears.

'He will pay with his head for such treachery,' the Prince observed. 'Like the men after Northampton.'

'Yes.'

'I will execute him myself!'

'It may be that you will, but now is not the time to discuss such matters. Go to your tutor, who will be awaiting you.'

Regretting my sharp lack of patience, I steadied my determination to push ahead with this battle. There must be no doubts. This realm must be brought round to acknowledging who was the true ruler of England, even if it meant more bloodshed. With God's will, it would be the last.

With my blessing but my absence, our troops marched out from York to the South, without Henry. We waited, as must always be the case when battle loomed. My lord Henry prayed, spending long hours on his knees. It was Palm Sunday, celebrating Christ entering into Jerusalem.

'I will enter into London, as Christ entered into Jerusalem.' Henry was so certain of victory. 'But not on an ass of course. The Londoners will rejoice, just as they did when we held the Love Day. It will be a time of peace for all.'

I could not pray with him. I could not find the words, and simply hoped that the Blessed Virgin could read what was in my heart. There was no need for me to fear the outcome. Victory would surely be granted to us. Had I not called on all our great families in the North to send us aid, to come in person with all haste. The letters were signed with Henry's own seal and had brought them flocking. We could not lose. We must not lose.

Would we hear the noise of battle from the walls of York?

I climbed there and looked out towards the South, taking the Prince with me after he had read to me efficiently enough from his book of Greek heroes. All was silent apart from the church bells and voices carrying from the streets below. Where would they fight?

Then snow began to fall, light flakes at first, melting on the shoulders of my cloak, on my hood, and then heavily, driving us from the walls to take refuge inside. The news would come to us when the battle was done and we were free to return once again to London.

It was bad. Worse than I could ever imagine. The words from my captains settled over me as if I were still standing in that snowstorm. Failure. Disaster. Bloodshed. Decimation for

Lancastrians. The two armies had met on the fields outside the village of Towton, not so many miles away.

My heart was as icy-cold as the wind, my mind as frozen as the glittering ice in the puddles on the river's edge. What was left for us now? Henry looked bewildered. My son was restless. All looked to me for guidance, but what decision should I make? What would my mother and grandmother have done during their days of conflict?

'Can we regroup?' I asked Somerset.

'No, my lady.' His face was grey with cold and the ignominy of loss. 'It was as bad a defeat as I have ever witnessed. We lost so many men. The field at Towton was heaped with our dead, so many great names of Lancastrian loyalties. The Earl of Northumberland dead. Devonshire and Wiltshire taken and executed. To remain here is not good policy, my lady. I swear they will be at the gates before the end of the day.'

'Will these walls not protect us?'

'You cannot rely on the loyalty of the populace. They might open the gates and welcome York into his own city.'

Of course. March was now the Duke of York. I glanced at Henry, who was listening but offering no thoughts.

'You advise me to flee.'

'Yes.'

I drew in a breath. We would become fugitives again, rebels against the might of the victors.

'I have failed.'

I said it before I could press down on such thoughts.

Somerset stepped forward, keeping his voice low.

'Do not admit openly to failure, my lady. I would say that all is not yet lost. At least you kept the King and the Prince here with you. If they had been on the battlefield they would be dead or prisoner. With them free, you have kept the royal line

164

of Lancaster alive. You can recover and fight again. But not here in York. You must go north.'

Indeed, I had been prepared for the worst, with our possessions packed ready for flight. My orders were now clear. No use repining, no use mourning our dead. Not yet, even when it was in my mind to visit that terrible battlefield to see for myself the devastation, as I had when we had achieved victory at St Albans. Was it not my duty to honour the victims of war, on both sides? But I dare not. I would mourn when we were safe. Now it was urgent that we flee north to Newcastle. And then what? To Scotland with our few remaining allies, collecting those I could of our friends to establish a Lancastrian court, perhaps across the border.

Why had we lost so disastrously? Was this God's punishment? I could not believe that. I must not. The rightness of inheritance must be adhered to. I banished any sense of my culpability, even when nausea lodged in my throat. As we set off, I surveyed our small number. Somerset and Exeter, on whom I must rest my command of an army in the future. Exhausted, ruined, lacking money and supplies, Newcastle was too close for a true refuge, too much open to danger. I must get Henry and the Prince to Scotland where we could survey our future in security.

'Where are we going?' Henry had asked at last when Somerset had departed to put our flight into operation.

'To Scotland.'

'Is it wise to leave England?'

'It is too dangerous to remain. We cannot risk our son falling into the hands of Warwick or the Yorkist upstart.'

His brow was furrowed. 'But we will return. Am I still not King of England?'

'Yes, we will undoubtedly return.'

I would not give up. I would never give up the fight, but I

must throw myself once more on the Scottish Queen's mercy, no matter the price she asked. I clenched my jaw. She would demand Berwick from me and I would have to hand it over. Now, seeing my weakness, she would probably demand more.

As we fled north the eyeless head of the late Duke of York watched us go.

His son was close on our tail.

A warning, if ever I needed one. We rode like the wind, as if pursued by the Devil.

## Anne, Countess of Warwick

It was a triumphal procession that rode into the bailey of our castle at Middleham where I and the girls awaited them, for the whole country had rung with the news of Lancaster's defeat. It was a mirror image of their earlier entry into London. There was Richard, leading his men, and at his side the young Edward of York, the new hero of the battlefield.

They dismounted, dispatched their troops to quarters in and without the castle and came into the Great Hall where they were made welcome, stamping their feet against the cold. Lady Alice clasped her nephew Ned to her bosom, relieved that we had not lost another child of York. Wine was drunk and food prepared while I followed Richard up the stairs to his chamber. I closed the door.

'You are unharmed,' I stated.

'Yes, thank God.'

Richard did not quite meet my eyes with his. I recognise subterfuge.

'Do I believe you? You were limping as I climbed the stair behind you,' I observed. 'When you dismounted, you grimaced.'

'It's nothing. An arrow in my thigh at Ferrybridge, just before the main battle at Towton. We were fortunate to hold the bridge over the River Aire, but lost too many men in the freezing water and an effective hail of arrows. It was a well-planned attack against us until we dislodged the Lancastrians. I was one of those recipients of the arrows. Fortunately not serious.'

A summary delivered quite casually, as if it did not matter.

'Not enough to keep you from the field at Towton then.'

'Nothing would have kept me from that, other than an arrow in my heart.'

I kept my distance as he allowed his cloak to fall from his shoulders. It was clear that he did not want me to fuss over him. So I would not. Or not yet.

'Was it as bad as they say it was?'

'Yes. And worse than that.'

A silence fell while he gazed out of the window, as if seeing sights that he wished were invisible to him. When he made no attempt to break it, it was I who did.

'Do you stay?' I asked as if he were a chance visitor.

'For a little while. We will entertain Ned as victor of the battle. And then I will take on the campaign of putting down the rebels in the North.'

All business and planning. I would change that.

'Do I tell you that I am delighted to see you, almost in one piece?'

'I never doubted it.'

'Do I remind you of how many times I have died a slow death in the last few days before we were told the outcome of the battlefield?'

At last he managed a shadow of a smile, turning away from the window. 'It seems many days since I heard such soft words. I am pleased to be here. You can help me unlace these metal plates if you are feeling grateful for my return. I seem to have lived in them for weeks. When not in battle there were always those on the road willing to lure us into ambush.'

Together we unlaced and removed them piece by piece, I playing the role of squire as I had done so many times before. Metal put aside, Richard stripped to his much-bruised skin while I ordered the bath to be brought and hot water fetched up to the chamber. He sank into it with a sigh, while I inspected the arrow wound in the fleshy part of his thigh. It could have been worse, but it was angrily inflamed and needed care.

'It has been well managed by your physician to remove the arrowhead, but I'll still anoint it and rebind it.'

'I know. You have always had some skill at wounds.'

As he relaxed, he began to talk, as I knew he would, the heat softening his muscles and his disciplined mind. He talked about the battle. About his plans.

'It was a desperate affair in snow. Thrice-damned Trollope got the reward he deserved, dead on the field.' Very little was spoken about the bloodshed but enough for me to know that it was a desperate fight, as I soaped his shoulders. I found a cushion for his head as his eyes began to close with the warmth.

'I must tell Ned...'

'Later.'

He slept, his striking features at last at rest, until the water cooled and I woke him.

'You haven't mentioned two crucial parts of this tale,' I reminded him as he applied a towel to his wet hair. 'Where is Henry? And more importantly, where is Margaret, since she will dictate what happens next?'

'Fled, all of them, with what is left of Lancaster supporters. Into Scotland, so I imagine.'

'Will the Queen of Scotland give them forces to return?'

'I doubt it. She has enough of a burden as Regent of Scotland, and her cousin the Duke of Burgundy will be keen for her to remain aloof from our conflicts. He wants an alliance with Ned against France. Burgundy does not want Margaret to return to England.' He thought about this. 'Or Mary of Guelders might be willing to make a gesture if she can persuade Margaret to hand over some of our northern fortresses. Whether Margaret will be willing is a different matter. It all depends on her determination to return and reverse the present situation.'

'Of course she will. You know that.'

As if I had not spoken: 'Nor do I think it will be a simple matter for her to win the support of friends in Europe, although Margaret will try. She will look of course to Burgundy and France. If our new King Edward, when he is crowned, shows himself to be a competent and strong ruler, they might fight shy of wasting money and troops on Margaret's cause. They will give their allegiance only where it lies in their best interests. Pray God that Ned shows himself worthy of their wagering for the future.'

Gripping the side-staves of the wooden bath, he pushed himself upright, scattering water-drops over me and the floor, wincing as he put weight once more on his injured leg. He used the dry towel that I held out to him, sitting while I plastered his wound with bruised leaves of water-betony, mixed with honey.

Richard hissed in sharp agony at my ministrations.

'It is good for you,' I advised.

'You always say that when inflicting pain!'

'And do you not always heal?'

After I had applied a wrapping of clean linen and tied it neatly, he donned hose and shirt.

'What now? Can you stay at home?'

Richard shook his head. 'You know what will happen. Ned

will show his face in the North and gather acclaim. I'll see him on his journey to Durham.' His smile was wry. 'Then he will go to London. He has a coronation to organise. My brother George will be at hand to see that things go well.'

'What of you? Do you not go with him?'

It surprised me that he would not wish to stand beside his cousin at this most important event. Seated on the bed to push his feet into his soft leather shoes, he regarded me as if thinking about it.

'No, I'll not be there. I will stay in the North, with my brother John. That's the good news. John is released from his captivity in York and will ride to join me. He managed to escape the horrors of Towton.'

'Which pleases me immeasurably. But surely the North will settle into peace now...'

He shrugged and stretched his shoulders. 'Despite all the difficulties for her, it is in my mind that Margaret will make every possible effort to return, or at least stir up those who will still support her. Some areas of Yorkshire and much of Northumberland are still loyal to Margaret. The northern marches could be up in flames before we can blink. I will stay here in the North, and we will keep the peace. This coronation will be carried out seamlessly with no detracting insurrection from the North.'

With this thought in mind, I felt that my life might just begin to settle around me, as the country became placid again with this new King. And yet there was one element that worried me as I watched Richard become preoccupied in preparing to head out to show a presence amongst those who might be polishing their swords and mustering their troops, for who knew better than I that Richard had mighty ambitions? He had lived for battle and the sword, but he had suffered defeat at St Albans and this skirmish at Ferrybridge, whereas Ned had two victories to his name at Mortimer's Cross and Towton. Young, golden, gallant, genial: without doubt he would make a magnificent King in comparison with Henry of Lancaster.

Did Richard envy the result of the success of his cousin? Ned would have the crown by the right of the Act of Accord. Perhaps Richard did not wish to be pushed into the shadows when the crown was placed on Ned's head. Would not Richard's achievements be obliterated against the backcloth of the golden glory of his cousin? He might see it better to carve out his own area of power in the North; a Neville kingdom in effect, with Ned's agreement. Ned was still very young and might not see the danger of such an acceptance of another power in the realm. Would he remain biddable after such victories on the battlefield, where men had learned his worth?

Richard had no more than thirty-three years to his name. What would he hope for in the coming years? In truth he had found no defeat too crushing for him. The coming years in the North would be rough and perilous for him but he would do it. Or did he see himself as the power behind the throne? Whatever the outcome, once more, I thought that I would see little of him.

I sighed a little. In spite of everything, I admired him more than I could say.

I arranged a rough and ready banquet for the returning victors before they went their disparate ways, where, thanks to Ned's enthusiasms, mummers performed a bloody battle in the semblance of a snowstorm from a shower of goose feathers, with much mock violence and fake death from those who wore the Lancaster sashes. Ned played the role of himself, emerging with the victor's crown and a bloody sword of wood and red paint. Everyone laughed. To me it seemed no laughing matter, even when a defeated King Henry fled the scene in his nether garments, dragging his wife and son with him, abandoning his crown as he ran.

Where would Margaret be now? What would she do? I knew that she would hate having to swallow her pride and ask for help once more, even from the Queen of Scotland. Particularly from a fellow queen. My future, as always, was in Richard's hands. It had always been so. Our daughters, too, would be dependent on his decisions over their future.

I watched him as he applauded the crude jokes of the mummers. What did he owe me? The loyalty of our marriage vows, the strength of his arm. He would fight for me, I was certain of it. Margaret had lost that certainty. She could no longer rely on the support of her husband, who was in flight with her and had no sense of the future or of what he had lost.

In a conflicted way, in spite of everything, I was sorry for her.

For good or ill, Margaret was now dependent on the Queen of Scotland.

# 17

## Humiliation and Triumph
## Go Hand in Glove, 1461

**Margaret, Queen of England**

I curtsied low before the woman who welcomed us. I might be Queen of England but here was a queen in her own dominion, and we were desperately in need of her help. Without her we were helpless. Henry bowed. Well prepared, so did my son.

When I last came for aid to Mary of Guelders, Queen of Scotland and powerful Regent, it had been in a need for money and troops. How trivial that now seemed. Now we had been forced to flee for our lives, our crown and throne stolen from us, our forces cut down in blood on the battlefield. We were in exile. If we were ever to return, I needed more than a purse of gold and a handful of soldiers. I needed the support of a full-scale invasion. But would this young woman with so many claims on her own position in this kingdom be willing to give it?

I assessed her, but politely, thinking that she had changed little in the months since I last saw her, whereas I felt careworn. When had I last used my mirror? My clothing, too, had suffered inordinately from the days and miles of flight. There the Queen stood, at twenty-seven years old, a woman of power, of influence as Regent for her young son James, a boy of ten years, standing beside her, as my young son stood beside me.

How similar our family situation, yet how different. Although her husband was dead, she held power here in this realm.

As before, she gestured that I should sit with her.

'You have returned to us, madam. I regret the need for your flight.'

'And I, Your Grace. Although my gratitude knows no bounds, that you will receive me again.'

'Of course. I know why you are here, madam.'

She addressed me, woman to woman, without a need for an intermediary, not even Bishop Kennedy of St Andrews who was her most influential counsellor. Cool, calm, Queen Mary was in control and was well aware that she owed me nothing. I wondered as I smoothed my creased skirts as I sat if it would be better if Henry was not here. Mary of Guelders and I could negotiate between us. I thought Henry would have nothing to say of any merit, but Queen Mary might consider that he held the ultimate authority in the making of an alliance.

'We are fallen on desperate times, Your Grace,' I admitted. She would already have been made well aware of our circumstances.

'Then you have come to a safe haven, Madam Margaret. I will not hand you over to your enemies.'

It was a relief to hear the words and to read the slight smile. We were safe. For the first time in days I drew a breath and felt no immediate fear of my enemies on my heels. The defeat and humiliation of the past was finished with. Now for the future. And the Prince's inheritance.

'I have spoken already with my counsellors,' Mary continued in her accented English. 'We will give you aid in your campaign to take back what is rightfully yours, madam. How much aid I am not yet certain. We must consider what will be an advantage to us. But before such heavy discussions, you must rest. And Lord Henry. I know that he has found the journey difficult. Then we will speak.'

Of course. Any woman in her position would be careful. This would not be an easy negotiation.

'I need to establish a court in exile, in Edinburgh, Your Grace. A place where I might welcome those who still are loyal to Lancaster. Will you allow that?'

She smiled again, yet her severe features gave nothing away. 'All will be arranged, madam. I have given orders.'

She clearly held all the strings of government, a woman after my own heart, although I suspected that she would wring the last groat from me in return. And indeed, the humiliation was not yet over, for we were dependent on her charity. I was determined it would not be for long. We would take back what we had lost. We would not remain here, a court in exile, for ever. But at least Queen Mary spared me the humiliation of having to ask for the most basic of necessities.

'You will have all you need, food and clothing and money for your servants. You will have a base for your household and those who will join you. A court of Lancaster in exile must be seen to have the possibility of return and future power. I understand that. I will provide it.'

'My thanks, Your Grace.'

I raised my head and returned her cool gaze, making it clear that I knew I was here under sufferance and disliked the necessity. Nevertheless, I would give leadership to those who joined the Court of Lancaster in exile. I would negotiate with Queen Mary.

I felt no reassurance from her calm mood. I had no sense of

whether she would come to our aid or not. What would we do if she turned her face from us, if she was persuaded to deny us shelter?

We made our journey to our new home at Linlithgow Palace, our first true refuge after the horrors at Towton, offered to us at the invitation of the Bishop of St Andrews until all could be made ready for us. We were grateful. A place of safety where I could plot our return. From there we moved to the austere Dominican convent in Edinburgh from where it was a simple matter for me to make overtures to the Regency Council of the young Scottish King. Thus I was summoned back into the presence of the Queen. It did not go well for me to be summoned, but I needed this negotiation.

'Do I meet with the Queen or do you?' I had asked Henry, knowing that he would dislike the need to make a display of his authority.

'Should I go?' he asked.

'Only if you wish it. Otherwise, do you give me the power to deal with the Queen in your name?'

Since I decided not to discuss with him the northern fortresses that might be forced to cede to Scotland, I was sent with his blessing. The Queen met with me in her Council Chamber, her Councillors flanking her in an heraldic array of power.

'My Council is not unwilling to aid your English campaign,' she began as soon as I entered the chamber. 'What can you offer us in return, madam?'

This time she kept me standing, as if I were a base petitioner. I swallowed hard on the anger that she would treat me with what I considered an inappropriate lack of courtesy as I gave a prompt reply.

'A firm alliance between England and Scotland, when we are restored to power, Your Grace.'

'I think that I need something more immediate, if my Council is to concur. It may be many months before you can claim victory, with or without my aid.'

I had thought about this.

'You know my offer, Your Grace. Have we not already discussed it? I will offer the hand of my son, Prince Edward, in marriage to one of your daughters. To the little Princess Mary. That will make for a permanent and powerful alliance between our two families.'

Edward was with me, standing formally at my shoulder in stern concentration. I had told him what I would suggest. His composure was a thing of wonder.

The Queen glanced to her right at the Bishop, who nodded.

'It would be a perfect alliance,' I said. 'When Edward becomes King of England, your daughter will be Queen. Consider the union between our two countries and the influence that would give us in European affairs, acting between the powers of France and Burgundy.'

'A tempting offer indeed.'

Mary pursed her lips as if in thought. Then her mild enthusiasm fell away, to be replaced by a keen brilliance of eye that warned me of what was to come. The tension in that silent room could have been sliced by a honed blade, while I was determined to remain as dignified as she. I needed this alliance, but I would not prostrate myself for it. Or would I, must I? She must know that as Queen of England I was a force to be reckoned with. Unfortunately, she knew that she had the whip hand.

'Do you realise, madam,' the Queen asked in soft tones, 'my cousin the Duke of Burgundy – of course you know that Burgundy is my first cousin – would advise against such a match? He sees an advantage in my keeping on good terms with the Yorkist powers in England. They may of course keep the throne. Your son may never become King. It may be that a marriage between our two children would be of no advantage to us in Scotland. I would be wary of following a different policy from the one suggested by my cousin of Burgundy.' She paused. 'Unless you are able to offer me another incentive to look kindly on you.' Another pause. 'Such as land.'

I had expected hard bargaining but what a blow this was to me. The room was silent except for the rustle of costly material, the clearing of a throat, while I sought for a reply. The Bishop tried hard not to frown. What could I say? In all honesty, I would confess. It would be of no surprise to her since she knew my predicament. I preserved my composure as I did what no queen would ever wish to do.

'I throw myself utterly on your mercy, Your Grace. I am desperately in need of Scottish help. As well as the hand of my son, I have the authority from my lord Henry to offer you the valuable northern fortresses of Berwick and Carlisle in return for your assistance.'

'It is a considerable gift between one ruler and another. Although perhaps it will be necessary for you to offer me more than a mere pair of fortresses.'

I would not commit myself. I remained silent before her direct stare.

'We will consider it,' she said at last. Mary inclined her head, then looked down at her loosely clasped hands where they rested on the table before her. 'I should tell you, an offer has recently been made for my own hand in marriage.'

She looked up in what might have been a challenge.

'Do I give you my best wishes?' I asked, instantly wary. 'To whom will you be wed?'

'Nothing is yet decided. I have been approached by Edward of York. Now King of England.'

'Has he been crowned?' I asked.

'My informants tell me that he will be crowned King in the month of June when all arrangements are complete. He was of course recognised as King after his victory at Towton. Your lord, once King Henry of this realm, has been usurped, madam.'

I inhaled slowly. All these negotiations might be for nothing. I felt the familiar spark of anger in my breast. He was already King, bar the placing of the crown on his head, and was already deliberately, viciously, undermining my position, offering marriage to Scotland.

'And will you take the Yorkist's hand?' I asked as if mildly interested.

'I am considering it.'

'But there is nothing for you to fear, madam,' the Bishop interrupted for the first time. 'You are safe here. You will not be handed over to any power in England, whatever decisions are made at this Council.'

'As long as you understand that my support cannot be bought cheaply,' Queen Mary added.

The Council meeting was over, leaving so much uncertainty, not least for my son.

'Will I wed the Scottish princess, *Maman?*' he asked as soon as we were free to return to our own domicile.

'It is possible,' I replied.

'What if I do not like her?'

'Princes marry for power. You will like her, I am certain of it.'

Who knew where the future would lead us? At least the Bishop was a man who stood in our favour and had replied to my anxieties.

\*

179

When I had recovered from my despair over our defeat at Towton and the blow to my pride at having to bend the knee before Queen Mary, I began to think and to plot, curbing my frustration with Henry, who seemed to lack all interest in what must be done if we were ever to step back onto English soil. He was more concerned with the state of his soul than the fact that his crown would soon grace the head of Edward of York.

'I feel that it is urgent that I pray and be assuaged of my sins,' he said. 'So should you, my dear wife. God will listen to us.'

How hard it was to keep my temper and my patience, but by now I had had much practice.

'God may well listen, but it is Queen Mary who is central to all our hopes. It would be far better if you showed a determination to return to England and take back what is ours.'

'How can I do that?' For once the confusion seemed to leave him and he saw the reality of it. 'We have no army. Has our Scottish sister agreed to supply us with sufficient men? Will she provide the gold with which to pay them? A fleet in which to transport them?'

'Not yet.'

'Then you must tell me when she does, my dear Margaret. Until then I must pray.'

'You might consider having a discussion with the Bishop of St Andrews,' I suggested. 'He is sympathetic to our cause as well as being a fervent man of God.'

Henry prowled around the large and comfortable chamber that had been allotted to him, stopping to place his hand on the gilded prie-dieu in the corner before continuing to pace, frowning at his inner thoughts.

'Would you not wish that?' I asked.

'No.'

'Are you not comfortable here, my dear lord?'

'No, I am not.' He came to a halt before me. 'I wish to go to a place of quiet and prayer. This is too busy with visitors and politics, with endless comings and goings. I need peace in which to concentrate.'

I took his hand in mine, keeping him still beside me.

'Do you not wish to take back the crown?'

'I found little pleasure in wearing it. It worried me. I did not like the disputes with the men who would give me advice. I would rather be a monk.' He gripped my hands tightly now. 'I could do that until our return to England is certain. I would like that, and you will tell me what is happening. I have given you the authority to treat with the Queen. I will be more use praying for the outcome.'

'*Maman* says that I will wed the Scottish princess,' Edward announced, having come into the chamber.

Henry's frown deepened. 'Does she? I don't think I have agreed to that.' He looked at me. 'Why did you not ask me?'

I gave up, agreeing to his immediate departure to the priory at Kirkcudbright on the coast, a place of peace and serenity, where he could embrace the monastic life. I wished for such serenity in my life, but it was not to be. Since I could not depend on Queen Mary, into my hands had fallen the need to consider alliances in Europe, sending off diplomatic missions. I would do it. And when my seven-year-old son was full grown, England would be there for his taking.

Did it matter to me that while I directed our loyal Lancastrian commanders to resist sieges, to lead armies and leave on dangerous diplomatic missions, Henry abandoned me to travel to the quiet of monastic life? Sometimes I felt so very lonely. But since there was no one to support me, I began to construct a list of those who might come to my aid. Henry and I were related to so many influential families in Europe. Would not one offer us succour? Sicily, or Castile, or Portugal. Since Burgundy was hostile, the best source of help for me would be France. I dispatched Somerset to the French Court to test the friendly ear of King Charles VII, but Charles's death changed matters. It was clear from the beginning that my cousin, the wily King Louis XI, was unwilling to commit himself to any aid that might not fall to his advantage.

As days bled into weeks, with no decisions in Scotland to be made, I wondered if I should consider escape to France, taking my lord Henry and my son with me. I might, but was warned by our supportive Bishop that the seas were patrolled by Yorkist ships. It would be dangerous in the extreme; we must remain in Scotland. Besides, if I took refuge in France, how difficult would it be for me to return to England? We must do the best we could, but my hopes had fallen into a pit of near despair. The Duke of Burgundy continued to encourage the Scottish Queen to abandon the marriage plan between Prince Edward and the Scottish princess. I knew what was happening. The Duke wanted an alliance with the Yorkist usurper in England against Louis of France. He did not wish Scotland to stand in his way. Any alliance with me would be a complication he could well do without.

In England the Yorkist rebels grew stronger. Jasper Tudor and Exeter fled into exile in Brittany, my reliable ally Somerset in exile in Burgundy. What hope for us? Many once-fervent Lancastrian supporters were bending the knee to Edward of York. The promise of a pardon was very persuadable. Even the heavens seemed to have turned in favour of the House of York with a progress of eclipses and strange stars.

Some days when I arose from my bed, isolated and alone, I thought of the past, of Countess Anne. She did not write to me, nor I to her. What would we have to say to each other? I would bemoan our exile and place much blame at Warwick's feet. She would gloat in their success.

Then I thought not. She was not a woman who gloated. Yet she must still feel the victory of Warwick bringing the Yorkist usurper to the throne. We were so far apart: I struggling for the very existence of my family while she enjoyed the future for her daughters in the marriages that Warwick would arrange for them.

I detested Warwick with every bone in my body, with every drop of blood in my veins.

But I wished I still had the friendly ear of his wife. I felt that I had no true allies in Scotland, no one I could trust with my innermost thoughts. At least with Henry saying his prayers in Kirkcudbright, it was a relief not to have to break my fast with him and listen to his prayers. Far more useful to create persuasive words for King Louis. He really was my only hope for restitution if I could but persuade him.

Had Countess Anne stood at the coronation in Westminster to witness the creation of a new monarchy, a new royal family of York? I seemed to be at the centre of the dismantling of the power of Lancaster. A wave of bitterness swept over me. It lived within me and made me poor company.

## Anne, Countess of Warwick

It was generally held to be true that Richard, Earl of Warwick, had created a king. With advice, support, and military backing from Richard, Edward, Duke of York, became the crowned King of England on the twenty-eighth day of the month of June after the victory at Towton in April.

I attended the coronation at the behest of Richard. Or

whether he wished it or not. I thought it would be politic to show a Neville and a Beauchamp presence. It also pleased me to meet up once again with Duchess Cecily and Countess Alice.

'Why is my son not here with you?' demanded Countess Alice.

'There is rebellion in the North which claimed his presence. I am here in his stead.'

'Did he forbid you to come?'

I smiled, and so did she. 'As a dutiful wife I will not reply to that.'

'Perhaps it would have been best if he had been here,' suggested Duchess Cecily as we readied ourselves for the ceremony in silk and damask and cloth of gold. Butterfly head-dresses fluttered in the breeze. 'There are many who will not approve of a son of York as King. We should have solidarity in numbers, and the formidable Earl of Warwick is the most crucial link in the chain of gold that we have created for the House of York.'

'Why would it matter whether Richard is here or not?' I asked. 'Your son will wear the crown.'

'If they are militarily hand in glove, they must be seen to be so.' Duchess Cecily was forthright. 'It will discourage opposition. There must be no suggestion of a rift between them.'

'There may be much wisdom in what you say, but I assure you, there is no rift.'

I did not see what harm there would be in his absence. As Richard had said, it was in Ned's interests that he stay away in the North and put down any dangerous insurrections. The ceremony could proceed quite well without him.

Indeed, it was a ceremony of great splendour, with much public acclaim. Duchess Cecily glowed with pride as the crown was placed on the head of her son where he sat enthroned on the gilded chair of state in the centre of the nave of Westminster Abbey. If ghosts from the past were present at the ceremony, it was the tragically dead Duke of York, but perhaps my lord of Warwick also stalked the shadows. He might be absent, but all knew his presence in these propitious happenings.

There was a little frown between Duchess Cecily's straight brows as we followed her son out into the city.

'What troubles you? Is this not a day for rejoicing?'

Duchess Cecily regarded her son, who was beaming at the crowd, catching a flower tossed by a woman in an azure gown. 'My son is of a flirtatious disposition. He needs a wife.'

I followed her line of sight. 'Ned is enjoying the occasion. He is not yet twenty years of age.'

Duchess Cecily was not persuaded. 'It is enough to take a bride and beget an heir.'

Which I reported to Richard on my return home, to find him in residence at Middleham, in deep conversation about supplies and military necessities, with our steward in the Great Hall.

'There was much discussion of it, of a womanly nature,' I announced as the steward departed.

'Women's gossip.' Richard was unimpressed.

'Ned, of course, said nothing. He was too busy catching flowers and sweetmeats from any damsel in the crowd who wanted to catch his attention.'

'And I suppose there were many. Who did you decide on?'

'The general consensus was a foreign princess. Countess Alice thought French, although your Aunt Cecily looked towards Burgundy.'

'I concur, of course. A foreign bride would be the best choice. It's always dangerous to tie an ambitious English family to the royal throne. Too much power in one place.'

Which struck me as ironic since the Neville family firmly surrounded the new King. Could the Nevilles en masse, and

Richard in particular, not be accused of exerting too much influence on the new King? I said nothing except:

'I think that you should have been there.'

'I doubt I was missed.'

'I think you were. I think Ned needs reminding of who put him where he is today. Ned no longer, but King Edward, and full of self-importance, as he might expect.'

'I doubt he will forget.' Richard was unperturbed.

I considered, recalling my impressions of our new King. 'The commons love him. They adore him. His height and broad shoulders, his bright hair, they all appeal to their desire for a King of renown who can lead an army into battle. They hailed him as if he were a god of the old stories.'

I wondered how long it would be before he wished to cast off any restraining bands. He might prove to be a formidable force. Perhaps Richard should take care. And I said as much.

'I will. Do you fear for me?'

'Not yet. But one day perhaps. Today you can rely on his gratitude and his appreciation of your good sense, which you will use in his interests.' I said what was in my mind. 'It seems to me that Ned will have his own voice in who should be his chosen bride.'

Richard's voice gained an edge. 'If he has any sense he will listen to good advice.'

'I expect that he will,' I soothed, sorry to have disturbed the atmosphere.

'Will I not always use my influence to support our new King? If it means fighting battles, then I will do so.'

'Let us not speak of battles tonight.'

He linked his fingers with mine. 'No. Not for tonight. Tomorrow is time enough.'

Slowly, we walked through the Great Hall towards the

staircase that would take us to our private chambers. It was good to be home.

'Do you remember the day when we were wed?' I asked, the thought leaping from nowhere into my mind.

He laughed, his hand tightening around mine. 'Not with any clarity. We were very young. And you had been promised to me since we were children, so it was not unexpected.'

'Do you recall your promises to me?' I asked.

'Of course. The same as in any marriage vow. To love and to cherish you ...'

'Until death us do part according to God's holy ordinance, and thereunto I plight thee my troth,' I finished it for him.

'Why have you asked me that?'

'I'm not sure.' I frowned. 'Unless it was witnessing Ned's flirtatiousness at first hand.'

'I am nothing like Ned.' Richard slid a glance in my direction. 'And before you ask me, I have fulfilled those vows I made to you.'

'I was not questioning your loyalty, although I swear there are few couples who do keep their vows. I suspect that Ned will find it impossible to remain faithful to one woman, within or without marriage.'

'And do you suppose that Margaret has always been loyal to our sometimes witless King Henry?'

'She would swear that she has,' I replied.

I wished that I had not started this. We were treading on difficult ground here. Did we not both know the rumours, and where they had originated? It was Richard who cast oil onto these troubled waters, to make all serene again.

'Today the late Queen's affairs are not ours. And neither are Ned's. Let us, in memory of our youthful selves, fulfil our own holy vows once more.'

ANNE O'BRIEN

I was more than ready to consign Margaret to the shadows. The fulfilment was most pleasurable.

'And how has life been in the North while I have been absent?' I asked when at last I lay with my head on his shoulder and our breathing had settled to normality.

'Bloody. Brutish. Treacherous. Uprisings snapping at my heels to left and right with every step,' he admitted.

Richard punctuated each statement with a kiss to my palm.

I was sorry that he found such satisfaction in leaving me to put those risings down.

188

# 18

## *York and Lancaster Come to Terms with the Future, 1462*

**Anne, Countess of Warwick**

'I am not really garbed for a court appearance,' I said.

I had been inspecting a cellar where water was seeping in through old stone-work, causing a threat to the barrels of ale and tuns of wine stored there. My hair was tied up in a neat coif. Richard, returning here to Middleham after one of his journeys to quash a minor skirmish, had sought me out to present me with a gold and jewelled collar, carelessly fitting it around my neck so that it lay and glinted on the dark cloth of my gown.

'Spoils of war?' I asked, squinting down at the array of gems. There were cobwebs and dust on my cuffs and hem, strangely at odds with the flat glimmer of sapphires and rubies on my shoulders.

'Certainly not. Bought with my own gold from a craftsman I discovered in Hexham, although the seller was more than willing to part with it to get his hands on coin. What do you think?' He pulled me into the faint light from the high chink of a window and walked round me. 'It looks well enough to me.'

'Can you tell in this dark cellar? But it is indeed magnificent.'

'You look surprised,' he observed.

'It is not the celebration of the day of my birth. Nor is it the day on which we were wed. Or, to my knowledge, when we were betrothed. To what do I owe this largesse? Have you the money to waste on such fripperies?'

Even so, it pleased me. I allowed my grimy fingers to stroke the precious stones.

'That and more.'

'But your campaigns surely bleed us dry.'

He smiled, proving that the campaign had been successful. 'Do you realise how much coin comes into our coffers every year?'

'No.'

'I'll not tell you. In case you waste it, as you say, on fripperies. I am allowed to waste some of it on my wife.'

Which made me smile too.

'There. Your smile is brighter than any gemstone,' he said, taking my hand to lead me from the cellar.

'I am flattered. And indeed, I thank you for it.' I kissed his cheek, then wiped away the cobwebs. 'You may buy me as many collars as you wish.'

After which, with Richard busy elsewhere, I stowed the collar in my jewel casket, where it lay beside the ring sent to me by Margaret, a ring I had never worn and never would. Two strange jewels indeed, to keep company with each other. My interest was sufficiently piqued with Richard's gift that I made it my business to consult his man of business. Were we as wealthy as Richard had intimated?

'How much coin do we have coming into our coffers, Master Stephen? What is the value of the land that we own? It seems that I have forgotten, if I have ever known.'

Inviting me to sit, Richard's clerk, well versed in all such matters, opened a ledger where there were columns of figures, turned over a few pages, and then pointed with his quill at the bottom line.

'You understand, my lady, that with the accession of King Edward, all your attainted estates have been returned to you. Furthermore, with the tragic execution of the Earl of Salisbury, my lord the Earl of Warwick has inherited his father's estate. And then of course there is the sad death of his mother, Lady Alice, earlier this year, her inheritance and dower has come into our coffers too.'

We had lost Alice, Countess of Salisbury, who had died in a fierce bout of cold weather that had settled on her lungs.

'So much!'

I read the figures, my eyes following my finger down the column.

'You are the wealthiest family in the land, my lady. Spectacularly wealthy, in fact.'

It was staggering. My lands, the Warwick inheritance, brought Richard over five thousand pounds every year, the Neville and Montagu inheritance from his own family estates a further two thousand. With an annual income from all sources of over ten thousand pounds.

It was not that I was unused to such wealth. We kept an impressive private household of twenty thousand retainers, spread between Middleham Castle and Sherriff Hutton, as well as at Warwick, but our most lavish establishment for entertaining guests was in London, at the house called L'Erber, a palatial stone edifice where Richard enjoyed entertaining guests. I smiled a little at the memory of the days, as a young bride, when I had first taken residence there, visiting the spacious kitchens. In amazement I had regarded the carcasses that were turning on their spits, the fat dripping and crackling, filling the chamber with smoke and the scent of roasting meat.

'Do we truly need six oxen for our household?' I asked.

'Indeed we do, my lady, at the Earl's command. And this is just for the start of the day. No one is turned away from our door who comes to break their fast.'

'How many do we feed, of the populace of London?' I had asked a young Richard at the first opportunity.

'All those who come to our door. The poor can take away as much meat as they can spear on a long dagger.' He regarded me with solemnity. We still did not know each other very well. 'Do you object?'

'No. I merely needed to know.'

'Good. We also have guests for dinner today, the Mayor and some of the Aldermen. Come and meet them. It does no harm to win popularity from those who govern the city.'

Oh, Richard already had an eye to winning favour as a great magnate, and already had a reputation for open-handed largesse. We could afford it, yet nothing could have prepared me for this column of figures, even my memories and the heavy weight of the jewelled collar on my breast before I had consigned it to my jewel casket.

'This annual income is indeed vast,' I remarked.

But I would rather have had Lady Alice's company than any number of jewelled collars, as I missed her. I was attracted by the frown on Master Stephen's face.

'What is it?'

'It is indeed vast, my lady. Perhaps I should not say...'

'But I wish that you would.'

'I am not given to gossip, but it will not surprise you that men in this land say that your lord is the real ruler of England rather than the young King. Bishop Kennedy of St Andrews, who has been negotiating a possible alliance with the Earl to heal the rifts between England and Scotland, has been heard to say that it was clear who was the governor of the realm of England. And it is not young Ned!'

I supposed it was true enough. I remembered Richard's shadowy presence at the coronation, absent but still a powerful entity, demanding to be heard. I did not like the implication.

'He is no longer young Ned,' I remarked lightly, 'but King of England.'

Master Stephen cleared his throat.

'There are jokes too – if that is what you wish to call them – coming out of the French Court. Dangerous ones.'

He looked as if he wished he had not spoken.

'Then you had better tell me those too.'

He shrugged lightly. 'They say this: they have but two rulers in England. Monsieur de Warwick, and another whose name has been forgotten.'

Which certainly gave me pause for thought.

'Which our King Edward will not enjoy.'

'No, he will not, despite his lack of years. It is he who wears the crown and he will be jealous of it. I am wary of saying this, my lady, but perhaps your lord should have a care. It is so easy to make enemies in a time when kings change.'

'Is that a warning?'

'I suppose in a sense it is.' He bowed his head. 'I meant no disrespect, my lady. I thought you should know.'

'And I must thank you for it.'

It gave me much food for thought. Wealth and power brought success, but it also made enemies. Master Stephen was right in his assessment; perhaps Richard should have a care. Old Lancastrian families might have been quick to bend the knee to the new Yorkist King, but old loyalties did not always die. Any rumours of a Lancastrian return would cause them to resurrect, and Richard would of a certainty become a target for their arrows.

'Are we very rich?' Isabel asked as Richard departed once more for Hexham.

'Yes, I expect we are.'

'Will I have a new gown?'

I regarded her ankles. 'I don't see why not. You seem to grow an inch every month.'

'What will it mean for us if father is very rich?' Anne asked.

'It means that a whole string of handsome young men will ride up to our door to ask to wed you.'

She smiled as if it pleased her.

'Did father marry you for your money?' Isabel asked.

'No, he married me for my family name. The Beauchamps are very important.'

'Were you not rich then?'

'I was not. My money and my title came after your father and I were wed. What a honey-pot I turned out to be.'

'And now it all belongs to father.'

'Yes.'

'Does it matter to you?'

Isabel's questions had suddenly become surprisingly pertinent to a daughter of a noble house. She was growing up.

'No. It is what happens in marriages.'

She looked unconvinced.

'Thank you for the collar, but there is a more urgent demand on our money.' My final words to Richard as he had turned north-east towards Hexham. 'Your mother is buried in the family tomb in Bisham Abbey, but she is alone.'

He did not need more explanation from me.

'And I should bring my father and brother home from Pontefract.'

'I am sure of it.'

'It has been remiss of me. I will do it. You are always my conscience.'

And after this prestigious reburial, there would be matters of marriage to discuss.

## Margaret, Queen of England

In the end, when all my Scottish hopes had withered on the vine of Queen Mary's reluctance, I sailed to France in desperation with 290 pounds of Mary's money in my purse, a commission to act as my lord Henry's envoy, and in company with my son. With Warwick intent on negotiating an English truce with the Queen of Scotland, I needed more help than the Scottish Queen could offer me, even if she did make up her mind to it. She might have promised me her goodwill, but I could not trust her to keep my son safe at her Court in my absence. Henry remained in his monastic seclusion. I thought he would be safe enough until I could return. There might be no logic to that, but there seemed no need to drag him across the sea in reluctant company with me. I would be travelling far and fast, which would not be to Henry's taste, demanding to stop at every way-side shrine or cathedral.

I met my father in Angers where he offered me his hand in greeting, a platter of bread and stewed venison in red wine, a bed for the night in my old chamber, and nothing else. He claimed penury and seemed to have no belief in my situation. There would be no arms or gold coin from Anjou.

From there I travelled to the Court of King Louis at Chinon. As expected, he drove a hard bargain, even as he smiled at me in compassion for my loss of a kingdom.

'How valuable is my help?' he asked as he settled me on a cushioned chair with a cup of wine and musicians playing softly in the background, much as if this were a social visit between cousins.

'My son's future might well depend on it,' I replied.

'Then what will you be willing to give in return?'

'What will buy a fleet from you?'

'I think my price might be too high.'

I did not like his smile.

I discovered I had little choice but to bow my head in agreement. If I wanted French aid I must pay the price. Or England must pay it. I agreed to hand over the valuable port and fortress of Calais in return for a French loan of twenty thousand livres, and Louis would finance an expedition. The bargain I made with Louis was not mentioned in the official agreement between us, announced five days later in Tours. It would be damaging to the Lancastrian cause. England would never agree to it, but it was the price I had to pay for a hundred-year truce between England and France. I would willingly hand over Calais if the crown was restored to my lord Henry.

These were days of anticipation, when victory seemed to be a certainty, for which I gave thanks. Never had I dreamed that I would plot my own destiny on the outcome of conflict on a battlefield.

I returned to Scotland in late October, with a fleet of forty-three ships, an army of over one thousand men led by Pierre de Brézé, and a heart full of hope. My forces were fewer than I had hoped for, but the late autumn weather was on our side, clear and fine. Nothing would stop us. Loyal men were gathering to my banners, either in support of my son or in hostility to the despised Warwick. This was what I had lived and prayed for over the past year. London was almost in our grasp even if there were many miles to cover to achieve our conquest. We shook out our royal banners, the red and blue and gold brilliant in the autumn sunshine, and began to march; the northern castles, Alnwick, Bamburgh, Dunstanburgh, surrendering to me when they saw my approaching force. Why had I been so anxious? The days of Warwick and the Yorkist usurper were assuredly numbered.

Until all went awry, in a manner over which I had no control: November storms at sea wrecked my French vessels, followed by news of the approach of Warwick from the South with a considerable army. It was no moment for rejoicing that the Yorkist usurper had been struck down with some painful skin complaint at Durham, forcing him to keep to his chamber. I might rejoice at his discomfort, but Warwick was campaigning, planning to raid into Scotland with his brother John, Lord Montagu. The castles we had taken with such joy were all lost in a deep despondency that settled over my army.

'What do we do now?' Henry asked, brought out of his monastic seclusion to be part of the army marching on London.

'We return to Scotland,' I said.

In utter despair, I might have added.

All made worse when my commander, the Duke of Somerset, abandoned his allegiance to me and turned Yorkist. He feasted and went hunting with the now-recovered-to-health Yorkist usurper. They were jousting with each other. I damned him for his treachery. All my hopes and dreams had foundered, while Henry seemed to have little comprehension of how great the disaster might be, for what was there for us in Scotland now?

## Anne, Countess of Warwick

All was sufficiently settled in the North that we travelled south from Middleham to Bisham Abbey, the ancestral base of the Neville family, where Richard had arranged for his father and brother to be solemnly reinterred, their tragic bodies brought from Pontefract with great panoply to where they truly belonged. The horrors of the Battle of Wakefield would be overlaid with Neville dignity. Now the family was restored, buried together at Bisham.

Richard and I stood side by side with the girls, while prayers of committal were said and cloth of gold was spread over the plain slabs for Richard Neville, Earl of Salisbury, and Sir Thomas Neville, until effigies could be made to give glamour to these Neville men, both lost in so terrible a manner.

'I will be buried here too,' Richard announced when the cloth was in place.

'But not yet for a good few years.'

I did not wish to be morbid or over-sentimental. The usual anxiety was building in me. He was about to leave again. Not quite those stressful days when I was as anxious as any wife seeing her husband in armour six days out of seven, when I saw him at all; when he was travelling daily the twenty-seven miles between three sieges and his base at Warkworth, while Ned suffered from a painful bout that caused him to scratch and groan of God's affliction on his skin. Richard's absence this time would be of a far more peaceful nature.

'How long will you be in France?' I asked as we turned away from the sad mementoes, but not before I had placed a sprig of autumn roses at the feet of the superbly carved Lady Alice, beside the small dog on which they rested. I placed my hand on her cheek, admiring the carving of her soft features encased in veiling, which looked as if it might stir in the slightest puff of wind.

'I pray not long.'

He frowned as he surveyed the imposing abbey buildings.

'What is it? A problem?'

'No, or not that I can see. Ned is capable of ruling without me. It is time, and more, that I search for a suitable bride for him. It is time that he set up his own household and got himself an heir. A French princess will be better than most, although I fear that Louis will test my negotiating skills to the limit. He prefers to keep his options open in his relations with England and Burgundy.' Richard grimaced at the coming prospect. 'It is like a mummer juggling balls of different sizes, dropping them all over the floor. Louis has remarkable sleight of hand. Not to mention his need to consult the court astrologer at every step. How many comets does he need to see, to indicate whether to offer a French bride to Ned or not?' Richard was frustrated but optimistic. 'But a French bride seems a good plan and England would settle into stability with a new king and an heir.'

We walked slowly back to the private chambers.

'Do we know where Henry is?'

'Fled back to Scotland, it seems, and long may he stay there. There is no hint of another invasion on the wind.'

'And Margaret?'

'Still petitioning endlessly to attract aid to enable her to return to England. She'll get no more from Mary of Guelders in Scotland.' The twist of his lips was self-gratifying. 'I have just concluded a truce with the Scottish Regent.'

I had not known. Here was power indeed.

'Is it signed?'

'Yes.'

'You might tell me.'

'I do.'

'Only when you remember. Wives are so unimportant.' I shook my head to ward off any excuses. 'Do you think that Margaret will return?'

'No, I don't, in all honesty. She will get no help. And with Ned wed to Bona of Savoy there will be even less chance.'

So that was his plan. I believed it. I believed it would happen.

'Do not forget out daughters,' I reminded him. 'They are still very young, but it would be good to have an understanding with powerful families.'

'They are uppermost in my mind. After the King. And you, of course.'

Wives were so unimportant, I had said. Except for their dowry and the sons they would bear. Margaret's situation was untenable in Scotland. She was penniless and powerless. It was hard not to be compassionate, and yet I hoped that she failed in her mission. To have her return to England again with a foreign army would undermine all that Richard and Ned were trying to create.

So Richard would go to France and I would return to Middleham to pick up the reins of my household. I would sometimes be lonely, but it was nothing new. The demands on my time in the running of Middleham were constant and I was well versed in it, enjoying the addition to our family of Richard of Gloucester, Ned's youngest brother, to continue his education as a great lord. Sometimes Francis Lovel visited too, and we became a lively household enjoying the hunting, the boys engaged daily in their military pursuits. Nor did they neglect their books, but they also sang and acted out the stories of the mummers' plays with much enthusiasm. It was good to hear youthful loud voices in the gardens and stables.

When Richard came home to us, as he did intermittently,

he joined the boys in their military games, exhibiting the art of attack and defence with sword and dagger, encouraging them to master the cut and thrust that might just keep them alive in battle. It was an element of Richard's life that I had rarely seen, and I relished it in spite of the need to apply unguents to bruises and abrasions.

Diccon and Francis became the sons I had not borne. They were as much a pleasure to Richard as they were to me.

At least Richard would find no opportunity in France to don his armour unless it was to make an impression in a tournament. I hoped that his diplomatic demands would keep him at the negotiating table.

## Margaret, Queen of England

I watched the shore of Scotland recede into the sea-mist. When I shivered, it was not with the unseasonal cold that struck at my bones, for this was July and good sailing weather, but at the fear in my heart. Would I ever return? I must not think of that. I had made up my mind to a step that I had never wished to take. As the land disappeared from my sight except as a dim line on the horizon, a memory struck hard, of my recent meeting with my lord Henry in his chamber, when I had carefully considered the words I would use.

'My dear Margaret,' he greeted me.

I saluted his cheek. His hair needed combing again, his robe, as plain as that of any monk, should be exchanged for one of better quality. I must speak with his body servant. That Henry had no thought for his appearance was not important. He was still the rightful King of England and one day he would wear the crown again. I was determined on it. That was the only reason behind my decision.

'We need to speak, my lord.'

'Is it important?'

'It is vitally so.' I drew him to sit beside me, taking the pen from his hand, placing it on the desk so that he must listen to me. 'I am going to France. To St Omer.'

'Why St Omer?'

'Because a French embassy from King Louis has agreed to meet with an embassy from Edward of York. I fear that Louis is intent on making an alliance with him; I cannot permit it. We are in desperate need of help if we are ever to return to England. The Scottish Queen will not help us. My father refuses. Burgundy is too closely engaged in negotiations with the Yorkist upstart. Louis is our only hope. I cannot let this meeting in St Omer be successful.'

I seemed to have spent my life travelling. I fought against the weariness of it all as Henry sat and thought about this.

'Will we ever get my crown back?' he asked eventually.

'We must. Your son must reign as King – after you, of course.'

'But what will you do to persuade Louis?'

'I know not, but I fear that if I do not go, Louis and the Yorkist will come to some agreement that will damage our cause irreparably.'

He considered this, eventually looking up with a beaming smile as if I had offered him some particularly enjoyable sweet-meat.

'Then you must of course go. What do I do? Do I come with you?' He looked anxious at the prospect.

I had thought about this. Would it not be for the best if he travelled with me and I could keep him safe? Would it not be the best policy to find him some safe haven in France until times were better? I thought not. If our ship was wrecked, or stopped by English pirates, I could not guarantee his life.

'Remain here, my lord. Give leadership to those who will still fight for us.'

I held out no hope at all.

Henry frowned. 'Will you return?'

'Of course. With an army. And significantly larger than last time.'

'What of my son? Does he stay with me?'

My decision on the future of Prince Edward had taken no time for me to reach.

'The Prince comes with me. We must not allow any chance of his falling into English hands. That would really be a disaster.'

His smile became gentle, full of understanding. 'You are very determined.'

'I must be.'

Yes, we could be shipwrecked, driven to the bottom of the sea in a storm, or taken prisoner in a chance attack by pirates. It was a gamble I would have to take. I could not risk the Prince falling into York's hands. He must remain under my eye.

'I will miss you.'

'And I you. It will not be forever.'

There was sadness in his face, but then it cleared.

'I will pray for you and your safekeeping. When do you leave?'

'Tomorrow. The Queen has offered me a ship.'

'I pray that you will achieve your heart's desire.'

My troubled heart softened. He was a good man, but he was not a good King. We sat together, hand in hand, as we used to do when I was a young bride. We spoke of the past, of the losses, of our dear son. Then I left him to his prayers.

Now here I was, abandoning him, and guilt had a hard hand. I must have some stratagem to rescue Henry out of Scotland to join me in France. But not yet. He must remain a valuable figurehead for those in England who still looked to Lancaster as the rightful King. My lord Henry would act as a glowing beacon for those who would still rise to our cause. I imagined him now, on his knees at his prie-dieu, his voice soft and low as he offered up petition after petition for our safety and our return. It was a good decision to leave him here.

Yet it still gnawed at my mind. Should I not have brought him with me? Would it not be safer for all of us if we were as a family in France?

I looked round at the small group of loyal supporters. Would they remain loyal to our cause? Somerset had abandoned me for the sake of a pardon and the return of his estates from the Yorkist upstart, the removal of the attainder against him. I despised him for it, yet I had to understand that some men valued their inheritance over past loyalties.

I turned my mind to the burden to be faced in France. I must try again to persuade my father. I must not allow Louis to make his never-ending excuses. I must stop him breaking the Treaty of Tours he made with me. I must do all in my power to stop Edward of York making an agreement with France not to aid each other's enemies. I must stand in the way of a similar agreement between England and Scotland.

What a terrible position to be in, watching my potential allies slip away if I failed.

I knew that Warwick was greatly in favour of a French bride for the Yorkist. That would not be to our Lancastrian interests. The name Bona of Savoy had reached me as a possibility. Would Burgundy then remain my only hope? I doubted that Burgundy would ever be prepared to help me.

When a weariness, as thick as the mist, curled round me, I shook it off. I could not afford to give in to despair. When did

I last take to my bed with no worries, no concerns, sure of a night's sleep? I could not recall the last time. My days and nights were never-ending worrying and plotting. Perhaps one day.

The misty outline of land had vanished.

'When will we return?' The Prince's voice at my side, his cold hand pushed into mine.

'I do not know.'

'But we will come back.'

'Yes. We will come back.'

How could I sound so certain when nothing was certain in my life?

But I would never call Edward of York King of England. I would never do it. It would be poison on my tongue.

# 19

## *Threats at Home and Abroad, 1464*

### Anne, Countess of Warwick

'What has he done? What has he done to stir you to snarling fury?' I demanded.

It could only be one man who had caused Richard to ride into Middleham with a scowl as heavy as the clouds building on the horizon. A storm was brewing from the North, and in my husband's mind. He threw his reins to his squire, planted a brusque kiss on my cheek, and marched into the Great Hall. I knew that he had been to Reading, where Parliament had been meeting last month. I could think of no event there to light this fire. Margaret was in France still, no doubt wearing out her patience, dreaming of an impossible invasion. The rebels in the North were keeping their heads down. I did not know where Henry might be.

Thus it could only be young Ned, our King, who had applied a burning brand to this conflagration.

'Not here,' Richard snapped when I lengthened my step to walk with him. As if I would have been sufficiently unwise to engage him in conversation in public when the air around him steamed with suppressed emotion. Fury, I thought. Richard did not have a short temper, but I knew when to keep a still tongue.

I followed him to his private chamber in the east tower. This was serious, unsettling. Not the loss of a castle or the depredations from a troublesome neighbour. Something had stirred this particular pot to boiling point. The lines that bracketed his mouth and cleaved the space between his brows were deeply scored. I had not seen this anger since news of the death of his brother Rutland and his father the Duke of York. And even then he had not been quite so uncontrollably furious.

'What has ruffled your feathers?' I took possession of his cap and gloves, at last risking a clap of thunder. I had already gestured that our servants stay clear. They had not needed the telling.

Richard slammed the door behind us.

'Edward. Young Ned, by God! Our crowned and anointed King. The youth I led to the throne, for whom I fought battles, for whom I have spent the last months in tight French negotiation, with what I thought were excellent results. The one who should be on his knees in gratitude to me, for a French alliance and a French bride.'

'What has he done to cast this fly into your honeyed cup?' I repeated.

I handed him a fly-less cup of ale, which he downed as if drowning in a desert. Handing the cup back to me, rather than flinging it at the wall, he wiped the back of his hand across his mouth and stood with his hands fisted on his hips.

'He is married.'

'Already? Is it not then Bona of Savoy?'

'It is not, and I am made to be taken for a fool. Even worse, he has been married for some months, since the first day of May, in fact. And the whole kept secret except from her thrice-damned family. A private marriage in the middle of a wood if the rumours are true. God help us and save us from such dull-witted decisions!'

He downed another cup of ale on a growl, while I pressed him to sit in the nearest chair with a hand to his shoulder, which he did reluctantly. I sat on the arm to keep him there.

'Did I not warn you that Ned would have a voice in his choice of wife?' I said. Richard bared his teeth in another snarl. 'And who is the lady in question?'

'Her name is Dame Elizabeth de Grey. Elizabeth Wydeville before her first marriage.'

'Wydeville,' I repeated, curling my fingers into the layers of his brigandine to keep him still. This was quite unexpected. It would cause ripples through the Court if Ned had chosen such a woman to be his wife and the Queen.

'Elizabeth Wydeville,' I repeated, piecing together all I knew about her, and none of it acceptable if discussing the Queen of England. 'I know the Wydevilles well enough, a minor landed family of distinctly Lancastrian persuasion. What in God's name would drive Ned to marry a Wydeville, however well-born Jacquetta might be?'

'Exactly so.' The whole of it poured out with a hefty dose of Neville pride overlying it all. 'A family of little breeding. A family dedicated to Lancaster in recent battles. What's more, she is no virgin princess, a fit mate for a King of England. The woman's late husband, Sir John de Grey, died fighting for King Henry at St Albans. She has two sons. What was Ned thinking? That he could turn his back on the French Princess Bona of Savoy, and take this woman to his bed on a mere whim. He thinks that he is King and so can do as he wishes. I say that he cannot.'

'But he has done it.'

'God's blood, he has! What's more, it is all legal with priestly blessings and there is nothing that can be done about it. Is he a May-Day fool to be so taken in? Or am I the fool to have trusted him to make a rational choice? He certainly did not see the need to take me into his confidence. He loves her, he says.'

'And what did you say to our love-smitten King?'

'Not what I was thinking! How I managed to keep silent I know not.'

I was impressed. Richard could be as outspoken as the next man, but Ned was no longer the young man who looked up to and admired his cousin. He wore a crown and had a sense of his own power after victory in battle. And had wed to please himself.

For a moment I felt envy of his situation.

'And does Mistress Wydeville love Ned?' I asked. 'Or Mistress de Grey as I should perhaps call her.'

'Who's to know? She might love being Queen of England more,' Richard glowered into the empty cup still in his hand. 'They are a family of ambition.'

'Ned has great charm.'

'God damn him for his charm!'

I thought about what the problem was here in Richard's mind as, escaping my clutch, he stood and began to strip off his travelling gear, dropping it as carelessly as ever on the floor.

'I think it will make no difference to your influence over him. He will still look to you for advice. You will still be his magnificent cousin. Your position is safe enough.'

'I trust so.' He stood with his back to me, staring out through the window at the blustering showers that had arrived and hid the view of the hills. 'You would have admired my sangfroid in the circumstances. I swallowed my ire and, at our King's behest, I escorted Mistress Wydeville into Reading Abbey where I presented her to the magnates and commons as their sovereign lady and Queen of England – bar the coronation. By God, it took some effort to pin a smile on my face! And through the week of celebrations, with the lords bending the knee on every side. I can understand why Ned might wish to share her bed. She's comely enough. And her mother is doubtless high-born. But marriage is beyond good sense!'

Then he turned his head and stretched out a hand towards me.

'Forgive me. It seems that I have come home in bad humour. You deserve better. Fill another cup of ale and come and sit with me.'

Which I did and we exchanged less contentious news. Then on a thought, even though I knew it might relight the fire in Richard's belly, 'Will King Louis feel slighted, that the Lady Bona has been rejected? Will he reconsider his proposed alliance with Ned?'

There was no expected eruption.

'Who knows what Louis will do? He is not called the Spider for nothing, weaving his tortuous webs. He might, of course, in a fit of chagrin, offer help to Margaret to fund an invasion, just to punish Ned.'

'It was a thought that had crossed my mind.'

'But I doubt it,' Richard added. 'I think Louis is careful how he spends the little money he has, and an alliance with Burgundy is a glittering jewel for him.' He continued to frown but the anger had gone. 'I still think I can conclude a treaty of friendship between Ned and Louis. And if Ned is happily ensconced in marriage, perhaps he can turn a blind eye to my extending my landed interests into Wales.'

It had been a sore spot with him. Richard had relaxed, the bad humour dissipating. He was still the counsellor at Ned's right hand. Surely Ned's new wife would make no difference to us. Ned would never cast aside Richard's advice.

'What is she like?' I asked.

'Very beautiful,' he admitted. 'Of course Ned was attracted. But why could he not just take her to his royal bed, or even commandeer hers, assuage his sexual itch, and then make a match with Bona of Savoy the legal one? There would be nothing to complain about in taking a royal mistress.'

'And do we attend the coronation?' I asked with deceptive sweetness.

'By God, we do. And we will smile from its beginning to its end!'

In the spirit of unity Richard and I planned to attend the coronation of Elizabeth Wydeville as Queen Elizabeth, to be held at Whitsuntide in the coming year. We would not make more waves than were necessary, although the storm clearly still surged in his gut. At the last moment he announced that he would not go.

'You must.' No good would come of his absenting himself, as he must know.

'I am sent on an embassy to Burgundy,' Richard said with some relief behind his smile. 'Louis of France is blowing hot and cold, as we expected, and Ned wants to tie Burgundy into an alliance. I am to persuade the Duke that it would be a good wager to draw England into his net. I am not sorry to be absent from the Wydeville spectacle.'

'So I go alone.'

'I suspect that you will be better without me!'

And what a spectacle it was. No expense had been spared by a besotted king, while our new Queen Elizabeth had every ounce of beauty and charm her subjects could have wished for. And certainly every inch of ambition. From widow of Sir John de Grey to Queen of England was quite a step. She had an eye to her own importance, clad in royal purple with a gold coronal on her hair, despite the necessity of walking barefoot through the ceremony. The feast was sumptuous, those present required to kneel when serving the Queen with the vast array of dishes that made up the three courses. This daughter of Lord Rivers had been raised to untold heights.

The Duchess of York was not present. Her silently expressed view of this undesirable marriage matched Richard's. She was not so silent when I visited with her in Baynard's Castle after the event.

'I will never condone what my son has done. He has sullied the fair name of his father. A Wydeville would never be an appropriate bride for Edward. I will never forgive him.'

I thought that she might when Elizabeth gave birth to a son and heir.

There was no reason why his marriage should make a difference to us, but the impressions at that ceremony and banquet were overly disquieting, not least the overpowering little group of Wydevilles, the Queen's family, who had come to celebrate. The Queen's parents, her brothers and sisters, her two sons from her first marriage; it was an impressive group, although some were still very young. Well dressed, comely, would they not anticipate rewards for Elizabeth's new rank?

I foresaw a distinct menace appearing on our horizon, making me consider what I should tell Richard. Families, particularly young ones, demanded marriage considerations. But then, perhaps I should leave it alone, for my worries might never emerge into full-flown danger. Even if they did, Richard would already be aware of any threats to us.

And then came an incident that made me consider picking up my previous correspondence.

## Margaret, Queen of England

Dreams were made to be broken.

All I achieved in St Omer was a gift from Philippe of Burgundy of a diamond, of some significant worth, and two thousand gold crowns, as well as a warning not to return to England since the seas were swarming with Yorkist ships.

'What do you do now, my lady?' he asked, the pity in his face enough to make me consider a sharp reply. Instead, I chose diplomacy. There was only one choice for me to make.

'I go to Anjou.'

I must, against all good sense, throw myself once again on my father's mercy. Even my chancy Scottish ally, Queen Mary, was dead, a mere thirty years to her name, leaving her son in the hands of Bishop Kennedy until he came of age. The thought travelled with me. What would happen to my son if I died now, before my time? Who would stand for him? Not my father. Who would raise money to restore him to his throne? I did not even have a regal coronet to my name, much less a crown; all had been sold to raise money, long since dissipated.

Another worry to keep me from sleep.

My father gave me a pension of six thousand crowns and the loan of a chateau, which I accepted, at the same time as I refused to bow to his cynical observation that a full-scale invasion of England could not be achieved in the blink of an eye, or even in a matter of weeks. Or perhaps ever. Thus once again I established my Court in exile, this time at the Chateau of Koeur at St Mihiel in the duchy of Bar. I had done it before in Scotland. I could do it again. I hated it, but I must make my followers welcome when they crossed the sea to join me. At least it proved that my cause was not homeless. I had many visitors.

I could not complain of my new life, but how small and mean it was compared with the luxury and grandeur of my life as Queen in England? Little had been spent on my chateau in past years; my father's gift proved to be hardly enough to feed those dependent on me, all crushed into the few rooms. I began to know the bite of poverty, for I had no money of my own. But there was still hope. My lord Henry was still living without duress. We managed to exchange letters. He was free and there were men in the North who would fight for him.

As for my precious son, he talked of nothing but cutting off heads and making war, as if he were one of the old gods of war.

Surely the Blessed Virgin would not forsake me.

Surely she would keep us all safe until we could return to our inheritance.

But then my son, my dear son, fell ill and seemed close to death. Such a fragile thread, all hopes for the House of Lancaster hung on his frail life.

The Blessed Virgin abandoned me. Everything I had prayed for, dreamed of, worked towards, fell into a black pit of distress, of hopelessness, driving me again to my knees.

'Blessed Virgin, take pity on me.'

I prayed beside him. I employed a carpenter to construct a shell of wood around and over his bed to keep out the light, which hurt his eyes, and the draughts that made him shiver uncontrollably. My physicians could work no miracle. He became more wretched with fever by the day, his fair skin covered with a rash of ugly abrasions that wept and grew into agonising pustules. I spent the endless days beside him with no fear that I would be afflicted with the dread disease.

The Blessed Virgin did not listen to me. If my son died, how would I spend my life? What purpose would I have? In those days I gave no thought to what might be happening across the sea in England. In the end I sent a courier hotfoot to my father, begging that he would send his physician.

'Save my son. In God's name save my son.'

I repeated the words over and over again on the page. In response the physician arrived with his potions and promises of a miracle, but I read the fear in his eyes.

'What can you do for my son?'

He explained gently, as if I were an ill-educated woman who could not understand.

'A most advantageous use of the herb pennyroyal, my lady. The leaves are bruised and steeped in wine to cleanse foul ulcers. To drink it will ease the boy's pain and help him to sleep.'

'Will his face be scarred?'

'My tinctures will cause any marks around the eyes to fade.'

He was so certain. I was not, and as the days passed I feared the worst. My son's poor body became thin and wasted, and I wept openly until I was sent from his chamber, in fear of the disease afflicting me and bringing my death.

'My lady...'

I awoke from a restless sleep in terror. The physician.

'Do not tell me that he is dead.'

'He is not. He sleeps at ease.'

He would live, but I was too exhausted to give thanks in prayer.

'Will I still be King?' he asked petulantly as he drank one of the potions. 'I hate this. Do I have to drink it?'

'Of course you will be King, my son. And yes, you must drink it.'

'When can I go hunting?'

'When you have regained your strength. Now drink.'

He did so and fell into a restful sleep, which did not assuage my anxieties.

215

As I had vowed during those dark days, when my son was well enough to be left I went on pilgrimage to St Nicholas de Port to give thanks before the powerful relics of St Nicholas, brought there from Italy. I had little money to give but I offered what I could on the altar with my endless thanks. Sons were a blessing but a terrible curse when death hovered over them. I could not shake off that fear; would the illness recur?

As I travelled home to my borrowed chateau I crossed the path of a royal courier travelling between King Louis and my father. He doffed his herald's cap, beating the dust from the gilding on his tabard as we drew rein.

'Some snippet of news that might interest you, my lady. From England.'

'Then tell me. I am in need of good news.'

With my son's return to health, once more my thoughts must of necessity begin to pick up my plans for the future.

'King Edward in England has married.'

My ears pricked up at this. 'I doubt that this is good news for me. Who is the fortunate lady? Is it indeed Bona of Savoy?'

'No, but I know not her name other than Elizabeth. She is an English lady from a knightly family. She is a widow.'

'Are you certain?'

'Yes, my lady.'

Unexpected news indeed. I could not think of any English woman who might be worthy of such a position, and certainly the York upstart would not wed a widow. I shook my head as if to deny it. But then the repercussions overcame my lack of knowledge of whom she might be. If she was fertile, what matter the name of her family? This would mean that he would have an heir of his own blood, to push my own son even further from the crown. And of course York had two brothers, but both too young as yet to wed. But a widow…

'Does the lady in question have any children?'

'Indeed I believe so, my lady. She has two sons from her first marriage.'

My heart lurched at such unwelcome news. She was indeed fertile. My position became more difficult by the day.

'Tell me. Do you know where King Henry might be? Or the state of his health?'

'I have no knowledge of this, my lady. Is he not still in Scotland?'

I could discover no trustworthy information. It was some weeks now since I had received any communication from him. Recently there had been rumours that Henry had been taken prisoner. I did not believe them, not until the source was a voice that I could trust. There were too many people who would bring me sorrow. All I could do was keep my ear to the ground to discover what the feelings were in England. Any weakness for the usurper and I would rejoice. If this widow bride from a mere knightly family created a ferment of opposition, I would be the first to seize the opportunity it might offer.

I would immediately take ship. I would return.

I experienced a bright resurgence of hope.

Until a letter was delivered, an unexpected letter, after all the horrifying events of the past months.

# 20

# *An Exchange of Despairing Correspondence, 1465*

## Anne, Countess of Warwick, to Margaret, Queen of England

I am writing to you, with a word of warning, hoping that it will reach you at your Court in exile. You may of course have already heard of this from one of your informants, of which I am sure you have many, but I still felt a need to make all clear. Rumours can be false, intended merely to hurt. If it were my husband, I would wish to know. And if you were in communication with King Henry, as he once was styled, any letters you send might now go dangerously astray. You must take care what you write.

Is it disloyal of me to tell you this? I think not. It is compassionate, as you admitted once before, one woman to another.

Henry of Lancaster, once King of England, is captured and is now residing in the Tower of London. There is no threat to his life, but it makes your situation more difficult. King Edward and my husband, the Earl of Warwick, have a weapon that will be used against you if you try to return with insufficient force.

I do not know what your plan is for the future.

How was he captured? This is the truth of what
happened. He was caught in flight in the wild county of
Lancashire, and from there brought to London. I know this
for the truth because my lord of Warwick escorted him, it
has to be said in triumph, through the streets, Henry's feet
bound in unkingly fashion with leather to his stirrups to
prevent his escape.

There is no need to fear for his life. He is, I think, more
valuable alive than dead to King Edward. He is allowed
visitors. He is free to read and pray. I think he is not
unhappy.

I do not envisage that this will change your plans in any
way. I should make you aware that there are no loud voices
of opposition to King Edward of which you could make
use. You will be aware that our King is wed to Elizabeth
Wydeville, who was wed as Madam de Grey. He is turning
more and more to this Wydeville family for advice. They
have become fervently Yorkist even though the new Queen's
first husband died fighting for Lancaster on the field at
St Albans. Now it is in their interests to be Yorkist. Such
changes we see.

You have my concern for your life in exile. I would not
be easy in it and neither will you be. I cannot wish you well
in your strategy to return, for I think that it would bring
death and disaster to my family, and an unlikely success for
yours in the circumstances.

I know that you continue to regard my lord of Warwick
as your most deadly of enemies. I think that you should also
look to the Wydevilles, for they have no affection for you
and your son.

Why am I giving you advice? I feel taken up with events

outside my control and it troubles my sleep. Perhaps you feel the same. May the Holy Virgin bless you.

Perhaps you must accept that the Wheel of Fortune has finally turned against the House of Lancaster.

Anne

Countess of Warwick

## Margaret of Anjou, Queen of England, to Anne, Countess of Warwick

By the Queen.

It is not in my heart to thank you for this, but my conscience dictates that I must. It is an unlooked-for kindness from you, Countess Anne. I am grateful for your letter, although the news is grim. At least I now know that it is true, and not mere rumour. I know that you would not spread untruth merely to reduce me to despair.

My poor lord Henry will be a sad pawn to be used in this political game. I know that he will agree to any suggestion made by the Yorkist usurper. He has no element of judgement left in him, only his prayers bring him comfort. He is a gentle soul who should never have been called on to be King.

Is it treasonous for me to admit that? Does not everyone know it? He would have made an excellent priest or monk. He no longer has the will to govern, even though he might like to wear the crown that is his by right. All I can do is pray for him.

I will never abandon my quest to secure the royal inheritance for my son.

What of my life in exile? It lacks the comfort to which I had grown used. It is not the residence of a Queen of England, but the cramped rooms are improved for me by the fine gardens that stretch along one side of the chateau and give me solace when I can escape from those who take refuge with us. I must not complain.

Sometimes when I wake in the dark of the early hours, when worry overcomes me and drives sleep far away, I think that I will never return. My son will never wear the crown. I was told that forces loyal to me received a crushing blow at the Battle of Hexham. I need an army and a fleet. I need money to pay my supporters who will come to my banner when I land in England. I need a commander for my army; the loyalty of Somerset can never be taken for granted again after his flirtation with the Yorkists, although I should be grateful for his return to me.

In those dark hours all seems impossible.

My son grows strong again after a severe illness. I thank the Blessed Virgin. Today as I write I feel strong, too, and I believe that he is destined to become King of England. I am just returned from pilgrimage to offer my thanks and petition for spiritual aid.

A Wydeville wife for the man who usurped my lord's throne, you tell me. I knew only that her name was Elizabeth. It horrifies me. I suppose that she will prove fertile with him. The Yorkist usurper will soon have a clutch of children to take the throne after him, but I vow that I will not let it happen. I must not. I must hold to my task even when hopelessness fills my days. I am on my own with my own future to negotiate.

I still regard the Earl of Warwick as my enemy and will never be won over to see otherwise.

I can barely tolerate the thought of the daughter of Lord Rivers wearing the crown of the Queen of England in my stead. It is my right to wear it as my lord Henry is still King. Elizabeth Wydeville lacks the noble birth to make her a suitable bride and consort for a king. I have respect for her mother, Jacquetta, the Dowager Duchess of Bedford, who was one of those who came to escort me to England as a bride, but the Rivers family has no merit of its own.

I will never abandon my position as Queen of England.

I will never kneel before Dame Elizabeth de Grey. How can a woman of such inferiority be raised to the heights of Queen?

I can write no more. All I see is dark days of destitution before me.

What will happen to my son if I die?

Dismay colours my days and the writing of this letter.

Margaret

Queen of England

# 21

## *Perilous Journeys in England and France 1469*

### Anne, Countess of Warwick

I was writing when Richard entered the muniment room at
Warwick Castle where all the documents relevant to the
Neville-Beauchamp inheritance were stored. I looked up, but
could read nothing in his expression except an arch of brows in
surprise to see me there. It was not my usual domain. I knew
that we had had a recent royal courier, but as to his purpose I
could not guess. I had matters appertaining to our family on
my mind.

'What did he want?' I asked, putting down the pen, frowning
at the ink on my fingers.

'I am summoned to Court. Ned is keen to see me bend the
knee.'

Elbows on the desk, ink wiped away, I folded my hands and
rested my chin on them.

'I had noticed that you have not been to Westminster, or
wherever Ned is holding his Court, for some time.'

'No.'

He perched on the edge of the desk as if he intended to stay.

'Thus your absence has become a matter of comment.'

'I imagine it has.'

'Why would that be? Why have you, it seems to me quite deliberately, stayed away from Court?'

His eyes continued to hold mine in what I could only interpret as a challenge, daring me to disagree.

'Because there is no purpose in my going.'

I sat back and threw down the gauntlet.

'So I was right. Ned has summoned you before.'

'Yes.'

'And you have not gone.'

'No.'

I knew partly the reason. Richard's negotiations with Louis had been cast into disarray, to Richard's private humiliation. Richard's attempts to achieve a French marriage and a French alliance had both been abandoned after much time and effort on his part. He was not in a mood to appear amenable. Reading the intractable set of his mouth, I felt the brush of temper.

'Is it wise to refuse an order from your King?' I asked.

'I see no wisdom in riding the length of the country for that same King to ask for my opinion and my aid, and then refuse to act on it.'

This was dangerous stuff. My temper flickered into life but I kept my voice even.

'For God's sake go, Richard, or you will be at war with him as well as with the Lancastrians.'

He showed his teeth in acknowledgement of my needling, picking up a knife to sharpen my pen, smearing ink on his fingers.

'Ned can't afford war with me. There are too many men in England who will follow me into battle.'

I would not step back.

'If you challenge his authority he might just lock you in the

Tower with Henry. That I could not tolerate, and neither could you.'

He shrugged as if it mattered little, but it was not difficult to read his dissatisfaction, his restlessness, as he stood and prowled, throwing down both pen and knife onto the table, picking up a book here, a manuscript there, until he returned to look over my shoulder. It worried me. I was used to Richard's overwhelming confidence, his belief in what he was doing. The muniment room suddenly had an air of menace, as if some dark foreboding had entered the room. It positively bristled with unrequited ambition.

'I don't often see you with pen in hand,' he remarked, since I had picked it up again.

'I rarely have the need. I dictate my household needs to my steward. But we have two daughters. I am planning marriages.'

He picked up the list. It was still a short one, but the product of some days of consideration. All the heirs of magnate families, of a suitable age and disposition, who might be considered appropriate to take our daughters as brides. They were from families that we knew well. They would make excellent alliances for the future. Here they were:

Henry Stafford, Duke of Buckingham
Viscount Bourchier, cousin to the King
Lord Grey of Ruthin, heir to the Earl of Kent
William Herbert...

I had run out of ideas at that point. So few who might be considered important enough for a Neville marriage. Was Richard thinking of a French or Burgundian connection? I did not know. Would he even consider Ned's younger brothers if we could achieve a dispensation because of the close relationship? But Ned might not be in favour of such an alliance. The margin was filled with scrolls and flowers, and many blots from an ill-sharpened pen, but they had failed to spur my imagination to more possible suitors for the girls.

'Would any two of these heirs to wealth and power be suitable for Isabel and Anne?' I asked.

Without a word of agreement or denial, Richard tore it in two, strode to the fireplace and cast it into the flames, a short, sharp gesture of disapproval. He watched as it caught fire and fell into ash.

'So much for my hard work,' I complained. 'Did you not approve of them? We need men of influence and strong noble connections. Or is it that you look abroad, to France?'

He did not reply, except to say, 'It is too long since you have been to Court. I think I'll take you so that you can see what is happening.'

'Obeying the King's summons at the same time, of course.'

'But that is not my purpose. How many sisters of our new Queen grace the Wydeville family?'

'Why?'

'Think about it, my usually percipient wife.'

So I thought.

'Three? Four?'

'Try harder!'

'I will not guess!'

He took hold of my hand and pulled me to my feet.

'You will not need to guess. Nor will you need a list.' At least there was a breath of a return to his good humour. 'We leave for Court tomorrow.'

It was indeed many months since I had been to Court. It was to be a lesson in failed diplomacy for me to absorb and appreciate. In recent months there had indubitably been a setting aside of

Richard and the Neville family. Now I understood why Richard had not galloped a path to Ned's door in these recent months. It was as clear as the glass in my new ivory-backed mirror, within a day of our residence at Westminster. King Edward had adopted the Wydeville family, pushing his erstwhile supporters into dissatisfied opposition, a dangerous situation that I did not see clearly enough until I returned to Court.

Against all good sense, in spite of all he had done, Richard, too, had been pushed aside. Sir Richard Wydeville, father to the new Queen, had been appointed Lord Chancellor. Richard's strong support for a French alliance was indeed abandoned and Ned pursued one with Burgundy instead, supported by Rivers.

It was like watching a mummers' play, where masks were swapped and traded, as royal approval moved from one family to another. A mummers' play where the main players were Wydevilles. A face now prominent at Court was the Queen's brother Anthony Wydeville, the famous jouster, now Lord Scales through his marriage to the Scales heiress. Lionel Wydeville was endowed as Bishop of Salisbury, while Edward Wydeville was created Admiral of the fleet. Titles and offices had been handed out with ease. It was whispered that Rivers would be made Earl Rivers and Lord Treasurer. Power indeed.

Richard had received none.

How busy the Wydevilles had been.

Then there were the marriages.

The Wydevilles had five daughters as well as Elizabeth. The Queen's sisters had a need for husbands. Ned had agreed to every one of the Queen's suggestions.

'I see what you mean,' I remarked under cover of the celebrations, the feasting and drinking, that always seemed to surround Ned.

'I am sure that you do.'

All my prospective heirs snapped up. Buckingham, Bourchier, Ruthin and Herbert, all wed to the sisters of the Queen. That little knot of anxiety grew claws as I recalled Richard's fears of a powerful family surrounding our King. The creation of a Wydeville clique at the centre of Court and the government was here before our eyes. How influential they had become.

'Who is left for our daughters?' I asked when Ned and his new friends left with falcons and hounds to enjoy a morning at the hunt.

'We will see.' Richard's brow was dark, his right hand clenched around his gloves. 'I am in no mood for hunting with the Wydevilles. When my cousin has returned and has time for us, we will have an audience with Ned.'

I had no knowledge of what he intended, although I should have seen it for myself. Had Richard asked my opinion? No, and I was unsure what my reply would have been. When Richard requested an audience with Ned, we were invited into the armoury where Ned was overlooking the state of his armour.

The cousins exchanged an embrace and courteous words while I received a warm salute to my cheek. There may have been a gleam in Ned's eye, but Richard's absence was not touched upon, except for Ned to issue a subtle but pointed invitation.

'Come and measure swords with me, Cousin,' Ned challenged. 'See if my skills have improved in your absence.'

'If you mean skills with sword and dagger, I doubt it,' Richard replied. 'But then you have been fostering a wider spectrum of skills, I notice.'

Neither was averse to a friendly contest. How often had I seen them wield sword and dagger against each other in past happier days? But this time there was an edge as keen as that of the swords in the clash of metal, the thud of booted feet, the slide on the tiles. They were still evenly matched, although Ned's conspicuous height gave him an advantage; what he gained in reach, Richard overcame in experience. I had no fear for either of them, even when Richard's sword was caught between the hilts of Ned's weapons. Richard cleverly disengaged and continued the assault. I could be proud and admiring of both.

Until Ned dropped the point of his sword to the floor, cast his dagger down on a bench, and stepped back.

'You did not come here to challenge me to a duel, Richard. What do you want of me?'

'I am here with a proposal to put to you, my lord.' Richard, replacing his own sword and dagger on the bench, was cool and respectful after his long absence.

'Then speak it.'

'I suggest a marriage. For my daughter Isabel, who is now of marriageable age.'

So that was the reason for this meeting. I should have known. Perhaps I did. I tried to look complacent, as if it had all been discussed between us.

Ned raised his fair brows in apparent surprise, which I did not trust to any degree. 'Do you need my consent? Is it not within your own dominion? Unless you have chosen some unsuitable foreign family who will drag us into wars...'

When Ned showed his teeth in a smile, I decided that he had become manipulative and cunning in his maturity.

'I do need your consent,' Richard said. 'I suggest a marriage between my eldest daughter and your brother George of Clarence.'

A silence, indubitably as sharp-edged as the sword that Ned now dropped to join his dagger. He tilted his head as if considering it, his face blandly accepting of such a suggestion. I held my breath. Richard simply stood, fingers lightly clasped around the jewelled links of his belt.

Ned shook his head in friendly fashion.

'I have in mind Clarence's marriage to a foreign princess. A network of alliances against those who would usurp this kingdom. I do not look for an English bride.'

'Would it not be an advantage to unite our two families even closer in blood than they already are?' Richard suggested, equally calm, as if such a negotiation happened every day. 'If you are looking for allies in any coming conflict, a close friendship at home might be better than looking to France or Burgundy. For both of us.'

I watched as Ned's lips pressed slowly but firmly together. Even I could see that the King might not desire such a close liaison between the two most powerful landowners in the Midlands, Clarence and Warwick, creating a block of Neville-Plantagenet interest there, with Richard a dominant force over his youthful would-be son-in-law. No, Ned was not in favour and expressed himself forcefully, picking up the sword again to run his fingers over the gold-worked hilt.

'I will not give my consent. You must look elsewhere for your daughter. There are other families with sons who will welcome your overtures.'

'To ally with a Neville? To ally with the family of the Earl of Warwick?' Richard's eyes were dark with emotion. 'Show me the son and heir of a powerful English family who would be acceptable to me. There are far fewer since you have promoted the family of your wife.'

The silence could be tasted, like the harsh tang of metal.

'I will not discuss it.'

'Which I regret.'

'You ask too much of me. I do not yet have a son. If my

brother George becomes King after me, your daughter would be Queen.'

'Yes, she would. Would a Neville queen be so undesirable?'

'I have no wish for it.' He cast the sword down again with a distinct clang. 'I have said no.'

Richard bowed and we would have departed, leaving, it seemed to me, all in the balance, except that Ned's voice stopped us.

'I have a need for your diplomatic skills. Perhaps we could discuss it.'

I left them alone. Would Richard be willing to disobey his King? Would he retreat in cowed obedience? Ned was intractable; Clarence was still his heir, the future King, until the Queen gave birth to a son.

'What have you done?' I asked as soon as Richard joined me. 'Only alienated the King.'

'He has been alienated from me ever since the Wydevilles appeared on the scene.'

'Keep a sweet tongue, Richard.'

'I have. It goes ill with me.' Richard managed a smile. 'Ned still has need of my talents. Ned wants me to play a diplomatic role in the journey of his sister Margaret from London to Dover, on her way to her wedding with the Duke of Burgundy.'

'What did you say?' I asked as we rejoined the courtiers at play in Westminster's Great Hall.

'That I would consider it,' Richard replied. 'I gave no answer. Nor will I yet.'

A sudden presentiment crept over my skin of what would happen if he refused. We had fought enough battles, shed enough blood.

'Do it, Richard. For the sake of peace between our families.

Do it! Smile. Grit your teeth and take Margaret to Dover. She is a fine girl and you can talk to her!'

For a long moment, as we watched Queen Elizabeth dance with her brother Anthony Wydeville, as elegant a dancer as he was a jouster, I thought that he would refuse. Instead, he turned his head and smiled at me.

'I will, of course. I thought I would simply make Ned wait for my reply. Now will you come and dance with me?'

I did so, and as we followed the slow, gliding steps of the carole dance I thought all would be well, in spite of that slight suspicion that Richard was working on his own intricate plans for the future. We would find another suitable husband for Isabel. Perhaps it would indeed be good policy to look abroad.

I must simply rest on Richard's good sense and diplomatic skills. I executed a complicated dance-step to perfection but without much satisfaction. Pray God my husband could keep his ambitions in check.


## Margaret, Queen of England

In my borrowed chateau at Mihiel at Bar, loneliness wrapped me around like the folds of a velvet cloak. My life grew barren of emotion other than duty and thwarted ambition. What was there in my existence to encourage me to rise from my bed? What satisfaction soothed me to give me comfort when I retired to sleep?

I knew some would say that I had much to be thankful for, so many blessings to lay hope at my feet and beckon me into a future when all would be well. Yes, I valued the advice of my commanders. Where would I be without them? Probably a prisoner in the Tower with my lord Henry, at the mercy of the Yorkist usurper. They had saved me and supported me here in exile. But there were days when I yearned for more than the loyalty from the men who had sworn their duty to the House of Lancaster. I yearned for soft words from those who might have a care for me. From my family. From those who had more than the pursuit of their own power and position in their words. The women who came into exile with me were of great value, but they were not so close that I could open my heart to them.

One day my son would speak his mind and advise me on what I should do, but he was still young, far too young to take on such a burden. I would not ask it of him. Perhaps one day when he had been blooded on a battlefield, then I could pass some of the burden to his hands. I prayed that he would survive the battles that assuredly faced us for me to do so. And there was not only the impending clash of arms for my son to overcome. A recurrence of the dreadful disease that dragged him into a fever and blighted his fair skin filled me with terror. He had recovered with no apparent harm to his energies, but one day he might succumb again, and where would my hopes be?

Henry was far beyond my influence, incarcerated, acting at the demands of the Yorkist King. Even when he had been free to travel with me and ride at the head of his army his words had had little value. He would compromise, make amends, be openhandedly generous, praying over the sins of his enemies. He had no sense of the bitter reality of life where those who surrounded him would use him for their own gains. How often had he forgiven Richard of York? How often had he welcomed him with open arms when it was clear to all that he desired his crown? The image of that fatal Love Day still rose like a nightmare in my mind. Henry was incapable of making any decisions, even to the robe he might wear. I would never be able to turn to him.

Who was there left for me? My father, some would say, since I had come to his Court, but my father was as guided by self-interest as any man I knew. He would not help me. Then why not Louis of France? He would make alliances with whomsoever would bring him influence and wealth, making smiling promises, then turn his back and abandon those who suddenly seemed to be of no advantage to him. He would abandon me. In my heart of hearts, I knew it. I remembered too well how he mocked me to the delight of the Milanese Ambassador, when I last appealed to him. Oh, I was told about it, with some measure of enjoyment in the words of the teller.

'Look how proudly she writes!' he had sneered, fluttering my letter as if it were of no moment, when I had abased myself and begged him for help. 'She thinks that fair words will wring gold and arms from me. Has she learned nothing in her tumultuous life, when all has been lost to her?'

I had nothing to offer him in return now. My relationship with him, cousin to cousin, was shattered beyond mending.

Where was my pride, my strength of will? It had all been trampled into dereliction. I could see no way forward.

There were some days when I envied Countess Anne, envied her comfortable life with her family. What decisions did she have to make other than the running of her household, what they would eat, the health of her children, the state of the hangings in her Great Hall at Warwick Castle? Although I might detest him, Warwick was a capable man, a good husband, a good leader. Countess Anne might find it trying to be constantly obedient but there must be some comfort there when her needs were considered.

There was no one to consider mine.

'Blessed Virgin, give me strength and fortitude for the future. How will I return? How will I rescue Henry? What of my son's inheritance? How many years must I sit here and watch the conflicting relationships in Europe?'

The Blessed Virgin seemed unwilling to listen to me.

I was lost in a desert of shifting sand. There were no paths, no guiding stars. Or more truthfully, I was like a ship without a rudder.

## Anne, Countess of Warwick

'I do not agree with this,' I said. I discovered that I could barely breathe for the sheer audacity of this strategy that could be the undoing of us all. 'You are putting us all in danger.'

Richard was unrepentant.

'I am planning our future security.'

'With the King collecting his army against us for sheer wilful disobedience?'

'He will not.'

'I think you underestimate his temper.'

'More like to sink his disapproval in a cup of ale. Or the bed of his lovely wife.'

It should have been an occasion of great rejoicing for me, seeing my elder daughter wed. It was not. It was an event that blasted a warning to all who were willing to listen, which Richard clearly was not.

'I think it more likely that the King becomes your enemy,' I said, refusing to be persuaded.

My combative husband had sent me a message to Warwick Castle to bring the girls and meet with him in Dover, where our exchange of opinions had occurred. We would cross to Calais where we would remain for some months. Since Richard was still Captain there, there was no element of surprise, even an anticipated enjoyment in a fortress that I knew well with people with whom I had a long acquaintance. We were met on the quay, Richard full of energy and the success of his campaign. With him stood George of Clarence, the royal Duke, magnificently dressed and well mannered, bowing to me and our daughters, helping us onto the vessel that would take us to Calais. Although neither as tall nor as handsome as his brother Ned, there was a slick air of satisfaction about him.

I knew immediately what this was all about. I did not need it explained to me. What surprised me most was that Duchess Cecily was to sail with us.

'How can it be that the Duke of Clarence should accompany us?' I asked with praiseworthy sweetness. After all the fuss of departure, I stood beside Richard on the deck as the walls and towers of the Calais fortress drew steadily closer. It was summer and good sailing weather. 'And Duchess Cecily too. Can I even guess what you are planning?'

'You might.' He leaned negligently on the bulwark, deliberately keeping his gaze turned from me. 'Are you surprised?'

'I was there when Ned refused your request.'

'Which I refuse to accept.'

'You did not tell me. Did I not deserve to know? Isabel is my daughter. You have made this decision in your usual high-handed manner.'

I felt aggrieved that he should have arranged this without my approval, but more specifically without my knowledge. Not that I should have been surprised. Did he not conduct all his campaigns without my opinion, and was this not simply another part of his campaigning, to keep a tight hold on power? That

I and our daughters should participate was simply part of his scheming.

'You knew what was in my mind, Anne.'

'I know that Ned will never forgive us,' I said.

'He will, once it is done.' Richard at his most saturnine.

'He did not seem in a forgiving mood when you first suggested it.'

'It will tie us to him and he to us. It will strengthen us against Wydeville aggrandisement. Do you not approve? He cannot object to Isabel. She is as well born as he is, and far more valuable than a foreign bride. That was a mere excuse to push me aside.'

I thought about this, aware of Anne and Isabel and Clarence in deep conversation, sheltering out of the wind. Isabel was laughing, Clarence responding, Anne watching with a sparkle in her eye. They knew each other well. It would not be a match against Isabel's wishes. She flirted beneath her lashes, enjoying the young man's attention.

My approval? It meant nothing. After all those years of marriage, how my confidence, my sense of my position, my role in our household, was shattered.

'Why did you not tell me? That is what I resent, Richard. Was it because you knew I would object?'

'Yes.' He was bluntly forthright. 'I thought it would be easier to get you all to Calais without argument. Forgive me. Your opinion, one way or the other, will not change my mind.'

'Then I will not give it.' But I did anyway. 'You could be digging our grave here.'

'How would that be possible? Once it is solemnised, what can Ned do but accept and rejoice with us?'

'How could you be so blind? Clarence might admire you, and see the value of Neville estates coming his way, but Ned will never agree now that you have challenged his authority so blatantly.'

'I see the future very well!'

'I don't like it!'

'You don't have to like it!'

So here we were, in a spate of bad temper, to celebrate a royal marriage, which we found politic to hold in Calais away from Ned's watchful eye. He had forbidden it, but Richard was determined to bring it about without royal consent. I should have been full of joy for Isabel as we made that short journey across the Channel to Calais, taking Richard's brother George, Archbishop of York, with us to conduct the ceremony. How difficult it was for me to rejoice, despite Isabel's high spirits at her forthcoming wedding.

I considered the family connection of the young people, one thought sticking like a burr in a dog's pelt.

'They cannot wed,' I said, pleased to put a spoke in Richard's wheel. 'They are related within the bonds of consanguinity.'

'They can wed if they have a papal dispensation.'

'Which you have? Of course you have arranged that too!'

Another step he had taken without my knowledge. I wondered how much it had cost him in gold to persuade the Pope to comply.

Richard closed his hand over my wrist, his impatience with me and the situation palpable.

'What do you expect me to do? He has handed all those whom we might seek to the Wydeville family. What choice is left to us? Our daughter deserves a man of blood and recognition. What better than a royal prince, who is my cousin? When I die, the Neville estates will be of great value. And your Beauchamp lands too. Our daughters need husbands of the highest rank.'

I could argue against none of that reasoning. I changed direction.

'Why Calais? Or need I ask?'

'Why indeed. Out of Ned's immediate sphere of influence.'

'But Ned does not agree, and never will. The fact that you acted in secrecy will make it even worse. What will come of this, Richard?' Fear was beginning to overcome my petulance. 'I am afraid. For you. For all of us.' I watched my daughter and Clarence again. Isabel shone with happiness. Clarence seemed perfectly conversant with the idea of this marriage to his cousin. 'Will Clarence happily thwart his brother's plans for him?'

'He will if it means inheriting my lands through Isabel.'

I sighed. We had a marriage to celebrate, whether I liked it or not. Richard slid his hand down and took my cold hands and held them together, palm to palm within his own gloved hands, as he had so often in the past when we were at one in thought and deed.

'Ned will come round to the idea.'

My bout of anger seemed to be draining away, since it would achieve nothing but an aching head for me. I took refuge in my cabin, small as it was, until we reached land, and considered my face in my mirror, searching for answers that I could not discover.

Instead, I sought out the Duchess. Her expression as I tracked her down to the bow of the ship where she was anticipating the landing, was not welcoming.

'Do you support my nephew in this?' she demanded.

'No. I think it is a mistake. Do you approve?'

'No. I approve of nothing that Warwick is doing at present.'

I might have leaned beside her, but the Duchess's face was unforgiving in its austerity.

'What is he doing that rouses you to such ire?' I asked.

239

'He is hurting me to my soul.'

'Will you tell me?'

'No. I will not speak of it. I swear it will be the death of me.'

She turned her face away from me so that I left her to her morbid thoughts, returning to my own concerns. What damage would this marriage do to our family? There was nothing I could do to prevent it, nor could I heal the apparent rift with Duchess Cecily, although she did bring her minstrels with her to play at the marital feast.

Thus my daughter was wed, with some minor celebrating, in Calais and in direct defiance of the King. A surprising number of English nobility and their wives joined us for the event. Richard presided with appropriate gravity, Clarence was high-spirited, while the Neville brother the Archbishop solemnised the marriage with due reverence. Isabel glowed with her achievement in being wed to a royal brother, Duchess Cecily cast a sour gaze over all, while I participated as I must. Did I like Clarence? Confident, ambitious, gifted and attractive, he appealed to Isabel. Yet I saw the glib, shallow, spoiled eighteen-year-old youth beneath the charming façade. So far, he was under Richard's spell and would agree to this marriage, which might increase his power against his brother. Why would he cast his lot in with Richard rather than the King, who would give him all the power he desired, all the land he coveted?

Another element to this marriage that did not bode well.

Throughout the whole of it, smiling and welcoming, I fulfilled my allotted role as wife and hostess, controlled and capable in making our guests feel at ease, obedient to the demands of my family. I had been raised to see my own future in a marriage to a man who could hold my inheritance in a strong hand. There were days when I envied Queen Margaret her strong will; her ability to take hold of a threat to her position and bend it to her own desires.

Had I ever done that in my life?

Richard would laugh at the idea.

In all honesty, what good had it done Margaret?

# 22

# *Family Cataclysm After the Battle of Edgecote, 1470*

## Anne, Countess of Warwick

'Open the gates.'

I ordered the gates of Warwick Castle to be opened, the portcullis raised, since the banners outside were Neville and ecclesiastical. Here was Archbishop George Neville, last seen at my daughter's wedding in Calais. With him was a visitor I would never have expected, and in no state of grandeur or habitual flamboyance. The banners of York were absent.

Never had I lived through a time of such upheaval and the constant ripple of fear. The muted pleasure of the wedding celebrations was jettisoned by the following day, by which time Richard and Clarence had dispatched a manifesto to England. I read it before it was sent. I suspected that this offering was Richard's sop to my pride. On perusing it, I clamped my lips shut. What value in expressing my fear? Richard had a further campaign in mind and would follow it, with or without me.

The document condemned the power of Ned's evil ministers, naming Earl Rivers, calling on the men of Kent to join Richard at Canterbury in outright rebellion. There were apparently already uprisings in the North, ostensibly led by someone named

Robin of Redesdale, but in effect organised by Richard's affinity in the region. While I and my daughters travelled to Warwick Castle, Isabel regretful at being separated so soon from her new husband, Richard applied himself to challenging the King. This was no different from any other campaign, I castigated myself when I was regrettably acerbic with the servants, but there was a terrible air of treasonous insurrection about this one that was quite different. I could not see where it would end. I could see only a distant battlefield. I could see only disaster.

But now, in Warwick, with brisk orders for wine and food to be laid in one of the antechambers off the Great Hall, I was down in the bailey before they had even dismounted. It was a formidable escort, but then it would need to be, since here was Ned, our King. He looked dishevelled and displeased, surrounded as he was by Neville's henchmen, but he managed a smile for me as he swung down from the saddle.

How quickly he could summon an air of charm when he needed to, and yet beneath the charm I could read a tight-held fury, something above and beyond the fact that he was Richard's prisoner, which was bad enough.

'Good day to you, Countess Anne. You have me here a re-luctant guest. My lord of Warwick desires my company – when he arrives. Believe it or not, I am under his jurisdiction.'

'My lord!' My only reaction was one of shock that it should have come to this.

'Once you called me Ned.'

'Once you were not my King! Nor were you under restraint in my castle!'

He laughed, the same youthful expression of mirth that I recalled, but the lines engraved around his mouth and between his brows I did not recognise. There was a temper here beneath the enforced charm; there was a deeply engraved maturity and acceptance that all was not well in his privileged world.

'Do I ask pardon, my lord? Or welcome you?'

The sudden upset of what had occurred had robbed me of a suitable response.

'A welcome would be good. I should be thankful that my feet are not tied to my stirrups as Henry's feet were. I am here under duress, but must be thankful for small mercies.'

'We have no plans that you should suffer discomfort during your stay here, my lord,' George Neville replied, full of recognisable clerical pomposity.

'Except that I am not free to make my greetings to the Countess and then depart.'

I did not know what questions to ask. Nothing was writ clear. It was our clerical visitor who made all terribly smooth for me.

'Let us go indoors before we entertain the servants to a greater degree.'

He patted my arm, which displeased me even more, but I kept silent.

'What has Warwick done?' I asked him, when the door was closed against eavesdroppers.

'There has been a battle, my dear Anne, at Edgecote. My brother Warwick is well. Earl Rivers is not. Nor is his son. Other notable Lancastrians, too, have paid for their poor advice to the King. My nephew Ned here will spend a few weeks with you.'

'What he has not said is that I am his prisoner,' Ned announced. The laughter had entirely dissipated, as had the youthfulness. 'As I said, I am brought here under duress and told that I will remain here at my cousin Warwick's pleasure, God damn him!'

'A prisoner, forsooth.' I swallowed, my throat suddenly dry. Here was the disaster I had been expecting, but how could I have foreseen that I must entertain the King, held captive under my own roof? Was this not treason?

'So I am led to understand. What do you think your husband will do? Depose me, lock me in the Tower with Henry, and make my brother Clarence King? That would be a coup for your family. How valuable that marriage has proved to be, the marriage that I expressly forbade. Your daughter Queen of England, and I still alive. Or perhaps my lord of Warwick might even arrange for me a quick death.'

I knew nothing of these presumptions but would not admit to it. Nor could I admit that Ned's reading of the situation might be more than accurate. So Rivers was dead, as well as his son. Richard had taken vengeance indeed.

'How can you think such a thing,' I replied, as cool and calm as any woman welcoming a guest. 'You are right welcome here, whatever the circumstances, and your life is under no threat. I will ensure your comfort. I doubt it will be for long.'

While I prayed that it would not be.

The Archbishop beamed. 'You will be safe enough here, my lord. You will be well guarded.'

'From whom? The only enemy I see is the one who owns this castle. And the only reason I will be well guarded is so that I cannot escape.'

Leaving Ned to a platter of bread and cold meat and a cup of ale, since his appetite was in no way diminished by his capture, the door remaining guarded to prevent any attempt at escape, which to me appeared ridiculous, I demanded some information from George Neville.

'What are Richard's plans?'

'I don't rightly know,' he admitted. 'My orders were simply to keep him under surveillance.'

'And where might your brother of Warwick be?'

'I think he will not be long in coming to collect his prisoner.'

'I hope to God he does. I like not having a king incarcerated under my roof.'

And indeed it was not for long. Richard arrived to take our reluctant guest to Middleham. This proved to be a brief stop on what appeared to be yet another campaign to stop the country falling into insurrection. He would be gone by the next day, taking Ned with him.

'What in God's name are you doing?' I demanded, *sotto voce*. It would not do for the household to hear their lord and lady at loggerheads, although it would not be for the first time.

'Making our own position secure. It will be safer to have him in the North.' His smile was cynical and without warmth. 'Has he been good company?'

'Remarkably, in the circumstances, since he fears that you will plot his death and hand his crown to Clarence.' I could not prevent my exasperation showing in my tone, in spite of my determination to keep the peace. 'Is it true that you caused the death of Rivers and his son?'

'Yes. They have been duly executed. Rivers was a threat to my own position in this realm. Was it not essential to stop this constant whittling away of my authority? I must accept the Queen, but I don't have to accept and bow the knee to her endless family.'

'What will you do with Ned? Kill him too?'

'It is not yet my plan, even if you think it might be.'

'I think I might no longer know you!'

A flare of temper that ended any further discourse.

The final meal together was uncomfortable with long silences.

'Where is my lord of Clarence?' Isabel asked at one point between the perpetual appearance of courses that dragged the meal from one hour to the next.

'In London,' Richard replied. 'He sends you his loyal affection and his hopes that you will soon be together again.'

I did not believe it for a moment, but Isabel seemed pleased enough.

'Isabel is carrying his child,' I announced deliberately, to stir a reaction that was not made up of polite nothings. 'We should rejoice.'

'Some good news then,' Ned replied with praiseworthy composure. 'I offer you my best wishes.' He slid a glance to Richard. 'Is this child the future King of England if you have your way?'

'It is not my intention ...'

'Who can know what your intention might be, Cousin. I always thought that you were the one man in the realm that I could trust.'

Which ended all conversation between us.

When Richard departed early on the next morning, taking Ned and the Archbishop with him, my bed having remained cold, I offered an equally chilly farewell.

'I will inform you when the child is born. Unless you, too, are dead by then. What happens when you release Ned? Do you think you will return to being King and Counsellor? I would watch those brandishing daggers behind my back if I were you.'

'I always do. It is my intention to remain in the best of health and return to you.'

He did not offer me a farewell kiss, nor I to him.

'What is the issue between you and Ned?' I asked. 'Beside the fact that you have taken him prisoner.'

'A family matter. It need not concern you.'

'Duchess Cecily knew of it. At the wedding. She was remarkably hostile towards you. She knew of some plot of which I am ignorant.'

'Yes, she did.'

'But you will not tell me.'

His features were hard, as if touched with frost.

'I will tell you when it becomes necessary.'

There was really no good to come of this.

Nor was there. Richard's allies began to desert him. To deal with the northern uprisings, since Richard did not have the ultimate authority to summon a major force, with trouble snapping at his heels from every direction, he was forced to release Ned from Middleham and allow him to resume his crown. How would they ever work together after this?

I began to pack our coffers for flight. I could see no other hope for us.

Sooner rather than later, I prayed, since Isabel was by now in a fragile state of pregnancy. We would, I presumed, take refuge in Calais once again. I did not think that Richard would ever consider claiming sanctuary at the Court of King Louis, nor would the Duke of Burgundy welcome us into his dominions. Calais it must be.

As for the family matter with which I was not cognisant, nor was likely to be in the near future, it seemed to me that I was hemmed in by a conspiracy of silence.

Which did not trouble me overmuch until, at the turn of the year, there came an unexpected visit to Warwick Castle from Duchess Cecily, travelling in a blue-and-white cushioned litter, probably the same one in which she had travelled to welcome the newly returned Duke of York in better days, but still she came with all her customary arrogance. I helped her to alight.

'Do not tell me that you were just travelling nearby and decided to visit me,' I said, recalling the charged atmosphere at

Calais, even as I drew her into the warmth of my chamber where she might sit and recover from the journey.

'I would not insult your intelligence, my dear Anne.'

'Then enjoy our hospitality and unburden yourself.'

She sipped the wine, but for a little while we sat in silence as if the Duchess was considering what to say. For the first time I thought that her comely face had been hardened by the passage of time. Then she sat up, straightened her shoulders, and turned her sharp eyes on me.

'Our families are at war. But we should not be.'

'Then there must be honesty between us, my lady. What was the issue at Calais when you were hardly in a celebratory mood, in spite of the travelling mummers? Did you consider your son's marriage to my daughter to be reckless?'

'Not as reckless as my son Edward's marriage to the Wydeville woman. Besides, Isabel is wealthy and my god-daughter. How could I object?'

'Yet something disturbed you. Something soured your mood. What has Richard done? Apart, that is, from raising arms against Ned.'

'There are rumours.'

'There are always rumours.'

'This one from the Milanese Ambassador in France. I suspect Warwick's hand in it. It usually is.'

I could not disagree. 'I imagine that Richard is planning on deposing Ned and making Clarence King, with Richard as his Chief Counsellor, of course.'

'Ha! If that were the whole of it!'

I raised my brow in silent query. What indeed had Richard done?

'To achieve the restoration of Warwick's power behind the throne,' Duchess Cecily explained concisely as if every word was drenched in poison, 'my name has been dragged though the marital mud. Ned, it seems, is not the son of my husband. He is a bastard, begot during an affair I had in Rouen with a common archer named Blaybourne, during my lord's absence. I can only imagine where that rumour began. Who has the most to gain from it? Clarence, of course, but I doubt he has the wit to concoct such an attack on marital fidelity without help. My nephew is the one who has become a polished proponent of propaganda. He smeared Margaret's young son readily enough. Now he has smeared mine. If Ned is illegitimate, he cannot be King. But Clarence can.'

Would I believe it? I swallowed a mouthful of wine. Of course I would.

'I can make no excuses for him.'

'Neither of us can.' She raised her chin so that her veils shivered. 'As for an archer called Blaybourne! Would I so demean myself?'

It made me smile, in spite of all the tragedy of this broken family.

'No, you would not.'

'It seems to me that we should hold fast to ties of family where we can. All is about to be smote even further asunder than it already is.' When Duchess Cecily became biblical, it meant she was much disturbed. 'I understand that Warwick has released my son and the crown is back on his wayward head.'

'So I understand.'

'He and Warwick will never work amicably together again.'

'No.' Any wish to smile had vanished. 'There is nothing we can do, is there?'

'No, nothing.' Duchess Cecily put down her cup with a distinct snap. 'Let us talk of happier things, of Isabel hopefully carrying a healthy son for Clarence. And where you will discover a match for your daughter Anne.'

We did our best, but the clash of temperament in the kingdom hovered over us. At least Duchess Cecily agreed to stay overnight before continuing to London. Although our conversation had had sharp moments, she had not felt the need to wipe the dust of Warwick Castle from the soles of her shoes. She left me with my hard-won peace all disturbed. Yes, I was certain that this harmful rumour would lie at Richard's feet. No good would come of this. Duchess Cecily looked as troubled as I when she gathered me into an unexpected embrace.

'Sometimes, my dear, grief is too hard to bear.'

'Sometimes it is impossible,' I agreed, 'and I see no end to it.

Nothing about this visit had encouraged me to believe that yet another flight to Calais did not hover over us. What would I say to Richard about this attack on his aunt's good name? I did not know. Nothing I could say would make any difference. Were we not already at odds?

# 23

## *French Exile and Family Tragedies, Spring 1470*

### Margaret, Queen of England

'Events may be turning in your direction, my dear cousin. Or at least holding out a fragile hand of hope.'

Louis enjoyed any opportunity to scrape at my weakness. I tried to forget his previous discourtesy, which was well-nigh impossible, but I now had a lifetime of compromise. Leaving the rural fastness of my borrowed chateau at his invitation I had taken up residence at the French Court at Angers, enjoying the luxury, urged to accept the offer by flocks of rumours that had swirled and settled like migrating birds. I could not afford to reject any offer that came my way. Even so I found it difficult to be gracious,

'The only manner in which they might turn in my direction is if the House of York is wiped from the face of the earth,' I replied. 'And I would prefer an invading army at my disposal rather than an empty hand.'

I was really in no mood for polite discourse. Louis continued to smile.

'Neither is possible yet, perhaps. But hear me, Cousin. I am in a position to inform you that there will never be a reuniting between Edward of York and the Earl of Warwick. Which is good news for you.'

'Warwick is no fool.' I might not like him, but I could never dismiss his political acumen. 'Warwick might see the need to heal the old friendship with the man he made King. They might be hand in glove again before the end of the year, while I malinger here. As for the situation that my lord Henry finds himself in, I cannot think of it. Is there nothing you can do to obtain his release?'

Louis shook his head and handed me his most recent missive.

'It is said that Warwick has abandoned Edward. It is said that Warwick is in flight from England.'

It did not seem to matter to me. Rumours were as strong as the aroma of the midden at the French Court in the heat of those summer months. Warwick's disaffection. The restoration of Edward of York to power. The return of my lord Henry to the Tower after the brief restoration of the King at Warwick's hand. And yet so harmful to the Yorkist cause was this nugget of news that I could not ignore it. Surely there would be an advantage for me in this unsettled state in England?

I worried over it, as a cat would worry over a particularly vicious rat that would not die.

Louis was pleased to tell me that Warwick had fled, leaving behind all he possessed. His son-in-law, the despicable and untrustworthy Clarence, was with him and all his family. Of course I knew where he would take refuge. I had first thought Ireland, where York had once taken up residence, but that would have no appeal for Warwick. His connections with Calais were strong as Captain of the garrison. He would land there and lick his wounds until he could see a way to return again. It would bring me no gain to have him in Calais. I needed allies in England, men who could lead an insurrection so that I and my son might return. I was becoming increasingly bitter, increasingly intolerant of Louis's refusal to give me ships and men to fight.

'Perhaps you should send out a courier to waylay the once-mighty Earl and invite him to negotiate with you,' Louis said with a malicious little twist of his lips. 'Warwick might be just the man you need to ease your return. If you are willing to reward him sufficiently for his efforts, of course. My astrologer suggests that this would be good policy for you.'

I stood, pushing back the cushioned chair with a grating of wood against the impressively flowered tiles.

'I will not. I will never do that. His name is engraved on my soul as my nemesis. He will always be so. I care not where he is or what he does.' I made no attempt to hide what was undoubtedly a sneer. 'Your astrologer offers false reading of the future.'

I stalked from the room. So they were in exile. I would not think of Warwick's fury at his ignominious expulsion, but Countess Anne did infiltrate my thoughts. She would be in exile too. She would know exactly what I was suffering. In a strange way it pleased me that I should not be alone in my isolation. I wished her well of her diminished life in Calais.

## Anne, Countess of Warwick

We were in flight. The wind howled and the waves were vast, tossing our vessel. Never had I made for the haven of Calais in such a storm, in all the years I had travelled and lived there. I huddled in our tiny cabin with Isabel and Anne, in a vessel not much larger than a merchantman. Richard had no need of us on deck and it was too dangerous. Anne clung to my hand. Isabel whimpered. She was close to her time and all I could pray was that we would make landfall before we were all stricken with catastrophe. This was no place to give birth, and not for a young girl bearing her first child.

'Talk to your sister,' I said to Anne.

I would struggle up to the deck, cloak and hood wrapped around me, and see if Calais was in our sights. I would try to be courteous to Richard, in spite of our recent clash over the dangers into which he had tipped us all when my relative peace at Warwick Castle had erupted into the cataclysm of a hasty departure. The northern rebellions that should have trapped Ned on his unexpected return from exile were crushed, which left us in immediate threat and precipitated a hasty visit from Richard.

'We are not safe here,' Richard had announced.

'So I understand.' I regarded the hasty arrangement for de-parture around us. 'When do we leave?'

We had done it before. At least we knew there was a safe harbour in Calais, a sanctuary where the girls and I would be secure until better times. Anxieties rumbled, although the practicalities swamped them.

'As soon as you can finish packing your coffers.'

He was preoccupied in sending out orders, my presence an irrelevance. I felt anger building inside me.

'How could you do this to us?' It was rare that I challenged him in this manner. 'You realise that Isabel must be near her time? I do not even know where she is. Not with her husband, that is clear.'

At last he looked at me.

'Clarence has sent Isabel to take refuge in the Bishop's Palace in Exeter. She is safe enough, but we cannot leave her there. She will fall into Ned's hands where she might become a useful pawn for him. We will collect her on our way to Southampton to pick up the *Trinity*. She and Clarence will come with us.'

The truth of it spared me any need to argue, but still I made my thoughts clear.

'Was this not always going to be the result?'

'Of what?'

'Of you issuing a challenge against Ned's sovereignty? Of you threatening what he saw as his birthright.'

'It was not his birthright. Without my support and military interventions he would never have ousted Henry and seized the crown in the first place. Our great magnates still saw Henry as the rightful King. Ned, young as he was, needed more than just a victory on the field at Mortimer's Cross. I thought I could hold on to power and keep Ned in exile in Burgundy, but with Burgundy's aid, Ned is back and keen to punish me for my disloyalties. You know this.'

'I do know it. I sometimes wish you would put your family before your personal ambitions.'

'Are they not one and the same?'

'On this occasion they are not. It shreds my belief that you can ask that question, when to drag Isabel across the country and the sea could be critical to the health of her and the child.'

'She will be safer with me than if she remains in England.'

There was no arguing with him.

'All I know is that I no longer recognise you.' I had said it before; it was becoming increasingly true. 'Your ambitions are out of hand, Richard. Could we not be satisfied with our lands and the loyalties of our affinity without challenging the King? Do we not risk losing everything we own? What value for us to be in Calais if we cannot return? I swear that Edward will never again look on you as a friend and adviser. If he condemns you as a traitor, our lands will be confiscated and we will be exiled for ever.'

Intemperately Richard dragged me aside from the busy servants where he could express himself without being overheard.

'What is there left for me in England, Anne? Ned has built up the Wydeville interest beyond all recognition, even with the death of Rivers and his son. What is there for a Neville? He listens to no one but the family of the Queen. I am banished to within the borders of my lands.'

'Once you would perhaps have been satisfied with that...'

Although I could not recall such a situation for many years.

'Once, I had not tasted power. Do I now live away from the centre of power after experiencing its glory? I was not born to retire and live out my life privately, supervising my estates. Am I not the most powerful, the most wealthy magnate in England? You have known me all my life. You know what I am. And yet you say that you no longer recognise what I have become. I would say that you know me very well. I will not have my hold on my lands challenged. Now, do you come with me, or do you remain here until Ned's troops march up to the door and demand admittance? Without doubt he is marching from York and is hunting me down. I cannot risk a battle.'

'If I said that is what I would do, that it is my greatest desire to remain at peace here in Warwick, would you leave me here? Isabel could join me.'

Richard huffed a breath. 'Of course I will not leave you here. I need to know that you are safe. And it is not safe for you to remain in England in the present circumstances. I cannot leave you here, Anne.' He scowled at me. 'Once, you would not have questioned coming with me.'

'Once, I did not have a daughter close to her time to consider.'

'She will be well enough. We will care for her.'

I caught his arm as he brushed past me to answer a hail from without. As sudden anger shattered my self-imposed restraint.

'But hear me, Richard. If aught happens to her, I will never forgive you.'

I did not think that he heard. Or if he did, he gave a good show of ignorance.

We fled south, all of us, leaving Richard's artillery train for safekeeping in Bristol, where he could recover it when events changed, he said.

'So you plan to return.'

'I will return,' he stated as if there was never a doubt of it.

Our conversations were brief and brusque, lacking in any warmth. Richard was driven and I was unforgiving.

I knew why Clarence was so firmly attached to Richard. If Richard could persuade England of Ned's illegitimacy, then Clarence was the heir, even if Ned eventually produced sons of his own. I had not challenged Richard over this. I had not even spoken of what I had learned from Duchess Cecily. What was the value of me creating even more division between us? There was enough bad blood without adding more rumour and bitter discord.

All I could do was set myself to flight and a successful escape, intent on the safety of my daughters.

It was not to be a smooth venture. We were repelled at Southampton, where Richard's new ship, the *Trinity*, was lost to us, but eventually, tired and travel-stained, we were forced on to Exeter where we collected Isabel and commandeered a new ship. At last we set sail out of Ned's reach for Calais. Although the seas were growing more and more threatening to our small craft, my mind settled as we came into sight of the harbour that I knew so well. The castle, the chambers that awaited us, gave me reassurance. Isabel would give birth to her child there, and Richard would open up negotiations once more with Ned, returned in triumph from exile. Surely my fears could not be realised, that Calais would be our home for ever, or at least as long as Richard could keep hold of it? The clouds on the horizon were as black as those in my mind. If he could not, we would be homeless, seeking refuge at some foreign court. The sea surged, a blustery wind shivered the sails.

Was this some terrible augury of disaster?

I hid my fears for the sake of the girls.

'We will soon be ashore. Don't worry, Isabel. Your child will be born in safety, in Calais.'

Isabel sighed wanly. I clasped her hands in mine while Anne brought a cup of warm wine for her, to still her anxieties.

'Could I not have found refuge at Warwick?' she asked, not reassured. 'Surely I would be safe there.'

'Your father says not. He thinks the King would starve you out.' I would be loyal to Richard whatever was in my heart, and probably he was right in his decisions. 'Nor could you have stayed at Exeter. It was too weak a refuge for you.'

In the act of donning my cloak to see how close we might be, my fingers stilled on the jewelled clasp, and my heart leapt in my throat. There was no doubting the sharp sound of cannon fire.

'Blessed Virgin! Protect us in our hour of need! Don't move from here unless your father sends for you.'

I left my daughters to discover Richard and Clarence on deck, leaning over the rail, peering through the gloom towards the shore. I joined them, staggering as the ship lifted and fell with the waves.

'Who fired that?'

'From Calais. A warning shot, it seems.'

Richard's expression was impossible to read as I went to stand beside him and saw a small boat being put to sea from the quay and being rowed towards us. I recognised the man on board from the livery of his servant. Reaching us, they climbed aboard. We did nothing to repel them. They were not the enemy, but Sir John Wenlock, well known to all of us and Richard's second-in-command in his absence. He bowed to me and to Richard.

'Well?' Richard demanded. 'Would you fire on me? You cannot refuse me entry to my own port.'

Seeing the anger brighten in his face, I closed my hands over the rail, white-knuckled with the dangerous tension of this meeting. If the tumultuous seas were not bad enough, this was an unlooked-for development. Wenlock replied in flat tones that suggested he might not approve, but he had no choice in the matter.

'I regret the need to refuse you permission to land, my lord.'

'Am I not Captain of Calais?'

Richard had to shout to make himself heard over the wind and waves.

'So you may be, but I have direct orders from the King, my lord. You are not permitted to enter.'

I saw Richard take a breath. 'And if I insist?'

'Our cannon will sink you.'

'God's blood man! I have my daughter here, about to give birth to the King's nephew. Here is the King's brother.' He flung out an arm to indicate Clarence, whose face was probably as stricken as my own.

'Still I cannot disobey, my lord. You must put in elsewhere. Not at Calais.'

Thus, so simply, our safe haven was denied to us. A sudden sharp wail from the cabin below, loud enough to be heard through the storm, took my mind from this.

'Isabel!'

I fled down to the cramped, airless cabin, to where my daughter had begun her labour to produce this child. Above my head I heard the noise of our reluctant guest leaving. Commanding Anne to once more clutch the hand of Isabel, I returned to the deck to accost Richard.

'It is as I feared,' I informed him. 'Isabel is in labour with this child. We should land.'

'Which is not possible.'

'What do we do? Fight out way in, or return to England?'

'Neither seems a viable option. There is an alternative.'

I knew what it was. There was only one.

'You consider taking refuge in France.'

'Of course. It has its complications. We will be at the mercy of Louis, whom we must beg for succour. Who knows what price he will demand?'

'Then I leave you to make your decision. I must return to Isabel.'

He stopped me, with genuine concern. 'How is she? Is she in any real danger?'

'Too soon to know. A first baby. It may be quick or dilatory.'

'Pray that it is a son,' Clarence said, his gaze still on Calais even though it was now beyond our reach.

'Pray instead that your wife survives the ordeal and the child is born in full health,' I said, no longer prepared to be polite. 'She should never have been put in this situation, as you both know. But then, when does a man consider the comforts of his womenfolk?'

I had no patience with either of them.

It became an essay in despair. Not all the holy relics tucked beneath the thin straw mattress, not all the talismans that I had brought with us for just such an eventuality, to place around Isabel's neck; not all the draughts of efficacious feverfew in warm wine could give my daughter ease from her fears or the pain, or aid her to bring the child alive into this world. He was born after hours of agony, although more quickly than I had feared. He was small, with wisps of dark hair when we cleaned away the blood, his skin bloodlessly pale in death. He had never drawn a breath.

'Can I see him? Let me hold him,' Isabel demanded as we bathed and cleansed her pain-racked body.

I wrapped the child in a fair cloth. There was no cry, no breath. No life. While Isabel wept over him, I signalled for my waiting woman to take the child away and wrap him securely for the journey onward. Then I went up on deck again. We were still anchored off Calais, but more ships had joined us, many of Richard's own under the command of his nephew Thomas Neville, who had come on board.

'At least I have some support,' Richard said with grim acceptance of the futility of it all. 'Wenlock has sent wine to give sustenance to Isabel.'

'She needs more than wine,' I said with no attempt to soften the blow. I was beyond that. 'The news is bad. The child is still-born.'

And I began to weep hot, angry tears. I could not stop them as they mixed with the rain and the salt-spray, my breathing short and painful. I wept for Isabel and the dead child. I wept for the emptiness of our exile and the loss of everything we knew and loved in England. I wept for the crushing of Richard's ambitions and his need to go cap in hand to the French King. I wept for the uncertainty of our future. I wept for myself, for my inability to save this one life that would have brought joy to Isabel.

Immediately Richard came to me, his temper pushed aside, and folded me in his arms, sheltering me from any prying gaze. I stood there in his embrace, rigid in grief and helpless anger.

'There was nothing we could do,' I said when at last the fit of weeping became no more than a sob. 'The child was a boy. He was perfect, but so small. You almost had a grandson.' And in a moment of absolute despair: 'I have failed in this too, to keep this child alive.'

Richard's arms tightened around me and I felt his lips warm against my forehead.

'I will not accept that. I know you could not have done more. You were given an impossible task, beyond the skills you have, beyond the skills of anyone faced with such a calamity. You saved Isabel, when she, too, might have died. She will bear more children to carry on the Neville line.'

I could not be soothed. Nothing could dispel the hopelessness that engulfed me.

'He was so small. He could not draw breath. What will become of us?'

'We go to France. I really have no choice. Is Isabel safe?'

'Yes. She is weak and fretful but will come to no harm.' I forced my distracted mind to return to what needed to be done. 'The child needs to be buried.'

'What better than a burial at sea? What do we call the child?'

'I think it must be George.'

'I regret the child's death,' Clarence said dutifully, but offering no other regret.

'So do we all.'

He did not ask to see Isabel.

Richard took over the ordering of the rest of that tragic day. 'We will put into the safety of the Seine, at Honfleur. But first, before we deal with Louis, we will take up the concerns of our own family. We will bury this child here at sea and consign him to the care of the Almighty.'

Our priest named the child and he was given the dignity of a burial in the stormy waters, wrapped in a Neville banner, the white saltire shining out against the red, the only suitable heraldic cloth we had to hand. I thought it appropriate enough. When Clarence lowered the tiny body into the surging grey of the waves, I was struck by the harsh grooves on Richard's face, from the loss, and from the decision he had been forced to make, throwing himself on the mercy of King Louis. After the prayers, when the child had been committed to God's care, I joined him at the rail, turning our backs on Calais as we set a course for the mouth of the Seine.

'I regret that our flight should have brought us to this,' he said. 'I remember that you said you would never forgive me if Isabel suffered.'

I sighed, recalling my words all too clearly, but he had taken the burden of my grief onto his own shoulders, and for that I must forgive. Even when he appeared to be ruthlessly lawless, he had a care for me.

'I should not have said that.'

'But you felt it in your heart.' He raised my chin so that he could read my face. 'Can you forgive me now that the child is dead? Or will this day for ever stand between us?'

'Nothing could have saved the child,' I admitted, accepting at last what had been inevitable, and for which Richard was not to blame. 'Even if he had been born on land and in the comfort of a bedchamber, his hold on life would have been tenuous. He was too small to live.'

'It would have been an easier birth for Isabel on land. If I had allowed it.'

'Perhaps.' I agreed with him, but I would forgive him. I did not need to say it. Richard knew. He always knew what my emotions were. I touched his face, barely visible in the dark shadows. 'All we can do is look forward. Will Louis receive us?' I asked.

'I doubt he will be enthusiastic.'

'But he will not turn us away,' I said.

'No. Louis will decide first how valuable I might be to him.' He flexed his shoulders, as if casting off the sad events of the last hours, looking ahead to decide how valuable our stay in France might be for us. 'And until we know for sure, we will use Honfleur as a base for some valuable raiding on Burgundian ships in the Channel.'

I should not have been surprised that he would turn it to his advantage. Of course he would. I returned below to give the news to our daughters and dry Isabel's incessant tears with encouraging advice, whether I believed it or not. But as we neared the mouth of the Seine, Richard summoned me on deck, drawing my arm through his, leading me to the prow.

'There is our refuge, our safety.'

I considered the placid waters of the river, the prosperous little towns along the banks.

'There we can stay, if Louis is in a mind to allow it. We can regroup and consider the future. Isabel will recover her health, and you your clear sight of what is due to our family.' He looked across at me, willing me to share his confidence. 'It will not be for ever.'

A little breeze ruffled his dark hair and my veils. It was soft and gentle, as was the touch of his fingers as he lifted my hand to his lips in a gracious salute.

'Are you content, my lady?'

So formal. I smiled at last.

'I am content.'

'And you are my entirely well-beloved, whatever the future holds for us.'

Words that soothed my heart-wrenching emotions, so that I clasped his hand before allowing him to escape and return to matters in hand. I must accept the turn of the Wheel of Fortune, for good or ill. Richard needed my support just as much as I needed his.

## Margaret, Queen of England

Would these recent events play into my hands after all? Everyone with an ear to gossip was quick to tell me of events in the Channel: the loss of the child, the failure of Warwick to take refuge in Calais, the problem of exactly where he might serve out his exile. I regretted the infant's death, as any mother would, but my thoughts were elsewhere. If that branded me hard-hearted then so be it. The choice of landfall for Warwick was of major interest to me, as was Louis's reaction if my enemy requested sanctuary in a French port. I must make it work for me if Warwick stepped within the circle of my present scheming.

'What will you do if Warwick lands in France?' I asked Louis. 'Calais has turned him away. Will you do the same, or do you invite him to make a base here?'

'I will welcome him, of course.'

Which was indubitably a lie. The accompanying glint in Louis's dark eye was sly. The last thing Louis wanted was Warwick setting foot on French soil. Warwick's presence would make difficulties in Louis's relations with either Burgundy or England. Better that Warwick return to England as quickly as might be. I knew that Louis would not promise him much aid. He did not have the money to fund an invasion to send Warwick home. And yet, would this not open wide a door for me, if Warwick could be drawn into my net?

'What is it that you wish for, Margaret?' he asked abruptly when I made no reply. 'Are you in need of an alliance with him?'

I appeared to consider. My reply was suitably ingenuous.

'Not with Warwick. It surprises me that you ask. I will never consider an alliance with Warwick.'

'I think that you might, and I will be fascinated to see how you manage it. He detests you as much as you detest him. On the other hand, Warwick has cut his ties with King Edward irrevocably. He might see the value in having your support to return.'

'Do you really think that Warwick will hop so easily from York to Lancaster?'

'Why not? If he has sense, he will. If it will suit his ambitions.'

I let a little pause develop again. 'He might see the value. I never will. Would I ever be willing to welcome Warwick into the Lancastrian fold? Do not ask it of me.'

But I would consider it. It was a fascinating possibility.

'I must consider the price the Earl of Warwick will have to pay for my friendship,' I said. I would take no immediate actions. I would wait and watch. I would not dance to Louis's tune, or Warwick's – or only if I had no alternative. I lifted my hands in open appeal.

'If I decide to speak with the Earl and come to some arrangement with him, would you help towards an invasion?'

'I will consider it.' He repeated my own words.

He was as sly as ever. But then, so could I be. I would not willingly open my mind to the probing of Louis's inquisitive fingers.


## Anne, Countess of Warwick

Coming on deck for some much-needed air, I walked into a fierce confrontation between Richard and the Duke of Clarence. The wind swept away some of Clarence's heated words, but I heard enough to keep my distance.

'I see what will happen: once in France, you will make an

alliance with Queen Margaret. You will agree to fight to restore her son to the throne.'

'You see more than I do.' Richard was trying to keep the exchange on an even keel. 'I have made no such agreement.'

'I can see it as clearly as that bank of cloud threatening yet more rain.' I feared that he would be in the right of it. 'You lured me with false promises,' he continued, his handsome features becoming obliterated as he became angrier by the minute.

'I made no promises, merely held out possibilities.'

Clarence shook his head, refusing to be placated. 'I was to become King of England in place of my brother.'

'It is still in my thoughts.' I watched as Richard's hand closed on Clarence's arm, to hold him still. 'But times have changed. You know that as well as I.'

'It is my right! You said that my brother Ned is illegitimate, which makes me King!'

'You have to accept what can and cannot be achieved.'

But Clarence, now far out of control, snatched his arm away from Richard's grip and raised his gloved hand in a fist as if he would strike Richard. I watched in horror, anchored to the distance I had taken from them. Would Clarence indeed strike? And would Richard allow so inappropriate a gesture from this angry young man? Clarence might be tempted beyond all good sense, even though it would achieve nothing but a further deterioration in relations. Richard was not a man to accept so physical a response.

Nor did he. With the swiftness of a hunting raptor, Richard grasped Clarence's wrist and held it hard, immobile, until Clarence's fist opened and he took a step back. Whereupon Richard, without a word of condemnation, released him.

'Forgive me,' Clarence managed to say.

'I will, but I advise you not to repeat it. My patience is not without end.'

Seeing me as a witness to this little episode, Clarence flung round and strode away across the deck, a petulant young man who had suddenly lost all vision of his future as King of England at the same time as he had lost control of his actions. Where would Clarence give his allegiance now, if he were fool enough to strike out at the one man who had promised him the throne? I did not trust him. In my heart in that moment I accepted that I never had trusted so self-centred a youth.

His removal gave me the opportunity to approach Richard and voice the new layer of anxiety that had wormed its way into my concerns.

'He could be a dangerous enemy,' I said, turning to watch Clarence lean against the rail, to look back towards England.

'I know it,' Richard admitted. 'He could become a treacherous weakness in our planning. What do I do? I see no value in an alliance with him, as things stand. I will not pretend otherwise. Surely you agree.'

'Of course, but it was a cruel dismissal, Richard. Perhaps you should not have encouraged him so blatantly in the first place. At least you did not strike back, but Clarence now sees himself as being robbed of a crown. Do you tell your daughter that she will never be Queen of England?'

Richard frowned. 'I would rather you tell her, but I suppose that I must. I think that she will find it hard to accept, but as a strong-willed Neville she will come to terms with it. As for Clarence, he will have to live with our new future. He is no longer of value since we are all about to become dependent on the intricate schemes of Louis and Margaret. They will never accept Clarence as the future King.' He stared at the figure of Clarence, who, his shoulders hunched, stood with his face turned deliberately away from us. 'You do not buy a hawk without trying it for flight first. I tried this hawk of Clarence and found it wanting. I'll not fly it in our campaign to return to England.'

When the captain of the vessel called, Richard left me to consider such a bleak reversal in our son-in-law's plans. Indeed, Richard had no choice but to paint the realities for him, but how viciously cruel truth could be. Where would it drive Clarence? I could imagine him kneeling at Ned's feet, petitioning forgiveness, begging to be restored to his brother's side in this never-ending war. We had doubtless created another enemy here, one that could no longer be managed and soothed. And even more terrifying in my thoughts. What would Clarence's possible *volte face* do to Isabel's loyalties? I could not bear the thought of losing my daughter if she chose Clarence over her own family. A cold numbness spread through my heart, forcing me to see the reality of it. After all our losses of the past few days, I could not prevent the slow beading of tears on my cheeks.

# 24

## *The Turmoil of French Exile, 1470*

**Anne, Countess of Warwick**

We took refuge in the Seine estuary on the first day of May, when the sun shone with warmth on our shoulders, the little waves dancing with silver light. Some would have said it was a good omen. Not I, nor Richard, whose cynicism had deepened with the years.

'Will Louis invite us to Court?' I asked.

We had been welcomed by the Admiral of France as Louis's representative, but there had been no invitation to visit with Louis.

'I think not.' Richard displayed remarkable sangfroid about the situation. 'Louis is bound by a treaty not to help the enemies of the Duke of Burgundy. Capturing Burgundy's ships makes me just such an enemy.'

Only too true. Richard's fleet of ships had been quick to attack and board any Burgundian ships that had crossed our path. But with no one to deny us, we landed and took up residence in the town of Valognes in Normandy where we received a courier. Louis suggested that it would be best if Richard departed, perhaps to the Channel Isles, out of Burgundy's sight.

'Better for whom?' I asked when the courier had gone, with Richard's weasel words of acceptance of the advice.

'For Louis. He will not meet with me publicly. I am too dangerous a guest.'

'Surely we do not have to move on again.'

'I did not say that. We will remain here where I can plan an invasion of England. Keeping this foothold on French soil will commit Louis to some sort of action. I doubt he will drive us into the sea.' He regarded me across the sparely furnished chamber in the little fortress where we had taken residence. 'What do you think he will do, my percipient wife?'

I did not have to think for long. 'I think he might just drive us into the sea.'

But Richard did not agree. 'He'll not waste money on such a campaign. He'll have other plans in his devious mind.'

'Which are?'

'I'll not talk of them yet.'

'I can only trust that you have read him correctly.'

We were traitors now in England, where we might forfeit our lives if we were ever foolhardy enough to return. All our lands and possessions were lost to us. If we did not return, as we well knew, a life of privation and charity in exile faced us, lurking on the edge of the French Court. Much as Margaret, once Queen of England, was living on the charity of Louis. Meanwhile Clarence was restless and ill-tempered, Isabel still prone to bouts of tears and Anne impatient at being ordered to keep her sister in a good mood. Richard was plotting while I . . . I tried to preserve a tolerant façade when all beneath were layers of despair and desolation.

Yet Louis did not drive us away, whatever plan he had for us. A sense of chivalry prevailed. After a month's silence and inactivity, on the eighth day of June we were invited to visit with him at his Chateau of Amboise.

'We are honoured,' I remarked sharply. 'Do we all travel there? What changed his mind?'

'As I said –' Richard appeared astonishingly complacent '– he has a plan.'

'And I presume so do you.'

I knew it. I knew exactly what his plan would be. There was no future to be gained in reconciliation with the Yorkists, so it had to be Lancaster: an alliance with Margaret.

'My enemy's enemy is my friend, someone said,' was the only comment I was prepared to make.

What would be in store for us now?

I would have liked a conversation with Margaret. Was she to be part of this scheme? I kept my own counsel. At Amboise I suspected that all would be revealed, but whether we would appreciate the revelation was a precarious matter. We were dependent on Louis's good will whether we liked it or not. And what role would a vengeful Margaret have to play?

I did not like the prospect of the price that either would demand we suffer in atonement for our support of York. Had we not paid enough already in these past weeks?

## Margaret, Queen of England

I had expected this. A private letter from Louis, not announced by a courier or herald. While I remained in Angers, Louis was entertaining my enemy at Amboise. By my own choice, I would not be one of the number to welcome him. But here was a letter of intent from Louis, which perhaps it would be unwise for me to ignore.

*It would be an advantage to you, Cousin, if you came to Amboise. A discussion with the Earl of Warwick might aid your return to England and the reclamation of a crown that rightly belongs to your son.*

*I know your thoughts on this, or I believe that I do.*

*Do not waste time in thinking, or making excuses, but come.*

I read it through a second time.

'What is it?' the Prince asked, leaning over my shoulder as I sat at my desk, writing to those English lords who would welcome us back. I handed it over. His survey was more rapid than mine had been, but he was still young and saw no further than the mention of his own situation.

'Do we go? Do we go today?'

'Eventually, perhaps we will, but not yet. Not today.'

I would not commit myself. I was still reluctant to dance to anyone's tune other than my own. Neither the piping of King Louis nor the demands of the Earl of Warwick stirred my feet beyond each carefully plotted step.

I burned the letter. There was no need to keep it. Or to reply.

King Louis and the Earl of Warwick could wait.

## Anne, Countess of Warwick

We were welcomed to the mighty Chateau of Amboise with much attention, being feasted as if friends of long-standing. We ate with Louis and his wife, Charlotte of Savoy, who had obviously been instructed to smile on the womenfolk in the party and engage us in trivial conversation while Louis and Richard broached the more serious concerns. I kept more than half an ear on their exchange of political views, and the rest on Queen

Charlotte's never-ending opinions on the tapestries and the culinary expertise at the French Court. It took much concentration on my part but was of inestimable value in keeping me abreast of what Richard might be thinking.

'What are your thoughts of the future, my lord?' Louis launched into the questions with the first course, at his most urbane as he ate his way through a dish of broiled venison in a rich pepper sauce.

'To return to England and take back what is mine.'

'It may be more difficult than you expect.'

'I do not presume that it will be easy, Your Grace.' Richard put down his knife and raised his cup in a silent toast to the King. 'It will be a campaign that requires much careful strategy. King Edward will have tightened his grip on the country in my absence. I still have loyal henchmen there, of course. My brother will call out his forces in the North.'

Louis ate a spoonful of pike in galentyne. Then another. And then here was what we had expected. He placed the spoon gently in his dish.

'I have in mind an alliance for you, my lord.'

'Indeed.'

'It may not be quite palatable to you.'

'Do I guess, Your Grace?'

'No need for guesswork for those as politically astute as you, my lord Warwick. An alliance between you and the Queen of England, my cousin Margaret that is, would be of advantage to both of you at this difficult juncture.'

Richard kept his countenance perfectly serene; once more he raised his cup to his lips and sipped the rich wine from Bordeaux as the second course was brought in, in vast array. I knew that he had no interest in the food.

'There has been no possibility of an alliance in the past,' he observed. 'Why should it be any different now?'

'In the past the two of you have not both been forced to suffer exile at one and the same time.'

'In the past we have been enemies. Are we not still adversaries?'

'Times change, my lord.'

While I ate a fried fig pastry, then admired the vibrant Flemish tapestries that told the mystical tale of the Lady and the Unicorn, pointed out to me by Queen Charlotte, Richard sat in silence, then said, as I knew he would:

'Tell me what you envisage, Your Grace.'

'That you agree to work together to restore King Henry to his kingship. Any plans to make the Duke of Clarence King in his brother's stead should be abandoned.'

Upon which I, too, abandoned any true appreciation of the Lady and her strange horned companion as well as a cherry pottage that had arrived before me. This was becoming a discussion of some political danger. Louis inclined his head in a breath of courtesy towards Clarence. I turned in my chair to give them my full attention, leaving Queen Charlotte to discuss with Isabel the French predilection for trailing skirts and unwieldy hennins. Clarence was sitting, struck dumb, none too pleased that the discussion continued around him. For what had been said in so many words: his hopes of the crown of England at Richard's hands had just been dealt a final death blow.

'And what does the Queen have to say, Your Grace?' I asked, before Richard could. 'Is she in agreement with this proposed alliance?'

'Do you suspect that she will not snap it up with both hands, my lady?' Louis did not wait for my reply, which was as well since I was unsure. Margaret would detest such a need, but she was just as politically astute as Richard. 'Although we have yet

THE QUEEN AND THE COUNTESS

to discover her true thoughts. I have asked her to come here to Amboise. All will be laid out in the open for your joint perusal.'

'And has she yet arrived?' Richard asked, as if expecting the Queen to emerge from the shadows.

'Not yet. The inclement weather was an excuse, although it is still high summer.'

'When she does, then we will discuss the possibilities,' Richard agreed, all amiability. 'If she does not, if she will not consider an alliance with me, as her arch enemy, then I will arrange my own return. A rising in the North under my brother's hand will occupy King Edward while Clarence and I return and muster our troops. Until any agreement is made with Lancaster, I would say that the Duke of Clarence has a fair claim on the English throne.'

I looked down into the dregs of my cup. Here was Richard as devious as Louis. I knew Richard's mind. He would return to England by whatever means presented themselves. And if it was Margaret's hand in his, then he would grit his teeth and do it. I glanced at Clarence, who had continued to sit silently through this discussion.

What was he thinking? He would desire to return as heartily as Richard did. And would doubtless take Isabel with him. I suspected that she would be more than willing to accompany him. Another uncertain development for me to worry over.


## Margaret, Queen of England

Another letter from Louis, as I would have expected.

> I would be pleased, my dear cousin, if you would come soon to my Court.

*It is becoming a matter of urgency.*

*The Earl is here but sees a need to make a swift return to England. If you linger in Angers you may be too late to make an alliance with him.*

*I may make a decision without you.*

Which he was perfectly capable of doing. And I might not like the result.

I considered the fear that had lodged like a stone beneath my heart. If I engaged in an alliance with Warwick, might I not be guilty of alienating some of my own Lancastrian support, men who blamed Warwick for the deposition of Henry? Without doubt, some, such as Somerset and Exeter, preferred an alliance with Duke Charles of Burgundy, which I considered untenable.

I must do what was best for my lord Henry and for my son.

I liked neither prospect.

Meanwhile I must turn my thought to my son, now approaching his seventeenth year. His education must not be neglected even though we might be in exile and my thoughts preoccupied. He must still become proficient in all the skills essential for a king of renown, which he would undoubtedly become.

It was not always an easy task, as even I had to admit. Sir John Fortescue, his tutor, was waiting for me next morning when I emerged from the chapel after the service of Lauds. He looked ill at ease, his frown severe enough that my heart quickened its beat. I indicated that he should walk beside me since it was clear that he needed to unburden himself to me.

'What is it, Sir John?'

'The Prince, my lady.'

'Is he in good health this morning.'

I had already been aware, to my annoyance, that he had not been in the chapel for Lauds.

'Undoubtedly. But I think that you should see.'

I raised my brows in query. It seemed that I had been neglecting my son.

'Does he no longer listen to your advice?'

'The Prince has moments when overweening pride governs his words and his actions, my lady.'

I sensed the problem. It would not be the first time.

'Has he been riding his new stallion into the ground again?'

'I fear so.'

My son had just returned to the stable-yard when we arrived. Abandoned, his horse, a fine bright bay with dark mane and tail, stood with its head lowered in sweat-stained exhaustion, sides riven with spurs and bleeding. As for my son, he had a sword in hand and, with the flat of it, was belabouring the well-born youths who had been appointed to bear him company when out hunting. I heard his cries of victory when they turned and ran from him. They would not dare hurt him of course in retaliation. They had been warned of his importance.

'Edward!' I had to call twice to bring him to heel. 'My lord Edward!'

He loped over towards me, face alight, eyes as sparkling as precious gems, hair in dusty disarray.

'Did you see, *Maman*? They ran away. What cowards they are.'

'I saw very well. I also see that your horse has suffered from your riding of him. Are you responsible? I think you cannot deny it?'

I allowed my eyes to move slowly down from his face to the bloodied spurs on his heels, daring him to make an excuse. He did not even try.

'Yes, *Maman*. I must learn to spur my horse on, for when I

am King. When I lead my troops into battle, I must be at the front of the charge.'

'So you must, my son.' In spite of my pride in him, I made my disfavour clear. This was no way for a prince to behave. 'You must also have a care for your mount. It will not do for you to damage him or cause him to disobey you.' I took hold of my son's arm to draw him closer. 'Nor must you attack your companions unless you are taking part in a tourney. They cannot retaliate because you are an English prince. You must treat them with respect. Do you understand me?'

His frown mirrored mine.

'But I am more skilful with a sword than they are.'

'That was not skill, my son. That was brute force since they were unarmed, and so unworthy of you.'

Edward's frown became a scowl; he was unwilling to admit it.

'You must learn courtesy and respect,' I said. 'You must learn the good manners of chivalry. It is not worthy of you to treat those who would be your loyal friends with coarse manhandling. A king would not do so. Do you understand me?'

The scowl gradually faded as he accepted the truth of what he had already seen in his short life.

'Yes, *Maman*. I should have done better.'

I nodded, pleased with the response. 'Now take that horse into the stable and see to the wounds. There will be an ostler to help. Repair the damage you have done in your ride. I will come and inspect your handiwork later. Give me the sword.' And when he did, although reluctantly: 'Why are you not at your lessons?'

'Because I must practise my military skills. My duty as a future king is to fight the battles for his subjects.'

'But you must also know the law and be able to judge them rightly. You need to study your lessons too.'

'Of course. Forgive me for my neglect.' He bowed to Sir John. 'I will come to you when I have tended my horse.'

'Good,' I said. 'You have learned that lesson well. We will continue this discussion at supper.'

'Yes, *Maman*. And we will talk of the law.' He looked back as he prepared to run off. 'May I take the sword and clean it? I promise I will take care of my horse first.'

'And tomorrow you will kneel with me in the chapel at Lauds.'

His face fell. 'Of course, *Maman*. I have been remiss.'

I handed over the sword with a nod of acceptance. How different he was from his father, so full of energy and visions of military zeal. I looked at Sir John.

'Well?' I asked when we were left alone.

'He talks of nothing but cutting off heads and making war, my lady.'

'As he will have to do.'

'But he must not neglect his books, absconding at every opportunity.'

'I agree. I will speak with him again.' I smiled. 'Between us we should be able to create an exceptional king when the day comes.'

I returned to my chamber, not a little troubled by Sir John's words. The executions after the Battle of St Albans had had a lasting effect on him. Perhaps he had been too young for me to put the power of life or death in his hands, even though the House of Lancaster might just depend on his warlike attributes. I could not be too hard on him, but I would not tolerate such thoughtless cruelty to his horse.

Now I must face Louis.

In a sudden blaze of temper at the challenges that faced me, not least my son, I raised my hand and swept the silver cups and the intricately painted slipware dishes from the table in my chamber. A horrified satisfaction swept through me as the dishes smashed on the tiles. But that was short-lived as I regarded the devastation. Now I regretted my loss of control, acknowledging that any success in the future would depend on iron-clad will-power, not foolish destruction. Besides, it was my own loss, for I had long admired the little plates decorated in yellow ochre birds and blossoms. I signalled to one of the servants to clear up the debris, leaving the room to avoid her condemnation of so unworthy a gesture on my part. I had been quick to take my son to task. I should have known better than to indulge in such a display of unwarranted passion.

Next day I set off to Amboise, taking the Prince with me, determined to teach him, and myself, some stern lessons in statesmanship. But I might just be prepared to come to an agreement of sorts with Warwick. If it enabled me to return to England, I might be prepared to make a pact with the Devil himself.

## Anne, Countess of Warwick

Margaret, we were told, had arrived at last at Louis's Court on the twenty-ninth day of June, to begin negotiations. Richard was not there, a decision quite deliberately made on Louis's part. Louis, we understood, had agreed to act as go-between, which some might say was an impossible task, but perhaps worthy of admiration, if Richard was not present until Margaret had shown some softening in her hostility. Margaret did not trust Richard; Richard did not trust her. Neither trusted Louis not to act out of self-interest, and all might rest on the advice given by his astrologer. There was no meeting point between the three of them and the reading of the stars could cast all into doubt. The vision of our permanent exile in this small town of Valognes grew more and more vivid in my mind and I hated it.

Clarence was kept out of any discussions. What could he add to them? He prowled the town and the rooms of the small chateau in growing dissatisfaction, threatening to return alone to England.

And then came a change.

Richard was summoned to the Chateau of Angers to meet personally with the Queen. I travelled with him.

'Do we know what is being offered?'

'I cannot imagine,' Richard admitted but looked relatively more cheerful than of late. 'Louis is keeping his cards close to his chest. I anticipate a long discussion with many hard words.' He paused. 'And at the end of it, a hard-won victory. I will not be beaten by a woman's whims. There can be only one outcome, for both of us,' he admitted finally. 'If we are to launch an invasion of England, Margaret and I must join hands in agreement, however distasteful we may find it.'

'Which might be your opinion,' I added as the towers of Angers came into view, 'but will Margaret be at all willing? And what will be my role in this clash of temperament?'

Richard awarded me a speculative glance. 'When I am exhausted from Queen Margaret's recalcitrance and Louis's cunning, when I can barely keep a civil tongue in my head, it will be your task to continue to smile and smooth out the burgeoning enmity, as if a Lancaster–Neville alliance is the one thing on earth that we both wish for.'

'Am I capable of such a miracle?'

'You may be our only hope.'

There was no answer to that.

# 25

## *The Cathedral of Angers,*
## *25th July 1470*

**Margaret, Queen of England**

'Is it at all possible for me to trust you to keep the agreement that we have just made?' I demanded of my French cousin.

Louis looked weary, the lines beside his long nose deep-etched as if he lacked sleep, but even in weariness, he was not to be trusted. Perhaps his astrologer had been delivering warnings.

'Of course. I do not break my word,' he replied. 'I can only offer prayers that neither will you.'

The negotiations were over. Fifteen days of hard discussion and disagreement, with Louis attempting to hammer out all sharp edges. Under pressure I had agreed to this meeting in the great cathedral at Angers, on this the twenty-fifth day of July. I would make this alliance with my enemy because I could see no alternative, however much I despised the necessity. The Earl of Warwick would invade England in the name of the House of Lancaster, rescue my lord Henry and take back the throne for him and our son. But before I would willingly place my name on this heavy document there were terms.

I would make them as stringent as I could. I would not sign easily.

Candles were being lit on all sides of the nave and chancel to illuminate what we had come to witness here before the high altar. The arrogant and proud Earl of Warwick had already been informed of what was demanded of him. I would destroy his pride. I would cut his arrogance off at the knees. And God would bear witness to what we would do here today.

There would be no retreat for Warwick.

Would there be for me? I would contrive a possibility of taking back control of this agreement that we would make, if affairs did not go to my liking. I must keep control. For at the heart of it all? I had agreed to an alliance, a marriage settlement between my glorious son, Prince Edward, and the younger Neville daughter Anne, even though I could barely tolerate the thought of such a union with the family of the Earl of Warwick.

'We could have done better,' I complained to Louis, who had furthered this marriage. 'Had I not offered to take the Scottish Princess Mary as the wife for my son?'

'And nothing came of that, my dear cousin.'

I slid a glance in Louis's direction. 'Do you not know? The Yorkist usurper, King Edward as he claims to be, has offered his daughter Princess Elizabeth as my son's bride, in an attempt to win my acceptance of his robbery of our crown.'

'Could you even consider it? And don't begin to think of foreign princesses, dear cousin. Anne Neville is a bride too important to reject.'

I sighed and held his gaze.

'I have no choice, do I?'

'None to my mind. She is well born. She is an heiress. She will bring you the Neville alliance.'

I knew in my heart the value of what I was prepared to do. Such a marriage would tie Warwick to our campaign as no other could. His daughter as Queen of England? How could he refuse? I might detest the plan, but it would win for me a leader to rally my supporters in England, once they had decided that they could trust him. They would accept him, of course, with my banners behind him. As for the alliance itself, Prince Edward at seventeen years was of an age to wed. Anne Neville was not whom I would have chosen as a bride for him, but with a wife who might hopefully soon be pregnant, the Prince would win hearts and minds of any who were still unsure of supporting Lancaster. She was fourteen years old, thus old enough to become a bride in more than name. She was not uncomely. Neither love nor affection was to be considered in such a marriage. Prince Edward was my chief diplomatic strength on which to wager, the King in this dangerous game of chess. A grandchild would strengthen my hand.

Louis was very persuasive.

'Can you see a better means of returning to England? You need this alliance, Margaret. You'll get no better.'

'I agree with you,' I admitted in the end.

'You amaze me, that we have a level of agreement at last.'

I smiled thinly. I would not tell Louis all my plans. I would never chain my son to a marriage that was of no value to him. There were ways of annulling an unwanted marriage.

## Anne, Countess of Warwick

It was done. Louis had forced Margaret's objections into some form of submission, while Richard had swallowed his pride to accept the agreement with Margaret. What would it mean for me? My daughter would be Queen. One day we would return to

England and reclaim what was ours in lands and titles. It was a strong argument, but what a price Richard had to pay!

She kept him waiting for her agreement, demanding that he submit himself to an apology for all his past actions of hostility against her. Even more vindictive was her decision to keep him on his knees for so long that some of the candles around us guttered and had to be replaced. The ignominy. The humiliation of it for a man as proud as the Earl of Warwick. But that of course was why she insisted.

At first I was unsure that he would comply. But what choice did he have? We needed the Prince to gather the Lancastrian support to his cause. Without it, Richard could not even consider an invasion.

Margaret's expression was sternly immobile, her face a study of bland acceptance, masking the hatred and distrust. It choked me as Richard simply knelt, spine straight, one hand on his sword hilt, awaiting her sign of recognition that he might rise to his feet. I was merely an onlooker, but it hurt me too.

Oh, we waited. Did she not find pleasure in it? Then a sign. A lift of her regal hand, whereupon Richard stood and bowed his acceptance.

Was I able to smile my approval throughout? Oh, I did, as if I were a painted and mindless poppet as the ceremony continued. Prince Edward and Anne, neither present here with us, were officially betrothed by proxy. We were all now committed to this alliance.

I thought of my daughter just growing into womanhood. She would accept, as would the Prince. As Margaret and I had both entered into marriages arranged for us, I prayed it would bring happiness, or at least some measure of contentment. Happiness was not a pre-requisite of such marriages.

Richard and I had been fortunate, but I admitted to little hope for this union. For the Prince, this marriage would be simply a means towards a much-desired end. Although he was still young, I saw little gentleness in him for dealing with a new and youthful bride.

I considered the empty spaces around us, for there was no throng to witness what we did this day. What would this mean for Clarence? He had thrown in his lot with Richard, hoping for power, seeing none at the hands of his brother. If he had hoped to be restored to England as perhaps the next King under Richard's aegis, all his hopes were now shattered into sharp shards, to cut and wound. As I had feared, Clarence and Isabel were the casualties of these bitter politics. But Anne would be Queen of England. All Clarence would get was the title Duke of York. He had nothing now to gain from the Lancastrian campaign. I might consider it a bad decision from Richard, but Clarence's ship was not one to which we could tie ourselves. The question was what would Clarence do when he heard the news that this alliance was now signed and sealed. The crown that Clarence had for so many months desired as his own, he would now never wear.

The main actors in this play moved towards the altar, to the jewelled casket that contained fragments of the true cross. One by one they placed a hand there and swore an oath. Each would uphold the alliance made this day in Angers Cathedral.

I was cold and full of dread. I could see no holy aura around this setting, this agreement. All I saw was the possibility of it being smashed in two, by a sword on a battlefield.

I knew Richard's concerns without his telling me, although he had done so. We had lived together long enough that he would not keep it secret from me. Nor could I argue the case with him, for I was in agreement with his disquiet. Could he guarantee the restoration of his estates and power when Lancaster resumed the throne? Or would he be instantly rejected, once Margaret had what she most desired? Richard wanted the formal marriage ceremony of our daughter and the Prince as a precondition of his departure.

I feared that he was being used, but he saw it of benefit to him. During exile Margaret had become harder, lacking any finer feelings of soft compassion. I understood her fears and anxieties but there was none of the gentleness of a young girl left in her. I recalled some of our past conversations, our past letters, when we had found some element of agreement and even conciliation. There was no meeting of minds here now.

## Margaret, Queen of England

When I had thought that all was settled and we could now withdraw, when I could at last almost taste the triumph of my schemes on my tongue, the calm of the cathedral was rent by a harsh demand, undermining any possibility that all had been decided on.

'So far you have dictated the terms of this alliance, my lady. I have agreed to all you have asked. Now I, too, have a demand to make.'

It was Warwick, his back to the altar, outlined in the sunlit colours from the great east window, but with his face in shadow. I stood and looked at him, waiting. What demand could he possibly make at this stage in our alliance? Had he not agreed to my terms?

'It is my wish that Prince Edward accompany me in the campaign to retake King Henry's crown. It is important that your Lancastrian followers see their own figurehead at my side. He must sail with me.'

Should I not have expected it? My thoughts tumbled one over the other, all to the same conclusion. I would not accept Warwick's demand. I would not. I would not trust my son to Warwick. What if Warwick trampled all over our agreement as soon as his feet were on English soil? What if he made new terms with the Yorkists, to hand over my son as a prize of war? I could not even consider it. I would not send him to England with Warwick. We would not sail until the future was assured for us. To sail too soon was to make the Prince vulnerable to betrayal and perhaps death. I could not contemplate it.

I spoke, keeping my voice appropriate for this holy setting.

'The Prince will not sail with you. I do not give my permission. He will follow later when all is secure. Only then will he arrive to act as Regent for his father, King Henry.'

I realised what I was saying as the words came from my lips; the first time I had acknowledged in public that Henry was incapable of ruling. So be it. My son would shine as the new King's Regent.

'I will send Jasper Tudor with you, the Earl of Pembroke,' I continued, not wishing to stir up Warwick's antagonism again. 'And the Duke of Somerset. They will call on the Lancastrians to rally to your side. You do not yet need my son.' I would not hand myself over completely to the Earl of Warwick's devious strategies. 'I will not be persuaded.'

Warwick hunched a shoulder, his expression bleak.

'You will offer nothing in compromise? Will you then agree to this marriage taking place before I leave these shores? I think that you must, as a sign of your good will, if you expect me to invade in your name.'

No, he did not trust me. I could understand. Our signatures meant little compared with the lifetime of adversity and death that loomed over us.

'Very well.' Oh, it was a hard concession to make. 'They will wed before you leave.'

'An excellent thought,' Louis, come to hover at my side, added in relief. 'The young people will wed at my chateau at Amboise. We will celebrate this momentous coming together of two powerful families.'

It was agreed. Warwick did not like it but what choice did he have? I was satisfied. I would hold the whip hand here. My son would not sail at his side.

## Anne, Countess of Warwick

Richard and I remained in the cathedral when all had gone their disparate ways, to rejoice or bemoan what had been agreed. The shadows whispered round us. The distant sound of sandalled feet did not disturb us as one of the priests came to douse the candles. The few candles remaining on the altar spoke of the holy witness to what had been achieved.

'Are you satisfied?' I asked.

'Yes.' Richard's reply was immediate. 'God's blood! My knees will still feel the imprint of those cold stones when I am in my grave. Fifteen minutes, I swear, that she kept me waiting in abject degradation, admitting all my past sins against her. You will earn your exoneration in victory. Wasn't that what she demanded of me? It heats my Neville blood. Margaret and Louis between them are a formidable force. But it will work for us. I will make it work for us.'

'I know that you wanted the Prince to sail with you.'

'Of course she would refuse, but they must follow soon; moreover, I cannot wait for a lengthy time before the wedding. I must return to England before any more time elapses. If I can take Ned by surprise, it will be to my advantage.'

Oh, it was in my mind. What if we failed? But I could not think of failure.

Yet I did. If we failed, would Margaret try for an annulment of this marriage? She did not want it and if she gained nothing from it, I knew her well enough to know that she would seek a way out of what she would see as an entrapment for her son. Would it even be consummated? It would be so easy to gain an annulment from a marriage that was in name only, a papal dispensation in return for a purse of gold.

I dare not think of failure, because to do so would put Richard in danger.

He took my arm.

'Let us leave. My knees are sore. I would rather fight a battle than spend another day in treaty-making with Margaret.'

'Although you have to accept that she was driven by a need to protect her family.'

'And the power. God keep her from breaking her oath. If she does, I will be left high and dry.'

It was the first time that he had shown any overt anxiety for the future. It worried me far more than Margaret's possible failure to honour her promises. As we stepped down from the chancel to the nave, I was aware of a darker shadow amidst the many. It did not take great insight to know who it would be. I did not hesitate.

'Leave me here a little while. I think today's events need divine intercession.'

'But not too long. I have an invasion to plan, a battle to prepare for...'

He left me to face his nemesis.

We stood face to face, two women in exile. Two women for whom the future was obscured. Two women who saw no pleasure in what had been done on that day. For the first time since I had known her, Margaret seemed uncertain of her future path. It was I who broke the silence, and even then, it was not a statement to evoke acceptance of this uneasy alliance.

'I do not know what to say to you.'

'Nor I to you.'

There was no exchange of courteous titles here today.

'You are rarely without words,' I said.

'You are quick to make your thoughts known.'

A little silence, broken only by the soft flap of wings of some bird trapped high up in the darkness above our heads. I looked up. I, too, felt trapped. Perhaps so did Margaret. I shook my head. There was no room here for compassion or understanding. Richard and I had been drawn into this net of Lancaster weaving.

'This is not what you wanted, is it?' I asked, although it did not need to be a question.

'No. It is not.'

'Nor I. It is a precarious marriage for a young girl. Particularly when it is not a desired union.'

Queen Margaret stiffened, although I could not read her features, for she had approached from the shadows. 'It is not my intention to cause her harm.'

'Who is to know what awaits any of us in the future? Harm comes in many guises.'

Now she stepped forward so that I could see the grooves of

weariness beside her eyes, the indentations of what might be long-hidden despair.

'I wish your lord well in his campaign.'

'Of course.' The bitterness that had lived with me so long now all but overwhelmed me. I shivered. 'I am cold. What use in continuing this conversation? Your future depends on my lord's success.'

'His only hope of return is my support. I merely wanted to say that...'

'What did you want to say?' I asked when her words dried before she could utter them, but Margaret turned to walk away. Driven by the tumult of emotions within me, I stepped towards her and I touched her arm.

'I trust that you have not sent him to his death.'

'He would have gone anyway, with or without me.'

Which was probably the truth of it.

'Why did you return to talk to me?' I asked.

She shook her head. 'I do not know. Perhaps in recognition that we are both in a dangerous morass of events over which neither of us has control. Perhaps in recognition that tragedy for one or both of us may be the undesired outcome of this terrible strategy that we have agreed on today.' Surprising me, she held out her hand towards me, palm extended. When she spoke, it was as if the words hovered between us against her better judgement, yet she still had a need to speak them. 'Forgive me if I have caused damage to you. Once, I hoped that there could be an affinity between us. It was never possible, was it?'

Drawn against my will, I placed my palm against hers. How cold they both were, yet I was moved to speak with more honesty than I had ever intended.

'I regret that it should end like this.'

'As do I. I have no clarity in my vision of what will happen next. Mayhap we will both suffer loss and inconsolable grief.'

She walked away, the soft slide of her shoes on the tiles the only sound until it faded into silence. I was left amidst the smoking candles, but could find no words to offer up to God in petition. All was despair.

# 26

## *An Agonising Parting:*
## *Château d'Angers, Late Summer 1470*

**Anne, Countess of Warwick**

This would be our final farewell, here in the Chateau of Angers, before Richard left these relatively safe shores for England, to wage war. It was August and it might be many weeks, even months, before we were together again. We had much experience of such partings and knew to guard against too much emotion. What could be said that had not already been said between us throughout our wedded life together? Best to keep to the unstable situation here at the French Court, where our daughter Anne's future still hung in the balance, her proposed marriage still not actually solemnised before a priest.

Richard was writing while I sat silently at some distance from him. I watched the movement of his hand, the tilt of his chin, the frown between his brows. He was restless, unsettled, and not pleased with the unfolding events. I knew each gesture so well. Soon he would recall that I was sitting here, look up, and speak to me.

I folded my hands in my lap, resisting the urge to interweave my fingers together in utter terror of what might be the result of this invasion.

What if I never saw him again? What if he was drawn into a battle that proved fatal? What if... I could not consider it. It was too painful. I chided myself for foolish worries. Had he not always returned to me? The invasion would be a success, Richard would take power in the land, driving the Yorkist King Edward into exile. All the Warwick and Neville possessions would be restored to us and one day in the future our daughter Anne would be Queen of England, standing proudly beside the new Lancastrian King.

I frowned down at my lax hands. Richard had not won all his battles on land in the past. At sea he had a gift for bringing his enemy to its watery knees, but on land he had suffered reverses. I must not think of that. I must have made a movement because Richard looked up and across at me.

'What is it?'

'I don't like it,' I said. 'It may be an important marriage for our daughter but still I cannot like it. She is just another pawn in the game of the Lancastrian adherents. A game that Margaret still commands.'

His eyes sharpened with a glint of light from the window. 'Or are Margaret and her son merely pawns in my game?' Then he sighed a little as if there were matters he did not wish to contemplate. 'Or perhaps we are all mere ciphers in Louis's infernal plotting.' He cast down the pen, leaning back in the chair, pushing his fingers through his hair before flexing his shoulders. 'I will assuredly make it my campaign. Ultimately, once my feet are again on English soil, I am not answerable to either Margaret or the French King.'

I don't know you any more, I thought, but did not say it, as I had done once before. Yes, you have always been ambitious, but this is beyond anything I recognise. You will make enemies on all sides. You are driven, and will see no compromise. What use in my saying anything? You may not seek the crown for your own head, but you desire the power that goes with it.

He stretched out his hand to me and I went to stand with him, linking my fingers with his, aware that his ambition was creating an overwhelming tension in the room. Once our return to England would have been a bright dream for the future; now it seemed to me that the edges were dark, Richard's aura even darker. Now that his plan was about to be put into action, energy was almost visible around him, like a corona around a winter moon. Richard's battle gear had been packed by his squire, the documents, except the one letter that he had been writing, were in a leather bag, placed there by Richard himself. There was nothing more to do, to take up our time, to take up our thoughts, except to say farewell.

'Do you tell me that you are at ease with this alliance?' still I challenged him.

'No. It is a diabolical clasping of hands. But if we can get Prince Edward to the throne, it will be of supreme importance for our daughter. She will be Queen of England one day. And for us too. Because of Ned's perfidy we are landless and power-less. The Earl of Warwick must achieve his true recognition. Can we live here, in exile, forever, on the whim of Louis? We cannot. Nor would you wish it.'

My thoughts moved on to the next few weeks, whether I wished it or no.

'I don't like the prospect of your invading England, where there will be an inevitable clash with the King.'

'Which King? It won't be Henry. He is beyond clashing with anyone other than his priest.' A wry smile touched his mouth as Richard turned from me, folded the letter and fixed it with wax, impressing it with his seal from his ring. 'There is so much ant-agonism between us, here at Angers, so much lack of trust, not least with Louis. But the rewards could be great. And without this alliance with Margaret we might never be able to return. I do not have the resources alone. I do not have the support in England. But Margaret and her son have a claim to the loyalty of all those who are tainted with Lancastrian fervour. That will be to our advantage. You know that.'

'But do you trust her? Do you not think that Margaret will take the first opportunity to have this proposed marriage annulled? A papal dispensation will be sought, whatever cause she can find to step back from it.'

'Perhaps. But not until she has what she desires most. The crown restored for Henry.'

'Or for Edward, her adored and precocious son.'

'Our son-in-law, when eventually they make their vows. Which they will, even in my absence.' He handed the letter to me. 'Margaret needs me, and I can make myself indispensable. She cannot afford to antagonise me if she wishes to return to England. Her followers are not strong enough without my leadership. Thus this nasty alliance in the first place. Sometimes the most unpleasant bedfellows are necessary.'

'Like fleas, lice and bedbugs.'

'Ha! I will do my best to avoid those, though I doubt I'll have much success. One of the worst aspects of campaigning. Now I think I am ready.' Pushing back the chair, he stood, took my face between his hands and kissed me. 'Let us part in good heart. Don't let the poisonous atmosphere here at Angers come between us. We have enough enemies.'

'I will never be your enemy.'

What strange path of fate had brought us to this. From fervent supporters of the Yorkist cause and King Edward, to an ally of Queen Margaret, planning an invasion of England in her name. From shedding Lancastrian blood, to setting off to drain blood from the followers of York. The terrible submission of our lives to the Wheel of Fortune drove me to speak.

'I have to say this. I had promised myself that I would not show myself as a weak and ineffectual wife, but I will say it anyway. I don't want you to go.'

He drew a finger down my cheek, over my lips, as if to recall their shape.

'We have parted often enough with danger on our horizon. I have been in battles before. Why should we not come out of this with a victory? Are there not any number of stalwart allies to come to my banner in England? My brothers are to be relied on. Lord Fitzhugh will play his part in my planning. I think Ned does not have the strength of purpose that he once had.'

'He will when his crown is threatened. And yes, I fear for your safety. My fear is one of desperation.'

'And I am touched by your concern. It has not been an easy life for you.'

'I was never promised one.'

'It was a political marriage. Not one of love. But we have found a strong alliance together. I could not have chosen a better wife. I will never see you as weak and ineffectual. You have been my strength and my sanctuary. To whom should I return? To whom should I declare my loyalty for all time?' He took my hands in his, palm to palm, as if making a sacred vow. 'I have known you all my life. I cannot imagine living in England without you. You will return to me there and, with peace, we will settle into some sort of stability. If you need my promises, I promise you that.'

'A promise that I will accept with my whole heart. What do you need from me?'

'What I need now is for you to send me to England with

your blessing. I cannot bear your doubts when all around us is awry. Do you have that courage? Do you have that confidence in me, to send me off with an assurance of my victory? That is what I need.'

'Of course I will send you with my blessing, and my belief in your final victory. Be certain in my faith that you will prevail.' I hesitated but I had to say it. 'I do not trust Clarence.'

'Neither do I. It is my thought that he will rapidly come to terms with his brother.'

'You knew that would be the outcome. As soon as he saw that you would not strive to make him King in Ned's place. Could he not have been handled with more cunning?'

Richard shook his head. 'It was a decision I had to make, and Clarence was the one who had to pay the cost of it. We both knew that he would never accept being less than King. He will make terms with his brother as soon as we are returned to English soil. What will he ask in return? To become heir to the throne if Ned has no male heir? I think it is what he wants. Once he was satisfied in giving his loyalties to me. Our daughter's marriage to the Prince has changed all that. Clarence will not be an ally of mine. There is nothing in it for him. He will change his allegiance as fast as an arrow from an English archer's bow. Self-interest always drove him.'

'Poor Isabel. She does not speak to me of Clarence's ambitions. I think that she no longer trusts me.'

How it hurt my heart that such deep chasms had been created in our family by death and lack of trust.

'Will you travel with Margaret, when the time comes for you to join me?' he asked.

'It is not yet decided. I have no wish to be parted from Anne, but once she is wed, then I must live with the thought of her joining Margaret's household until she can establish one of her own. It seems that I will be parted from both our daughters. I promise that I will come as soon as I can, even if I must commission my own vessel.'

'There speaks my resilient wife.'

I held Richard's letter in my hand, knowing its content. It was his decision to place Anne in Margaret's keeping during his absence. Not in mine but in Margaret's. It hurt but I knew it to be the best decision if this marriage was ever to happen.

'It may all be over before you arrive,' Richard said. 'Ned driven out and Henry in possession of his crown once more with me at his shoulder. Pray for my victory.'

'Do I not every day? What do you do when you have dis-embarked?'

'Whatever is necessary.'

'Tell me. So that I might imagine it when you are far from me.'

He sat in a window seat, pulling me to sit beside him on the dusty cushions.

'I have already set it in motion. A rising in the North under Lord Fitzhugh to draw Ned's attention. While he is busy there, all I have to do is slip through the blockade on our ships in the Seine, and land on the South Coast. All I need then is good weather. Oxford and Pembroke will be with me and we will rouse the country in the name of King Henry the Sixth, hoping that thousands will flock to us. Meanwhile my brother Montagu will march down from the North. We can catch Ned between us, and take control of the country.'

All perfectly planned. Could anything go wrong?

'And then?'

'Force Ned to come to terms. If we cannot take a firm hold on him, he will flee. Whatever the result, we will re-crown Henry, which will immediately solidify Lancastrian support. There is one thing that you can do for me.' He took my hand and raised it to his lips. 'Will you do all in your power to persuade Margaret and the boy to sail to England as soon as possible? She and her son are the strength behind the cause. Without her we are weaker. I know she is reluctant, but perhaps you can wear her down. If the Prince is on English soil, it will provide us with the figurehead to replace hapless Henry. And if we can trust Louis to continue to give Margaret his money and his support, I see no reason why we should not secure a momentous victory.'

'And what of Elizabeth? What of the Queen?'

'Either she will flee with Ned or go into isolation, into sanctuary, in Westminster. I do not fear her, or her children. Nor do I feel vindictive towards her. She will be safe enough.'

All so reasoned and well considered. I could not sow any more seeds of doubt, such as the impossibility of trusting Louis to honour his promises. Or the difficulty of prising Margaret away from French soil before her son's inheritance was guaranteed in the shining gold of a throne and a crown. I would do what I could. And then, because I wanted to know the answer:

'Are you ever afraid?' I asked.

'Yes.'

Briefly, the line between his dark brows deepened, and I knew he would admit to me what he would admit to no one else.

'Yes, I am afraid. Not of battle or death. More of mishandling events, of the men under my command, as I did at the battle when we lost control of King Henry. Of failing to see what needs to be done, and doing it well. As I failed to do in that second battle at St Albans. That is what I fear. But that need not trouble you.'

We clasped hands and exchanged a kiss, lips to lips.

'I could not have asked for a better wife.'

'Nor I a better husband.' I pressed my forehead against his shoulder. 'Did you hope for a grand passion?'

'When I was very young, but age shows the advantage of a close friendship and a loving care.'

'You have always had that from me.' I sat up and delved into my embroidered purse. 'Before you go.'

I pinned a talisman to his breast. A bear and ragged staff based on the livery badges distributed to Richard's affinity. They were of pewter. This I had had made in Paris, in gold and bright enamel. The bear had ivory claws and a ruby eye.

'Do you believe in the power of a talisman?' he asked.

'Of course. It will keep you safe and bring you home to me.'

'I will value it beyond all my jewels. Except you, the brightest jewel of them all.'

He walked to the bed, from where he lifted his great sword, unwrapping it from the oiled linen so that the light flickered along its sharp edges with a baneful message of death. For a long moment he looked at it, running his finger over the gilded hilt and the cabochon-cut sapphire that glittered there, before strapping it to his belt. Then he turned and walked back to me, as if driven by some inner unease.

'If we don't meet again, Anne...'

I placed my fingers against his mouth to stop any such consideration, driven by fear that such a line of thought would ill-wish our future. He removed them and kissed my palm, then enclosed my hands between his own in intimate possession, his eyes searching my face as if for perhaps the first time in his life he needed my reassurance.

'What is it?' I asked, pressing our joined hands against his heart that beat so steadily, so firmly, as if it would beat for ever.

'It must be said, my dear Anne,' Richard said. 'If we don't meet again – through shipwreck, or battle, of even some dire fever that might strike either of us. There is no perfect ending. There are an infinite number of endings. *À Dieu*. God keep you and bring us together again at last.'

He left me staring at the empty room, remembering only how age had crept up on both of us. Richard's hair, once dark, had been threaded with grey. How many times had I sent him to war with my blessings and my prayers for his safety? I had learned to live with it because he had always returned. I trusted his good fortune. Never had I been overwhelmed with distress as I was now, the dread that Richard was facing a cataclysm that he could not control. All I could see was loss and sorrow, created by blood and carnage on a distant battlefield. The premonitions were dark and ominous. Did he see these premonitions too? The thought struck like an edged sword in my heart, and I could not bear it.

'Perhaps, once we begin to fight and struggle to demand what we see as our own,' I said into the emptiness, 'there are only sorrowful endings. How will I live until I know that he is safe and will be returned unharmed to me?'

I did not see him sail but remained at Angers. It would have done no good for either of us, only intensifying the pain of parting.

## Margaret, Queen of England

Every day I waited for news. Every courier was sent to me, whether he came from England or even from Burgundy. I could not escape my suspicions that, shrouded in silence, Louis was planning a disadvantageous Burgundian alliance.

'In God's name, can you not tell me? Do you not have even the slightest rumour of events in England?'

My constant demand of every herald or courier.

The reply was invariably no.

I was short on patience and hope. If Warwick could not pave the way for me and my son to return, I would destroy all pretence of this mockery of a marriage. My son would not wed the daughter of a man who could not fulfil his promises to me, a man who had proved himself to be my enemy time and time again, no matter what Louis advised. If Warwick could not guarantee a victory for us, if he could not rescue Henry from the Tower, then I would not risk all on a return. I would stand before the altar and forbid the marriage.

'Where is the Earl of Warwick?' I asked.

For all I knew he was still on the French coast, still waiting for the storms to abate to allow him to sail. The anxiety ate at me. This was the best chance we had, the only chance. And all hung on the ability of a man I had called my foe, and still did. Louis had been gracious enough to provide us with sixty ships and a capable French admiral. Surely Warwick could out-sail the English blockade and reach the coast of England?

But all depended on the storms that swept in from the West.

And what would Warwick achieve when he reached England?

I fretted, pacing my chambers, through the latter days of September, barring the Prince and his betrothed from my door. The Countess wisely made no attempt to approach it. I would have remained, shut away there, until Louis sent a message, taking issue with my ill temper. It was delivered by a servant repeating it word for word, his face inscrutable.

'From my lord the King of France. I am taking out a hunting party. Your son will come with me and so will you. And the Neville women. You cannot sit here and worry over something that cannot be changed. Get your women to dress you for the hunt and be in the courtyard in an hour. Do not try to think of an excuse.'

It would have been beneath my dignity to do so.

It was invigorating. I had forgotten the thrill, the exhilaration of the speed and excitement of the hunt. For those few hours when we rode with the hounds along the bank of the River Loire and into the woods, I pushed aside the concerns that plagued me, but on our return, they were waiting for me, hovering like a bad odour from uncleaned garderobes, waiting to engulf me once more. One of the many couriers approached, Louis waving him towards me with bland cynicism.

'Well?' I slid from my mount so that we were on a level. 'What of Warwick?'

I sensed the Countess pushing her mare towards me but ignored her.

'The Earl has sailed, Your Grace. We are told that he has landed in England. On the thirteenth day of September. We have the news that he had disembarked, with the Earls of Oxford and Pembroke.'

'Was he well received?'

All would hang on this.

'The Earl has raised the royal banner that you gave him, my lady, and has roused the country in the name of King Henry. I have no proof of it, but it is said that thousands are coming to support his banners.'

I clasped my hands together in prayer. I had to give praise where it was due. Warwick's invasion had been a mastermind of planning.

'Has he marched on London yet? Where is King Henry?'

'I know not. It is thought that the Earl will have reached London by the end of the week.'

'Does that satisfy you?' Louis asked, appearing at my side.

'It is good news.'

But I was not yet ready to take ship. I was not yet ready to risk my son on a chancy enterprise. It would need more than rumour that Warwick was marching to London to get me to take that risk.

# 27

## Slow Progress at Amboise, December 1470

**Anne, Countess of Warwick**

The news was good, as good as it could be in the circumstances, but Isabel fretted.

'We should go home,' she said, unable to settle to her needle-work or reading. 'I wish to return to my husband. I wish to return to England now.'

I struggled to maintain restraint in the face of her growing restlessness. Of course I understood her desire to go home.

'So do I wish to return to England,' I said calmly. 'Your father says not yet, not until it is safe. You must accept the dangers and be tolerant of them.'

'Will it ever be safe?' Isabel faced me in a sudden flare of temper. 'You cannot keep me here for ever against my will. I am a married woman and can make my own decisions to return to my husband, if it is my wish.'

I stopped setting the gold stitches in the edge of a veil that Anne would wear for her wedding.

'Of what value will it be for you to return now?' I asked gently. 'You will probably just get in the way of military matters.'

'But I am of no value here! My lord of Clarence has been

abandoned by my father and King Louis. I have no part to play in the outcome of this cruel game of crowns and kingdoms. Why should I not go?'

I had no answer to that. Her interpretation of the situation was superbly accurate.

'You could be captured on your journey, killed even by some misadventure.' I attempted persuasion in empty words. 'It would be ill-judged for you to even contemplate such a journey as things are. All I can advise is for you to be resigned to remaining here.'

'As you have been resigned?' she responded, her eyes suddenly alight with battle. 'What good has it done you, Mother, throughout your life? All those weeks and months when you have had no knowledge of where the Earl might be. Whether he be dead or alive. What good has it done you to be patient? Fortitude has got you nowhere other than being an abandoned wife.'

Isabel's reply was vitriolic. Where had she learned such a challenge to authority, such caustic language? I thought that I knew well enough, living in the shadow of Queen Margaret. I tried hard not to curl my fingers to the detriment of the fine veiling. Nothing would be gained from my allowing my temper to match Isabel's.

'It has been necessary for me to exert self-control, to concentrate on overseeing the household when your father has been absent. Sometimes that is all that is demanded of a woman.'

'Has it brought you happiness?'

It was a fiery arrow, loosed without warning. A body blow. I could not think of an answer that would not simply make matters worse.

'Why should you advise me towards patience? The Queen has

no patience,' Isabel added, as if I might mirror my behaviour on that of Margaret.

'And what has that brought her? In either happiness or satisfaction?' I replied, casting aside the veil as I stood, the needle that I had stabbed into the cloth glittering balefully. Temper rippled under my skin in spite of all my good intentions.

'It will bring her happiness if she wins the last battle.'

'And what if she does not win? Then we will all lose and be cast into abject darkness. Don't hold up Queen Margaret as an image for me to copy. I will not do it. And neither should you. I thought that I had raised you to follow the path of good sense.'

'It was not good sense to take me across the sea when I was near my time with my child.' Tears shimmered in my daughter's eyes. Although with true Neville fortitude she forbade them to fall, it was an experience that had not faded for her with time. 'That was not good sense. It was cruel. The child was lost to me. I can never forget that.'

My daughter Anne, entering the chamber on a rare visit from Margaret's household, merely added fuel to the flames.

'The Queen will not leave,' she announced, looking from me to Isabel, stooping to retrieve the veil and restore it to me.

'Which does not surprise any one of us,' snapped Isabel.

All rested of course with Margaret and her unpredictability.

'This marriage of her son to me eats at her,' Anne continued with a frown, settling on a cushioned stool, smoothing her damask skirts; a new addition to her wardrobe, I noticed, and costly, with panels embroidered with red roses. 'I think she did not wish it ever to happen. She has no liking for me. She would still look elsewhere for a bride for the Prince, from the high-born families of Europe. What is stopping my marriage happening now that Father is in England with an army? King Louis chides her frequently. Will not you speak with her?'

I might agree with my daughter, but there was no value in my adding my spoon to stir the pot. If Louis could not move Margaret, then there was no hope that I might.

'When the dispensation arrives, then you will be wed,' I assured her. 'We need it. You are related within the degrees of consanguinity. You share an ancestor in John of Gaunt.' I tried to remain hopeful, for my daughter's sake. 'The Queen cannot change her mind now.'

'The Queen can do exactly as she wishes!' Isabel marched from the room, with a final retort. 'As I will do. I reject your advice. I will return to England as soon as I can.'

I sighed a little. At least I need not fear a battle. Ned had fled to Burgundy, leaving Richard in control of events in England. All we needed now was Anne's problematical marriage to take place and for me to acquire a new royal son-in-law. But of course, however encouraging I might be, Margaret was quite capable of changing her mind.

'Does the Prince treat you well?' I asked Anne when Isabel had taken her simmering presence out of the chamber. 'Is he kind? Does he talk to you?'

'The Prince ignores me. It is humiliating.'

'It will change when he gains the crown.'

'If he does. You cannot know that.'

What a heavy weight there was in my mind and below my heart. I felt that I was losing both my daughters to ungovernable forces, to the Queen's selfish indecision and the unknown events in England. We were living in a strange oblivion, without boundaries, without any sense of where we would be next week, next month, next year. It was beyond any solution that I might bring to the problem.

I could have wept for my daughters. Instead, I picked up the veiling again and folded it carefully, rescuing the needle as my thoughts swung back to Richard.

*God keep you safe, Richard. May he guide your steps to bring peace and amity to England.*

What an empty prayer that would be. I did not believe that it was possible.

I could not claim that exerting tolerance had ever brought me happiness.

## Margaret, Queen of England

'Do I have to wed her?' My son's voice once again became querulous at the last minute as we gathered in Amboise for this solemn event. 'Do I have no voice in this decision, *Maman*?'

'Yes, you will wed her. And unfortunately, you do not have a voice. It is decided.'

'Was I not to wed the Scottish Princess?'

'That is no longer useful to us.'

'She is the daughter of our enemy.'

'Who has become our saviour.'

'She has no royal blood. She is not a worthy bride for me.'

The Prince was falling into a morose, bad temper that clouded his comely face. I brushed it aside.

'She is the price you must pay if you wish to recover the crown. It may be yours by right, but it is in the hands of the Yorkist usurper. We need Warwick to lead our loyal forces against him.'

For once I lacked forbearance with my son. I had had enough arguments with Louis. I had been forced to accept, so must the Prince.

'You will wed her and get her with child. She is young and healthy enough and will give you a son. She is also well-born

313

enough to stand beside you as Queen when you are crowned King. You should also know that she is not without royal blood, and thus deserves your esteem. There is also her wealth, which will not be inconsiderable.'

Of course he could not disobey me.

How long had it taken us to get to this point? And yet I wished it had never come to pass. I had been forced into it, for without this alliance, Louis would prove more than reluctant to give us aid. I needed more ships, men-at-arms, money.

I must accept this marriage.

The holy words of the nuptial commitment echoed beneath the arches at Amboise as the Prince and his bride took their vows. She was very young, but if she could bear a child it would be yet another strengthening of our cause. Another heir of Lancaster. I must accept that Henry would never rule effectively again.

The final blessing was given by the Grand Vicar of Bayeux. It was a relief that I did not have to tolerate a more festive occasion. Warwick and Clarence, the major players in the game, were absent. A handful of French nobles had put in an appearance to witness the deed, but none of my own family. Most importantly, Louis was present, beaming on the young couple, a glint of mischief in my direction. He had got exactly what he wanted.

Edward was growing tall, I realised, as his father was tall. His face was bright at the attention lavished upon him, although his disapproval of what had been asked of him became once more evident by the sullen downturn of his mouth as the ceremony ended. Now we must all wait. I needed assurance of Warwick's triumphs in England before I committed myself and my son to returning. All threats must be removed. I would not risk his life until they were.

The Countess of Warwick was watching me. For a moment

I caught her eye. What did she think of this travesty? We had deliberately not spoken, for what bitter words were there to say that had not been said already? I looked away. She was unimportant to what awaited us in the future. This was merely a political marriage, as both she and I had experienced. I watched the young couple exchange the marital kiss. If Warwick failed, I would cut this marital knot with an instant annulment. I would not allow this mockery of a marriage to tie me, or the Prince, into an alliance that was of no value.

How hard and unfeeling I sounded in my mind.

Forgive me, Blessed Virgin. I must remain strong and dedicated to my cause.

## Anne, Countess of Warwick

It was done; they were wed. For good or ill, my daughter was now Princess of Wales; one day she would be Queen of England. My heart should be full of joy, of pride in what Richard had achieved for her, but there was no joy in me in spite of the fact that in the end all had gone smoothly, the dispensations had arrived. The chapel here in the Chateau of Amboise witnessed the union, under Louis's sanguine eye. Whether Louis had consulted his astrologers I was unsure. I wished Richard was here as I stood witness to my daughter's regal union, but then it was perhaps better that he was not. My face was set with a species of rigid acceptance of a marriage that was of no pleasure to anyone here present, yet must take place.

What did my daughter Anne think about it? For so young a girl, she was remarkably reticent, calmly self-assured as she made her oath before the cleric. She, too, knew all about political marriages and was obedient to the demands made on her. At least she had met Edward before they stood together at the altar.

'I don't envy her,' Isabel whispered. 'He is arrogant and opinionated.'

'But you have your own cross to bear with Clarence,' I suggested. 'Clarence is as ambitious as any man I know, except perhaps for your father.'

'George resents my father giving his support to the Lancastrian Prince.'

'I know. But sometimes political decisions are wounding. At least he cannot change his loyalties and offer them to his brother, as long as his brother is in exile.'

'But what if Ned returns?' Her glance was sharp. 'We both know that he will, however much we might pretend that he will give up his crown for good and stay in Burgundy. Father will have to face him some day.'

It was a thought that I had already been forced to acknowledge. It surprised me that Isabel was so politically aware that she would voice it, but then she was a young woman of intelligence who would see the future as clearly as I.

'When that happens, then Clarence may feel that his loyalties are conflicted.'

There was a little silence as the newly wed couple were led out of the chapel by Queen Margaret.

'I wish my baby had not died.'

There were tears on Isabel's cheeks, and no happiness in her eyes. A first child lost and her husband departed with Richard. There was nothing I could say to offer her contentment.

'There will be time for more children when we return home.'

So many complex strands of unhappiness. As Duchess Cecily had said, sometimes it was indeed beyond bearing.

*

I imagined that Margaret had offered up silent prayers on that day of the hunt, when we learned that Richard had made landfall. So did I. And even more after the wedding, when news began to trickle regularly into the Court at Amboise. Louis, still in residence with us, was thoughtful enough, or devious enough, to deliver his news to me as well as to the Queen. All that Richard had planned had come to pass, for on the sixth day of October he entered London, his campaign a success, his brother Montagu marching down from the North.

'Where is the King?' I asked. 'King Edward, that is.'

'He has fled the country, to take refuge in Burgundy and sue for help. He is still there, and Warwick is in command in England. He has called a parliament and the old King Henry is released from the Tower and once more wears the crown. The Readeption is quite an achievement by your husband. The Queen has taken to sanctuary with her children.'

Surely I need worry no longer.

'Have you told Queen Margaret?'

'Yes, of course.' Louis's smile was as guileful as ever, showing his teeth. 'She is even now giving thanks for this blessing, although I told her that King Henry appeared weary and without his usual strength. Still, he was cheerful enough when he was led through the streets of London. It is the Earl of Warwick who holds the power in the country. It may be that my cousin the Queen will consider leaving these shores at last. It will be a relief for you.'

It would indeed. There was no reason why we should not return to England. I expected Margaret to begin immediately to organise, with Louis's aid, a fleet to take us home.

Margaret said nothing.

Should I have upbraided her? It would achieve no effect.

All I could do was wait.

But as the days passed, the moment was approaching when I could remain in France no longer, whatever Margaret chose to do. I was not tied to her reins; I must exert my own authority as Countess of Warwick. Meanwhile I continued to be dragged wherever King Louis wished us to go. In December, after the wedding, instead of preparing to sail to England, we were transported to Paris, where a splendid reception had been laid on for us at Louis's command. I despised it. I smiled and donned an amenable mien with my court robes, but I hated every minute of it, for had it not been made crystal clear that Margaret could not be trusted, even over the marriage of her only son?

'Was your marriage consummated?' I asked Anne, without finesse. 'Did you share a bed?'

She shook her head. 'Oh, we shared a bed for form's sake, and were blessed by the Bishop, sprinkled with holy water, but then we were separated. The Queen did not wish our marriage to be complete.'

'Did she say why?'

'We all know why.'

How politically astute my daughter had become, and as forthright as her sister. Nor could I fail to see the bitterness in her face, that she should have been made an object of the Queen's political ambitions.

'I am sorry,' I said. 'It is an humiliation.'

'Are we not all pawns in the game being played by Queen Margaret?'

'Yes.' Why not be honest? 'If your father fails, she will have your marriage annulled.'

## Margaret, Queen of England

I sent for the Countess of Warwick, because in the end I knew I must. It proved to be a chilly meeting.

'I think that the time has come when we should sail for England,' I announced.

My jaw was clenched hard. I was still uncertain, but Louis demanded it. In the interests of an alliance between England and France, Louis needed me to return to take up my position as Queen of England at Henry's side, expressed so forcefully that I could withstand his blandishments no longer. I had thought that the Countess would be grateful. She was not. Her reply was short and sharp, redolent with an authority that she usually kept well hidden in my presence.

'I think that it is more than time, my lady. We should have gone weeks ago.'

'I will not commit my son until I know that all is likely to fall out to our advantage.'

The Countess was unimpressed by my old reasoning.

'You should have sent him with my lord of Warwick, even though you still do not trust him. The Prince would have been in the care of the Duke of Somerset as soon as he landed. You trust Somerset, do you not? I consider it a fatal mistake to allow yourself and the Prince to remain so long in France.' Usually so soft-spoken, the Countess's words cut the air between us to ribbons. 'You should have been there with the Prince to give leadership to your supporters. You should have been at my lord's side and so should the Prince, to encourage those who would fight for you. It seems to me the height of cowardice to wait until the battle is over.'

'There was no battle.'

'You did not know that. No one knew what would occur.'

Never did I recall her offering such plain speaking.

'I will take no criticism from you, my lady.'

'Yet I will give it. My lord of Warwick was of the strongest opinion that you, the Queen, should have sailed with him. You know that too.'

'I will not imperil my son's life until I know that all will be well. Victory must be assured before I allow the Prince to take his place at the head of our armies in England. Until that is so, I will not sail. I take no orders from Warwick.'

'No, you will take no criticism from anyone. I hope it will not prove to be your undoing.' She raised her head, her expression perfectly controlled despite her hot words. 'I wish to speak to my daughter Anne. It is my intention to travel immediately. I would wish her to come with me.'

'I will travel only when all is set in place to do so, and I know what I will face when I get there.' I was adamant. 'It is your choice how and when you return, my lady, but your daughter will travel with my son. You may make your farewells.'

Her criticism annoyed me, perhaps because I sensed a grain of truth. Should we have committed ourselves earlier? But I would never admit to it. I could at least be gracious over the Countess's farewell. It did not end as I might have hoped. Here was antagonism but I could not overcome my hatred and mistrust of Warwick. I could not be compassionate towards his wife, despite the past.

'I am sorry that you could not trust my lord the Earl, when he is even now risking his life for your cause.'

'I will only trust him when he leads my son to the throne of England. I will only trust him when the usurper of York is either dead or banished for ever, and his brats removed with him.

They may join him in exile if they wish, but live in England as a constant threat they will not.'

'I see that you do not consider restoring your husband to the throne again. It will be the Prince, not Henry.'

She was uncannily quick. I straightened my spine. The decision must be made, and I had made it.

'We both know that my son will make a far better leader. My lord's misadventures have robbed him of his ability to rule. There will be a regency. Now go and say farewell to your daughter. I am sure that you will be able to arrange your own ship to take you to England.'

'Why did you refuse the consummation of the marriage? Do you hope to annul it?'

'Yes.' The brutal truth.

The Countess curtsied, then walked to the door without another word.

'Countess Anne...' She halted but did not turn. 'I am sorry it has ended in this fashion.'

'So am I,' the Countess replied. 'Ambition is a cruel ally with intemperate demands. I hope that I can find it in me to forgive you, if your tardiness brings disaster to all of us. If your wilful decisions bring unhappiness to my daughter.'

'I swear that I will not need your forgiveness. Victory will wipe out all sins.'

I hoped that she would turn back, to acknowledge my certainty of our ultimate success. She did not. It was only afterwards, when I remembered our clash of wills, that I recalled that the Countess's voice at the end had been strained, perhaps with suppressed tears.

# 28

## *Return to England, March 1471*

**Anne, Countess of Warwick**

The weather continued to conspire against us. The winds blew from the West and the waves thrashed on the shore. Was this God's judgement on a campaign that was blighted from the beginning? I could not believe it. I must hold to my faith in Richard's abilities to bring all to fruition.

With Louis snapping at her heels for her tardiness, Margaret finally agreed on the need to sail and we travelled together with her son and my daughters to the coast. Any joy I felt in it soon died a death. Three weeks of attempting to cross the Channel while storms raged and Margaret procrastinated was a blight on all of us. In the end, patience drained as water through a sieve, forcing me to make the decision to return to England separately, and alone. We would be reunited in England, but at least I could sail alone and would not have to suffer the waspish tongue of Margaret and her perpetual plans to seize the crown once more for her son.

I had had enough of Prince Edward too, with his enthusiasms for war.

My daughter Isabel had already braved the winter weather

and gone on ahead. I could not dissuade her. Perhaps I did not try too hard, although I did try to plant a seed of doubt.

'What good will it do?' I appealed to her good sense.

'I know not, except that I need to be with my husband. I know that you think he will renew his allegiance to his brother. Why would he not? He will get nothing from a victory for the Lancastrian Prince. But I should be with him when he does it, even if it means that I join the ranks of my father's enemies.'

'That is the one undeniable truth that you have uttered,' I replied, helplessly, in despair, as I knew full well that she would carry out her threat. 'It will divide our family irrevocably.'

'Then divide us it must, but I cannot wait here.' For the first time I saw her own thwarted ambitions in her bleak expression. The joyful young girl who had entered into marriage with Clarence had gone for ever. 'Once, I would have been Queen of England at Clarence's side. Now you have decided that the honour should go to my sister. You do not need me here any longer. So let me go.'

'Then I will wish you well, since I must.' A thought came to me. 'I have something to give you, which may or may not be of use, but take it anyway.'

Since we were in my own chamber it took me no time to open my jewel casket, much denuded now of precious gems to pay for Richard's invasion, but there at the bottom was the gleam of emeralds and rubies in the ring once sent to me, so long ago now, by Margaret.

'Keep this,' I said, pushing it into her hand, closing her fingers over it. It once belonged to Margaret and was given to me as a token of some kindness between us, many years ago. Who knows what the future will hold for you? It may be that one day you will need this symbol of loyalty to Margaret of Anjou.'

'I doubt it.' The curve of Isabel's mouth was contemptuous,

but she did not return the ring when she left me and commissioned her own ship, as Duchess of Clarence, to carry her home.

I should have gone with her, of course, but I did not. Anne was still firmly clenched in Margaret's strong grip. My family was falling apart, but at last, unable to wait any longer, with a ship commissioned, I left France. Richard had sent for me and I refused to remain at Margaret's whims. She did not come to see me embark with my small household. We had said all we had to say. I regretted having to leave my daughter, but Anne would of necessity travel with Margaret as the wife of the heir. Had not Richard officially consigned her to Margaret's care? It was fitting that she should travel with her husband. I did not fear this separation from my daughter, merely regretted the necessity.

For a bleak moment as I boarded the vessel, it seemed to me that I had been separated from all whom I loved, but I would turn my face to England, to home, and anticipate that homecoming with joy. I would be restored to Richard's company. Perhaps I could even find some means of speaking with Isabel, although her loyalty to Clarence and his desire for the crown was clear. Our farewell had not been the loving one between mother and daughter that I could have hoped for, but surely it could be remedied, and Anne would soon follow.

So many relationships to be healed, but was I not skilled in healing?

Thus I stepped aboard with confidence and all the courage that Richard believed was part of my nature. Soon I would be in England again when all things would be possible. When all would be put right.

## Margaret, Queen of England

This was a day that I would inscribe in my Book of Hours with joy. This was the day I returned to England at last, free of King Louis, free of my father, successful in bringing the heir of Lancaster back to English soil. Prince Edward, a gold coronet glinting in the sun as it rested on his brow, stood with me on deck as we survived the storms and came to landfall in the port of Weymouth.

The fourteenth day of April in the year 1471.

'Give thanks that we are returned,' I told him. 'Surely God is with us and our cause.'

I said nothing to my daughter-in-law who stood beside my son.

'Where is my mother?' she asked.

The girl was searching the quay for signs of the vessel that the Countess would have sailed in.

'I know not.' The ship would be long gone, even if it had docked here. 'The Countess will join us, or she will not. What does it matter? My captains will now face the usurper and remove him for good.'

The news of events in England had been encouraging. Yes, the Yorkist usurper had fled from King's Lynn, abandoning his wife and children to take refuge in the Tower. My lord Henry had been released, to be crowned King again, albeit a puppet at Warwick's beck and call. The fact that a new Yorkist prince had been born to Elizabeth Wydeville did not trouble me unduly. None of these events seemed likely to stand in our way. I would refuse to listen to any false warnings from those who feared taking to war again.

All I could think of was the future. If Henry was too weak to wear the crown then my son would take it, with acclamations on all sides. He was of an age and a perfect knight. He would be a most acceptable regent for his father.

The sun broke through the storm clouds, spilling light onto us and onto the fair land before us, and I knew that we would be successful. The Prince's coronet became a halo of golden light. We would give thanks to God. I smiled at my daughter-in-law, my good temper restored. All my anxieties could be pushed aside. I had lived with them for so long, through exile and fears that we would never return. Here we were, home, with victory in our grasp.

As long as the Earl of Warwick could be relied on to deliver that victory into my lap.

## Anne, Countess of Warwick

The turbulent voyage had finally ended for me in Portsmouth. Despite the ferocity of the storms, I had travelled well as I always did, even though we were driven further east than we would have hoped, but eventually we made land-fall. Margaret would surely step ashore further west, so I must travel to meet up with her. I prayed for her safety and for that of my daughter Anne. Isabel was now probably on the road to London to join Clarence.

Great anxiety had travelled with me, nor did it leave me when I disembarked. I had heard no word of Richard. I could not sleep, even though I accepted gratefully the hospitality of the kindly monks at Beaulieu Abbey who welcomed me to their silent spaces and gave me a bed and food. Did it surprise me that they would open their gates to a weary, travel-worn woman in garments stiff with sea-salt whose loyalties might be suspect?

'The Earl of Warwick will reward you well for your kindness towards me,' I advised the Abbot, who proved to be not reluctant. Indeed, he was uncomfortably honest in his dealings with me, his warning echoing in my ears so that I was soon sick to my soul. How brief the journey from hope to despair. How unsettling the news awaiting me.

'It is not good news for you, my lady,' the Abbot advised when he had drawn me into his private quarters.

'Is my lord of Warwick in danger?' My first thought.

'It is possible. There is no certainty, but it is my duty to warn you. King Edward has returned from his exile in Burgundy. He has invaded in the North and landed at Ravenspur. He has received help from his brother-in-law, the Duke of Burgundy. He was well received as he marched south. We understand that he has entered London.'

'What of King Henry?'

'He is King no more. He is sent back to the Tower. He is safe enough, but the crown is no longer his.'

'And the Duke of Clarence?'

'We think that he has made amends and swears loyalty once more to his brother the King.'

Then the crucial question.

'What of the Earl of Warwick and the Lancastrian army?'

'I know not, my lady, but King Edward is once more in control in the city. There will be a battle for certain. King Edward will not draw back from vengeance on those who took the kingdom from him. They say that he is determined to spill the blood of those who would threaten him. It may be that a battle has already happened.' His kind eyes sorrowful on my behalf, he clasped the heavy silver crucifix on his breast. 'Forgive me, my lady. I should not have worried you, before we know the truth.'

'I think that I needed to know,' I replied.

As the Abbot had intimated, I could see no way forward for Richard that would not bring conflict and battle. What should I do now? I retired to my small chamber to contemplate what I had heard.

Duty demanded that I travel west to meet up with Margaret and my daughter. Clarence's loyalties were more than in doubt with his brother's return, and where would that leave Isabel, torn apart in her own loyalties? How long was it since Richard and I were parted? Six months. Six long winter months. Not so different from all the other times in our married life that we had lived with land and sea separating us, but this time it was different. This time I was haunted by a dark imagining that all would not end well, for any of us.

Yet why should it not end well? If Richard could still bring King Edward to heel and restore King Henry once more, then we could return to Warwick and Middleham and settle into a hard-won peace. Sitting in the little room, no more than a monastic cell, deep in my heart I accepted that it could never happen. All the portents were against us.

Richard must know it too.

And yet, as I had set foot on dry land, there were no threats, no bad auspices, no harbingers of death. The sky was clear of louring clouds and the sun shone after the storms. There was no foreshadowing of distress or despair. No rumbling of thunder from the East. No ravens or intemperate howling of a dog. Once I might have thought that my arrival here on Easter Sunday was a good omen.

I was past the belief in good omens.

## Margaret, Queen of England

Once disembarked in Weymouth and the final remnants of nausea abated, I sent out proclamations to men of the West to gather to our banner. Then I rode straight to Cerne Abbey in Dorset where Edmund Beaufort, Duke of Somerset awaited us, as well as the Earl of Devon. Their welcome was a balm to my heart. But not all the news was as encouraging. Somerset carried the rumours that the usurper had returned to England with aid from Burgundy, and that he was already in control in London. My lord Henry was once more consigned to the Tower.

I could not allow it to distress me. I could not think of it. Time to make plans.

Only then did I ask after the Countess of Warwick, if she had survived the voyage. It was thought that she had put into the harbour at Portsmouth, from where I expected her to journey to meet up with us. I put all thoughts of her aside. She could add nothing to our endeavours now; she had no power. Meanwhile, I sent out couriers to discover the whereabouts of the usurper and of Warwick. I must put my trust in him once more, for without him we were lost indeed.

We would not lose. We could not. I had been eight years in exile and almost a full year in planning this return. Now we would see the results of it and celebrate our success.

After giving thanks in the abbey, the Prince at my side, with a lighter heart, I supposed that I must make contact with the Countess. It would be the depth of ingratitude not to do so.

## Anne, Countess of Warwick

It was Easter Sunday, the fourteenth day of April, when I requested writing materials from the Abbot and began to write. Whether it would ever find Richard I did not know, but I felt the need to tell him of my circumstances and that of Margaret as far as I knew. In my heart I knew that it would never find him before we were reunited, and yet there was a compulsion in me to set down what had happened since we said our farewells.

I wrote it in my own hand. This was no content to lay before one of the abbey scribes.

*To Richard, Earl of Warwick, from Anne, Countess of Warwick*

*I know not where you are, but I trust that you will find this to be of value and perhaps a comfort. I have arrived in England at last and await news of you. The situation compelled me to sail alone. Storms beset my vessel, such that I was forced to land at Portsmouth. I have now taken shelter in Beaulieu Abbey, before joining Margaret and our daughter with the Prince, who made landfall in Weymouth. That is where you might send a courier, when it is possible for me to rejoin you.*

*We made landfall on the fourteenth day of April, which was the Sunday to celebrate Easter Day. Surely that would be a good omen. The Abbot says that it must be.*

*It is so difficult to imagine where you are and what you are doing. Are you perhaps at Warwick? I think not, and I doubt that you are in London. I hear that Ned is returned and has taken control of the city and of King Henry once more. At least you will be safe from Yorkist attack in Warwick Castle or even Middleham, although I know it is not in your character to hide from danger for too long. After all, your purpose in returning was to challenge Ned and restore the Lancastrians to power.*

*I imagine it will all end in battle. I will pray for your safety and the success of your challenge to the Yorkists.*

*I have missed your company over the last six months, even though I should have been used to it. Anne is mostly in the household of Margaret and the Prince as you would expect. All was undertaken with chilling protocol with Anne's marriage to the Prince at Amboise. Margaret accepted the necessity, but she continues to baulk at the need for this close connection with our family. This, of course, is not news to you. What Anne thinks I do not know; she keeps her own counsel. I had not realised that our younger daughter could be so strong willed.*

*The marriage has not been consummated. Margaret looks for an escape if you fail. She plans an annulment. We knew this would happen.*

*I have nothing to say about Clarence. We hear that he has stepped across the divide between York and Lancaster once more and sold his soul to his brother. What will he gain from it? Does he hope to become Edward's heir if the new male child does not survive?*

*You can tell me all when we meet up again.*

*We should have come to your aid earlier. Margaret was recalcitrant; the fault was hers. We should have come to England to win men to your cause. But what point in admitting fault now?*

*Have I ever said how much my heart is engaged with you and your campaigns? Love is never something we talked about. It was not a requisite in our initial meeting as children, in our marriage, nor in our life thereafter, and yet I cannot believe that you do not have the strongest affection for me, as I do for you. Love takes many forms. Your care and well-being is always*

331

*uppermost in my heart and my mind. It is now as I await news. I live in hope that we will soon be together again.*

*Sadly for our daughters, victory for one side will bring heartache for the other. I fear for them both in the future but accept that I can do nothing for them. Did we not know this when we arranged their marriages? Conflict is a terrible thing, denying happiness on one side, awarding it on the other. Victory for one daughter will be distress for the other. I find it difficult to consider the future.*

*I have now come to the end of the parchment allowed to me by our careful Abbot. Would it be a terrible thing if I admitted between the two of us that I do not care who wears the crown as long as you can sheath your great sword and look to your castles and your estates again? Have you ever done this in your life? Perhaps you will find it wearisome after so many years of pursuing the Neville cause. I doubt you will ever give it up.*

*God bless you and keep you safe.*

*May I hear your voice once more. You will never leave me. You will never fade from me. You will never die for me.*

*Your loving wife,*

*Anne*

*Countess of Warwick*

I read it through. And then again. It did not say what I wanted it to say, but what was in my heart I could not put down in words. I was afraid for him. I lived with terrible premonitions of death and disaster, but there were no marks of tears on the page to give him any concern. I had taken great care that it should not be so. I could not burden him further with my fears, since it would be a weight on his soul that he could well do without. Meanwhile I would bear it, the fear that I took to bed with me at night and that lurked in the shadows when I awoke in the mornings.

I would bear the looming sense of terrible loss for him, so that he might fight unhindered.

In the end I folded it and applied my seal. I needed a courier from the Abbot, but where to send it? I thought Warwick Castle would be the obvious choice. I doubted he would be in Middleham if crucial events were happening in the South.

# 29

## *A Tragic Outcome at Barnet,*
## *Easter Day 1471*

**Anne, Countess of Warwick**

How could I ever have foreseen what would happen, the terrible, the tragic overlapping of events? It was on the same day that I wrote my letter to Richard that the news reached us in Beaulieu. I was in the Abbot's chamber, discussing my need for a courier and where he should go. It was evening, growing dark, and the room was ill-lit by a single candle. I could barely see the courier's face but the atmosphere in the room resonated with disaster as he fell silent. He bowed. No shuffling of feet, he removed his felt wide-brimmed cap and held it clapped to his chest. He acknowledged me, standing in the shadows where I had retreated so that the Abbot could deal with this matter of business.

He, a young man without livery, had been riding hard.

'There has been a battle, my lord Abbot, my lady.'

It was suddenly cold in that room, so cold. I felt it clammy on my face.

'There has been a battle, at Barnet, on the morning of Easter Sunday.'

'And what was the outcome, my son?' the Abbot asked gently.

The courier's face told it all. The Abbot had already taken my hand and was leading me to a stool as if he knew the content of this message, pushing me to sit. But I resisted. I would stand to hear what was said.

'King Edward is victorious,' the courier all but croaked, his throat dry with dust.

'And the Earl of Warwick? Where is he?' I asked.

I closed my hand hard around the Abbot's soft grip. I could not meet the courier's eye. I had had no warning of this. No premonition. No mournful owl-hoot at noon. No crack of thunder from the East when the sky was cloud-clear.

'The Earl is dead, my lady.'

All I could do was draw in a long, slow breath and fight for composure. In that moment I was beyond emotion, beyond words. Beyond any feeling. I released the Abbot and my hands fell to my sides, open-palmed as if in petition to the Blessed Virgin who could still intercede with death.

Richard was dead.

'And his brother, too, my lady. Lord Montagu. When I left the battlefield, King Edward was in the process of dispatching their bodies to Westminster, where they will be put on display to prove their demise.'

I raised my head. Surely this could not be? It was possible to be mistaken, identifying those who died on a battlefield. My only hope was in my eyes, in my words, even though I knew in my heart that my hope would be confounded.

'Is there any chance that you are wrong? That the Earl and Lord Montagu escaped? Is that not possible, in the thick of the battle? Could they have taken refuge elsewhere?'

He did not hesitate.

'No, my lady, I regret to say. I saw the bodies. They were both cut down on the field of battle. There was no mistake on my part, nor on that of the men who desired the death of the Earl.

335

They knew exactly who it was that they attacked and wounded to death.'

All my attempts to persuade myself that all would be well had been worthless.

'Thank you. Thank you for the truth.'

I clenched my hand around the letter I had written and still held. Without another word I walked unseeingly back to my chamber where I lit a candle with hands that trembled, then held the letter to the candle flame and burned it to ashes. All I had written was gone in that moment of fire. He would never read it. He would never know of my care for him.

Then I blew out the candle and sat in the dark, ignoring the quiet knock on the door. A letter, travel-worn and torn at one edge, was pushed beneath it. I recognised the distinctive angular writing. Perhaps the courier had it with him and forgot to hand it over. But now here it was.

I could not read it. Not now. Not yet.

Helplessly, I looked at the stained message. What would I do now? A light had gone out of my world. I would live a shadow life. I would also live in fear. Who would protect me now? I was alone and without help. What would be my future as the widow of a traitor?

I could not even think about the futures of my two daughters. I must, but not yet.

All of my being was centred on my loss of Richard. Of his brutal death on a battlefield, his body to be stripped and displayed in London to prove that he no longer lived.

I continued to sit in the dark, and eventually allowed tears to come.

I had his final words to me in my hands.

I should read it.

Not yet. Not yet!

## Margaret, Queen of England

'No! In the name of God, no!'

I cared not the attention I drew to my person as the courier repeated his news, stunned as I was with the destruction of all my hopes. The battle had been fought hours before I had even landed, while I had been full of rejoicing, of schemes and planning. Had we not been celebrating our return? Even the storms had eventually settled into compliance. Warwick would lead those who supported me, and I would march on London with my son at my side. My lord Henry would be rescued. The House of York would be defeated and driven once more into exile. If not put to the sword.

I could not grasp what had happened.

I shut myself in my chamber and cursed the now-dead Warwick for his failure to bring our plan to a victorious end. How could he have failed so desperately?

All was now awry in my mind. Edward of York had strengthened his hand on the crown with those terrible events at Barnet, while my main hope lay, a stripped corpse on the stones outside St Paul's, a warning to all who might support Lancaster. My lord Henry would once more be under his control. All I had planned for was dust beneath my feet.

'It cannot be. How can I believe this?'

Fury and despair were a lethal combination. What to do now? I could speak to no one. My temper was uncertain. I banished the Prince from me. I could not bear to set my eyes on his wife. Did she mourn the loss of her father? It mattered not to me.

Should I turn tail and return to France? I could not.

When I had regained my senses I sought out Somerset, who was waiting for me.

'What do we do?' I asked my commanders, Somerset, Devon and Exeter, who remained at my side. 'What in God's name do I do now?'

It sounded weak that I should ask, that I needed advice. Would not the usurper turn immediately from his victory at Barnet towards the West, to destroy me utterly? He would have been told that we had landed. The only hope for the House of Lancaster lay with me and my son. We must take matters into our own hands. There would assuredly be a battle, but would we have the power to defeat the Yorkists after Barnet?

Somerset replied without pause. He, too, had been weighing the odds of our victory, and he answered my silent concerns. He was worryingly grave, but he saw only one choice for us.

'This is what I would say. Collect your followers, my lady, and march into Wales, where the Earl of Pembroke is collecting a force. Meet up with him. Warwick's death could just work to our advantage, since there were many who had been unwilling to trust him. Now you, and you alone, will lead the opposition to Edward of York. There will be no conflicting loyalties. One decisive battle against the Yorkists will solve all difficulties. You and the Prince will return to London in triumph.'

So clear cut. So obvious a decision to make. It calmed me. My mind became clearer.

'Yes. Yes. That is what we should do. We will fight.'

I put my hand on his arm, looking across to where the Prince stood waiting, his face alight with anticipation. My son, too, was keen to fight in his first battle. How he had grown in recent months, almost unnoticed since I had been taken up with French negotiations. Here was a young man, his skills with sword and on horseback worthy of any knight. Although he had no experience of directing a battle, I knew that Somerset would not neglect him in the thick of the warfare. My heart quailed a little. What mother would rejoice at her only son riding into battle against a man such as Edward of York, a man with a reputation second to none? But it must be so. My Prince was now broad of shoulder, his height considerable, his hand clenched around the chased hilt of his sword; he was no longer a child to be biddable to his mother, even though his hair still retained that infant fairness that would remain with him all his life. Now it was cut neatly against his skull to make the wearing of a helmet in battle more comfortable.

'What do you say, my son?' I asked. It seemed right to ask him. All I did was for him, for his rightful inheritance.

'We fight, *Maman*,' he replied simply.

'Then that is what we will do.' I turned to Somerset again. 'What route do we take? Where would we meet up with Pembroke?'

It was a relief that he had already planned it in his mind.

'We go north to cross the River Severn at Gloucester. It may be that we can take Edward of York by surprise. He may be weaker than he thinks after Barnet.'

I was immediately taken up in the planning. Did I cast a fleeting thought towards my daughter-in-law, whose father was now dead? Or towards the Countess of Warwick, who was widowed and in a dangerous situation? Fleetingly, but I had no time to stretch out a hand of friendship of conciliation or condolences. Nor could I wait for the Countess to journey to join us. She must make her own decisions. She must secure her own safety. All my thoughts were with my coming campaign when I would defeat the Yorkists and see the crown placed on my son's head.

I cursed Warwick for his loss.

I should never have trusted him. I had no compassion.

# 30

## *An Exchange of Correspondence After the Battle of Barnet*

### Anne, Countess of Warwick, to Margaret, Queen of England

My heart is broken.

As so often in the past I think that you will have no need of this news from me. You will know by now the destruction of all your plans. You will have been told of the terrible repercussions of the Battle of Barnet. The Lancastrian hopes have all been laid waste on that battlefield by Edward of York, who is once more King of England.

I have little room for compassion within my heart.

There is room for nothing but grief.

My lord of Warwick is dead.

I know that you will care little for my predicament, only that it puts a halt to your campaign. I am sure that you are already replotting what to do next. I know that you will not regret that he is dead in your service, except that it has put a halt to your immediate march on London. He was always your enemy in your eyes. The loss of his life will not matter to you, while I cannot come to terms with it.

Every morning when I arise I have to face the knowledge again. I have to accept it.

I have taken refuge in the abbey at Beaulieu, otherwise I fear that I will be taken prisoner. I cannot see my future. All I can feel is resentment that we were dragged into this disaster, although that was my lord of Warwick's fault as much as yours. All I can ask is that you take care of my daughter. She is in your hands and her safety is yours to command. It seems that Isabel is lost to me too, for she is at Clarence's side at the Yorkist Court.

God keep you safe. It is my duty to pray for you, but I can see no future for you and your son, or for me. Unless you can defeat King Edward on the battlefield, what hope is there? Perhaps I should pray for that event, but it does not come easily to me to pray for yet more bloodshed. I no longer care who rules England. I have lost too much. Perhaps one day I will, but not yet.

I miss him. I do not know what my life will be now. I could shriek my grief to the four winds, but what good would that do?

King Henry is a prisoner in the Tower, but at least he's still alive.

I wish that we had never taken exile at the French Court and fallen into the web of King Louis, although my lord's ambitions cannot be denied. I cannot wash away the blame from his decision to return. But you should have sailed earlier. You should have made landfall and summoned England to my lord's support.

There, it is written. I can blame you. I can never forgive you for leaving my lord so long without your support, and that of your son. May God punish you for your spite in neglecting what should have been done, through selfish motives. You were willing to use him but not to stand at his side. He stood and died on a battlefield while you held back until you could smell victory on the wind.

I will never forgive you.

Treat my daughter with kindness if you decide to annul the marriage and arrange a more powerful alliance for your son with a foreign princess. She does not deserve ill-treatment. She was a pawn in the marriage games that we all play.

Anne

Countess of Warwick

## Margaret of Anjou, Queen of England, to Anne, Countess of Warwick

By the Queen.

Your news is not new to me. I have no time to write more than these few lines. All is still to play for, for it is my intention to meet the Yorkist usurper on the battlefield. First I will meet up with Pembroke and his Welshmen, which should give me sufficient strength. Somerset is enthusiastic and so is the Prince.

Your grief touches my heart even though you blame me and I found it difficult to see Warwick as a trustworthy ally. He gave his life for my cause. I must be grateful, although I regret his failure.

You will probably hear of the outcome of my campaign. I march north into Wales to collect forces. Pray for our success. My son will assuredly one day be King.

May God bless our campaign with victory.

I trust you will be safe behind the sacred walls of

Beaulieu until I am in a position of strength to invite you to come to our Court to be reunited with your daughter.

The Earl of Warwick could never have been anything but my enemy. We agreed to our alliance through pure self-interest. I will take no blame for it. Are we not all driven by ambition?

Your daughter Anne is with me and safe. She will be treated kindly. As for the marriage, I have not yet decided. It can wait until after our ultimate victory.

Margaret

Queen of England

# 3I

## *The Death of All Hope, 1471*

### Margaret, Queen of England

This would be the moment in my life when my ambitions would be fulfilled. Our battle strategy was confirmed and, with no time to lose, we marched north as rapidly as we could, to join our forces with the Welshmen under the Earl of Pembroke. So many men swarmed to my banners and to those of the Prince. I could not have dreamed of such a following. My lord Henry was the rightful King; the support for him was heart-warming, and for my son, who rode at my side to acknowledge the cheering. We would cross the River Severn and face the Yorkist usurper in battle. We had been victorious before, would we not be so again? The recent disaster at Barnet would not colour my emotions. I imagined the victory, followed by our return to London, rejoicing, where I would release Henry from his Tower prison. The Prince would ride beside me. The Yorkist captains whom we captured would be dragged behind us in ignominy. Edward of York also, unless he met his end on the battlefield. An unmarked grave would do for him, I decided in my most bitter moments. Yes, this is where we would impose the future of Lancaster on the country.

Of course I sent out riders, to test the lie of the land. I had no intention of being taken by surprise by a Yorkist force, as Warwick had been in that second confrontation at St Albans.

As I waited their return, I recalled the past, remembering being accused of inappropriate behaviour for a woman, taking over the reins of power when Henry became incapable of making decisions. That had been nothing compared with the royal decisions I made now. To fight or not to fight. It had been such a burden of years and I was weary, but this was the moment when all my efforts would be sanctified by God in victory. Would I not be hailed as a true Queen of England, saving the realm from those who thought only of their own power?

One of the outriders returned.

'Edward of York has a force ahead. He is intent on stopping your crossing of the River Severn, my lady.'

I had not wished to fight at a river crossing. There would be danger, when soldiers could as easily be drowned as cut down.

'Then we must fight here, where we are camped.' I looked around to assess our position. 'Where is this? What is the church tower?'

'Tewkesbury, my lady. That is the tower of the Abbey Church. It is also possible for you to cross the Severn there if we prevail against the enemy.'

'Then so be it. It will be written as a triumph in the annals of the House of Lancaster, lauded by the chroniclers. Do we engage now, or do we wait for Pembroke's forces to arrive?'

There were differing opinions, but it was Somerset who prevailed, arguing that there would be no value in our waiting. I sought out my son, who had already heard the news and was crowing with his vision of his leading our forces. I watched him talk with my captains and knew in my heart what must happen. Prince Edward must fight. It would be important that he take his place at the head of the army despite the danger to his life.

Edward of York had won renown as little more than a youth on the battlefield at Mortimer's Cross. My son could ride and handle a sword as well as any knight in my army. He must win his renown here at Tewkesbury.

'I will fight,' my son announced. 'It is good that we fight now and do not wait.'

I could not prevent him. I would not prevent him, even though my heart quailed at the prospect of allowing him to so risk his precious life.

'So you will, my son. You will bring us victory.'

I would not be on the battlefield. I would leave the ordering of our forces to Somerset. Meanwhile our troops must rest and prepare. There would be no quarter given on either side. I sent my son off with a salute to both cheeks, proud of his martial vigour, his armour shining in the low sun.

'God be with you and strengthen your arm, my son. Follow orders from Somerset. You are yet young, and lack experience in these matters. Return to me with all the glory of a victorious prince. You carry with you your mother's love and your father's hopes.'

What more could I say to him? I had no amulet to give him, no banner, nothing but my love for him. He knelt before me to receive my final blessing.

'We will prevail,' he asserted. 'I will send news to you of our victory before the battle-day is out.'

I sent him off to battle, while I, with my household of women, took refuge for the night in Gupshill Manor, a small house within close distance where we were made welcome by a family of loyal Lancastrians.

## Anne, Countess of Warwick

I was existing in a strange state of inactivity, afraid to venture out of my self-imposed sanctuary. My emotions, too, were as if frozen. All hope for the future was overlaid with a thick coating of grief and fear and dread that impeded any clear thought. I had no news of my daughters and I dared not travel.

I did not know where Margaret was, or my daughter Anne. Or indeed Ned. No visitors to the abbey brought any news other than that there would be another battle somewhere in the West. I was there to waylay merchants and clerics alike. Surely someone would know about the march of armies or the outcome of a distant battle? Whoever won, one daughter would be on the winning side, the other probably afraid for her life. What mother would not live in dread with such a prospect?

For the first time in my life I sat in hopeless inactivity.

There was no news from Margaret. How could there be? All her energies would be driving her to meet up with the Earl of Pembroke and engage Ned in battle. All I knew was that Ned was a formidable fighter, and now that he had a son to fight for, he would be like a wolf in a sheep-fold when he engaged with the power of Lancaster. All my future would rest on what happened when Margaret's forces met up with Ned's army. If Margaret was victorious then I could travel to join her in London. Had she not said that she would welcome me at Court? If Ned claimed the victor's wreath, then my future would be in his hands. I would be the widow of a traitor with a punishment hanging over me.

I wept for my daughters.

I did not even know what they had done with Richard's body.

I could not bear the thought of dismemberment, as York and Salisbury had suffered.

'Can you not discover for me?' I asked the Abbot.

'I will try.'

'And you must tell me the truth.'

I might not be able to bear it, but it was better than false accounting. I would not be lied to. Not even for the sake of my heart.

I found myself hoping that Margaret was victorious in the battle to come. But did I truly want that? At least it would release me from this isolation, in effect what had become a semi-captivity.

I kept Richard's letter close to my heart. Still I could not read it. I was a coward and feared to have to shoulder his intimations of death.

## Margaret, Queen of England

The battle was played out without my involvement in the fields around Tewkesbury. I had done all that I could, all that might be required of me, riding through the ranks to give encouragement before leaving all in the hands of Somerset.

'Take care of my son. He is your Prince and your future King.'

My final words before I retired to Gupshill Manor, to wait in the small comfort that it granted to me.

The noise of battle reached us close after dawn: the roar of the forces on both sides, the crack and explosion of gunfire. It was impossible to tell how our men fared. All we could do was wait for news. My daughter-in-law waited with me. Then I heard hooves in the courtyard and footsteps on the stair into the hall where we stood, faces turned towards the door as it opened. A liveried messenger from Somerset emerged, red faced and out of breath.

'You must not stay here, my lady. Somerset says that you must leave.'

'I cannot.'

'If you stay, you risk being taken prisoner.'

'Is it as bad as that?'

'I fear it is, my lady. As it is, we face defeat. The Yorkists unleashed a vicious onslaught on the centre of our troops. It has become a rout. Many of our men have drowned in the River Severn. As we speak, our commanders are falling back towards the abbey. They hope to take sanctuary here, but you must not stay. It would be one more burden on them to protect you. They fear what might happen to you if you are taken by the vengeful Yorkists. A sanctuary has been arranged for you, beyond Tewkesbury, called Payne's Place. They have been told and are ready to welcome you. You will be safe there.'

'But I cannot leave the town.'

'You must, my lady. Indeed you must.'

The noise of war was drawing closer.

'What of my son?'

He swallowed visibly.

'I know not for certain. The Prince was left in command of the centre ground, facing the charge of Richard of Gloucester, brother of King Edward. It was a deadly attack and our line could not hold. When King Edward surged forward to meet up with his brother, it became a headlong flight of our men, with only the Prince left to rally them.'

'Why did no one come to his aid?' I demanded, seeing in my mind's eye the developing carnage on the battlefield. Would my son have been abandoned by my commanders? I could not accept it.

'It was an impossible task.' The courier's eyes fell before mine. 'I have no knowledge of what became of the Prince, my lady. I cannot hold out any promise of good news.'

Despair overwhelmed me as the permanence of death seemed to loom at my shoulder. It was all I recalled as blackness encompassed me. I was told later that I fell to the floor, my senses compromised, in a faint from which I could not be roused.

# 32

## *Two Pieces of Correspondence After the Battle of Tewkesbury*

**Margaret, Queen of England, to Anne, Countess of Warwick**

By the Queen.

I am alone here and all I can think to do is to write to you, so empty are my days. Here is the truth of it. All is at an end.

My son, my beloved son, on whom all my hopes had rested for so many years, is dead. Prince Edward is dead.

My captains are executed, dragged from their sanctuary in the abbey by the Duke of Gloucester, and put to death in the churchyard as traitors and rebels, without trial or any form of justice. Somerset was beheaded in the marketplace. The Yorkist upstart has had his revenge for bloody deeds in the past.

My army is defeated.

King Henry is once more in the hands of Edward of York.

But what does that matter beside the terrible loss to me of my son? I lost my senses after the battle. I had to be carried in a litter from Gupshill Manor. I am ashamed of

my lack of mastery over my emotions when my forces had
given their lives for me and my son.

For three days, after moving from one loyal manor house
to another, I have been brought here to Little Malvern
Priory, a small religious house, where I might hope to be
safe, but there will assuredly be wagging tongues that will
no doubt inform the victorious Yorkists. I expect to be
taken prisoner and to be escorted to London. You might say
that I should flee from here, but where would I go? Who
would take me in? I cannot inflict myself on any more
Lancastrian families.

Your daughter is with me and there is no need to fear
for her life. Her sister, Clarence's wife, will negotiate for her
release, I am certain of it.

What will happen to me? I think that no one will plead
for my life.

My son's death is the final humiliation for the House
of Lancaster. There will be no more heirs of my body. My
mind cannot step over that one supremely tragic event at
Tewkesbury.

What do I do now? All I had dreamed of and hoped for
is gone.

Bloody Meadow indeed.

Pray for me, Countess Anne. Pray for me, as I pray for
you. We are both women who have no control over their
future. You are in as much danger as I. Stay safe in your
sanctuary. I think I will not be safe here for much longer.

I do not seem to be able to weep, to mourn him as I
should. Why can I not? Should I not weep and cry out in
agony and rent my clothes as the women of Greek tragedies
were wont to do when their heroes were mourned? He was
all I had left. All the care and love I had spent on raising

this perfect Prince has been for nothing. I recall the day I gave birth to him in the Palace of Westminster, when my lord Henry was too addled in his wits to even understand that he had a son to carry on his name. But I knew that the birth of a male child was my greatest achievement. Now my golden Prince who no longer draws breath deserves that I should fall to my knees, my head bowed down to the ground. And yet I cannot. I am frozen, all emotions dead within me.

I should have been able to preserve his glorious life and live to see him being crowned King of England. My young Prince so desperately desired to fight and I could not stop him. I knew that I must not. He was of an age to be bloodied on a battlefield.

But at what terrible cost? Those precious years brought to an end in a battle charge.

Now, for the first time, I understand how you must feel at the loss of the Earl of Warwick. Now you have my compassion, but I can write no more.

Margaret
Queen of England


## Anne, Countess of Warwick

I read Margaret's letter. It left me strangely cold, despite all her suffering, and for the first time I discovered the impossibility of replying. My words would have scorched the pages until they flared into flames. She had lost everything, but so had I. And what of Richard's final words to me? I could no longer leave that long-neglected letter unread. At last I had the courage to open it, although my hands trembled at what I might read. Did

I wish to see his final words when they might be full of despair and intimations of defeat? But I could not leave it unread.

It was not a long letter.

*From Richard, Earl of Warwick, to Anne, Countess of Warwick*

*To my dear wife,*

*There will be a battle.*

*I reassure you that I anticipate a victory. We far outnumber the Yorkist forces, and are well supplied with ordnance. We also have King Henry with us, kept safe at the rear, but still he will give heart to the Lancastrian forces. The Queen's captains are confident.*

*Tomorrow is Easter Sunday, which we will celebrate to give thanks before the battle. I regret the Queen's tardiness in coming to England and the absence of the young Prince, but it cannot be changed.*

*When all is over and we have proved our might and the rightness of our cause on this battlefield at Barnet, I will travel to be reunited with you. You will ride with me into London in triumph beneath our banners of Neville and Beauchamp. I swear that we will not be parted in this manner again.*

*I have read through this letter a second time, knowing that it tells you little, and nothing of what is in my heart at this moment when death faces us all. What more can I write? I think that we said all that needed to be said when we parted in France.*

*Pray for me, my dear Anne. You have all my loyalty, as I know that I have yours.*

*I will send this to the South Coast, hoping against hope that it meets up with you.*

*Richard*

All so innocuous. A confident assertion of a victory.

All lost for Lancaster, for Richard and for me, on that dread field at Barnet.

I wept over it, as I had not been able to weep before.

And when my weeping was finished, I was left to consider what Ned would do with me as a traitor by association. Nor could I banish the fear of what he would do with Queen Margaret when she finally fell into his hands.

# 33

## *A Cruel Imprisonment*

**Margaret, Queen of England**

I was discovered in my refuge a handful of days after the battle. It had only been a matter of time. There was no safety for me now in England. I had no friends to come to my aid.

This refuge had been arranged for me in Little Malvern Priory, a poor religious place of fewer than six monks, with little physical comfort, but at least it was shut away from the world in the low wooded hills. I did not care where I might be or about any lack of comfort. I shut myself in my cell-like room, paralysed in horror. In a single day I had lost all my most important commanders, captured and later condemned to execution by York's brother the Duke of Gloucester: Somerset and Devon, as well as all the men of my household who had shared my exile and my fight to restore the Lancastrian inheritance.

My only consolation was that the usurper Edward had pardoned the common soldiers. The blame was not theirs. They would not be hacked to death. Nor had he dismembered or displayed the bodies of my captains. It was poor consolation, but I could not bear the thought that it would be done.

Consolation? There was no consolation for me. Or for my

lady-in-waiting, Lady Katherine de Vaux. Katherine, too, had lost her own husband in the battle.

I knelt before the bare crucifix on the wall above my bed. I could not think, I could not make decisions. One terrible gamble we had made in facing the Yorkist usurper. All lost on a battle-field. I had lost him; I had lost everything. I could not even think of Henry. He was of no help to me now, returned to the Tower. Did he even know that his son was dead?

'But do you know he is dead?' Anne asked. 'How can we be certain?'

Did I know for certain? I had not seen his body. I had not been told by any man who had seen him fall. Did the faintest seed of hope live within me? I clung on to it as a drowning man would hold fast to a rope thrown to him by a would-be rescuer. There was no grief expressed on Anne's calm face, but I held to the hope she offered me.

As the days passed with no further news, that seed withered and died.

What would I do now? I had no care for the clothes my women brought to me. I refused all meals until chivvied into eating for my own health. What did my health matter when I had nothing to live for? What would happen to me now?

All I could do was wait until Edward of York discovered where I was. I could only wait until he came to take me into captivity.

'Why do you not flee to France?' Katherine de Vaux suggested. 'It can be arranged. You can take ship from Bristol.'

'I cannot. I cannot make the decisions.' How hopeless I was. My mind refused to grasp the future. 'And if I leave, does that not finally stab the cause of Lancaster in the heart? I do not even know that Louis would want me back on French soil.'

They came for me, of course, and the Prior had no choice

but to allow this armed force at his gate to enter. A forcible abduction, if that is what it could be called, at the hands of Sir William Stanley.

There was only one fact that I wished to know.

'What is the fate of my son?'

His smile was cruel indeed.

'He is dead, madam.'

Now I knew. I must accept and abandon all my foolish hopes.

It was necessary for them to drag me from the Priory. I could not even find the words to resist the men with the Yorkist and Stanley emblems on their garments. How my spirits had fallen into an abyss. My tongue was stilled, except for one question:

'Tell me what has happened to my son's body?'

'I know not. It hardly matters.'

I knew not where they were taking me. London, I supposed, to the Tower. I did not care as they handed me into a litter and pulled the curtains close.

Instead, I was escorted north to where Edward of York waited for me. I still would not call him King. He was breaking his journey at Coventry, I was told, after putting down a rebellion in the North. That is where they took me, to my horror.

It was the last place I would have wished to be taken under guard: Coventry, my secret harbour, in the centre of my dower estates, a place where I had enjoyed my authority after Henry had been stricken by his illness, and where I had feted my son in his childhood. As we rode through the streets of the town – for I was forced to exchange the litter for horseback so that I might be seen by the crowds – I recalled the pageants that had welcomed us and heaped praise on us, lauding my position as mother of the heir. St Margaret slew a dragon in my honour. I was compared with the Blessed Virgin Mary herself. Henry had been with me, but all the praise and glory had been centred on me and on my son.

Now the crowds were silent to witness my arrival, or perhaps they did not even notice this small group of soldiers with the even smaller group of women held tight in their centre. I closed my eyes and allowed them to lead my horse. I had no wish to remember the agonising past. How far I had fallen.

Edward of York looked exultant when I was ushered into his presence in the chamber I had once called my own, decorated with the same Flemish tapestries, vibrant with leaves and flowers and strolling knights with their ladies that I had had placed there. I saw the flash of victory in his eyes before it was quickly veiled. Was I not still Queen of England? I had not been deposed. I would refuse to recognise his kingship. I would not kneel or bow my head. I would not answer his questions. It seemed that my pride was not as dead as I had thought.

But no, it would not be wise to use my pride as a challenge. My life now hung in the balance with this man. He could order my death if he so wished, or keep me in perpetual imprisonment.

He rose from his chair when I entered, tall and broad, brazen with the authority that he had stolen. His two brothers were with him – the three brothers of York together in authority, all my enemies in one chamber. I surveyed them. Edward, no longer the lithe young man, his face and body showing the signs of high living, if tales were true. Clarence, smugly self-satisfied from the outcome of his change of loyalties; here was a man I would ignore. And then Gloucester, an unknown power in the land, slight and dark with an uncomfortable intensity about him. These were the men who would determine my fate.

They no longer showed traces of battle, no remnant of royal Lancastrian blood on their hands or their fine clothing, except that I could see it. It was as if the stains would remain there for eternity. I stood before them, straight-backed, hands linked loosely at my waist, refusing to acknowledge any one of them. I might be defeated but I would not kneel before them. I regretted the well-worn state of my garments when they were garbed in sumptuous velvet and damask, jewelled chains gracing their shoulders. I was the crow in the midst of this trio of brightly arrayed jays, without decoration or jewel, enveloped in the dense black of mourning. Would they laugh at me, sneer at me? I raised my chin a little higher.

'My lady. I trust you travelled well. I think that you were not put under any improper coercion.'

The usurper inclined his head. So he would show me some due respect after all. His welcome held no crudity in it.

'My lord.' My voice sounded light and dry to my ears as if not often used. 'It seems that I am your prisoner.'

'Yes.' He surveyed me from head to foot. 'You look weary and travel-worn. Come and sit.'

I did not move. Any show of compassion would reduce me to unwelcome emotions, but he held out his hand and I found myself placing mine there so that he could lead me to a chair with carved back and arms, a soft cushion to ease my aching bones. Yes, I was weary, unbearably so. I sat, and he pulled up a stool so that he might sit beside me, indicating that his brothers should withdraw from us.

'Rest a little. You have had too much to bear, my lady.'

How could he show me such pity, weakening my defences against him?

'What do you know of what I have had to bear?' I demanded, horrified to hear my voice raw with loss and grief. His concern might have soothed my heart. He could afford to be generous. I was his prisoner and the Lancastrian cause was dead. But I raised my head, forcing myself through my weariness to meet him eye to eye.

'What are you intending to do with me?'

'I have not yet decided.'

'Execution?'

How harsh and unwomanly my voice, my demand to know the truth.

'I do not execute women,' he responded roughly.

He eyed me. He had aged since I had last seen him, power and conflict engraving lines on his brow and beside his mouth. I had ruffled his composure but he was still in command. I drew in a breath.

'I suppose that I must be grateful for my life. But will you give me my freedom?'

'No. Not that. You are too dangerous an adversary, even when heart-sick and weighed down with weariness as you are now.'

No, of course he would not free me.

'I wish to see my lord the King,' I said.

'Later.'

I knew that I would have to fight him for my future, and so I did.

'You have no right to keep me in captivity.'

'I have every right. You waged war against me.'

And I would say it. 'And you killed my son.'

I dropped the statement into the silence. For a long moment Edward of York considered the palms of his hands.

'You have killed my son,' I repeated. 'How can I ever forgive you for that?'

'I do not require your forgiveness, lady. Your son challenged me in battle. Death is the penalty.'

'He did not deserve to die. He should be King of England.'

I heard my voice rise to echo from the softly tapestried walls.

The usurper did not hesitate.

'I am King of England, by law and victory in war. Traitors pay with their lives. Do not try my patience, my lady. You, too, are a traitor. Just as you are too dangerous to allow freedom to travel in England, your son was too dangerous to be allowed to live. You must know that. I have no wish to spend my life looking over my shoulder for a Lancastrian dagger aimed between my shoulder blades. Even if I allowed him to go into exile in France, I would have no deliverance from his threat. You raised him well, my lady, to hate me and mine.'

'I swear that you will never live in peace.'

'I have every intention of doing so.' His quick smile held no humour. 'That is why I must make a decision about your future.'

'I am still Queen of England.'

'No longer.'

'Then what am I?'

He smiled wryly. 'You, my lady Margaret, are nothing but an embarrassment to me. I have no wish to be deemed an ogre.' He stood and raised me to my feet with a hand around my wrist. 'There is a chamber prepared for you. Tomorrow we go south to London. There will be a guard on your door, but you need not fear ill-treatment. Your women already await you there.'

And then the one question I must ask.

'What have you done with my son's body?'

His face became stern at my presumption.

'Do you suggest that I would treat the Prince gracelessly in death? There has been no despoilment. He has been buried within the abbey at Tewkesbury, in the chancel, with some ceremony as you would have wished. His name, carved for all time, marks the place where he lies.'

'I wish to see it,' I demanded.

'That will not be possible.'

'I would have wished to see the crown on his head!'

'It could not be. Be satisfied. The boy rests at peace in hallowed ground.'

'And what of his widow? What of Anne Neville? What do you do with her?'

'That has still to be decided. There are other voices raised on her behalf. All our business here is finished. Now go, for I have matters to attend to.'

It was a comfortable chamber to which I was escorted, one that I remembered well.

I slept like the dead.

My humiliation was not yet complete. I was escorted south, staying at Yorkist manors and religious houses, until we arrived in the city. Edward of York had arranged that he would enter London in a triumphal march to impress the populace, surrounded by his victorious retinue. I was to be the gilded jewel of his triumph. Before it all, I was paraded in an open litter through the streets. There was no hiding, no means of drawing curtains to shut out the cheers and the jeers. The Yorkist was popular, he and his two brothers. His success at Tewkesbury was celebrated in ale and meat pasties. There was no mourning for my cause or for my son's short life. Those who cheered would be drunk on the Yorkist victory and wine and ale by nightfall. For me they deserved to roll in the gutters in dregs and vomit.

I stared blindly before me, refusing to respond, refusing to listen to the catcalls and gibes, the crude comments. Twenty-six years ago I had been similarly paraded in a litter, come for my wedding, my long hair virginally loose over the shoulders of my cloth-of-gold gown. That had been my own victory march. Now I was defeated and grieving, garments in a sorry state. I was put on show like a mummers' bauble for the populace who cheered my ignominy.

I would not respond. I would show no emotion.

On our arrival, when I was helped from my litter and escorted to my chamber in the White Tower, I looked up at the blank walls. My lord Henry was here too somewhere. Would I be allowed to see him? *I do not execute women*, Edward of York had said, but would he execute Henry, now that he had both of us in the palm of his hand? In the strength of his reclaimed crown, he might consider it an act worth the doing. Power and ambition would warp any finer feelings.

'I wish to see my husband the King,' I said to the steward who accompanied me to my chamber. I did not know him. He had not been here in the Tower when I had lived here as Queen.

'It is not permitted, my lady.'

'Will you ask King Edward?'

I almost choked on the name, on the title, but surely he would allow it. I did not know where Anne was. She had not travelled with me from Coventry and was no longer part of my household. It did not trouble me. She did not carry my son's child, and so could never be of any value to me; my compassion for her was fleeting. I had been led to understand that she had been put into the care of the Duke of Clarence, who would take her to stay with her sister Isabel. I presumed she would be treated well. There had been no farewell between us. What would I have to say to her? She had meant nothing to me but a means to an end.

As I had been in my own marriage.

It was late evening when there was a knock on my door. Such courtesy being unexpected, I looked up from where I sat with my psalter on my knee, open but unread, with no wish to be disturbed into false courtesies, but I nodded to Lady Katherine de Vaux, who went to open it. I heard a low-voiced conversation, then the door opened further and my visitor walked in, a servant accompanying him with a hand to his arm.

Immediately I was on my feet, the psalter cast forgotten on the floor with a flutter of the illuminated pages.

'Henry. My dear lord.'

I could not believe that I had been shown such favour, but here was my lord Henry, who blinked at me in the shifting candlelight.

'Margaret? They said that you were here. I did not believe them. Where is our son?'

Memories swept back. Memories of our early years together when there was much care and affection between us, when he had been young and fair, an admirable king, before clear thought abandoned him.

'Margaret?' he repeated. 'Have you come to take me from here? Where will we go? Where is our son? Is he not here?'

I walked to take his hands in mine as his servant stepped back. How insubstantial they were within mine, how the years pressed down on him, his hair thin and unkempt, his outer robe little more than threadbare, the fur edging moth-eaten. Had they no thought for his regal birth, his coronation, his godly blessing? He was a mere husk of the man I had wed. His face was gaunt, his expression worn with care, even when he managed a smile.

'I cannot take you from here,' I said.

'Why can we not leave?'

'It is the wish of the King.'

'But am I not King?'

'It is the wish of Edward of York.'

'He is very kind to me. He sends me books.'

I could not reply to this. What a sad remnant of the young man I had once known.

'Will they let me visit you again?' he asked.

'Of course. I am sure that they will.'

I kissed his cheek.

'Where is our son?'

I swallowed. 'He is not here with me.'

'Where is he?'

'Did you not know that our son, Edward, is dead? He died bravely on the battlefield at Tewkesbury. He fought as any brave knight, as you would have wished.'

He looked away from me, then back again. 'Yes. I think they told me. I am sad.'

I was not sure that he did indeed know.

'I have prayed for his soul, of course,' Henry added. 'Will he be laid to rest here in St Paul's?'

'No,' I replied softly. 'But he has a fine resting place in the abbey at Tewkesbury.'

'You must come away now, my lord.' The servant stepped forward again and touched his arm quite gently. 'We may not stay long.'

'Of course.'

He turned from me as if he had nothing more to say.

Henry was led away, looking back over his shoulder, promising to speak with me the following day. Then he halted to pick up the psalter from where I had dropped it, smoothing the pages, handing it back to me with a smile. His feet shuffled on the floor.

How had we come to this? How sore my heart was within me.

Next morning, even before I had risen from my bed, a written message was delivered to me, brought by Lady Katherine, who had taken it from a servant. It was short and without signature.

The only information it imparted to me was this, written hurriedly in a clerkish hand:

*This is to report that Henry of Lancaster, once King of England, has died during the night. The cause was said to be death from a melancholy. He slipped away from this life before the royal physician could administer a draught to keep his heart beating. He died without pain and without any final words to be recorded.*

I sat, speechless and dry-eyed. Katherine left me alone.

Should I have questioned its veracity? I knew that his death was true, as surely as I sat in that room with the note flat between my palms as if to absorb the horror of the words. Why? Why did he need to die? For I did not believe that it was by chance. I would not question the death, but I would question its cause. Surely my arrival had had no influence on it. And yet had I not anticipated it? It should not have been a surprise.

I summoned Lady Katherine with a lift of my hand.

'Do you know any more about this?'

'Yes, my dear lady. His body was discovered in his chamber this morning. The physician who came to see him thought that he had died just before midnight. The King decided that you should be told.'

'He allowed me to see him yesterday.'

'Yes.'

'I did not know it would be for the last time.'

How cruel is ignorance, when deliberately created. I simply sat and considered my emotions. Grief? Little. Regret? Some. It would have been better to send him to live out his days in a monastery, but even I knew that would never be. What had Edward of York said of my son? Too dangerous to live. So I supposed was Henry, but it was difficult to believe. Who would now rescue him and place the crown on his head once more? It seemed to me that Edward of York was safe enough.

As for Henry, there was never any depth of love between us. Once in the early days of our marriage there was a soft affection, but that had died. Respect had been difficult when he could no longer shoulder the burdens of kingship, and yet I had done all I could to care for him and restore him to what was his by right. I had protected his son until I could protect him no longer.

Casting the note aside, I stared at the palms of my hands as if I would see my future there. What did Henry's death make me? It had undermined every argument I might have. Now I was even more of an embarrassment. A childless widow with no claims at all on the crown of England, Henry's death had destroyed my cause completely. I was helpless, penniless, entirely dependent on Edward of York's mercy, of which I suspected he would have little.

If only Anne had carried my son's child. It would have given me a light to shine as a beacon in the future. But I had not wanted that, and so I had wilfully forbidden the consummation. I had not wanted my son tied to her.

'My lady?' It was the Duke of Gloucester who had come to the door, severe of expression but bowing courteously. 'My brother the King wishes to speak with you. If you will accompany me.'

He made no mention of Henry's death on that short journey. This time Edward of York was alone, when Gloucester left us together.

'Did you kill him?' I asked.

'No.'

'Did you give orders for his death? I swear it was not ill-health that took him from this earth.'

Edward of York shrugged as if the how or why were of no importance.

'The physician said that he died of a melancholy after news of recent events, of the death of his son and your capture. He died of a broken heart, I suppose.'

'Exacerbated by a knife in his flesh. Or, more likely, a dose of poison in his wine.'

Edward of York swept the idea away with a flamboyant brush of his hand. The light from the window at his side brought into relief the fleshy face and thickened neck. This was not the graceful boy I had known at York's side at the battle that never happened at Ludford Bridge.

'An irrelevance,' he said, his tone grating. 'I have decided what to do with you, madam.'

'To join my husband in death?'

'Did I not promise that you would take no harm at my hands?'

A leap of hope in my heart.

'Then send me back to France, if you will. To my father's Court. Or that of King Louis.'

'It might be considered. I would rather Louis offer you a home than I.'

'Then why not let me go?'

His smile was slyly contemplative.

'It will all depend on the terms. You are a penniless beggar, and thus must be provided for financially, whereas I desire recompense. You cost me much in death and bloodshed. Not least the blood of my father and brother. The discomfort of my mother.'

'Duchess Cecily could stand up for herself.'

'No matter. I will promise to begin negotiations. If Louis will ransom you, then I will consider an exchange, your person for a heavy purse of gold. Meanwhile, I will send you to Windsor.

You will not be free, you will be guarded, but will live in some comfort. You will leave tomorrow.' He regarded me. 'You do not seem inordinately grief-stricken at the death of your husband.'

'You do not know what is in my heart. I have enough grief in my life. I will mourn in my own way.'

And I would pray that Louis, in all his deviousness, would see some reason for coming to my aid. I did not hold much hope.

I was moved to Windsor where I could not fault the care for my comfort, although I could my lack of freedom. I was not lacking in news and discovered more about Henry's death, none of it changing my mind over who was to blame. The Bastard of Fauconberg, Thomas Neville, the illegitimate son of Warwick's uncle Lord Fauconberg, had raised a force to free Henry and restore him to the throne. The uprising collapsed but not before reaching London Bridge, far too close for comfort! Fauconberg was arrested and executed at Middleham Castle. This was what Edward had been doing before he met with me at Coventry. Such an uprising might be put down, but it had assuredly signed my lord Henry's death warrant.

Thus he had died on the night that I had arrived in London. The same night that Edward of York had taken up residence. I knew whose hand had signed the document, whose tongue had given the order.

He might still sign mine. I did not trust Edward of York, whatever he might promise. Would I, too, be murdered, one dark night, at Windsor?

I cursed him. I cursed him for the deaths of those at Tewkesbury, and now for Henry. For myself, I could only wait.

# 34

## *Freedom or Freedom Curtailed? 1472*

**Anne, Countess of Warwick**

Beaulieu Abbey became my home, at first my place of safety.

Then it became my prison.

Fears and nightmares lived constantly with me.

I had taken refuge there, until affairs changed and I could leave. Now there would be no leaving. I had thought to live in seclusion until I could make contact with my daughters, or until I might travel to Court to throw myself on Ned's mercy and claim back my dowry and jointure, and my Beauchamp inheritance. As a traitor's widow I knew that I must act with discretion, but surely Clarence, royal brother and my nephew by marriage, would be generous? Ned owed his crown to Richard, before the relationship soured. Then surely he owed me some compassion, some compensation? Would he not remember and treat me with dignity in my present situation? It was a cold, dark existence for me in the abbey, hemming me in with austerity. Ned had the power to release me from this.

I was dependent on the Abbot for my news and he was kind enough to keep me abreast of what happened in the outside world. What desperate news it was, some of which I knew, particularly the death of the Yorkist commanders, executed after the

Battle of Tewkesbury, the holy ground so drenched with blood that services were not permitted until it could be cleansed. The slaying of Prince Edward on the battlefield and the capture of Margaret, as well as the capture of my daughter Anne and her journey to London came to me piece by piece. Then there was the death of Henry, not unexpected given the ultimate Yorkist victory.

I had heard it all, and apart from the safety of my two girls, it was not important to me. Isabel, as Clarence's wife, would suffer no ill effects after the battle had wiped out the hope of Lancaster. Of my daughter Anne, now widowed and her ties with Lancaster severed, I was unsure, but I had no fear that Ned would treat her with disrespect.

I prayed that she would at least be reunited with Isabel.

As for the rest of the bad news, it was all in the past. I must secure my future.

The thought lived with me that Margaret's situation was as uncertain as mine; she was as effectively imprisoned as I. Now widowed and childless, her isolation was far worse than mine. At least my daughters were still alive and might come to my aid, although I grieved for both in my uncertainty and my loneliness.

'Tell me of my husband,' I urged the Abbot after Compline when he suggested that I drink a cup of wine with him in his chambers. Grief had been resurrected to surge within me when I realised all that I had not been told.

'But you know all I can tell you,' he said, unwilling to add to my pain.

'I know that he died on the battlefield at Barnet. That his brother died too. Tell me that he died bravely. Tell me how he was treated after death.'

'Do you wish to know?'

'Yes. What I imagine is far worse.'

'As for his bravery, I know not, but I imagine that he was. All I know was that the morning was thick with swirling mist, making it difficult to recognise friend from foe.'

That was not what I wanted to know. 'Was he brought down from his horse?'

'Indeed no. The Earl chose to dismount and fought on foot at the end.' The Abbot held my hands in his. 'What I do know is that the Earl's body and that of his brother were taken to London and exposed so that there should be no doubts of their deaths. They were on the steps of St Paul's Cathedral where a mighty crowd gathered.'

Quite as bad as I had thought.

'For how long?'

'Three days.'

I turned my mind away from that image. 'What happened to my lord's body, after the King had humiliated it sufficiently?'

I knew how the bodies of traitors were dealt with. I remembered the heads on Micklegate Bar. My heart was cold stone in my chest. I wept silent tears.

'Not as bad as you might think, my dear lady. They were taken to Bisham Priory. Your lord was buried with his family there. It is what he would have wanted. And you, too, would have wanted it for him. You cannot fault King Edward there.'

'I have no kind thoughts for the King who so willingly killed his cousins.'

'It had to be done. Warwick was too dangerous, my dear. You know that. You must accept it. There could be no remaking of an alliance between Warwick and the King after past events.'

It was true. Ned could never forgive. At least it was one worry taken from my mind. I imagined Ned taking his revenge by casting Richard into some nameless grave where he would be forgotten for all time, after exhibiting his body on gates and bridges throughout the country. Perhaps one day I would be allowed to return to Bisham to pay my own respects. Perhaps...

I had no real hope of it.

The weeks passed slowly. What of my daughters? Why did I hear nothing from them? Had they been turned against me? I received no news, no letters, no visits. It was as if I did not exist. One daughter had changed sides from York to Lancaster, following her husband. What had happened to the other after Tewkesbury? I had been told that Anne had been taken prisoner with Margaret, and now both were under Ned's control. Surely he would not confine my daughter to the Tower, whatever might be Margaret's fate. Fear gnawed at me with the teeth of a rat.

It was time that I stopped dwelling on the past and looked to my future. I could not remain here in perpetuity.

In a moment of clarity, I realised that I could expect no dower from Warwick's estate since he was regarded as a traitor, but I still had my jointure settled on me at my marriage, as well as the vast Beauchamp and Despenser inheritance that was still mine by right. I knew what I needed to do. I needed to come to Ned, to the King, to claim those rights. I had done nothing wrong. I had not betrayed him. I had taken sanctuary for my own safety. Even though I had been bound by duty and obedience to my husband, I was no traitor.

The Abbot's question broke into my unsettling conclusions. How long had I been lost in my own thoughts, sitting here in a patch of weak sunlight in the quiet of the cloisters? At this time of the morning they were empty, the monks busy with their own work in the scriptorium or garden, the novices raising their voices as they learned to sing the response for the Mass. Otherwise the only sound was the twittering of little birds seeking nesting sites in the carved arches of the stairway that led to the monks' dormitories. The Abbot had come to join me, taking a seat beside me on the stone surround, despite its lack of comfort.

'What do you wish to do, my lady?'

The cloisters should have been a tranquil haven, a refuge of serenity. There was neither tranquillity nor serenity about the decision I had come to.

'Claim what is mine,' I said without hesitation.

'I think it might be unwise for you to leave these walls where at least you are guaranteed safety. I can offer you no safe passage to London.'

I felt within me a strengthening determination. I would be weakly dependent no longer.

'I cannot live here all my life. I will have what is due to me. I will demand recognition of my status as the Beauchamp heiress. I will go to the Court and kneel before the King, if I must.'

What had driven me to this decision? A memory, not one of my own but one told to me frequently by my mother and grandmother; a family memory that would strengthen my spine against any adversity. My inestimable great-great-grandmother, the heiress Johane de Geneville, wife of Roger Mortimer, Earl of March, had been forced to fight for the Mortimer inheritance against all the odds when the Earl was executed for treason. She had lost everything, the lands, the castles, her titles. She had been successful in her battle for restitution against the third King Edward. So could I be. Johane had never given up the fight. How could I, her great-great-granddaughter, even consider it?

'I will travel to Westminster, to King Edward's Court,' I repeated.

'Then I suggest that you ask for safe conduct from the King.'

'Will you write it for me? A safe conduct for me to go to Court and petition for my rights.'

'I will. It will be sent tomorrow.'

I knew that he would keep his promise.

I waited for the reply.

It was October, when autumn was turning into winter with high winds to dislodge the final leaves, leaving them in piles to be swept up from the cloister at the abbey, when a reply was sent. It was the worst of news for me, and relatively quick to arrive. It had not taken Ned long to make the decision that would dictate the direction of my life. I knew it as soon as I saw the Abbot's face.

'You must come and sit. You need to be strong, my lady.'

It was after the daily gathering in the Chapter House when the monks had departed about their work and prayer. All was quiet, but it was the silence of cataclysm for me. I could sense it, blown in by the gales.

'I will not sit,' I said. 'I am not so weak. Tell me, for it cannot be worse news than my lord's death. The King has refused my safe conduct to take me to Court. I should not be surprised. If he can deny the freedom of the late Queen, he can refuse any pleas from me.'

'Worse than that, my lady.'

'How can it be worse, unless he plans to execute me in my husband's name?'

'Not that.' The Abbot shook his head in reprimand. 'Our King does not wage war on you, but I have received orders, my lady. You are to be kept here under my jurisdiction, in strict confinement. You will not be allowed to go to Court to sue for your inheritance, your jointure or your dower.'

I would not be allowed. Edward was denying me my rights. Bitterness choked me.

'And of course you must obey our King,' I said, any respect that I owed to the Abbot draining away.

'I must. I must in the King's name keep you here. It will not be an uncomfortable life, as far as I can make it, but you will have no freedom or the luxury you were used to as Countess of Warwick.'

'I am still Countess of Warwick.'

The Abbot's gaze held mine as he delivered the blow.

'In the eyes of the world you are invisible, my lady. Your lands and titles no longer belong to you.'

I considered this in mounting horror.

'Has King Edward taken them?'

'No. All your lands were occupied by the Duke of Clarence after Tewkesbury, in your daughter's name.'

The repercussions for me could not be clearer. A permanent restriction on my freedom, a lack of recognition, my lands in Clarence's greedy hands.

'Could you arrange for me to escape?' I asked. 'To go to Ireland, or even back to France where I might discover someone who will aid me?'

'I dare not, my lady, I dare not. I must protect my Abbey and my monks.'

There was no moving him.

I returned to my meagre accommodation, in the lowest of spirits.

A strange, unsettling piece of news had accompanied the King's refusal to consider my plight. I did not know what to think, whether to celebrate or mourn.

My daughter Anne, so recently widowed, had married Richard, the King's brother. She was now Duchess of Gloucester. I had not even known, and certainly had no control over this. Who had organised it? The King? Richard himself? I cast my mind back to the young boy who had been raised in my household at Middleham, who had learned to hunt and ride and fight and enjoy books, who had become as close as a son to me.

Was Anne a willing bride? It seemed so. Had there not always been a close friendship between them in their childhood? Not that it would matter. If the King had desired it, then it would happen. The two Neville-Beauchamp heiresses wed to the two royal brothers.

It would not take a soothsayer to read the King's mind.

My inheritance, and that of Richard, would be divided between them.

Such manipulation. Fury boiled within me in that holy place. I was helpless to change what Edward was doing. I was as helpless as Margaret, a prisoner.

I noticed in passing that I no longer thought of our King as Ned. The days of that family name were long gone. He had rejected me, and so would I reject him. Except that I would not sit helplessly here, entombed in Beaulieu Abbey. It was not right that my inheritance should be denied me. Nor my freedom. I would not accept it.

I took myself to the scriptorium where monks were working in the gentle atmosphere of the scratch of pens and the shuffle of manuscript pages, writing and copying, and I requested the aid of a clerk.

'Write this down for me, if you will.'

It was a list. I recalled writing a list of possible husbands for my two daughters, in happier times. This was a list of all who might come to my rescue. A list of all who might have compassion for my position, and some who would not but who must still be petitioned. A list of those who had been friends in the past and even enemies, but now had voices at Court where King Edward must listen to them.

There was no surprise here as I ticked them off on my fingers and the clerk wrote them down. King Edward and Queen Elizabeth, of course. The King's mother, Cecily, Duchess of York, who understood what it was to be widowed. Who had also been robbed of her inheritance after the debacle at Ludford Bridge. I added the King's eldest daughter Elizabeth, although she was but a child, an unlikely ally. Surely there were more who might listen to me? King Edward's sisters, the Duchesses of Exeter and Suffolk and Burgundy, should not be omitted.

'Anyone else, my lady?'

'Yes. And I will write to the Commons to tell them of my desperate situation. They may claim some influence over the King.'

Surely someone would come to my aid now that the war was apparently over. The women had all known loss and grief, many of them had known widowhood. Surely all would understand that I was no traitor. Some of them knew what it was to be driven to claim their rightful inheritance.

An impressive list? It was a poor showing. All it did was imprint the fact in my mind that I was truly on my own with few, if any, to stand for me, yet I would not be deterred. If I did nothing I would simply live for ever without hope. I must give myself that fragile chance of being rescued. First, I would write to the King. I would write it myself. This was not for a clerk to interpret. I would not kneel or bow low. I would demand what was mine, by law, by justice and by the right of inheritance. I would appeal to family, to events of the past. If I did not make this plea, I had the suspicion that there was no one who would make it for me. Richard had made too many enemies for me to expect even a single hand of friendship to be stretched in my direction.

*To my lord and cousin by marriage, King Edward*

*From your true liege woman, Anne, Countess of Warwick, who has never acted in any treasonable way towards you.*

*I have been robbed of my title, my inheritance and my freedom. How can this be?*

*I have never been attainted for treason. Nor was my lord of Warwick attainted, simply because you wish the Warwick inheritance to pass freely to our two daughters, and thus into the hands of your two brothers. I, too, should be allowed to take possession of what is legally mine as an heiress and a widow.*

*I retired to the abbey at Beaulieu to escape any attacks on my person and to pray for the soul of my lord of Warwick. I had no other motive. I am not here to plot and scheme. I have never plotted or schemed against you throughout my whole life. As my husband's wife, it was necessary for me to stand with him in his decisions, as a dutiful wife would. You will understand this.*

*I throw myself on your mercy.*

*By what manner of justice has the Abbot of Beaulieu been ordered to restrict my freedom? Sanctuary should not be a prison. I wish to be free to walk out of this place and choose where I should live. I wish to be able to leave without fear for my life.*

*I know what is my right to hold; inherited through my Beauchamp birth and my marriage to the Earl of Warwick, I know full well what should be my dower, my jointure and my inheritance.*

*I ask for your compassion, if you will remember the past when my lord of Warwick was the most loyal of royal servants. Did*

*not the Neville family spill enough blood to achieve the crown of
England for you?*

*Grant me my freedom. Grant me my lands and my wealth,
gracious lord.*

I signed it.

Sent it.

In my heart, was there any true hope that my appeal would be
heard? Would my lands ever be returned? In my heart I knew
that this petition was a lost cause.

'Why not petition your daughters, my lady?' The Abbot possessed a hope that was not mine. 'Should Duchess Isabel and
Duchess Anne not be the first recipients of your petition?'

But I was afraid to do so. Isabel would do nothing against
Clarence's wishes. As for Anne, I did not know. If her new
husband had an eye to my estates, he would not argue my cause
to his royal brother. I thought that Gloucester would certainly
make a claim for himself on behalf of his new wife. No, I would
not write to them, dividing their loyalties, but I would write to
their now-royal husbands.

I sent my petitions and set myself to wait again. Forever waiting. As the weeks passed without reply I challenged the Abbot:
'What if I disobeyed the King and travelled to Court anyway?'

'I will lock you in, my lady.' He was stern but overwhelmingly
compassionate. 'I can't let you go.'

'Tell me of the Queen. Queen Margaret, that is.'

'Queen no longer.'

'Is she in the Tower?'

'I understand that she is living in Windsor, under restraint.'

Was there any hope for either of us?

# 35

## A Gentle Imprisonment in Wallingford Castle

### Margaret, Queen of England

I was told of my lord Henry's interment. A brief description by a York herald was sent to me at Windsor Castle, for which I must thank King Edward. I supposed that I must now address him as such. Who else could be King? He would be King and his sons after him. There was no more pure Lancastrian blood left to claim it.

Of course I was not allowed to attend the obsequies. My presence might arouse emotions amongst any who still retained Lancastrian sympathies, solace that was now best buried and forgotten with the old King. Embalmed with wax and spices, wrapped in linen for burial, his body was carried through the streets of London to St Paul's to be shown to the crowds, then on to the Benedictine monastery at Chertsey Abbey where his earthly body was finally offered rest. The Yorkist usurper had no intention of allowing my lord Henry a tomb in St Paul's or in Westminster Abbey, where pilgrims of Lancastrian loyalties might flock, but at least he was given a burial place that he deserved, as the monk that he often wished to be. I hoped that he would approve. I could not think of the manner of his death.

The herald bowed and departed with much courtesy.

Who was I now? I had no claim on the throne, I had no one to fight for, and no one to fight for me. But I would never give up my claim to be Queen of England. I also was informed by that same herald that the few possessions I owned were to be packed into coffers. My confinement at Windsor had come to an end.

'Where am I to go?' I demanded of him. 'Am I to travel to France?'

My heart leapt at the prospect of returning to my homeland. There would be no comfort there for me, but better than the uncertainty of remaining a captive at King Edward's behest. If I returned to France I could take refuge with my father. Or even at the Court of King Louis.

Once in France I could decide on my future, but what it would be I could not envisage; the future was blurred with shadows for me, but there would never be a return to England. Since I had no claim on that throne in my own right, neither my father nor the French King would come to my aid. Desolation welled up in me again. I had no rights at all. I did not think that Louis would want me. Nor did I believe that Edward would ever allow me to leave England unless he was well rewarded for it, and Louis was not one for generosity unless it was in his interests.

'Where am I being sent?' I repeated, dreading that it was back to the Tower of London where Henry had met his end.

'You are to go to Wallingford Castle, my lady. All is arranged.'

'Wallingford!'

A tiny easing of the tension around my heart. I knew who lived at Wallingford. I might even be received there with some semblance of welcome and courtesy, not the cold politeness of the royal servants here at Windsor.

'You will remain in the custody of Alice de la Pole, the

Dowager Duchess of Suffolk, until more satisfactory and permanent arrangements are made for you.'

I would consider that situation when I was alone. I would never expose my fears and heartbreak to any man employed by the King.

'Then I am not to return to France,' I stated, perfectly calmly.

'No, my lady. One day it may be so, but the financial negotiations with King Louis the Eleventh are proving difficult.'

As I had thought: it might never happen. I might die here before Louis would be willing to ransom me. Meanwhile, King Edward would rather be rid of me in this manner than at the stroke of an axe for treason. And Alice de la Pole might indeed prove to be a friendly face. Once again, my spirits lifted slightly, until I recalled the treason she had committed in the past.

'I should tell you, my lady, it will still be an imprisonment at Wallingford. You will have no freedoms, and the Dowager Duchess will be under strict orders to keep you confined.'

'Do I take my ladies with me? I want Lady Katherine de Vaux.'

'The King has given no orders to the contrary.'

It meant much to me. I might have lost everything, but for the first time for some months my heart beat with a calm anticipation.

Wallingford Castle awaited me with what I could only consider a glowering hostility as I pulled back the curtains of my litter. It was a major fortress, surviving sieges and warfare over the years, frequently the residence of royals when its grey walls and turrets, as well as the impressive old keep, had been much added to by recent buildings. It had a reputation for luxury and the quality of its furnishings. As I was escorted through the imposing gateway it merely seemed intimidating. However luxurious the life within, it would be my prison.

And here was Alice de la Pole, Duchess of Suffolk, standing in her Great Hall, mistress of every inch of its antique splendour, the windows set with jewelled glass. It was as if time had stood still, or at least had taken a few steps back into the past. Here was a woman I knew well, or had known. She had been one of the women who had escorted me to England as a young bride. She had been present at the birth of my son. Aged now, her shoulders slightly stooped, her long features no longer smooth and smiling with youthful enthusiasm, Alice had lost her husband Suffolk to murder, his head and body tossed onto the beach near Dover by a riotous mob. A magnificent survivor, granddaughter of the poet Chaucer, Alice had outlived three husbands. I thought that her lined face, the deep grooves enclosing eyes and mouth, told their own story of the strength of will needed for her survival of such a lifetime. Would she be a friend to me? It seemed unlikely, even though once in the past she had been a most trusted lady-in-waiting.

Here she was, acting as my gaoler at the behest of the Yorkist King.

'I welcome you here as a friend and a guest,' she said. 'I imagine that you are a reluctant one.'

'How could you do it?' The first angry words I uttered. 'How could you sell your soul to the Yorkist upstart?'

'Not quite the initial response I would expect from a woman who will be my prisoner,' she replied with the wry twist of her lips that I recognised.

My attack had surprised me, but I made no attempt to rein it in. There was no humour in me. That was all dead.

'You betrayed the house of Lancaster! You tied yourself to the stirrups of York. How could you think of doing that? You are no friend of mine.'

Lady Alice was unmoved by my tirade.

'I stood in loyalty to my own family. You of all women know how important that is, in a political world. I was not free to make my own choices, as you have not been free to make yours.'

My anger did not abate at this show of reason.

'Tell me why you agreed to make such an outrageous alliance.'

The flicker in her eyes made it clear that she knew what I meant. Alice de la Pole, Dowager Duchess of Suffolk, had made an incredible decision that would deny all Suffolk's past loyalties. When she held control of her son's wardship and marriage, in an age where the wardships of wealthy young heirs were of such vast importance, she and Richard, Duke of York, had entered into an agreement for her son, John de la Pole, to marry Elizabeth, one of York's daughters.

'I saw the opportunity for an advantageous match.' Lady Alice took my arm and led me towards the stairs, explaining as we walked. 'And you have to admit, I could not have chosen better in the circumstances, since Elizabeth's brother is now King of England. I would do the same today and tomorrow. But that's in the past and has no bearing on the present, except that I am put in charge of your person. Come in and sit and allow your temper to settle, my lady. You will get no response from me through harsh words.'

'I note that you no longer address me as your Queen,' I accused her, unwilling to abandon the depth of my sorrow.

'Because you are no longer Queen of England,' she replied. 'I will address you as such if it brings you any comfort. My advice is to abandon the past with all its griefs.'

'I suppose that I have no choice.'

'None at all,' she replied cheerfully with a gentle touch to my arm. 'Best that you accept the situation and make the most of my calm temper, since you are weary and in bad humour.'

'I will never call you friend,' I said.

'You do not have to, but nor am I your enemy. Now sit and take stock of your new home.'

At least I did not fear her as a custodian while the King's negotiations with Louis dragged on. Obedient to her suggestion, I sat and took the offered wine cup, until my anger subsided and at last I held out my hands in friendship, as I had rarely done with women at my Court. I had need of a friend. Yet I must not forget that Alice de la Pole had given her allegiance to the Yorkist family, coming to terms with the Yorkist regime many years ago. Her son now lived comfortably at Court as the King's brother-in-law. Alice had survived, some might say without principle, whereas I had fought against York and now had no family at all. Perhaps she had shown great political acuity, whereas my marriage and my sense of rightness and duty had dragged me into a pit of despond. I must be careful what I said to her.

It was Lady Alice who put me at ease.

'Well, my lady, I may be your custodian, but it will not be a harsh punishment for you. I will ensure that your clothing is replaced, and you may use the services of the Dean of King Edward's chapel in Windsor for your petitions.' She was leading me up the staircase to the chambers that had been made ready for me, chattering all the time, although her steps were slow with age and pain of movement. 'Who knows how long it will be before some agreement is made for you? And here are the chambers I have apportioned to you and your ladies.' She eyed me. 'Your clothing is fit for nothing but to be cut into remnants. We will remedy that. I have linen and wool aplenty, as well as some fine green velvet ready to be sewn, and a box of sables.'

I looked around at the comfort: the clothes' presses, the luxury of hangings and bed covers, the highly carved and polished furniture, the gilded bowls holding *pot pourri* to scent the air. Everything taken from me was restored here for my pleasure.

'I am grateful.'

'You have lost much. I know it will weigh on your heart.'

It was a settling. Of my heart as well as my body, as Lady Alice talked about the Court, about her son, about the Queen and her children, until I raised my hand to stop the flow.

'Tell me one thing, if you will.

'Of course, if I can.'

'What do you know of the Countess of Warwick?'

'A sad case.'

The little blow to my heart surprised me. The distance had grown between us since grief had taken over my thoughts, but I had not envisaged this.

'Is she dead?'

Lady Alice shook her head.

'No, but she might as well be. She is a virtual prisoner in the abbey at Beaulieu where she took refuge after Warwick's death at Barnet. I have to say that King Edward has not been kind to her. He has refused her the right for her petitions to be heard, nor will he allow her protection for her freedom to travel to Court. There is, of course, the matter of her inheritance, the whole of the Warwick estate.'

I could imagine it would be an issue.

'And her daughters?'

How had I cut myself off so completely from what had happened to them?

'Both are alive and well, Isabel wed to Clarence, as you would know. Anne's situation you might not: she is now wed to the Duke of Gloucester.'

Powerful connections indeed. I wondered what this would do for the Countess's situation. Lady Alice answered my unspoken question.

'The King will do nothing to allow so much wealth and land to slip beyond his control. I wager the Countess will never have her legitimate inheritance restored to her.'

It was indeed a sad affair. Both the Countess Anne and I were now dependent on the questionable good will of King Edward, both dependent on his good offices. I did not trust him and neither, I was sure, would Countess Anne, even though she had once called him Ned. Perhaps, in hope, she still did, but I thought that she would fear him as much as I did.

For a few days I actually considered writing to the Countess again. In the end I could think of nothing to say that would diminish the desolation that was as cruel for her as it was for me.

# 36

## *A Deceptive Freedom, 1473*

### Anne, Countess of Warwick

A horse-drawn litter arrived to take me from Beaulieu. It was an impressive affair, with swags and curtains and cushions in heavy velvet emblazoned with King Edward's coat of arms, as if I were his possession. For my comfort it was pulled by four stalwart horses.

This rescue came at the hands of my daughter Anne and her new husband, the Duke of Gloucester. I welcomed it. My petitions had received no response, there had been no replies, but surely here was hope for the future since my daughter was wife to the King's brother? My inheritance was still mine. The King had made no claims against me. Could I not establish my own household and live as a widow with dignity and acknowledgement of my status? I considered where I might like to live. At Warwick Castle, or even Middleham. I had fond memories of days spent at Middleham. Or one of my own properties, my Beauchamp inheritance. For the first time for many months I could look forward as I said my farewells to those who had given me refuge, and my few possessions were packed into a single coffer.

'God be with you, my lady. Life has been trying for you.'

The Abbot pressed my hands between his own in a soft benediction.

'It seems that the Blessed Virgin will smile on me once more. I am not going to imprisonment. I shall be free to order my life as I wish it.'

'I pray that it will be so, my lady. I will pray for your perseverance and your acceptance of what is to come.'

'As do I.'

I could not quite read his expression, nor that of Sir James Tyrell, a henchman of the Duke of Gloucester, who had come to order my escort and was now waiting for me with distinct lack of patience. And suddenly I could not quite rid myself of the thought that there was a threat here to my livelihood after all. But was I misreading this situation? Perhaps isolation had made me too cynical.

'Where are you ordered to take me?' I asked as I prepared to be handed into the litter.

'To Middleham, my lady.'

Why had I worried? A warmth filled my heart. I would be at ease there until my life became clearer. I would be restored to my daughter Anne. Was this happiness that had crept into my cold heart? Perhaps not, but it was a satisfaction. But first I had a mission.

'I wish to make a diversion, Sir James.'

He frowned. 'I have no orders for that, my lady.'

'Yet that is what I wish.' I was still Countess of Warwick. I did not accept orders from a mere knight. 'It will not take long or be far out of our way. I wish to go to Bisham Priory.'

I could see him thinking about this. I raised my brows in haughty command.

'I will go to Bisham. I see no reason why you can even think of refusing my wishes.'

Thus he came to the conclusion that there would be no difficulty in giving me what I wanted, and so I travelled to Bisham Priory, as I had long wished to do.

On arrival I dismissed my escort, walking within the walls of the religious sanctuary, acknowledging the tombs that I knew so well. The previous Earls of Salisbury with their superb images carved in stone all lay at peace. And then more recent interments. My father-in-law, Richard Neville, Earl of Salisbury, killed after the Battle of Wakefield, beheaded at Pontefract, his body restored here. Beside him Lady Alice, his wife, whose grief I had shared.

How majestic they both looked. The metal plates of Salisbury's armour, the painted tabard with its red saltire on a white background, his head encased in mail, while it rested on a great jousting helmet. His feet on a favourite hound. And there was Alice, her hair neatly braided and coifed. A placidity that neither had known in life. I touched their feet in respect.

And then I moved on to the one I wanted to see.

Richard Neville, Earl of Warwick. Beside him his brother John, Marquess of Montagu.

Both cruelly slaughtered at Barnet.

No images here, merely plain slabs bearing their names. At least they had been properly interred, I presumed, with a priest committing them to God's care.

It was not seemly, it was not acceptable, that they should lie here without recognition of their earthly importance. I vowed to do something about it when I had the money to pay for effigies. I would send masons and sculptors to make memorials worthy of their proud names. I imagined Richard's figure in full armour as I had so often seen him in life, the shining plaques on arm and breast and thigh, the magnificent Italianate workmanship in the engraved cuirass and vambrace, in the gauntlets and sabatons. The great helm in which he went into battle. The bear and ragged staff on a banner laid beside him. It behoved me that Richard Neville should be remembered in death as the superb earl and knight that he had been.

I knelt beside the slab that bore Richard's name, regardless of the cold. I could not pray. What could I offer up to God when he was lost to me? There was no essence of him here. Any sense of Richard had been effectively destroyed when his body had been exposed on the steps of St Paul's. Still I knelt, in despair that I felt so little of his presence, when I had hoped that he would be restored to me.

'My lady ...'

Sir James had come to find me. Had I lingered there so long? Time had passed, and I was cold, so cold.

'Do you wish to stay longer, my lady?'

'No. Let us go on.'

'Let us indeed.'

I could not look back. What would be the good of that? I must look forward to a new life, a different existence, even if it proved to be a lonely one.

I did not know that it would be the last time that I would walk through the rooms and gardens at Bisham. I did not know that I would never see Richard's tomb again, nor be able to give it the majesty that it deserved.

He was dead to me in body and soul.

All I could do was remember the past, even when I wished that I could banish it.


Middleham Castle: our northern fortress, full of good memories, happy memories. Perhaps it would welcome me home. I felt my heart lift with every mile as, the litter curtains pulled back, the scenery became familiar to me. Never had I travelled this

393

route on my own, but still I could only anticipate the pleasure of familiar surroundings. I was released and my freedom was restored to me. This night I would sleep in my own chamber, order my own food and reacquaint myself with a place that had given me such a depth of family care and affection. If the shade of Richard walked at my heels, I would not complain.

There was no welcome. The clouds were low on the hills, smothering the valleys as if in mourning, and the rain pattered on my hood as I was helped from the litter. The walls were cold and grey, rain running down the stonework. No one came to meet me.

My daughter Anne was not there, the steward eventually informed me, absent in York in the company of the Duke of Gloucester, but was expected to return any day. Of course she was now Duchess of Gloucester. The circumstances of Anne's marriage remained shrouded for me except for servants' gossip, since my daughter had not wished to communicate with me about her new situation. I had received no letter from her. Perhaps she had been told to be wary of what she said to me. Perhaps Gloucester had warned her to have a care if treason continued to hang over my head. But she was my daughter. Of course she would welcome me to my old home. And tomorrow the sun would shine again on Middleham.

When did I begin to think of him as Gloucester rather than Diccon? When I was escorted home by Tyrell, perhaps. Or when I discovered that Anne's marriage to him had been arranged and completed without my knowledge. If I were honest, my journey north had felt like another surveillance rather than a homecoming. Stepping into my own chamber had not wrapped me round with the pleasure of memories I had expected. Richard did not walk the wall-walk with me. I was as strangely isolated here as I had been in Beaulieu.

Then, within the week, Anne was here, dismounting from a fine mare, looking sleekly radiant and delighted that I had returned, almost as if there had been no passage of time or series of tragic events since we had last parted at Louis's Court.

She stepped into my arms, then, with astonishing command and confidence, she invited me inside. It was strange to be welcomed into my own home, when I had already been in residence there for five days. We settled with wine and a comfortable fire in a chamber that I had rarely used, but one that, as I had already seen, Anne had refurbished for herself with new tapestries and cushioned furniture and extravagant banks of candles. My daughter made no attempt to bring the names of her father or Prince Edward into our exchange of reminiscences. It was as if she had deliberately banished them from her new life as Duchess of Gloucester. Were they both not the enemy in the eyes of her husband? But then probably so was I.

She was also quite forthright in guiding the conversation between us, which rendered me wary.

'I am sorry I was not here to bid you welcome, Mother. I have been in York with Diccon. You must be grateful that you are released at last. That you were free to leave Beaulieu.'

'Yes, it pleases me to be here.' I could think of nothing more to say about that. Then, because it was in my heart to ask: 'Did you agree to this marriage? Was it what you wished for?'

Not that she would have had much choice in the matter if it was a stratagem of King Edward. I felt a light barrier between us, as if she was as cautious as I, but she answered readily enough, her face brightening with a smile that I never saw when she wed Prince Edward.

'Of course. Why would I not? I was a widow, and too young to remain one without protection. I swear Diccon will prove to be a more comfortable husband than the Prince.' She added with

395

unexpected pride, 'I knew I was too important not to be sought as a bride. Better Diccon than any other man I know.'

'You know Gloucester well, of course.'

'Of course.' She smiled. 'How formal, Mother. You used to call him Diccon. There was always an affection between us when he was learning his court graces here at Middleham. You must recall the emergence of two energetic boys into our household.'

Still no mention of her father, and I ignored her reference to my formality since I could not explain it to myself. It was merely a feeling, a reading of atmosphere. Instead: 'You were not forced into this?' I persisted.

'Never.' She laughed softly. 'The Duke of Clarence would rather I had remained unwed. He would have stopped this marriage if he could. He had me kept under duress in his household.'

Of which I had had no news. So much had been happening. I felt suddenly helpless, powerless, ignorant of the undertones in this family. Indeed, in the kingdom.

'And Isabel was in agreement with this?'

Anne did not quite simper.

'Isabel does what her husband tells her. But Diccon would have none of it. Diccon wanted me and rescued me. And now we are wed.'

'Why did Clarence not want it?'

My daughter shook her head, unwilling to discuss it further and returned to the matter of Gloucester. 'Richard arranged for a dispensation for our marriage, because we are related within the bounds of consanguinity, and we wed secretly in St Stephen's at Westminster.'

'Did the King agree?'

'He did not object.'

Whatever the truth behind it, Gloucester had been keen for this marriage to take place. Our conversation moved to domestic affairs. It was comfortable enough, but I was aware that my daughter was keeping me at bay. She continued to be welcoming, concerned for my comfort, confident in her role as lady of Middleham Castle, but there was a brittleness about her of which I had no memory, but then she had suffered as much as I after the defeat at Tewkesbury and the death of the Prince, of which she spoke not one word, and I allowed her her reticence.

And yet…

'You knew that I was incarcerated in Beaulieu Abbey,' I remarked.

'Yes, I knew where you were.'

'Did you know of the letters I wrote to beg for intercession?'

'Yes, I knew.'

'Did you ever try to negotiate for my release, to add your voice to those who might rescue me?'

Her smile was engaging, compassionate. 'No. Diccon said that it would be better if you remained there in safety until all Lancastrian affairs were settled at Court. I knew that no harm would come to you.'

It seemed a reasonable reply, after all.

I could even pretend that the past had not happened. Or could I?


When Gloucester returned to Middleham towards the end of the year I realised how much time had passed since I had last seen him. He was no longer the young boy, but a man who had grown into the power placed at his door by his brother. He had effectively stepped into the Earl of Warwick's shoes in the North. He was still slight and would never be tall, but he had a supreme confidence and spoke with authority. Thin-faced, dark haired; more than any of his sons he reminded me of the dead Duke of York.

'It is good to see you here, Countess.' He dismounted from his horse, coming across to me where I stood beside his wife, and kissed my hand. 'I hope that you approve of me as a son-in-law. I'm sorry it was all arranged without your presence, or your agreement.'

His smile was gentle. I was circumspect: I trusted no one these days.

'As long as my daughter is content in her marriage, I have no complaint.'

'I think that she is.' They exchanged a warmer smile. It seemed that they were happy together. Then I, too, must indeed be content.

'I hope that you will find your new life here agreeable, my lady. We will offer you every comfort.'

'I should equally offer my thanks for your petitioning for my release,' I replied, giving thanks where it was due. I knew how to be diplomatic when it was needed. 'Without you I would still be tolerating monastic solitude in Beaulieu Abbey.'

He bowed his head. 'We thought that you ought to be restored to your previous home here at Middleham.'

Why did I feel that it would not be a choice for me, where I would live?

'I would wish to travel,' I said, to test the waters, 'to see my daughter Isabel.'

'Of course. But the roads are poor for travel at present. We will consider it when they harden with frost.'

Which I accepted. Middleham was my home. It had my hand on it from the past. Despite all my losses, I could be happy here. I was no longer subject to gentle captivity.

I walked from the courtyard into the hall in the company of my daughter and drank wine to welcome Gloucester. I should have been at ease. I should have been able to enjoy the new close-knit family that was being created here in my old home, yet I could not turn my mind from a new anxiety. What was it that hovered over me like a storm-crow with some nameless warning? What could possibly happen to me here that was worse than the wounds and losses I had already suffered in my life? I tried to convince myself that I was being irrational, that my daughter and son-in-law wished me nothing but good, but the storm-crow would not fly away. There was something for me here to face with dismay, if I could only reach out and touch it.

The wine and kindly words did nothing to ease the knot of panic that had become lodged in my throat.

# 37

## Doors Closing and Opening, 1475

**Margaret, Queen of England**

'There are moves afoot, my dear lady.'

Alice de la Pole, swathed in her habitual veil and wimple, took her seat at the table where we broke our fast. She walked with even more difficulty now, using a cane; the grip of her gnarled fingers and the lines that bracketed her long features spoke of constant pain. I knew that she suffered and had her physician beside her on many days. She must have lived for at least seventy years, although I would never be so impertinent as to ask her.

'I feel old this morning,' she continued. 'And do not say that I do not look it. I have a mirror that speaks the truth.'

'You tolerate ill health as well as you usually do,' I replied. 'You have more patience than I.'

'I was raised to be strong-willed.' She gestured to one of her women to pour a cup of warm spiced ale. 'It became necessary with three husbands with different degrees of male pomposity. But putting that aside, my news.'

She picked up a spoon, grimacing at the difficulty of curling her fingers around the stem as she dipped it into the bowl of mussels and leeks, seethed in almond milk, a favourite dish of hers, but one that turned my stomach so early in the day.

'You look uncommonly cheerful, Alice,' I suggested. 'Am I to return to Windsor? Or the Tower? You will be rid of me at last.'

I had been a prisoner in name and to some extent in body here at Wallingford Castle for well-nigh four years with no hint of change in my status, although Edward of York could no longer see me as a threat to him or the security of his family. I was forced to accept that the realm was at peace, Tewkesbury the last battle to be fought between York and Lancaster, for who would lead the forces of Lancaster now, after the slaughter in the abbey grounds? The Yorkist King and his Wydeville wife now had two sons, thus the inheritance was secure. Could he not let me go free? Any insurrection against him would not rest in my helpless hands. But in true scheming fashion he would still grasp every opportunity to wring gold out of France for my release; regrettably, the negotiations between England and France had come to nothing. I thought they never would. Perhaps Wallingford would be my final resting place.

'You have no faith, Margaret!' Alice chivvied. She was the only one left to me to call me by my name. We had abandoned formalities long ago.

'How can I disagree? I have no faith in the man you call King.'

'Then you should give him some generosity of feeling. At last he has signed a treaty with King Louis, the Treaty of Picquigny. The terms are interesting.'

'Then tell me.'

Dropping the spoon into the bowl, she drank a mouthful of wine before continuing.

'Edward and Louis have agreed to a truce and a trade agreement between England and France, to last for seven years. Louis will reward Edward with a substantial bribe if he will reject his claim to the French throne. And a yearly pension. The French King comes out of this very well.'

'I am delighted to hear it.'

I pushed the dish of unappetising mussels with its rank aroma away from me to the far side of the table.

'They have agreed to support each other with troops if they face rebellion at home.'

'Do they? I do not see how this will affect my life. I no longer have the power to raise a rebellion. And in whose name would I raise it?'

I really did not care. If Alice's ability to hold her cup had been less painful, I would have been less patient.

'The King has also agreed to his little daughter Elizabeth marrying the Dauphin, when she comes of age.'

'Then it is a most serious alliance between two unprincipled men.'

'You might say that, if you were not careful in choosing the words to pass your lips. I am always careful when enemies abound. Ah, but that is not the best of it.' Alice's smile widened.

I sighed. 'It no longer concerns me, Alice.'

'But it does! Louis has agreed to ransom you. At last, he will facilitate your return to France.'

My hands, engaged in applying a knife to a dish of winter pears, stilled. I looked up, demanding the truth. After four years I had almost given up hope.

'A ransom. How much? Is it enough to tempt your King? What persuaded him to let me go?' I asked bitterly. 'How much was the French spider prepared to pay? Or has it already been refused?'

'A miraculous sum, Margaret. One that King Edward would be a fool to refuse. Louis will hand over fifty thousand crowns in return for your illustrious person.'

Dropping the knife, I was stricken to silence for a moment.

'Am I worth so much to him?'

'So it seems. And I doubt indeed that King Edward will turn him down.'

No, Edward would certainly accept so vast a sum. For the first time since that terrible battlefield at Tewkesbury I could see the longings of my soul being at last fulfilled.

'It is interesting that Louis will pay so much,' Alice commented.

When she eyed me with a quizzical expression I knew that she was hoping for my thoughts on this. It was not interesting at all. I knew very well what the French King's plans would be. It hurt my heart. If I returned to France, Louis would demand that I turn over my inheritance from my father to him. When my father died and left me with the money and property that by rights should be mine, Louis would bargain with me. He would gain everything and I would be left with no inheritance. It would leave me living on Louis's charity.

I said nothing. I would not discuss it. It was all too painful, leaving me totally dependent on Louis's whims. Abandoning the pears, I picked up a brie tartlet and began to eat.

Another problem rose before me, like a miasma over the platter of cold meat that one of the servants had brought in for Alice's attention. Would there be conditions before King Edward would let me go? Would there be conditions that I could not bear to accept? I could not imagine what would be demanded of me, but cynicism lay heavily on me. I had learned that women were nothing more than helpless pawns in the governing of realms.

My freedom still seemed to be far distant.

'What is more important to you, Margaret? Your return to France? Or to insist on keeping your rights of inheritance, if indeed you have any?' Alice asked. 'There will be a royal official at our door before the week is out, I promise you. You must consider your reply to him.'

I sipped slowly from the cup of wine. I did not know what it would be.

'And don't tell me that you will be so stubborn as to refuse this offer. You will gain nothing by remaining here. My health is not good. When I die, where will Edward send you?'

'Do not speak of death, my dear Alice. There has been enough in my lifetime.'

'I will face it when it comes.' Her tone was sharp, her warning clear. 'We have lived amicably together. When I am gone, life might not be so pleasant for you. I suggest that you eat another of the brie tarts. It will sweeten your mood, since you appear to like them so much.'

I picked up another of the tartlets, brushing away the crumbs from the fur of my sleeves. Alice's advice gave me much to consider, but before my thoughts proceeded down the route of my ransom I asked, as I had once before:

'What can you tell me of the Countess of Warwick?'

'Nothing of pleasure,' she replied dryly. 'Unless you would happily wish the widow of your enemy ill. Her life is not one to relish. In the end, you had the better bargain when King Edward sent you to me. The Countess has not fared so well in her family home.'

True to Alice's word, a royal courier, in less than official clothing, came to inform me of what I already knew: I would be ransomed. I did not know the courier, and the lack of acknowledgement of my previous state as Queen of England was indicative of my present status.

'Does the King wish to see me?'

'He does not consider it necessary, my lady.'

Which made all clear.

'When will I be ransomed?'

'As soon as may be.' He bowed, his face grave. 'There are conditions, my lady.'

As I knew there would be.

'Will they be acceptable to me?'

He shrugged as if he really did not care. 'Your freedom depends on it, my lady.'

Lady Alice stood beside me as I absorbed the conditions, laid out before me by the King's man, clearly, concisely, as if I might have difficulty in understanding them. They were as I expected, stripping me of all that remained of my past. It was degrading. I lifted my chin and held his gaze as he listed the demands made on me.

'I have no choice, do I, unless I wish to remain in captivity?'

'You have none, my lady.'

I gave a brisk nod of my head. Had I not thought long and hard about this?

'You may take my acquiescence back to your King.'

'The King needs your signature, my lady.'

Anger could not quite be quelled. He needed my name on a document but would still not grant me the honour of a visit to Court. Because I must do it, when the courier produced a document, I signed it and added my seal from the royal ring that I still wore.

'You are free to go home now, my lady.'

'Go home?' I could not see it in those terms.

He bowed, taking the document with my compliance.

'There,' Alice said, when the door closed on his back. 'It is done.'

For a moment emotion welled up inside me.

'All that has happened since you escorted me to England as a bride, undone in one sweep of a pen.'

'I am pleased for you, although I will miss your company.'

She hobbled from the room and I sent for Lady Katherine de Vaux. I considered what I would ask of her.

'Do you wish to leave me now? Would you remain here in England with your family? There is no further loyalty demanded of you.'

She did not hesitate even for a moment.

'I can serve you in France. It is my wish. Unless you no longer need me.'

'You are the only constant in my life, Katherine.'

'Then I travel with you. If it is your wish.'

I studied her. She had been with me for so long. Although she had never stood as a friend to me, it would be a strange comfort for her to stay. I sighed in unexpected relief.

'Yes. It is my wish, and I thank you. Come with me.'

I sent a letter, before I left these shores for good. I did not know if it would ever reach her, but I felt the need to write it.

# 38

## *A Single Piece of Correspondence Before Exile*

**Margaret of Anjou, Queen of England, to Anne, Countess of Warwick**

By the Queen.

After all that has passed between us, I decided to write before I leave England for ever. I will never return. We will not see each other again. There will be no more correspondence.

I have gained my freedom. I am to be allowed to return to France after King Edward's negotiations with King Louis have come to lengthy fruition, Louis of course seeing it in his interest to give his permission for me to live once more under his surveillance. He has an eye to my inheritance, and I will have no power to stop him from taking it. He has ransomed me so that I might have a duty of compliance with what he demands from me.

I will fight to keep what is mine, but it will be hard.

What was demanded of me by your King to achieve this?

I was forced to renounce all claims I might have as once Queen of England. And why not? All my connections with

Lancaster are dead, after all. Why would I not wish to leave this country that has brought me nothing but ill?

Thus I have renounced all title to the English crown, to my dower lands, and to any other claims against the present King Edward. Legally I am no longer Queen of England. Not even Dowager Queen. I can lay claim to no English titles of land. King Edward owes me nothing. I return to France a penniless supplicant for King Louis's charity.

I know that you are under the jurisdiction of your daughter and her husband, although I cannot discover the true circumstances under which you live. I think that you are at Middleham Castle. Our situations are not so different, are they? Women of power who end their days subject to the desire and ambitions of others, and their own family at that. Women who as widows have the right to their own possessions, their dower, their jointure, but these possessions are craved by others and will be stolen from us. We have no power to resist and no one to fight for us. We have both been women of high birth and superb inheritance, only to have it taken from us.

At least you have grandchildren from your daughter Isabel. I envy you.

I have never felt more alone, although my loyal Katherine de Vaux will accompany me when I leave these shores. I cannot be more grateful for her generosity in staying with me. I doubt I will find much of a welcome at my father's Court. I have nothing of advantage to bring him.

I trust that you are in health and find some comfort in your life.

Do not forget the connection that we once found together, if it was friendship of a sort. How difficult it was for us not to be drawn into hostility and enmity. Some days guilt strikes hard at my heart.

I wish you well, and with thanks for some understanding in the past.

Margaret

Queen of England


## Anne, Countess of Warwick

There were frequent couriers calling at Middleham Castle for the attention of the Duke of Gloucester. There were no letters for me, although I frequently asked, when documents were delivered.

'Is there anything for me?' I asked the steward.

'No, my lady. Only for His Grace the Duke.'

Did I believe him? Sometimes I thought that his expression, although courteous, was less than honest.

'Would any letter sent to me be kept from me?' I asked my daughter.

'No, of course not. Why would you ask me that?'

'No reason.'

'Who would write to you?'

I could not admit that there was no one, unless Duchess Cecily felt moved to honour me with her thoughts on my present situation, but she, I understood, was devoting her now-pious life to God. She would have no interest in my predicament. Otherwise there was no one except for Queen Margaret. If she wrote to me, and I doubted that she would, I never received it.

What would I write to her in reply? There was nothing for me to say. And who would deliver it for me? I could trust no one to do so. I wrote no more letters.

# 37

## *All Is Not as It Seems, 1476*

**Margaret, Queen of England**

The twenty-second day of January in the year of our lord 1476. Another momentous day in my life, the day I was released from my captivity and set foot once again in France. An escort was provided by the English King under the command of Sir Thomas Montgomery, an individual with no conversation, but then I had nothing that I wished to say to him.

Alice de la Pole did not live to see me go before death took her. I shed tears. She was one of the few friends left to me. I had no reply from the Countess of Warwick, unsure of whether my letter had reached her before I began my journey to France. I was free, but dependent on others for my travelling, indeed for my survival. Katherine de Vaux accompanied me as she had promised. I had not realised how much it had meant to me that she should come with me. I was growing weak in spirit in my advancing years.

I wondered if the Yorkist usurper would still demand a final interview with me before he sent me on my way. What would he have to say to me? Nothing. He had received an exceptional payment for my departure, thus I was of no more value to him.

It proved to be a silent journey and a rough sea. I thrust aside all memories of the days when I first arrived, a young girl full of hope and happiness and ambition as Queen of England. I was no longer Queen of England. But I would not give up the title. I never would, but I would never return. This was permanent exile from a country that was no longer my own and did not want me. I deliberately turned my back on England and looked forward to the shore that grew ever closer.

I did not feel that I was going home. I no longer knew where my home might be. I knew what it was to be lost and alone and, if possible, my dishonour was intensified on that day in January. Rouen was cold and windswept when we arrived, and I was led into the vast cathedral where the dank shadows pressed down on me. Oh, the shame. The ignominy of it, although all was formally ceremonial with nothing demanded from me other than my presence. This was the formal transfer of my person, from English to French hands, as if I were a parcel of cloth from one merchant to another, a bundle of little merit. Two French ambassadors in heraldic robes made the first payment of my ransom, the gold coin clinking in a leather pouch.

All was not yet paid, but I was free.

And yet I was not. Without land and money of my own, how could I be free?

King Louis chose not to attend, which placed layer upon layer upon my humiliation, and even more when he kept me waiting in a small room outside his audience chamber in the familiar Chateau of Angers.

It was a return full of grief for me, for I remembered when I had last taken refuge with Louis, even though I did not trust him. Then my son had been alive and so had my lord Henry. Then there had been the hope that an invasion of England would bring me my heart's desire and restore the crown of England to the House of Lancaster. As manipulative as he ever was, Louis had given me a fleet and forces. He had arranged the negotiation with Warwick. However much I had hated it, I had been given the opportunity to bring my desires to fulfilment and restore Henry as King.

Now as I waited to be admitted to this final refuge, it horrified me to realise that I had no desires, no plans. I was as empty as a withered seed case, cast aside by the winds. Not even the spring April weather could have raised my spirits. Nothing except a need for recognition of my status, my birth, my own inheritance as a daughter of Anjou, however meagre it might be. I still had my pride as a princess and cousin of France. What would Louis demand of me, in return for the ransom that he had paid out for my person? I trembled at the thought, pulling my fur-lined travelling cloak tight around me, a final gift from Lady Alice before she breathed her last. I must not show weakness.

Still I was kept waiting without even a chair to ease my cold limbs. If he intended to debase me, Louis succeeded, but I knew I must not show emotion to any degree, thus I curtsied deeply, the rich velvet folds of the cloak spread around me, when I was finally admitted. I might not trust Louis of France but herein lay my future and I must treat him with the utmost respect and gratitude.

He approached and lifted me to my feet, all graciousness.

'My dear Margaret. It pleases me to welcome you to my Court.'

'I must thank you for the ransom, my lord. For my freedom.'

'It was my pleasure to rescue you, my dear lady.'

I struggled not to ask why it had taken four years for him to agree.

'I am grateful that I am able to return and make a new life for myself.'

'I wish you well in your new life. We must make it possible for you to settle here and live in some degree of comfort.'

Empty words. He was offering me nothing. Had I expected better? Before I could ask...

'I am certain that you understand; your mind was always a keen interpreter of politics.' Louis smiled but it was the snarl of a wolf. 'Your freedom will not come without a price, Cousin.'

'I am aware.'

This was his judgement. His demand for his magnificent gesture. Would he take everything from me?

'You are weary after your journey. We have arranged rooms for you here in the chateau, the same as you occupied before so that you will feel comfortable with the familiarity. We will speak again tomorrow, when you are rested and better able to accept my decisions.'

He would keep me waiting again, but I had no power or influence here. I must wait.

That night I wept.

Lady Katherine, who could not comfort me with soft words, left me to my misery.

My memories pressed hard on me.

So did my fears.


When I was summoned the next morning, deliberately clad in mourning-black to make an impression of a woman who had lost all, Louis was calm and grave, seated behind a wealth of documents. He invited me to sit, but he did not see a need to dismiss his servants, which I might consider an insult to my status, but to Louis this was merely a matter of business. A clerk sat at his side to record our agreement.

'You are not without resources, I see, Cousin.'

He allowed the back of his hand to caress the sable edge to my sleeve.

'I had a kind friend, who is now dead,' I said. 'It is not the generosity of Kings.'

'I fear that you will not find me overly generous in the disposition of your person.' He turned over one document, and then another, although I was certain that he knew the content without reading them anew. 'I have made my decision, Margaret. Your freedom cost me much. Nor can I afford for you to use any of your possessions from your father to set up a new court which might make difficulties for me. It would not be good policy for any resurrection of the Lancaster claim to the English throne. There are some who might consider it, such as the Tudor connection. They have strong support in Lady Margaret Beaufort for her son, Henry Tudor. I do not know what your thoughts might be on that issue. I do not want any Beauforts or Tudors making a pathway to any court that you might establish here within my hegemony.'

Lady Margaret Beaufort. Henry Tudor, her son. They meant little to me although I knew their claim on the blood of Lancaster. To aid their plotting to take possession of the English throne was not within my consideration. I realised that Louis was staring at me, waiting for my reaction. When there was none, he continued.

'What did you hope for in coming here to me, my lady?'

I considered what might be the least I could accept.

'An acceptance of my birthright as a princess, daughter of René of Anjou, as cousin to the French King. I would hope that my birth would recommend me to you, to restore my status and allow me an entrée to your Court. I could hope for somewhere that I might call my home for my final years, to live with dignity as Queen of England. And I would hope for a grant to enable me to live within that dignity.'

'You ask much of me. You are no longer Queen of England, and lack all influence.'

'But I hope that I do not ask too much, my lord. Are we not of one blood, you and I?'

He laughed softly, unpleasantly. Cold fingers stroked down my spine. Today I would know my fate.

'I am afraid that you ask too much of a King in my financially uncertain position. Here is my answer, Cousin. Here are my terms for your freedom and a future home in my realm. You will abandon all claims to inheritance of your father's estates in Anjou. You will sign over to me the land you now hold in your own name from your dead mother in the areas of Bar, in Provence, and in Lorraine. You must reject any hope of returning to the French Court. You are too much of a danger to me there. In return, I will provide you with a pension of six thousand crowns.'

For a moment I could not speak, as I absorbed what he was offering. He would strip me of everything I owned. The pension was a paltry sum in comparison. Was this to be my future? The weight in my breast, pressing down on my heart so that I could barely breathe, was a heavy one. Eventually I found my voice.

'If you take away my lands, where will I live? Surely there is a place for me at Court?'

'Not so. It has been agreed between myself and your father that you will retire to one of his castles, the Chateau of Reculée near Angers.'

It seemed to me more like a banishment than an acceptance as a member of Louis's family. He and my father had been in collusion. How dare they negotiate to reduce me to invisibility?

'Must I give up everything?' I asked, horrified at the fragility in my voice. 'These are my own possessions, in Bar and Lorraine and Provence, inherited from my mother. They are valuable. They would enable me to live in some comfort, independent of your generosity.'

'I know well their value, Cousin. They will recompense me for the amount I had to pay to bring you out of England. Better here than in Wallingford Castle, on hostile soil for the rest of your life. Fear not, I will not allow you to live in any discomfort, my dear lady. Besides, I do not think that you have any choice in the matter.' His gaze was quizzical, assessing, flickering over my face as if to search out any remaining weakness in me. 'I thought that after all your past suffering, you might enjoy a life retired from the political world.'

He knew me well. He knew I would not enjoy it.

'It is a fine house, I understand. You can keep a small household there.'

'My thanks, Cousin.' I stood and curtsied again, although I doubt that he saw the mockery in it. 'I am grateful that you have left me one establishment.'

'Of course. I could not allow my enemies to accuse me of leaving you homeless.'

There was nothing more that I could say. He had no care for me. He was not open to negotiation.

Following Louis's instructions, detesting the need to do so, I moved myself and my small household to Reculée near Angers, anticipating the life I would lead there. The chateau was small, suffering from neglect, and the pension was indeed a paltry sum. I would live in penury in this place I was forced to accept, as I investigated the unkempt chambers, the dust and the damp. I would indeed be isolated and powerless, just as Louis desired. Yes, I was free. There were no demands on my time. I lived with my memories of power and failure, of love and loss. I had been forced one way or another to give up everything. Once, I would have continued to fight to gain recognition of my place on this earth, but no more. My mother and grandmother might be damning of my lack of spirit, but it could no longer be rekindled. I had no one to live for, not even myself.

All I possessed was a pack of hunting dogs, my books and a casket of relics to remind me of my past glories. I was anonymous, faded from history. I grew sad and lonely.

Did I ever think of Countess Anne? Was her position any better than mine? I had no news of her situation. Was she allowed to visit the Duchess of Clarence and admire her grandchildren? It must be some comfort to her. I had no one. In a strange way I resented her good fortune.

Once, I might have written to her with an acerbic comment.

'Write to her!' Lady Katherine advised, almost bullied, to give me something to do, I suspected, and the anticipation of a reply.

What was there for me to write, to say to her? I was living out my life here, for months, for endless years, until the distant day when it was God's will that I leave this earth. I did not write. I did not think that anything I sent to her would find its way into her hands.

I had lost everything.

# 40

## *A Legal Death, 1479*

### Anne, Countess of Warwick

A time of grief? Oh, there were days that I wept, privately in my chamber, for my heart was sore and beyond healing. I was never to see my daughter Isabel again. In the short days of December, when we anticipated the celebration of the birth of the Christ Child, Isabel was dead after the birth of a second son, named Richard. One day we were rejoicing at the birth of a son, the following month we were in deep mourning for his mother; and then the child. He, too, survived only days before following her to the grave.

I had not seen Isabel since we had parted in France. I had never seen her two children, Margaret and Edward, my grand-children. I was simply informed of her death. All I could do was offer prayers for the rest of her troubled soul. Clarence had accused a woman of his household of witchcraft, to bring my daughter to her grave. My daughter Anne did not tell me of this but the servants here at Middleham did, as always quick to gossip and inform the woman who had once governed their household.

I damned Clarence for his selfish cruelty in dragging Isabel into the murky depths of witchcraft. I would give it no credence.

I covered my face with my hands to blot out the memory of our last farewell when Isabel was angry, driven by thwarted ambitions, while I had been unable to give her any comfort, when I had realised that the joyful young girl who had embraced marriage with Clarence with such enthusiasm no longer existed. How I regretted the coldness between us, caused by Clarence's ambitions and Richard's abandoning of him as an unnecessary ally after his agreement with Queen Margaret. I could understand Isabel's loyalties to her husband – did I not have my own over-arching loyalties to Richard? – but I cursed the need that had taken her from my side.

But that would not have changed this ultimate outcome of her death from childbed fevers. Isabel was lost to me. The bitter conflict created in France could never now be healed and I must mourn her until the day of my own death.

At first I did not believe it. I wished that I had been with her; surely I knew enough about the dangers of childbirth to prevent the deadly fever that attacked so many new mothers? She died without me and was buried at Tewkesbury, in the abbey where Queen Margaret's son had been laid to rest after the battle. Curiously I wondered what had happened to the Queen's ring that I had given to my daughter at that last meeting as some sort of talisman. Probably tumbled in haphazard fashion into Clarence's coffers, with the other jewels and mementoes belonging to Isabel.

There was less grief in my heart when I learned that Clarence, too, was dead under the charge of treason, meeting his end as a prisoner in the Tower. King Edward saw his increasingly ambitious and wayward brother as too much of a threat to him and the stability of the realm. My family was disappearing before my eyes. Cecily Neville had indeed withdrawn from public life, living at Berkhamsted, as chaste as a nun in all but name. She took no vows but chose to live in isolation.

I had not chosen that. It was forced upon me, for that was my lot at Middleham.

No visitors. No letters. No communications.

News of the outside world came from a great distance, and I began to suspect that it was filtered by my daughter and the Duke of Gloucester. I heard nothing of court affairs, of the old conflicts between York and Lancaster, of the lives of old acquaintances. It was like existing in a strange void, certainly one redolent of physical comforts, but also of a sharp ignorance, which grew stronger as the months passed. I discovered that my daughter Anne had no longer any love of gossip, of stories and scandals. When she was at Middleham rather than York we discussed affairs of the household and little else.

From the beginning it was made perfectly clear to me that she was unwilling to share any sense of loss over Isabel's death.

'Do you not care?' I asked, after giving her time to accept the sad news and perhaps even to approach me for comfort.

Oh, she said prayers with me, offering up petitions and masses for Isabel's soul, and expressed some acceptable concern over the future of Isabel's children, but then she became remarkably tight-lipped, even as we lit candles in the chapel.

'Yes, I care,' she replied, her tone not unfriendly. 'She was my sister. Is it not natural that I feel remorse at her death?'

'Do you not grieve that you will never see her again, or enjoy her company?'

'Of course. I remember the happiness of our childhood together.'

'And your father. You never willingly speak to me of him.

Her regard became level, even judgemental.

'I honour my father, and will always mourn his loss, but he

chose to fight for the wrong side. His death could have been avoided if he had aligned his livery and banners with York rather than with Lancaster.'

'He is still dead!'

'I know. I understand your grief. I light candles for him, as I do for my sister, but he made his choice, and one that I regret.'

I abandoned any further interrogation. Of what value was it? Surely these were Gloucester's opinions coming from my daughter's mouth.

There was one blessing in my life in this constant morass of sorrow. My daughter Anne gave birth to a son in the year that I joined their household at Middleham. I held him in my arms, wrapped against the cold, the only child of the new generation that it seemed I would know. I handed him to Gloucester, who rode from York to see his newborn son.

'What will you call him?' I asked.

'Edward, for my brother. Edward of Middleham.' There was pride in his austere face. 'Take him back to his mother and give her my thoughts and my love.'

It was a moment of satisfaction for me, one of few in those years.

Did I accept my confinement? For that was what it was, the issue that lay between us through all those years when it seemed that the gates of Middleham closed to prevent my freedom, just as forcefully as the gates at Beaulieu Abbey. It took me some time to realise it, but once I had, once I had seen Anne's reluctance, refusal even, to allow me any real choice in my life, it was as clear as day.

'I wish to set up my own household,' I informed my daughter, thinking that it would suit me better to live perhaps in York where I would not be so cut off from the world.

Her new son fussing beside her in his cradle, she regarded me with a solemn face, as if considering what to say.

'Diccon does not think it will be in your best interests,' she remarked at last, setting the cradle to rock.

'Why not?'

'Where would you find the money to establish yourself?'

'I am not penniless. Why would it be difficult for me?'

Her cheeks flushed, I thought with embarrassment.

'My jointure, my inheritance, both will give me the means,' I continued.

She became almost stern.

'I cannot explain it, Mother. You must speak with Diccon.'

'Cannot or will not?'

For the first time in many months I felt my temper rise within me.

'It is not in my power to allow you to go to York,' she said.

I withdrew from any further discussion between us, but I made it my plan to test the limits of my freedom here at Middleham. I ordered the steward to prepare a horse and a small escort, to be made ready to take me to Sheriff Hutton, one of the Neville castles. When I was ready, I arrived in the stables. There were no horses, no escort awaiting me.

'Did you not receive my request?' I was very polite to the groom who was forking hay into one of the stalls.

'I did. But you may not go, my lady.' Although his politeness matched mine, he was adamant.

'Why not?'

'It is not considered safe for you to travel.'

'Not even with an escort?'

'No, my lady.'

'Who ordered you to refuse my request?'

'Duchess Anne. She said that you must not go.'

Thus I was refused, courteously but firmly refused. I approached my daughter again.

'Why can I not set up my own establishment? Why am I not allowed to travel? Is this Gloucester's decision?'

'It is thought to be not safe.'

'Not safe for whom?' I demanded. 'Why are you party to this decision?'

She instantly deflected my accusation. 'The King does not think it wise.'

'The King or your husband? Or do you hold the key to this door?'

My daughter did not hesitate to hold my gaze, now prepared to use her authority as Duchess of Gloucester against me. How single-minded she had become, how much under the influence of her powerful husband.

'We are all of the same mind, Mother. Are you not at ease here, surrounded by people that you know well? What is there for you in Sheriff Hutton that you cannot enjoy here? Or in York?'

'I want my independence. I wish to be able to travel and visit. I wish to go to Court if it is in my mind to do so. I wish to see if my lord your father's tomb has been completed at Bisham. Yet it seems that the drawbridge of this fortress is raised to keep me in. Can I find no honesty in this place?'

'I will ensure that my father's tomb is completed as you would wish it.'

'But you will not allow me to return to Bisham Priory?'

'I cannot give you that freedom. You must speak with Diccon.'

The answer to every question, of course.

So I did speak with him. The Duke of Gloucester had acquired a kindly mien when it suited him, but behind it an ambition as strong as my lord of Warwick's, if not stronger. I addressed him as the Countess of Warwick, not as some powerless petitioner, seeking him out in the chamber he used for royal business in one of the towers. Surrounded by coffers and books, yet with all the extravagant furnishings of a great lord, he smiled a welcome and gestured to a chair, which I did not take. I stood before him with a straight-spined defiance.

'I am here on a matter of important business.'

'Then I hope that I can be of help, my lady. Are you sure that you will not sit?'

In the end I did so. It would be churlish not to.

'What reason is there for forbidding my right to travel? What right have you, or any man, to keep me here against my will?' He shuffled through the pages in front of him as if considering a reply. 'And do not tell me that I have misread the situation. I am kept here and denied the freedom to travel beyond these walls.'

His reply, when he looked up and met my gaze with a grave regard, did not surprise me.

'Here is the truth of it, my lady. It is thought that you might wed again. The King does not wish that to happen. It might just allow the possibility of a resurgence of Lancastrian interest in England.'

'I have no intention of marrying again.'

'You are only just past your fiftieth year. It might be possible. Other well-born widows wed more than once. Any man who is a supporter of Lancaster might think it good policy to wed you. As widow of the mighty Warwick you might be seen to be a valuable wife, a potential figurehead.' He frowned slightly, plucking a different argument from the air. 'Besides, you do not have the money to set up an establishment of your own.'

'I have my dower, the Beauchamp lands that are my own. I have sufficient funds to be independent.'

Gloucester discovered a document in the pile before him and silently handed it to me. He had known exactly where to find it all along. From the heading, it was written in 1473. An Act of Parliament. How many years had this been kept from me? Six years it had been hidden.

'What is this?' I asked as a cold fear settled on my shoulders like a winter cloak.

'Read it. It makes all things clear.'

He left me to do so, closing the door quietly behind him. And so I learned the truth of my predicament. Parliament had passed an act to give all my own lands to Gloucester and Clarence. They had been divided equally. All my petitions, written with hope, had indeed come to nothing. In spite of my demands, my requests, I had been stripped of everything by a vengeful king. And Gloucester had known of it, of course he had. He returned shortly with cups of wine, to find me sitting in his chair, the document flattened on the desk by my hands.

'I petitioned for my rights,' I announced, astonished at what had been done without my knowledge.

'Too late, my lady. It had already been decided, even before you wrote your first petition. Here, I thought that you might need this to fortify you in the face of this news.'

Had he meant to be kind? I did not think so; merely viciously practical. All became as clear as the light streaming through the window to cast its brightness on the document that created my poverty. When Anne entered the room to stand beside Gloucester, I knew they were together in this. I looked from one to the other. There would be no compassion in this room, only the stark emptiness of power and ambition achieved by my son-in-law.

'You were too well dowered to leave your wealth unchained,'

Gloucester said. 'Better to have it secure in mine and Clarence's hands.'

'And now with Clarence's treason and his death, all is yours. Did your wife, Anne, know?' I looked up at my daughter, at last understanding full well that she had known all along, but it was Gloucester who replied.

'Yes. She is in my confidence.'

Where was trust? I had trusted her, only to have it destroyed when I discovered on this day what they had done with my inheritance, when I was forced to accept the cruel manipulation of me and my property; it was all heartbreaking, my desolation particularly keen that my daughter should be a part of it.

What had they done? There it was in clerkly script before me. Parliament had been clearly put under pressure to ride rough-shod over all my rights. My land, my wealth, my property had been taken from me. As if I were – and there were those three terrible words as the clerk had written – *nowe naturally dede*.

My eyes focused on them, absorbing them again.

As if I were now dead. Dead! All my rights had been dis-regarded. In the eyes of the world, although still alive, I was a dead woman.

Even though it was there before me, I could not believe it. I could not accept it. The division of all the Montagu, Salisbury, Beauchamp and Despenser lands had been made between Anne and Isabel. Later the Neville estates too. While I was debarred, as if I were dead. Those words echoed and re-echoed in my mind. The terrible injustice of it, with no one powerful enough to stand against them and protect me.

I stood.

'Perhaps you would rather that I had indeed died, to solve the problem for all time?'

'It would make no difference. What you see before you is

426

the law,' Gloucester replied. 'The situation is not so desperate. You will always have a home here with us. You will always be welcome.' His austere face softened in a smile of great charm. 'There is no need for you ever to fear for your future.

And I believed him. I would have a home with the Duke and Duchess of Gloucester, but only because it suited Gloucester's purposes to keep me from making claims against him. I would be kept voiceless and weaponless. Beneath the surface grace of this formidable young man there lurked a fist of iron.

I looked at my daughter.

'Where is loyalty? Where is familial integrity?' I demanded, my voice sounding harsh in my ears. 'You knew of this and said nothing. You betrayed me. You, my daughter, deceived me and played me false.'

As my daughter had the grace to drop her gaze before mine, I made a silent vow in my heart. I would never again speak to her of my innermost feelings. I would not repeat my accusation against her, for it would bring me no solace, yet I dared not speak again of any of those matters that were of importance to me; I was not free at all. I must remain incarcerated. I must accept and be silent. Harsh words would achieve nothing at all, only more heartbreak.

Could I not resurrect those good times at Middleham, where I had lived with my young family with so much hope for their future? I could not. It became a place of grief and loss and imprisonment for me. The walls closed around me as firmly as those at Beaulieu. I had no income, no allowance of my own. No independence. No power as Dowager Countess of Warwick. I left the room to walk along the wall-walk where the wind lifted my veil but gave me no respite from the pain that had been dealt me. I found myself wishing that I had died at sea on the return from exile to England. Or at Beaulieu when the devastating news of Richard's death had reached me.

I stayed on the wall-walk as evening fell around me, unable to face my daughter and her betrayal of me. The bitterness rose as bile in my throat. There was no pretence of family loyalty any more. My daughter Anne had thrown in her lot with Gloucester, who had stripped me of all I had.

I still loved her, because she was my daughter, but I did not trust her. It was as if her expressions, her thoughts, her opinions, could only be glimpsed as if through a gauze veil.

On a sudden memory, as the banners above my head, resplendent with the white boar emblem of the Duke of Gloucester, were whipped by the wind; what had happened to the beautifully wrought Warwick bear and ragged staff that I had given to Richard? I supposed that it had been lost at Barnet, or thieved as booty as Richard lay helpless in the mud of the battlefield. It had been lost, as he had been lost to me.

I would have given that jewel to Anne's child, my grandson, in memory of his grandfather. Now I realised that it would not have mattered. Gloucester would probably have taken it from him, along with all the rest of my property, to obliterate any memory of Warwick.

Anger burned within me as destructively bright as the emotion that had driven Queen Margaret to wage battles in the name of her husband and son, battles that had brought the deaths of so many men. I snatched off my veil and tore it from hem to hem in a fit of mindless fury, casting the pieces between the crenellations, watching them as they fell to earth in a flutter of wind.

How futile, how childish a gesture, giving me no satisfaction. I knew that I could not submit to this ungovernable passion. I must keep my mind calm, my thoughts clear, seeking any action on my part that could restore to me what was mine. I must not allow myself to be compromised by helpless fears.

Easy to see the necessity, impossibly hard to take any steps against Gloucester's wishes. But I would not give in. I would not accept defeat.

Oh, Richard, what had my life become?

I descended to my chamber to pin a new veil over my hair with deliberate intent, a veil notable for the expensive gilding and embroidered gold crosses of the Beauchamp family. I would not be ignored. I would not be swept behind one of Gloucester's glorious tapestries. And yet, as I was perfectly well aware, all opportunities to right the wrongs against me had been stripped away by the men who desired my land and my wealth. Perhaps I must simply accept the realities of my life. How hard it would be to devote what was left of my life to stitchery and prayer.

## Margaret, Queen of England

My father died in the year 1481, four years after my return to France, but it did not alleviate my situation, unless my removal to the Chateau of Dampierre, near Saumur, an even smaller dwelling but one with attractive views, would please me. All my inheritance from my father passed immediately to the French crown before I could even make a claim on it. Louis seized it as his own. It was clear that I would remain Louis's pensioner. Pensioner or prisoner? There seemed to be little difference.

I had wondered if Louis would negotiate another marriage for me to a harmless French noble, so that I might disappear into some distant chateau in the French countryside. He chose not to do so. Thus I remained as his pensioner; I had no power, no land, and would not be sought in marriage again.

The years crept by.

I read my books. I put stitches into fine cloth. I walked in the overgrown gardens. I rode with my hounds in the extensive hunting reserves when I felt able to mount my docile mare.

There was no contentment for me. Once, long ago, I might have hoped for a friendship with a woman of almost similar status to my own. That had been destroyed through the force of circumstances and, I regretted, my own intransigence.

There was no hope, no rescue.

Queen. Wife. Mother.

All gone. All gone.

# 41

## *An End to All Suffering,*
## *October 1482*

**Anne, Countess of Warwick**

'There is a visitor come to see you, my lady.'

I never received visitors, or correspondence. If any letters were sent to me I presumed that they were intercepted. Travellers were turned away. Nor was I allowed to write, as once I had done. There were no more petitions from me, and my exchange of views with the ill-fated Queen Margaret had also come to an abrupt end. Of course it had. Were we not both prisoners of sorts?

I remained at Middleham Castle: once my home, my refuge; once one of the joys of my life with Richard and my children. Now I rose from my bed every morning, knowing that nothing would change, that everything would be the same until I retired again to my chamber after Compline in the chapel. My daughter Anne kept me company when she was in residence, and the child Edward, who was a gift to me, brightened my days, but I had no position in the household. No role to play. No authority that was recognised by the household other than the trivial requests that any woman might make. My life was restrained by the walls of this castle, as if it were a prison.

Or a shroud.

The legal distribution of my estates, due to the personal and despicable involvement of King Edward, had been effectively implemented as if I were dead. I could never forget that.

I was fifty-six years old. I was not dead, but I was invisible to the world.

Memories kept me stark company; neither agreeable nor gratifying, but worryingly vivid in what I might see as my failure as a mother to my two daughters. I remembered my daughter Anne as the young girl I had raised. Playful, endearingly open in her willingness to laugh at the mummers' antics, or mourn, grief-stricken, the death of a new foal. A child who would confide and whisper secrets or share her hero-worship of one of the knights in the tales of romance. Now when she sat with me in my chamber she was reticent, her thoughts and plans elusive, her gaze unwilling to touch on mine for any length of time. Some areas of her life she had deliberately shut away from me, as indeed, if I were honest, I had from her. We exchanged no intimacies. We did not attempt to speak again of Isabel. Of Clarence. Of the Prince or of her life under Queen Margaret's dominance. Nor did I speak with her of her father and his brutal death at Barnet. We did not even speak much of Gloucester where she had now given her loyalties. When we did, she smiled and agreed with every decision he made.

'That is all in the past,' she would say when I, perhaps foolishly, ventured to discuss Isabel's defection to Clarence or her own brief marriage with Prince Edward. 'What value in remembering a time of war and loss? Let us look ahead. It seems to me that all battles have come to an end. We will once more live in a realm of peace and prosperity.'

I thought that I knew her so well. I was mistaken. Events had changed her when she had become a Yorkist wife to one of the most powerful men in the land. Had Gloucester forbidden her to talk of the past, where there were dangerous areas that might rouse compassion in her for my present situation. Easier to talk of the delivery of barrels of wine to the castle than the sad fate of Isabel and the whereabouts of Isabel's children, probably at Court under the King's watchful eye since he was godfather to the young boy, Edward. The only occasion on which I saw her soften and become the girl I recalled was when she spent time with her little son. Then I recognised once again the playful and amenable girl I had hoped to raise.

Where once I would have trusted my daughter with my life, now I kept my own counsel, as she kept hers. It was a wearying experience of which I could see no end.

And yet, here was a change to the order of my day. A visitor.

It was thought best by the King, my daughter and the Duke of Gloucester that I should not communicate with the world. To my mind I was no danger to any man, except that to draw attention to my plight might become dangerous. What if someone decided to espouse my cause and fight for the restoration of my rights and my lands? Neither Gloucester nor his brother had desired such an eventuality since they were enjoying my wealth and potential power. Since Clarence's execution, Gloucester enjoyed it all.

For me, in those years since Richard's death, life was the loneliest I could imagine. My daughter and the Duke of Gloucester were rarely in residence since he had risen in importance at Court or travelled through the North where his power was strong. I could not be resentful, since Richard and I had worked so hard to bless our daughters with these most beneficial of marriages. I should not be resentful, but sometimes a knot of anger was lodged in my heart. I had lost Isabel to a cruel death, and Anne's allegiance was elsewhere.

The servant was speaking to me again.

'Do you wish to see her, my lady? The visitor?'

It was a woman, then. I could think of no woman who would visit me. My daughter had not waylaid her and forbidden her presence. My heart began to beat a little faster.

'And her name?' I asked, laying aside my stitching. Any woman with whom I might converse would be welcome.

'Lady Katherine de Vaux. She has travelled far.' A brief stare. 'The Duchess is away from home, to speak with the priest in the town. There is no one to stop you, my lady, if you wish to see her. The lady is most anxious to speak with you.'

The compassion of a servant was a sharp wound to my pride, to my dignity, but here was a name that I remembered. And no guard at my door to intercept my wishes.

'Then I will indeed speak with her.'

I stood and walked to the window to view the extent of my captivity – the impregnable walls and towers – but turned as the door opened. A woman I recognised from the past entered, her dark hair, now greying at the temples, covered with a travelling hood, her posture upright, her figure slight and still agile. Lady Katherine de Vaux, one of Margaret's closest women companions for many years. Elderly now, but still prepared to travel, probably at her mistress's behest. Or perhaps there was another reason. My heart tripped at the realisation of what it might be that had brought her here.

She curtsied, with all the grace I recalled from her days with Margaret.

'My lady. My thanks for allowing me to speak with you.'

'Lady Katherine.' I inhaled slowly, taking note of the remnants of grief on the woman's face. 'I think that there is only one reason why you would be here in England rather than with your mistress. And in such an obvious state of sorrow.'

434

'Indeed, my lady. My mistress is dead.'

I thought of this, the final breath of a woman with whom I had shared much experience, but whose ambition had brought death to so many of my family, and to one whom I longed for beyond bearing.

And I remembered Margaret as I had last seen her in France before I sailed home, her erect posture, her firm shoulders, her pale skin still unlined despite the travails of her years in flight and in exile, her masterful but elegant hands with their jewelled rings. Her auburn hair beautifully pinned and plaited. Her much-repeated assurances that her victory on the battlefield would win the crown for her son. How had she existed through her life of isolation, knowing that all she had once possessed had been lost to her? Powerless, penniless with no hope for the future. A widow and childless. I knew the pain of it even though once I would have called her my enemy. Once I had almost called her my friend too. How the fate of time had woven and then unwoven our relationships.

'I should commiserate with you,' I said, 'although I find it difficult. My most terrible loss can never be removed from her door.'

'My mistress also suffered grave losses.'

Which gave me pause to reconsider the words I should use to this woman.

'Yes, she did. Many would say that it was her own ambitions that caused such losses. If she had not pushed for battle at Tewkesbury, at least her son would still be alive, even if in exile.' I drew in a breath. There was no value in my opening these painful doors. 'Why are you here to see me, Lady de Vaux?'

'I have a commission from my late mistress.'

'Sit down, if you will.' I motioned for one of my women to pour two cups of wine, then indicated that she should leave

435

us. This was a private matter. She withdrew to the far end of the room, but no further. There were always spies within my household.

'Tell me,' I invited quietly, turning my back on any unwanted inquisitiveness.

'I am come from the Chateau of Dampierre near Saumur. Queen Margaret has lived there in difficult circumstances. She had a pension granted by King Louis, but she would be the first to admit that it was a poor recognition for one of his own family, a woman whom he had robbed of all her inheritance.' She stopped abruptly. 'Forgive me. It is not my purpose to burden you with any problems suffered by Queen Margaret.'

Queen Margaret? It might have amused me, but it simply made me sad. 'Did she still hold to that myth, even after all these years?'

'My mistress would never accept any other title. She was crowned and anointed in God's presence, which could never be destroyed. She never saw herself as other than Queen of England. Her lord Henry was always King, even when imprisoned.'

'Despite many who rejoiced to see the end of Henry's reign,' I said. 'So many fine men died because of her exploits.'

'Including my own husband,' the lady agreed. 'He died at Tewkesbury.'

She took a sip of wine as if to ease her throat, but it was clear that the grief was long gone.

'There is no point in dwelling on the past. For either of us,' I said.

'No. None. My mistress was granted a pension by the French King. She lost the rest; any inheritance she had was confiscated. She had nothing to leave of value in her will, even when she remembered those who had comforted her.'

'She knew that she was dying.'

'Yes, she knew. She was fifty-two years old. She died on the twenty-fifth day of August. She made her will three months before she died.'

'Was she ill?'

'She had become frail, in mind and body. She did not enjoy her incarceration. Her spirit, always so strong, could never accept it. She had begun to lose her hair. It was a great loss to her. Vanity, as she would admit, was one of her greatest sins. If you were to ask the cause of her death, I would say of a broken heart.' Lady Katherine looked down at a purse embroidered with the English royal emblems that she carried, opening it to extract its contents. 'I was bid to bring you this.'

A package was held out to me, well wrapped in leather against the elements.

'Most of her remaining goods were sold to pay her servants and any debts of her household,' Lady Katherine explained. 'Those debts that could not be paid, she implored King Louis to meet. Since he had taken all the wealth she might have inherited through her father and mother, it should be his burden to pay the debts, which I believe he has done. This treasure, too, should have been sold, if King Louis did not covet it for himself, but I was to keep it secretly and bring it to England.'

I unlaced and folded back the leather to reveal a roll, beautifully gilded and painted, marvelling at this magnificent work of art, which Margaret would have used for her personal devotion. What an intimate gift this was for her to send to me, the widow of her enemy. A beautiful, fragile object showing the Queen at prayer, kneeling at her prie-dieu. I looked up at Lady Katherine with astonishment.

'It is her prayer roll,' she explained. 'My lady used it daily

437

when she prayed for those who were dead and those she remembered from the past.'

'But why me? Why send it to me?'

'I do not know, my lady. Except that she has no family of her own who would value it. She thought it would not be lost or maltreated in your hands.'

I allowed the document to gently reroll itself, carefully rewrapping it in its cover.

'But you would value it, Lady Katherine,' I said. 'Why would she not leave it to you, who spent so many years in her company and service? I am sure that you were more friend than servant. Why not leave such a valuable possession to you? Far better than to leave it to the wife of the Earl of Warwick.'

'I would have valued it,' Lady Katherine admitted, 'but it was not intended for me. Sadly, she had nothing left to leave me. Perhaps my mistress has written why she made the decision.'

I discovered that there was a sheet of parchment tucked within the leather covering; it had fluttered to the floor.

'I will read it later,' I said, picking it up, slipping it within the folds of my stitching. 'This is a beautiful thing, and I will treasure it. It is not something I ever expected.'

It had created a warm place in my heart that she had thought of me at the end. It displaced my isolation just a little.

Lady Katherine laughed softly. 'You are fortunate that it has arrived with you. My lady willed her favourite hunting hounds to a neighbour who had given her friendship in these later years. I would not have enjoyed bringing them to England.' She shrugged lightly. 'King Louis claimed them all since my mistress had made him her heir. Not even one of the creatures was to go to Madame de Montsoreau in the end. You are fortunate to receive this gift. At least it was small enough for me to stow away in my luggage.'

'King Louis was not the kindest of hosts,' I observed.

'No. The Queen was of no value to him as soon as her husband and son were both dead. She had no claim on the English throne and nothing to offer King Louis as an intermediary. Who would speak with her? But at least he allowed her to be buried with her mother and father in Angers Cathedral, which is what she wanted.'

We sipped the wine in contemplative mood.

'Where do you go now?' I asked.

'I have friends who will give me a bed. I have my children.'

'But King Edward will not welcome you back.'

'No, perhaps he will not, but I think that I am no danger to him now. He will rejoice at my lady's death.' Her eyes caught and held mine. 'I think that you have a kinder life than the one my lady suffered at the end, unthought of and neglected.'

'Even though the law has designated that I am dead, and my lands given elsewhere? Even though I am not free to travel or make my own life?'

'You have a daughter and a son-in-law. A grandson.'

'Yes, I have Edward. He is a blessing to me.' I put down my cup and stood. There was really no more to say. 'Good day, Lady de Vaux. I wish you well on your travels and in making a home for yourself here. And my thanks for your long journey.'

My visitor turned at the door, looking back, as if undecided. Then said, 'My mistress grieved long and hard. She lived with sorrow and guilt in her last years. It is my thought that she deserved some compassion.'

I could not find the words to reply. As she left, my daughter Anne entered, having returned from her priestly discussion in Middleham. There was a faint frown at the departing guest.

'Who was that?'

'Lady Katherine de Vaux, with news for me. There is no

plotting to concern you. It is simply that Margaret of Anjou, once Queen of England, is dead.'

Anne's expression remained difficult to read. 'I suppose that I should feel some sorrow, but there is little in my heart. What a deviously manipulating woman she was. Why come to tell you?'

'Unfinished history between us, I suppose.' I was prepared to say no more, and my daughter could think what she wished. Lady Katherine would never return. I had had time to hide the roll with the letter within my stitchery. They were private to me and anything of value might end up in Gloucester's hands if discovered.

'If you will forgive me, my daughter, I will say a prayer for her eternal rest.'

'She was guilty of much bloodshed.'

I stared at her and replied with much sternness, 'The demands on her were almost too great for her to bear. And she lost much. As did I. And you, of course. You would not today be the wife of the Duke of Gloucester if Prince Edward had not died at Tewkesbury. We have all suffered in these wars, which ought to rouse our compassion, one for another.' I thought for the moment, accepting the truth of what I had just heard. 'Queen Margaret should not be forgotten in death. She was alone and without comfort. She has no one else to pray for her.' I walked to the door. 'I do not need my waiting women. Do not send them after me.'

Carefully folding my sewing, I climbed the stairs to reach the chapel on the second floor of the tower, where I knelt, conscious of the pain of passing years. When I was certain that no one had followed me, I unfolded the roll, and the letter fell out again beside me. I opened it, smoothing out the creases. It was written in an unknown hand, yet it had a feeling of power and intimacy that I remembered. Margaret's last letter to me, with the familiar opening line, full of courtesy and recognition of our status. I smiled. She had indeed kept to her title in spite of everything that had happened to her. King Edward would not rob her of it. He would never rob her of it now.

*Margaret, Queen of England, to Anne, Countess of Warwick, August 1482*

*By the Queen.*

*I have written this to you because I see death approaching. My ills do not go away; advancing age presses down on me. I have lived here at Dampierre sur Loire in no true discomfort, my enemies would certainly say, but life drags at my spirits and I feel a need to send this, even though I am too weak to use a pen.*

*Once we would have stood across from each other as enemies, as we did. Once we exchanged opinions of mutual support as wives of powerful men and mothers of children who would wed well and keep the family power intact. Those days are long gone when we wrote to each other. I expect that you still see me as the cause of your husband's death at Barnet.*

*As I doubtless was.*

*Yet who could have stopped the mighty Earl of Warwick from returning to England to bring the Yorkist usurper to heel if it was in his mind to do it? I could not. Neither, I think, could you. Warwick was as driven by his own ambitions as was I.*

*As the years have passed, I have considered our relationship. There are so many similarities between us, similarities that the years have not obliterated. We were both women of substance. We were both destined for political marriages, although my inheritance was far more important than yours, though your wealth was greater. We were both wed to men of high blood. We were players in the perennial game of chess when women were the pawns.*

*But then our lives diverged. Your lord had greater abilities than mine. He proved to be a leader of renown. Even I must admit to it. It must have been a comfort to you. But I gave birth to a son, a blessing. I know that you felt the failure of having only daughters. It drove you to your knees before the Blessed Virgin to beg for a son for Warwick. Do you remember when I was accused of taking a changeling child into my arms, to give Henry a son? I did not commit so heinous a crime, but it must have crossed my mind if I had indeed failed.*

*We have both lost our husbands, I lost my son, you a daughter, although there is still one to give you hope. I am unsure of your situation or comfort. I believe that your life is restricted, as is mine.*

*On some days I despair. I have so much blood on my soul and my hands. Sometimes, although it might be a sin, I look forward to my death. How many years will you have to pay the penalty for your marriage to Warwick? For his treachery? Your guilt or innocence cannot be proven, but you are punished as if guilty.*

*If you look for retribution for my deeds during my life, then I have been duly punished, far beyond even my enemies would dream of. I could compile a list of my sufferings. My son is dead. My husband murdered in the Tower. Rejected by my own father and by Louis of France. Robbed of all my past dignities. Robbed of all my inheritance. Powerless, penniless, lonely. It is the hardest burden to bear. I would accept it all if my glorious Prince, my Edward, could by some miracle be restored to me alive.*

*Yes, I am punished. Should I have abandoned my lord Henry to his fate? I fought for him and our son. I would do the same again.*

*As for you, my dear Countess Anne, perhaps you should have left your sanctuary and gone to Court and demanded a hearing from the Yorkist who wears the crown. You chose not to. It may have been the right decision, of course. I no longer have a judgement on affairs in England. How could you trust your King to treat you with grace? Yet would not your daughters have stood for you and argued your cause? As we both must admit in the cruelty of hindsight, you would never be allowed to keep your inheritance. I am sure that you read the situation better than I.*

*I ask for forgiveness and understanding for any sins that have harmed you, as I give mine to you. I have not always been so tolerant of the failings of others, but the approach of death is a great leveller.*

*May the Blessed Virgin protect and keep you.*

*When you read this, I will be dead and my earthly travails over. I must be glad.*

*Margaret*

*Queen of England*

*I will remain Queen of England in my own mind until my final day on this earth, and beyond. Enjoy the prayer roll as I have. It has given me great comfort. I trust that it will give the same to you. If you can aid Lady Katherine to any degree, I beg that you will.*

I sat for some time with the letter open in my hand, wishing that I could reply. So much truth there. I discovered that there were tears on my cheeks, so I must have wept. I wept for Margaret and for myself. Her trials were over. Mine were not and I could not see where they would lead me.

There were lessons here for me too.

She had been strong to the end and so would I be. I wiped the tears away, placed the prayer roll in a coffer for safe-keeping, and went to discover my daughter and grandson. Sometimes, despite his lack of years, I saw my Richard in the young boy when he rode his horse and picked up a wooden sword. I saw Richard in the tilt of his chin, in the furrowing of his brow when he was thwarted, in the stern Neville features that had begun to develop as the years passed.

As I folded Margaret's last letter, I repeated a vow, the one I had made on the wall-walk when I had first discovered the ultimate betrayal of property-rights. I would never give up my own battle to secure what was rightfully mine. I knew what should be returned to me, my Beauchamp lands, my dowry, my jointure. I would not have Margaret, even from beyond the grave, consider me weak. Perhaps I must start writing petitions again. There would be ways to smuggle them to Court. And I would do all I could to make contact with Isabel's son and daughter. They were my blood. Surely that could not be refused me. I would do it. Margaret had fought to the end. So would I.

Perhaps King Edward, now with two sons to follow in his shoes, could be persuaded to have mercy on me, despite that terrible blight of illegitimacy that Richard had stirred up. One day I might sit in my own hall, surrounded by my own people, secure in my inheritance. One day...

Hope was a transient thing. Even if I failed, I would not have Margaret believe that I had never even tried.

Meanwhile, I walked on the wall-walk of the castle, looking out to the hills, the clouds banking in the West and heralding rain. Lady de Vaux would have a damp journey to her ultimate destination, but she would not stay. She had no love for either of the remaining York brothers, she said.

A movement caught my eye in the shadows at the corner

tower. A figure. A shape. The lift of an instantly recognisable winter cloak, fur-lined with an enamel clasp, as if stirred by a quick movement. Was it real? I blinked, as a shower of rain swept across in the wind. Still it was there, the silver bloom of mist sparkling on his dark hair, on his shoulders.

There was only one thought in my mind.

I walked slowly towards him.

'Margaret is dead,' I said softly as if the figure hemmed in by cloud could hear me. 'I am still alive, but with no part to play in this life. You have three grandchildren. Your daughter Anne may be the one to carry the Neville flame into the future through her little son Edward.'

Of course there was no reply. I did not expect it. This was a myth, a dream, a mirage. A foolish longing on my part.

'I am lonely,' I said, a little louder. 'All I can do is petition for the return of what is mine by right. I must continue to fight to keep your name alive. I must live out my time as best I can. I will never allow you to be forgotten. You will always live for me.'

It seemed to me that the figure turned away. A smile perhaps, a lift of the hand that held the great sword with the sapphire set in its gilded hilt.

'I miss you more than I can say,' I said, as if my words would hold him still within my sight. 'I will never forget what we had together.'

But then he was gone and I was truly alone.

Suddenly the sun blazed through the clouds, picking out the grey lichen growing on the stones of the wall-walk. I spread my fingers over the coping. Richard would never grow old and sit by the fire in Middleham Castle with his grandchildren, to tell tales of war. I would never hear the clear timbre of his voice again, but perhaps the Wheel of Fortune would spin once more for me. Perhaps, in some distant day, I would resume my title of Countess of Warwick, my lands and wealth restored to me. And when I was at last free, I vowed that I would ensure that Richard's effigy at Bisham displayed him in the full armour he had so loved.

How foolish I was, seeking for victory in corners where all my freedoms were curtailed. I laughed a little sadly at the powerless emptiness of my dreams. And yet Margaret's letter had reawoken a spirit of desire within me. A song-thrush began to sing on the battlements of the nearest tower, such a paean of repetitive joy to touch my heart. I was still alive. There were men who would re-member me and my Beauchamp ancestors, men who would remember the mighty Earl of Warwick who had made such an impact in this realm. However futile it might seem, my heart settled a little into a steady beat, into hope.

It was time to put aside the aching emptiness of my life; it was time to become Queen Margaret's She-Wolf. I had an inheritance to fight for, and now I had discovered the willpower to do it.

# *Acknowledgements*

I have so many acknowledgements to make, and so many thanks to give:

To all at Orion Publishing, who have made me so welcome in my writing of historical fiction.

To Charlotte Mursell, my editor, for her words of wisdom and enthusiasm for my medieval heroines.

To Snigdha Koirala and to the whole splendid Orion Publishing team, who have launched into the world the intrepid women who star in *The Queen and the Countess*.

For Jane Judd, my agent, who continues to give me her advice and her support, as well as giving me the first review of my new book. I am very appreciative of her clarity and foresight.

To all at Orphans Press, who maintain my website and my newsletter, and come to my aid with all the technical knowledge that I do not have.

And finally, all my thanks to the women whose voices and opinions we hear through the turbulent years of the Wars of the Roses. They are the true heroines of *The Queen and the Countess*.

# *Credits*

Anne O'Brien and Orion Fiction would like to thank everyone at Orion who worked on the publication of *The Queen and the Countess*.

**Agent**
Jane Judd

**Editors**
Charlotte Mursell
Snigdha Koirala

**Copy-editor**
Francine Brody

**Proofreader**
Holly Kyte

**Editorial Management**
Anshuman Yadav
Jane Hughes
Charlie Panayiotou
Lucy Bilton
Patrice Nelson

**Audio**
Paul Stark
Louise Richardson
Georgina Cutler

**Contracts**
Dan Herron
Ellie Bowker
Oliver Chacón

**Design**
Charlotte Abrams-Simpson
Nick Shah
Deborah Francois
Helen Ewing

**Photo Shoots & Image Research**
Natalie Dawkins

**Finance**
Nick Gibson
Jasdip Nandra
Sue Baker
Tom Costello

**Inventory**
Jo Jacobs
Dan Stevens

**Production**
Ruth Sharvell
Katie Horrocks

**Marketing**
Katie Moss

**Publicity**
Sarah Lundy

**Sales**
Catherine Worsley
Dave Murphy
Victoria Laws
Esther Waters
Group Sales teams across
Digital, Field, International
and Non-Trade

**Operations**
Group Sales Operations team

**Rights**
Rebecca Folland
Tara Hiatt
Ben Fowler
Alice Cottrell
Ruth Blakemore
Marie Henckel